The Long Shadows

First published in the United Kingdom in 1997 by
Dewi Lewis Publishing
8 Broomfield Road, Heaton Moor
Stockport SK4 4ND

All rights reserved

Copyright ©1997
For the text: Alan Brownjohn
For this edition: Dewi Lewis Publishing
Front cover photograph: John Holden
Back cover photograph: Sandy Brownjohn

ISBN: 1 899235 21 3

The right of Alan Brownjohn to be identified as author of this work has been asserted by him in accordance with the Copyright, Designs and Patents Act 1988.

Acknowledgements

Page 5: Taken from *The Royal Hunt* by D.R.Popescu and translated by J.E.Cottrelli and M.Bogdau, published by Quarto Books Ltd in 1987.

Page 118: Taken from *A la recherche du temps perdu* by Marcel Proust translated by C.K.Scott-Moncrieff and published by Chatto & Windus. Copyright the Estate of Marcel Proust.

Printed and bound in Great Britain by
Biddles Ltd, Guildford and King's Lynn

Alan Brownjohn

THE LONG SHADOWS

DEWI LEWIS
PUBLISHING

NOTE

Each passage excerpted from Philip Carston's novel *A Time Apart* (Ridgbury, 1987) is introduced by the symbol ***. Places where the consecutive narrative of that novel stops and the narrative of this book resumes are indicated by the use of square brackets, thus [...]

The kind permission of Ridgbury and Co. for the use of the above excerpts is gratefully acknowledged. It should be emphasised that the fictitious members of that company depicted herein bear no resemblance to any real persons, living or dead, employed by Ridgbury in that or any other period, or to anyone employed by Paramore USA after their later acquisition of Ridgbury and discontinuation of that imprint.

THEN

"... The Danube was taking him down and what was incredible was that the sun was shining red as it was sinking into darkness, and the leaves were rustling, and there, rising, was the moon."

        D.R. Popescu: *The Royal Hunt*

ONE

– 1 –

It came to Tim Harker-Jones that on any morning after the age of forty-five you have to be a hero to get up.

Today his desultory, intermittent sleeping had left him scattered about the bed in the usual pieces. He had to instruct his brain to tell his contorted limbs that they could connect and move.

Once he used to be able to sit up in bed without using his elbows. So long ago... now his elbows were two absolutely essential bony props which he had to pull up from his hips and dig into the mattress alongside his rib-cage, so as to win leverage. They were his only means of lifting his aching, breaking torso into action. If his elbows ever failed...

Always now the inscrutable night hours brought this separation of the parts from the whole. Tim was increasingly aware that human structures could feel as if they came apart like chairs, or tables, or anything from which pieces sever themselves. That foot, that hand, that – why shouldn't it just drop off? Your body end up like a lot of separate numbered sections on a chart needing to be constructed again every day.

Or like, he thought, the incompatible, contradictory bits of a dismantled electric plug? Through which, by a ramshackle forcing together of coloured wires and brass screws and nuts and the catalytic supervention of a fuse, there passed the power to warm and to illuminate. Come on, fit it together again. Take the screwdriver of resolution to it. Elbows first.

To think of such a metaphor, Tim said to himself, shows that this old machine, while it is to me, still works. "There is some zest in me even yet", he whispered aloud to the bedroom. Come on then. You have a 12.50 flight to catch."

This was 8.30, an hour before Tim's preferred time of rising, on a dull winter Saturday a few weeks after a Christmas in the advanced nineteen-eighties. Some light came through the curtains and fell on the surface of his working table when he passed it, fell on an assignment no less piecemeal so far than his own waking body: the events of Philip Carston's life set down in summary on about fifteen sets of typed slips and a smaller number of piles of scribbled sheets. All that would need to be laboriously put together too. There were also some carefully typed sheets, a tentative draft account of Philip's earliest years; which he had spoilt.

The slips were typed because Tim was not yet beyond an electric typewriter and onto a word-processor.

The large pile of sheets was scribbled because Tim worked by making rough and rapid longhand drafts. The typed sheets were spoilt because Tim laboured with a mug of coffee constantly beside him; and tapping the appropriate key on his typewriter sent the carriage rocketing to the right; and late last night the carriage had sent his coffee flying over the pages he had typed during the afternoon.

"Bad luck," Sara had said casually. That was when he decided to go to bed. But he had his unintended revenge during the night. At about two a.m. he woke up laughing, laughing loudly, enough to wake Sara though she was a heavy sleeper. "What is it?" she mumbled at him. When he could stop laughing he told her. "A dream," he said. "I dreamt we went to a Greek restaurant. Called – the Hubris!" Tim said, giggling seismically, shaking the bed. "You wake me up for *that*?" said Sara.

Matters could be worse, he said now in a loud undertone at the wash basin. Although I need the time I am losing during this next two weeks, I also need a break. I realise that my trip might provide some ideas about one of Philip's more mysterious preoccupations; though Philip's interest in writing about an unnamed, fictitious country comes much later in his life.

As he paced around the duty-free store at Heathrow, Ridgbury's two thousand seven hundred and fifty pound advance seemed yet again a meagre return for his efforts in securing it.

"There will be a biography," said Philip's will (commanding and sardonic rather than hopeful), "and I should be touched to feel that my friend, the distinguished biographer Tim Harker-Jones, would be able to undertake it." But Dominick Paldrey, Philip's publisher, was under no moral or contractual obligation to commission it.

Of course Dominick had to accept Tim's phone call, three days after the funeral. But he did not respond readily to Tim's thought that they might lunch on the notion of a life. He tried to procrastinate.

"Tim, that would be an absolutely marvellous idea," he enthused, "but I don't know exactly *when*, 'in the near future' as you say, it could be. I mean –" ineffably pleasant, and agreeable, and evasive – "could we wait a bit? It's so soon after Philip's – Philip's vanishing... if we waited, like, till the spring –" this was autumn – "we might be able to gauge the degree of interest."

"I've got quite a lot on in the spring," Tim said untruthfully. "That's the only thing. This autumn's better."

Of course it was better; he had no work at all. Tim could hear Dominick sighing with annoyance at the other end, covering the mouthpiece, instructing someone else about some more important matter. Then he was back suddenly with false apologies, but at least conceding Tim a little of his invaluable time, perhaps just to get rid of the whole idea.

"Look Tim, what we *could* do," Paldrey said gravely and confidentially, as if he really felt he had to be decent about the dead novelist, "is to have lunch at *my* place on a *Saturday*. Even as soon as Saturday week? If that's as easy for you as coming here?"

At the door on the chosen Saturday Paldrey, in weekend shorts and Rhode Island University T-shirt, looked as if he had forgotten Tim was coming.

"Oh God! Step inside, then. I'm afraid it's a bit of a mess."

The corridor into the depths of the Paldreys' Victorian house still had the century-old floral wallpaper, infinitely tattered and soiled, everywhere worn or rubbed away by hands or heads, or the friction of furniture, or the heat of fires. Tim followed Dominick into a wide, knocked-through space that didn't seem to be any particular kind of room any more, not a lounge, not a study, not a playroom or bedroom, but all of them at once and nothing conclusively. There was a grand piano, but glossy magazines were piled all over its closed keyboard lid, and the top was cluttered with pot-plants, some dead, some still dropping petals.

And yet this room was only a route through to another room, approached down three steps and leading on and out to a long, downward-sloping garden. The second room seemed to Tim even more confused and unfocused than the first, no physical centre or definable purpose, nothing beyond the random acquisitiveness of its inhabitants. It had a hideously fashionable atmosphere, created by an array of junk all the time changed and updated. There was a table, for a word-processor and printer, and books and papers, but the room was also, down one side, the kitchen, and Dominick's wife, Alic, in shell suit and trainers, was sitting there in the only empty one of four wicker chairs, talking hard into a mobile phone.

From upstairs came a wild sound of children's voices and a young woman's voice vainly intervening. Dominick and Tim stood tentatively on the edge of this kitchen space (there was a smell of something cooked earlier in the day but no impression of imminent lunch) and waited for Alic to finish. When she suddenly did, she greeting Tim with a switched-on smile, and asked Dominick,

"Has Louie gone to get our lunch?"

"I don't know." And Dominick disappeared, leaving Tim to make conversation.

"A drink?"

Tim nodded firmly, and Alic opened a fridge door, pulled out a half-full bottle of Beaujolais standing up beside the milk, snatched three streaked tumblers out of a dishwasher, poured. She leaned back against the sink, sipped at her glass and grimaced, gave him a small hard stare.

"You've come to talk over something?" she asked.

"Louie won't go," Dominick said, returning. "She says they won't let her go. But really, she's scared to take them." Alic smiled at Tim with a shrug of despair.

"I'll go myself," Dominick continued. And to Tim, "Will you come – for the walk?"

Along the street to the Chinese take-away they talked about the weather and Philip Carston's funeral. Dominick said nothing at all about Tim's reason for coming, and Tim resolved to ask nothing until they were back and seated at the lunch table. But where could there conceivably be a table with space to eat in the Paldrey's house?

While they were out, though, Alic had solved the problem by clearing two more of the wicker chairs on the kitchen side of the room. They were to eat sweet-and-sour pork, bean shoots and rice on their knees; it could not be more relaxed and informal.

"About this idea, then," Dominick announced as soon as he had spooned out his meal roughly onto his plate and shaken soy sauce over the mound. "What's your line on it?"

Tim had prepared himself for the directness of the question. He knew that "your line" in Dominick's terms, meant fashionableness, saleability, "sexiness".

"Philip's secrets," Tim replied. He had absolutely no idea whether there were any.

Alic's mouth, Tim thought he could see out of the corner of his eye, dropped open for a mere second of incredulity.

"So what are those?" asked Dominick flatly; eating hard and not looking up.

"Few modern novelists cover so much human ground in their fictions," Tim said, deliberately using the kind of blurb-and-catalogue writers' phrases Dominick Paldrey might appreciate, might even have written. "We know less about people Philip actually knew and used for the novels than with any writer of comparable celebrity." Sometimes you just talk nonsense, Tim told himself.

For a moment or two Dominick and Alic Paldrey were

actually listening, and nodding; Alic had paused in her eating, and appeared to be thinking. She stood up, and replenished their glasses with the very last of Thursday's cold red wine.

Tim had to keep this up.

"I have a theory that his stay-at-home image," Tim said, "was a calculated cover for a certain amount of –" he must not exaggerate this – "of illicit travelling. It may be that he wanted to meet women he wouldn't have wanted to entertain at home." All this was the purest invention, though deriving from the range of successful women characters in the novels.

"Can you prove this?" Dominick was saying. Meanwhile, Alic, hearing the word "women", sensing a matter on which she might have an opinion, was standing a little taller at the sink, pressing her knees back to increase her height like a diminutive diva wanting to seem a genuine young man, a Leonora perhaps, or a Cherubino.

"Who *were* these obscure women then?" she demanded sharply.

"I don't know whether they *were* 'obscure'," Tim came back gently. "But they were certainly women. I want to find out who they were. I have some clues." He did not, but he congratulated himself on this answer.

"He had *reasons* for obscuring them," declared Alic, as fact.

Tim realised he needed to go along with Alic's assumption, because he was making unexpected progress.

"As I said, I'd want to go into all of that," he replied.

Dominick appeared to be thinking about something specific (unless his mind was wandering to something more urgent), because he was feeling in a pocket for something, shaking his head, then picking it up from the table, a letter.

"Do you know anyone called – called Simon Stonehurst? A theatre director? He lives in Carston's home town."

"I may have heard of him," Tim said. He hadn't.

"This could be a coincidence."

Good, Tim thought. He knew Dominick believed in the

significance of coincidences.

"He's written about doing a stage production there of something he's been sent – a script referring to Philip's novel *A Time Apart*."

The letter looked at first sight long and confident and pretentious, a bit bullying for someone asking favours about using passages from the book.

"Don't read it all. I'll copy it for you if you're interested. He's got some odd theory about Carston and the heroine. From a friend of his – a guy working as a diplomat in some Iron Curtain country or other."

"Well, she's one of the most mystifying characters he ever did. The main male character has a strong love affair with her. I'd want to look into her, certainly." He had never thought of this idea before, never imagined any foreign liaison of Philip's.

"Mystifying." Tim realised he had chosen the adjective well. Now both the Paldreys were looking at him with interest.

– 2 –

As if night had to begin at the very moment you advanced your watch two hours, the landscape below suddenly seemed to have gone black immediately; and the blackness, flying over the mostly empty terrain of the Carpathians, was total for something over half-an-hour.

Only when their landing at Otopeni Airport "in ten minutes" was predicted did isolated lights begin to appear below, signs of normality, people huddled into the routines of living hardly aware of the sound of the aircraft overhead, to whose passengers this arrival in Romania was important and full of uneasy fascination.

Sara had driven him to Heathrow. "Forgotten anything?" she said as they closed the door of the flat. "No," he told her. But then, remembering the talk with the Paldreys which had clinched the deal, he ran back inside and collected his copy of *A Time Apart*.

He had toiled during the autumn months making notes about everything he could remember of Philip Carston's early life, when they were closer friends, visiting the streets (if not the house, which had been demolished) of his childhood, going into his schools. In the minor public day school Philip had attended from eleven to eighteen, Tim was amazed to discover an elderly master who had actually taught him when he was himself fresh from the university.

Tim decided to work on the biography chronologically, trying to follow the reticent (and later on, reclusive) Philip from the early nineteen-fifties, when he knew him well at university, into the period when their lives separated and he ceased to know him very much at all. In the years of the last four novels (these included *A Time Apart*), all of which featured his adopted home city under the fictitious name of "Fieldenhurst," Tim and Philip had not even corresponded.

The smiles of farewell from the Tarom cabin crew at the top of the steps looked to Tim more restrained than the greetings given on entering the plane at Heathrow; as if to convey that in their own country they needed to be more cautious. Across the tarmac the air was misty and chilly; the crowd shuffled very quietly into the waiting bus which covered all of fifty yards to the terminal. At the edge of the tarmac, six or seven pariah dogs prowled in a small dejected pack, sniffing and scratching over a grass verge.

Now he was standing around, uncomfortably, with ninety or a hundred other people, mostly Romanian but a few of them unidentified English, in a small ground-floor hall with pastel-coloured posters on the wall: city squares, beaches, ski resorts. He was waiting for that soldier with a Kalashnikov to see him and his hand-luggage through the metal-detectors, 'Made in Belgium' he noticed.

Progress was slow, the examination courteous but thorough, and deliberately humourless. Beyond the small arch through which everyone had to pass, several items of baggage had been opened, as if the metal-detectors were not trusted to be rigorous enough. In front of Tim went a Romanian carrying a viola in a case. Case and instrument were scrutinised; the owner grumbled, the soldier noisily justified his actions, the owner entreated, the soldier took the viola, held it up in the unsatisfactory ash-grey light, shook it and listened, shook it again, listened again, then handed it back without a word. As he laid it carefully in its case, the musician turned to Tim and complained further, pointing openly at the soldier, not bothering to lower his voice. Except that the man was not a soldier, Tim now realised, because a group of real soldiers in khaki were standing restlessly in the background and this man's dark blue uniform signified the police.

Tim felt sure he would be officially met here. But when he entered the large upstairs concourse, up steep marble steps, he wondered how long his hosts would be prepared to wait. Only two out of six passport control windows seemed to be operating, and there was a long and discontented line at each. This hall, brown and clean and dimly illuminated, full of people, echoing with aggrieved voices, was neither cold nor warm; it kept you unsure whether it was one or the other, though the uniformed airport officials went to and fro in overcoats. Tim stood for some moments trying to decide which of the queues to attach himself to, glancing out at the space beyond the guarded barriers, full of more passengers and officials and luggage. Then he noticed out there a face looking eagerly in, which looked like an English face. He was too far away to see the name on the card the man was carrying so he went to the head of the queue.

When he read the words "Tim Harker-Jones", he waved at its bearer. At first the face went on staring anxiously beyond him. Then its eyes roved over Tim's face, not responding to the wave. Then it did a double-take, and broke into a grin of almost frenetic welcome.

"Go to the end!" he called, in a high-pitched English voice, incongruous and deeply comforting. "To the diplomatic channel."

Tim registered a tall, even gangling, figure in a light absolutely English raincoat, a young man with a healthy, enthusiastic glow around him. The diplomatic channel was a window like any other, but with no queue at it.

"Sam Taplin's laid low with a virus. He'll try to see you in a day or two. Did you survive the journey? I'm Nick – Nick Tillitt. 'Tillitt' as in Hertfordshire. Have you been on cultural visits to other places?"

Tim had never been "officially" anywhere abroad, and said so.

"This is an excellent one to start with. You'll be able to do anywhere after this," Tillitt loudly confided, guiding him to the luggage carousel. "You'd have been two hours – three – if you'd had to wait," he opined, very audibly. "Quite deliberate. Always happens to London flights when the Foreign Office has been naughty."

Heads turned in the waiting crowd, the faces of stocky men and women in solid leather overcoats and black fur hats. To listen, Tim assumed; so why did Tillitt not keep his voice down? Or perhaps they were just surprised to catch the sound of a foreign language spoken so volubly? "The F.O.'s suddenly latched onto the environmental tactic – destruction of the Romanian architectural heritage. Prince of Wales and all that. Whoops!"

Suddenly Tillitt leant forward with grotesque ungainly energy and pulled Tim's large suitcase off the carousel, having spotted its diplomatic labels.

"Any more?"

"Only one."

At the Customs, more quick smiles and explanations in Romanian from Tillitt, and a broad smile for him (of recognition and amusement?) from the sturdy woman at the counter, who did not ask for anything to be opened. And they were suddenly out into much colder air, in which Tim could make out a wide and empty avenue stretching far away into black distance.

Naturally he went to the wrong side of Tillitt's car.

"Ah, you're still in England!" Tillitt exclaimed. There

seemed something a little mad or manic in his glee at Tim's mistake. Inside the car – "They don't do this here, but I do," he said, buckling his safety-belt. It sounded to Tim like a small reminder that, while a cultural guest here of the British government, he should stick to British rules.

A couple of hundred yards down the avenue – "What does that mean?" Tim asked. It was the large roadside notice with tall red words: 'Ceausescu si poporul.' "Ceausescu and the people." Tillitt said. "And that one's 'Ceausescu and heroism.' You'll see those everywhere. Though not in the top hotels, strange to say."

"And what are those?" Buildings three-storeys high, cream or beige in colour, roofed with reddish tiles, plain shops at ground level.

"Some of the new apartment blocks." Tillitt continued. "A lot better than what they replaced."

"What did they replace?"

"An extremely muddy and dilapidated village. No loss."

"They didn't knock down things worth preserving?"

"No. Not here. Maybe one old church in the centre." Then he corrected himself. "No – wait a moment. I'm not sure they *did* lose a church at all. No – they lost nothing worth keeping."

Tim was surprised. Tillitt was certainly not keeping to the Foreign Office line.

"They tell you in the U.K.," he went on, still very quietly, "that the reconstruction of the old city of Bucharest is an act of socialist vandalism. Historic monuments bulldozed, churches smashed to rubble. You've heard that?"

"I have."

"Well, some of it's true. But, you know, they actually put one historic church on rollers and *rolled* it to another site intact. And a lot of the districts they demolished were virtual slums. Really they were no loss."

"So – so you're saying – saying some of that is – is *propaganda*?"

"Ah, not entirely. But it's only a part of the story, maybe not

17

the most important part. Have you been believing all of it? That routine Foreign Office stuff?"

Tim sensed that the whole conversation could be a test of his own views and responses. If Tim had, for courtesy's sake, agreed unequivocally with Tillitt, he would have revealed certain political colours. If he was prepared to accept these surprising assurances, he was gullible, yes? Not safe to leave for too long with plausible Communist foreigners? He felt wary of Tillitt.

"You have to believe a lot of it," he said. "But I shall be interested to see for myself."

Suddenly Tillitt altered his tack.

"You're a biographer?"

"Yes." Tim thought he could guess what was coming next.

"I'm afraid I haven't read any of your works." Tim had guessed correctly. "We've got a couple in the British Council library here. For some reason they're quite often taken out."

"Why should Romanians borrow them?" In asking, Tim felt he accepted the obscurity imposed on him by Tillitt's ignorance. But he was interested to know.

"There's not many biographies of writers published here. Not much biography full stop." (Was this true?) "Or certainly not *recent* lives. No one's life can possibly be as full of achievement and wisdom as our hero President's, and it would be invidious – or dangerous – to suggest it could."

"But President Ceausescu doesn't write plays, or poems. I can see why there can't be *political* biographies – "

"If our President *did* write plays or poems they would be marvellous. But although he doesn't, it's still *extremely* invidious to suggest that Mr. Ionescu might be as marvellous a playwright as Mr. Ceaușescu is a President. Then Mr. Ionescu becomes a public rival."

"Who is Mr. Ionescu?"

"A Smith, a Brown or a Jones who happens to have talent."

"What's happening *here*?"

They were nearing what appeared to be the city centre,

though everything looked impenetrably dark for seven-thirty at night. Tim was gazing at perilously unlighted holes and trenches in the road, piles of rubble, boarded-up lanes of the carriageway marked "M" at intervals.

"Extending the Metro. I give him that. It works well. What are you working on at the moment?" Tillitt suddenly asked, peering into the black of the empty streets.

Tim hated to divulge plans which might not be fulfilled, but since no one else would have been commissioned to do it, and he was a thousand miles from London, there was no harm in telling Tillitt that he was compiling material for a life of Philip Carston.

Tillitt jerked his head round sharply to look at him, swerved in the darkness, narrowly failed to hit an oncoming tram.

"Well! – *interesting*. Interesting," he exclaimed. Then he paused, exhaled oddly as if remarking something extraordinary. When he began to speak again there was something curiously cautious and inhibited about his tone. "We've got – we've got several of his novels in the library here. I'm sure you'll know one has been translated into Romanian. It's very popular."

"He's been *translated*?"

"Yes. Well – the one book."

"Which one?"

"It's funny, I can't think of the title in English." It was as if Tillitt was holding back some delicate or dangerous knowledge.

"I'll ask about it," Tim said.

"Actually biography rather attracts *me*." Tillitt started again. "Though writing plays attracts me more."

"Do you have ideas?"

A tired, courteous question.

"Only the vaguest." Evasively, perhaps? Tim merely grunted affirmatively. Tillitt, manoeuvring among traffic, seemed to be winding up himself to ask something.

"Do you know – know Simon Stonehurst by any chance?" he asked suddenly.

Tim nearly said, "That's some coincidence!" But he stopped

himself. "I know the name. I don't know *him*."

"Ah!" Tillitt said, almost with relief.

Tim did wonder, for a moment, about coincidence. Inside the luggage not opened by airport Customs, slipped inside *A Time Apart*, was the copy of Simon Stonehurst's letter to Dominick Paldrey, a mixture of entreaty and cajolery, hints about the topicality of his play project in view of recent events in Eastern Europe, and so on. "Basically" (a favourite word of Stonehurst's? He used it twice in the letter) he needed to get permission for the extensive quotations from *A Time Apart* used in the script without paying anything to Ridgbury as copyright owners.

"I'm due to leave here this autumn," Tillitt went on. "And I imagine I'll be back in England for at least two years. That might give me some writing time."

"Sounds quite suitable."

– 3 –

Tillitt pulled vigorously on the brake and became brisk and instructional.

"Hotel Vidraru", he announced. "I'll see you in, you'll find it quite comfortable. If you want a meal" – so there was no plan for them to dine together – "they may say they can't do it as late as this, but insist politely and I dare say they'll provide something. When they come to take the order, leave out a packet of cigarettes in a visible place. Give it to them when the meal arrives, *not* before. It helps for the next time."

The foyer was warm and quiet, with the quietness of people who didn't want to say anything very loudly. Men sitting in large armchairs in the semi-darkness were hardly talking at all. The posters offering attractive tourist trips to the Black Sea coast or to ancient Transylvanian cities did not look as if they could keep their promises.

At the door to Tim's reserved fourth floor room in a dim corridor ("Foreigners are always put on the fourth floor," Tillitt said) the key would not enter the lock, although the number undoubtedly corresponded: Tillitt checked it with a pocket torch.

"Wait there, I'll take it back."

Tim waited in the gloom. Someone, a man in a hat and a heavy overcoat, turned the corner in the corridor and trod heavily towards him as if with a purpose; but passed without looking up, thinking his own thoughts. There followed, after the successful turning of his key in a lock further on and the quiet closing of a door, several minutes of absolute silence. Then lift doors were opening again and Tillitt was returning, accompanied by a woman clerk from Reception – extraordinarily beautiful and firmly reticent – who took a different key to the lock of a different door, and opened it easily.

The room inside looked comfortable and reassuring, furnished in heavy yet serviceable style with a wide double bed (with handsome head-board), a built-in desk topped by a mirror and a wall-light, built-in wardrobes and cupboards, armchairs, television, telephone, a tiled bathroom with bath and basin and strip-illumination. Tim had no money to tip the woman for solving the problem and Tillitt guessed his thoughts.

"No need – she's too important," he said. "Look – I'm going to leave you now. This is your first instalment, which I'll be glad if you'd sign for" – an envelope of Romanian banknotes – "and Angela Cernec will be coming for you in Reception at nine in the morning. She's your guide and interpreter. She's very nice, one of the best we know, but be very careful – I don't need to tell you that." (So why had he told him?) "They wouldn't let us have her if she wasn't 'reliable'. She should have a car, and will drive you to the Writers' Union for your first meeting. Sam Taplin will try to take you for lunch."

Tim was alone for the first time since arriving... He now savoured that joyful moment soon after arrival in an unfamiliar place when you are left in solitude at last in a hotel bedroom with no more problems to face for a while, no compulsory social gestures to make. For about ten or eleven more hours, most of which he would use for sleeping, no further action was required of him. He was doing nothing wrong so he would not start looking for hidden microphones or cameras yet. He was not hungry yet. He might take a look at the television.

An efficient brawl was going on, in, he guessed from the clothes, the 1940's, in a lavishly expensive restaurant. Cloths were being swept off tables (everything strewn on the floor), tables were being overturned, chairs hurled, bullets from the revolvers of bulky men in dark suits were smashing into mirrors. These were Romanian actors, but dubbed English accents came out of their mouths. Because the film had certainly been made much later (in the nineteen-seventies?) it had an air of pastiche, though the mood seemed serious enough.

Law and order, which wore less expensive dark suits and carried more accurate guns than its enemies, was facing a final showdown with seedy, ruthless capitalist racketeers. Evil was bloated, but dauntingly agile and resourceful, a huge boss of some city mafia shown outside the restaurant in a large, unidentifiable car (and this was peculiar; Tim thought he vaguely recognised the street). Good was represented by the tall, vigorous Inspector, who had a face furrowed by experience of the world and strengthened by moral determination.

The telephone rang, very loudly, long single rings, very un-English in their volume and insistence. He had not expected this. Every feeling that he had come to a sinister place returned. Suddenly he was wide-awake. He jumped, sat up, leapt off the bed realising he had fallen asleep despite all the action on the screen because it now showed decorous folk-dancers and singers tripping in circles. He had forgotten he had seen a telephone in the room, even half-dreamed for a second that its strident bell was sounding in the film and was somehow a violent threat to his safety.

He picked up the receiver. What do you say into a foreign telephone unexpectedly ringing for you?

"Hallo, and welcome to our country, Mr Harker-Jones," he heard.

A woman, a welcoming strong Romanian voice speaking clear, perfectly-pronounced English.

"Hallo..."

"Hallo, I am Valeria, Valeria Ciudea, Carolina's editor at the publishing house." Carolina pronounced Caroleena.

A pause, as if she expected Tim to give a cry of delighted recognition. But who *was* this? And who was this "Carolina" he was assumed to know about?

"I know we meet to-morrow, in the morning at nine-thirty." (Do we?) "But I want to welcome you myself, on behalf of the publishing house. It is very exciting for us to have you here in Bucharest, so I am giving you your first official welcome by telephone."

"Thank you. You are very kind. But are you sure you –?"

Elaborately intertwining dancers in folk costume, female choruses, hands clapping a rhythm; and the telephone line going muzzy suddenly, so that the eager voice continuing its greetings became a far-off whisper in the earpiece: "Do you hear me? Do you hear me? Mr Harker-Jones?" Growing ever more faint and disconcerted until it stopped, and was replaced by a high-pitched droning. Tim replaced the receiver, thinking that whoever it was would without doubt call him again and explain.

But no second call came. He remembered the phrase from the standard warning given to first-time British visitors to Communist countries: "A local girl may be trailed in front of you." The words had brought back all of his adolescent attraction to, and terror of, mature and sophisticated older women – only they were now, since he was well into his fifties, mature and sophisticated younger, *foreign* women. So were the Romanians onto him already, an hour after he had settled into the hotel? Trailing in front of him a Valeria, a beautiful editor working for the Security – and a Carolina, too – whetting his appetite for their first meeting in the morning?

He went and bolted the door, prepared to leave it bolted if anyone knocked, in case it was the telephone caller, or even the entrancing woman from Reception enquiring about any needs he might have. He felt hungrier now but resolved not to try to order a meal. He could take a quick shower? No, he loathed showers, and besides there might not be hot water. He would leave all until the morning. He switched off the folk-dancing. He had some airport chocolate. He would read. But he had left his London newspapers in the plane. He scanned the fire instructions and failed to understand them. In bed, he read the hotel brochure, memorised the hours for (in English) "full-size breakfast", went through his programme.

Then he did remember, of course, his copy of *A Time Apart*. In its way, re-reading it would be appropriate because Romania was rather the kind of country from which the heroine in the book might have come. Tim smiled to think that he was embarking in reverse on the journey that girl (in summer rather than in winter) had made from Communist Eastern Europe to England.

He leant over to pick up the slim, shiny book, and pulled the bedside lamp a little nearer.

– 4 –

*** Katrin woke. Felt the fear of indefinable things that so often comes with forgetting where it is you have slept.

A bright sky; a sun dazzling her through a window. She thought she had been in England for days, meeting hundreds of strangers. But no, she had dreamed that, she was still on the plane.

She was on the plane, which had started for England, but was now heading back for her own country. She had dreamed that too. Now fully awake, she knew it was flying on and not back because no one around her seemed troubled. So why had someone woken her?

They had questions to ask her, that was it. She would be taken back without ever leaving the aircraft. Except that nobody *had* woken her. No one had been speaking to her. Her immediate neighbour (whom she had cautiously not even greeted) was asleep. A stewardess passing by was looking in another direction, pushing a trolley of duty-free articles. Katrin would not want to buy skin cream, or wine, for dollars.

If the cabin crew did not ask her questions it was possible that they assumed she was important. She was privileged enough to make the trip, so she must be. She could be watching them more than they would be watching her. No one would stop her entering London now.

She began to accept completely that the buildings and streets gliding along below her were real, and would need to be interpreted. They were only just fifty metres beneath her now, with the plane veering and wavering over them and everything coming vividly closer until – she felt it touch down with the barest of bumps and skim along the ground, a moment of infinite relief ending when she remembered it had yet to stop safely and switch off its engine. Soon she would be using English for the first time with English people.

Straight out of the plane into a sloping tunnel, then along wide sunny carpeted corridors. She held her small bag tightly, passing uniformed officials at desks where they appeared to have no purpose except to gaze at people passing them. Security, she did not doubt.

Signs directed her to passport control and immigration. One sign asked for citizens of the U.K. and the E.E.C. countries, who would go to the same desk. 'E.E.C.' meant 'European' she thought. So she joined the queue, which was moving quickly; but thought she should ask someone.

"Is this the right line for *all* Europe?" she enquired in English.

"Deutsch?"

Katrin spoke no German.

"Nein. Français?" she ventured.

"Oui."

She asked the question in French, was answered "yes" by the woman, "no" by her husband. There was a mild argument, ending in her being dismissed to the other queue, which was moving very sluggishly. She was as ancestrally European as anyone, but she was not allowed to go to that particular desk, where people were passing through with some speed.

She could see that the official at the new desk smiled. But the smile was not easy and gentle. It was all so slow. He had many questions for a black man with a red passport. Each person seemed to require several minutes' attention. The official smiled and smiled; but delayed and delayed.

Nearer, Katrin heard people reply in faltering or heavily accented English (she couldn't understand much of it) to sharp, repeated questions, asked louder the second time. The atmosphere in the large hall was not deliberately oppressive, and yet nothing was going to be easy.

She would open the bag she carried and they would see she had nothing but personal effects. There would be no medicines which could be scrutinised as illegal drugs, no book which could be questioned as subversive. Only a letter.

Again the official smiled, this time as he took her passport.

He looked charming enough, this clean young man with short-cropped hair, in a very white shirt and grey tie, and his smile looked more relaxed and sincere in greeting her than it had in dealing with others. But –

"What brings you to England?" he said suddenly.

Katrin jumped a little. *What* brings her? He must mean *who* brings her, doesn't he, since an invitation from 'Cousin' Dora had been required to secure permission? She didn't reply to his smiled question, but smiled herself, and felt in her bag for Dora's letter.

"What brings you to England please?" Repeated curtly.

"I have an invitation from – a relation."

"I don't want to know *who*, I want to know *what*. In other words, *why* you're here.

"Oh *why*. Well, it is for a small holiday."

"As a tourist, then?"

"Well no – yes." It was neither an 'official' visit, nor was she going on a booked holiday tour.

"You have friends in England?"

"Yes, my – my cousin."

"And you're staying –?" An unended sentence.

"Yes, I am staying. In Fieldenhurst, with my Cousin Dora."

"I mean you are staying *for how long*?" Wearily now, with a flicker of his eyes up to the ceiling.

"For two weeks. For a fortnight."

"How old is your cousin?"

"How old is her? Is *she*?" Her English was exact and she only floundered out of nervousness and subdued anger. "She is fifty. Fifty-five."

"She is not British?"

"She is British now. They are living – have been living – in England thirty years."

He raised his eyebrows, thumbed the pages of the passport, handed it back. Katrin stood, as if he intended to summon up Police or Security to ask her more questions about why she had a fifty-five year old cousin. But his smile had switched to someone behind her in the line.

She went out, following more signs, to reclaim her baggage, suddenly realising how endangered she had felt. But she experienced no relief. Now there would be more encounters to be nervous about.

And yet the Customs here were not suspicious of her at all. She read the notices slowly and decided she had nothing to declare. So she truthfully chose to push her trolley through the "green channel". Groups of Customs officers behind empty tables looked at the passing travellers but stopped no one. This was easy. At the airport in her own country when she was leaving everything in her luggage had been turned out and turned over. There had been endless scrutiny and endless interrogation, and the surreptitious passing of gifts.

She turned a corner and was out into a wide concourse, watched by a hundred people who were waiting, some holding up cards and placards with names. Would she recognise Dora from the photographs? Would Dora be displaying her name on a card?

She was not. Katrin immediately recognised her rushing forward, grabbing the trolley to push it for her. Dora kissed and hugged her lavishly, possessively. The greeting was meant kindly, and Katrin responded with relieved delight at being in safe hands. But the welcome was too warm. "Oh you poor thing, you poor, poor thing," Dora was pronouncing shrilly, as Katrin stared around her at a place she had only ever seen in films. Was that man on the horse in the huge poster advertising a tourist resort in the mountains? The woman in the bathing dress announcing a seaside place? No, they were publicising cigarettes and cosmetics. So why not show a packet of cigarettes, a jar of skin cream?

"Are you hungry, my dearest?"

"No."

Why should she be hungry? She had only had coffee and a roll when she got up at five-fifteen, but she had eaten well on the plane.

Surprise and concern filled Dora's heavy, over-kind features. Everyone knew that people were nearly starved in her country. She would only be not hungry if she was one of the privileged Party few.

"Was it a comfortable flight? How is Katrin?"

This other Katrin was Katrin's mother.

"She is well." She had not been well, but she was now.

"Does she have a doctor for her illness?"

Of course she had a doctor. They had sickness in her country, so they had doctors. And hospitals with highly-qualified surgeons, even if resources were limited. Had Dora forgotten so much, or understood so little, as a result of being thirty years away?

"She has a very good doctor."

"And your father is well?"

It was always "your father" in letters and on the telephone, enquired about as a second thought. He was a little bit disapproved of. He was a Party member. But so was Katrin, like any young person who wanted to get on.

"He is well, but he is terribly busy. I sometimes think it is too much – "

Dora was not listening, Katrin assumed. But in fact Dora was having her own thoughts. She was alarmed at Katrin's father's busy-ness. It must be sinister.

Katrin looked beyond her as they walked, her eye caught by a shop on this airport concourse dedicated only to – it only sold socks? Could you make your living, even become rich, by selling only *socks*? She did not believe this shop could survive.

"You will be warm and comfortable with us," Dora was saying now. Why should Dora imply that she might not have been warm and comfortable at home? Katrin began to feel captured. She hoped Dora would permit her to meet other people, not insist on being with her and watching her all of the time.

They went down a gentle slope towards a metro station. Here the walls were almost covered with advertisement pictures, looking at her insistently. Coaxing her into believing in their smiles. For example, here was one that advertised insurance; and that was strange. Did you pay for your insurance here, at the window where you apparently bought your tickets for the Metro – the Underground? Was that why the queue was so long and slow? No, the people were buying tickets for the trains. *Tickets*, for the Metro trains? The Metro at home did not have tickets.

– 5 –

Dora talked, and talked, in the underground train to their London terminus and after that, in the mainline 'Intercity' train all the way to Fieldenhurst. It was kind, but it was also overwhelming and tiring. Katrin had a seat on the inside near the window, but she was unable to see very much of the undulating early summer countryside because she would have had to turn her head away; and a wall of the long, open carriage blocked out *most* of the window and the seats were arranged like those in a plane or a bus, with little leg room.

"Today you'll want to rest, I know," Dora was saying. "But to-morrow you will meet some English friends who are coming to dinner."

Katrin was very glad of that, because she had not spoken any English so far, in four long hours in England, only overheard it. Tried to understand it in the terminology, in the brief exchanges, of assistants in the station shops, of passengers trying to locate reserved seats, of ticket inspectors. Tried to take in some of the English names as Dora ran through them: Dora was proud of her Englishness and English acquaintanceship.

"There is a very nice –" Dora hesitated. Then she settled for the English words, not thinking there was not any exact equivalent in her and Katrin's own language. "A very nice *estate agent* and his wife, Jason and Claudine."

But what was an *estate agent*, Katrin wondered. A collective farm secretary? An estate manager, as in Chekhov? If so, whose estate?

"He is very interested in books, and art, and plays. Claudine paints. And we have two other friends, a couple called Julian and Sam, coming, I'm not sure what he does." Katrin must have looked puzzled. "Oh, Sam is his wife. Samantha," she explained. "They are *so* helpful with the theatre –" Dora had been mentioning the Fieldenhurst theatre frequently, hinting that she herself had some important function in it.

Hedges, fences, fields with healthy-looking cattle casting short shadows passed them. Katrin would have been content simply to sit in silence and let England unfold, present itself to her, outside the window. She was intoxicated by its richness of texture under the afternoon sunshine; the fields were joyful water colours containing every shade of green.

"And we have a charming young civil servant friend who would like to meet you – he's coming to dinner too."

Dora made no reference to a wife, and Katrin began to assume, sadly, that this one was intended as a dinner companion for her; there would be three other couples at the table including the hosts. Dora had allowed her to think the dinner had been happening anyway, her visit was not the reason for it. But both the meal and the young civil servant (Richard Hendleton, twenty-eight or twenty-nine) sounded very deliberate.

The countryside became scrubland, gradually, with dumps of dismantled cars, the brick façades of small deserted factories with broken windows, bridges over busy main roads, the approach to Fieldenhurst.

The only guidebook to English cities she found at home had been very old. Fieldenhurst had a sizeable entry, but the development of industry in the city had only been mentioned in passing, not with the pride and the detail (pictures of machine tool enterprises and petro-chemical works) you expected in her own country. On the other hand, the deepest respect was bestowed on Fieldenhurst as an historic centre, with a castle, a cathedral, a prominent school, medieval street-lines.

"John will be meeting us," Dora said; all the words in English suddenly.

"But do you talk in English with John?" asked Katrin in English, smiling. John was not English either, he and Dora had left Eastern Europe thirty years before. 'John' was the English version of his name. Dora laughed.

"I forgot! It's natural to use English." Now she had relapsed into her own tongue, and Katrin begged her, "Please talk in English if it's natural, I want to practise."

"I think you will have plenty of practice with our friends."

When John, only ever seen in just one photograph, introduced himself, he was actually larger, more filled-out, had more character than the picture suggested. He was prepared, unlike Dora, whose bitterness coloured and reduced everything about the place she had left, to grant that Katrin came from a civilised country.

For example, "Do you want a bath?" Dora asked Katrin pityingly as soon as they were inside the front door of the smart little semi-detached house. John, bundling her luggage in behind her, laughed. "They do have baths where she's come from. I remember them quite well," he said.

When she was at last alone in the bedroom they had given her, in a kind of solitude at last, Katrin simply sat down and looked at it, as she would have liked to look quietly at so many things in these past few hours. This, then, was the place in which she would be sleeping her first night out of her own country. Since Dora and John had arrived in England with hardly any possessions, the contents of their house were all inescapably English. Katrin enjoyed them at first: the flowers in the wallpaper, the solid cabinet of drawers, the neat dressing-table with the glass top and the silver-handled mirror and hair brush, and the glass pot of hair grips covered by the skirts of a little smiling china lady. Very pleasing.

She supposed those pictures on the wall to be of characteristic scenes, the cornfields, the river, the sunlit old city streets of Fieldenhurst with the cathedral spire rising reassuringly over the rooftops. Dora would have had an icon at home; but here there was just a mildly religious pastel picture, a faintly haloed shepherd gazing proprietorially at a placid flock in an English-looking field.

Unpacking as neatly as she had packed was difficult. The bedroom, novel and charming when she had first entered and looked round, seemed cluttered and inconvenient, claustrophobic even, when she tried to find surfaces to set out the contents of her luggage, including the gifts of lace and table mats and tiny vases. And Dora came in, trying to be helpful. Having changed out of the clothes she herself had travelled in to Heathrow, she made Katrin feel that her own clothes, which she was struggling to find space for in the small bedroom, were not very colourful or varied, were only too visibly well-used. It was something she only rarely felt at home ...

... Clothes, again. During the rapid car tour of Fieldenhurst John had given her in the morning she had thought that you did not see people in the streets conspicuously wearing the garments displayed in the shops. Wondering now what to put on for this dinner with friends, she was still thinking about that trip to town. She had asked John so many questions and he had answered them all fully, with rueful patience and kindness. Where Dora treated her like the child they had never had, was too eager to please and to control, John let her talk, let her ponder aloud, smiled gently at her naivety or forthrightness instead of laughing out loud and correcting her.

At one point John had said, turning off the Ring Road and driving back towards the centre of town, "Dora will never go back." He said it without question, not in relation to anything they had been talking about; in fact they had been driving in silence for a time while he allowed Katrin just to stare at things. It had plainly been on his mind.

Katrin looked at him surprised.

"So would you?" she asked, she thought a little too boldly.

The rueful smile. They were into a traffic jam as they approached the city centre, which they had to cross.

"I would have liked to try once," he told her slowly. "Ten years ago – fifteen – when it was all better than it seems to be now, and more hopeful. And when we were younger. I think it is too late now." *

"You are British citizens." Katrin knew that, so it was not a question.

Note: Certain sentences at this point were omitted from Miss Predeanu's Romanian translation, published in Bucharest.

"And we are British citizens." He affirmed it neutrally. "Dora is in a way very lucky. She has forgotten that people in England fail to understand her."

"But she speaks English very well. Doesn't she?"

"Very well. Better than me!" Katrin was not at all sure of that. This big, gentle man was being as unassuming in this as in everything else. "I mean understanding what she is to English people. Dora lives the English life, she doesn't know that people don't comprehend our past. She thinks she looks as English as the rest of them because they accept her. I know that I am not and I am lonely because people fail to understand why I feel I am an exile. And, you know, they are not even interested in understanding. You would not want them to ask all the time but most English people never ask at all. That never worries Dora. She has settled down. She is involved in this little theatre. She is happy. Or 'lucky' is the word."

And then John smiled, having unburdened himself of what he called his "misplaced, misconceived nostalgia"; and turned the question back to Katrin which meant he wanted to compare what he had as a naturalised librarian in 'prosperous England' with what he might have known in their country if he had stayed, or returned.

Quite innocently the slim young woman had warmed to the older man, enough for him to feel he could talk to her candidly about the guests they were inviting to dinner in the evening, from which Katrin expected absorbing insights into English life and the English character.

"He sells people's houses for them," John said about Jason Simmingley, when she asked him what you did in England if you were an 'estate agent.'

"Sells houses? He doesn't manage houses – or an estate?"

"Nothing so responsible!"

"And they pay him for that? He can live by it? He doesn't have another job?"

John smiled, but did not let Katrin see.

"He lives by taking a percentage of what the buyer pays the seller. As the prices of houses are rising all the time, he is a rich man."

"And why don't people buying a house just go and talk to the people who want to sell it?"

"Ah – it needs several people to arrange the sale. The owners of the house need the estate agent to advertise their house as available for sale. If a lot of people are interested in a house the owner can sell at a higher price." She was shocked at this, for a moment; then nodded in understanding. "When people think they have a home to buy they go to a solicitor – a lawyer – and he arranges a contract."

"I see. It used to be like this at home, a long time ago..." She thought she saw. "Mr Simmingley's wife is an artist?" She seemed to recall Dora telling her something like that.

"Claudine paints pictures in her spare time," he said. "Artist is a strong word. I am a librarian in a public library, I invent tunes at the piano. But I am not a composer."

"And there are two people, a man and a wife, called Julian and Sam."

"Samantha. Julian is one of those solicitors. She works in a building society. And you will not know what that is!"

"So they all fit together?" she said after he had explained. "The people who lend the money for the interest, or take the percentages when houses are sold, they decide everything about where people can live and how much money they have left after they have paid the highest price for the house? It is true what you learn in my country! It is all controlled by money and who has it."

"In our country," he corrected her.

"Who is the civil servant coming this evening?"

"Richard Hendleton? He's a friend of Julian and Samantha." Apparently he was very pleasant and intelligent, though John found him reserved to the point of dullness; perhaps merely shy. John said nothing about his age or appearance. "He's not their special friend. These are all people interested in Dora's theatre.

35

The town theatre. They are called 'The Friends of the Theatre'. Dora is the Secretary of the Friends."

"Is it a state theatre?"

"No, but the state gives it some money. It is quite good – I suppose." He spoke as if he himself had little interest in it. "Dora enjoys it, I said that," he said, thinking they had somehow come full circle.

All of their conversation in the car had been in English [...]

– **6** –

"Er – coffee?"

Trying a foreign accent in the way he spoke the English word, as if that would render the term comprehensible.

"No am coffee. Tea?"

"Tea."

"Tea!"

"Yes, please. Er – rolls? Butter?" Tim was hungry now.

"Tea – rolls – butter – jam. Ham?"

"Yes, ham, thank you."

"Omelette with ham? Salad?"

"Oh rather, yes, please. Everything. Thank you."

Outside the cold sun shone on tall, formal, unidentifiable buildings which kept the elaborate grandeur of another period and converted it to present, Communist purposes. Tim's provisional schedule, brought from London, was beside him on the table – he moved it now to make space for the heavy teacup into which the waiter dropped a sachet of black Chinese tea on a long thread, pouring water on it from a porcelain pot. There was no milk, no lemon, only the tea. The rest of his order came with surprising speed. He ate hungrily.

He had slept well. This could even be something that felt like uncomplicated happiness. Sitting around in a foreign place with work forgotten. Except that strange connections with Philip Carston had cropped up in Tillitt's conversation, and there had been that odd phone call...

He found himself watching the waiters in case they were watching him. The restaurant was not busy. A large white-coated group of waiters loitered (he could see them when he turned round) near the kitchen door, and most of them were sending glances in his direction. There were smiles and laughter from time to time, and he had to tell himself they were not discussing him. There were hardly any other people in this large low-ceilinged room with the white tablecloths, flowers in glass vases, no one obviously suspicious or ominous, just one or two inconspicuous individuals in the shady corners, whom he could not see very well because the sunshine dazzled him.

"Good morning. Excuse me, are you Mr Harker-Jones?"

Where had she come from? He had not seen anyone entering, and crossing the room. She must have been there already. (Or come out of the kitchen? No.) Had she risen from one of the inconspicuous corner tables?

"I am Miss Cernec – Angela. How do you do?"

He stood up, and smiled. She was offering him a hand, at a level rather too high to grab and shake but also too low to bend over and kiss. A moment later, he supposed he should have kissed it when he had already given it a small, awkward tug in nervous greeting. But with a mouthful of ham omelette? Unprepared again...

"Will you sit down and have some tea? They don't seem to have any coffee on the menu."

But Miss Cernec waved to a waiter. "O cafea!" she was calling. And it came, almost immediately, greatly to Tim's surprise. Was she well-known here? Could she pull strings?

He was rapidly, instinctively, guessing her age. Early thirties? Or younger? A cool, thinnish, almost-but-not-quite pale face, with a practical look about the bright eyes. Short, but well-coiffured hair, that shone slightly. A direct manner of talking, with a suggestion of enacting a routine of welcome for the hundredth time. Impersonal; but Tim felt reassured by an implication of friendliness. She had the gift of making him feel he could rely on her.

And yet he had official instructions not to assume that friendly Romanians could be trusted. Not that he, Tim Harker-Jones, biographer of twentieth century 'literary' writers, had military secrets or business information to give away. But he thought that he would not tell Miss Cernec anything about last night's peculiar phone call. So he simply answered her questions about the flight, the hotel, the breakfast, politely.

"Mr Harker-Jones," she suddenly said with great deliberateness, as if about to announce something momentous. "We have to decide whether you would like us to go at the weekend to the Black Sea, or to the Carpathian mountains!"

"Which do you recommend as more interesting?"

"Both." The faintest outlines of a smile.

"Which is better at this time of year?" (Mid-winter, in effect.)

"Both are very good. It is what you want."

"Are the hotels warm?"

"The hotels are very warm. But we can wait until to-morrow to decide. There is time to buy the tickets. Have you finished?"

"We walk to the Writers' Union first," she said when they were through last night's revolving door and out onto the pavement. "Left, please. It is a nice morning of weather we have organised for you." The faint smile again.

Almost immediately, "That's –" He stopped and pointed.

"That's what?"

"That's the restaurant, I'm sure it is. In a film I was watching on TV last night. And this is the street. I can see it is – in daylight."

Miss Cernec seemed to have a trained impassivity for coping with visitors' unexpected reactions to her country.

"Well, I am not surprised if it is in a film. It is a very famous restaurant."

Into a wide, bare square now, traversed oddly for this time

of day by very few people, and very little traffic.

"What is that building?" Tim asked.

"I don't know."

Didn't she, or was she not prepared to say? He would persist, he resolved. She would have to know the one he nodded towards on their right, far across the open space, because it was crested by large skyline letters which he could only partly try to translate: TRAIASCA PARTIDUL COMUNIST ROMAN.

"What is that one?"

"You can see. It is the Party Central Committee."

He felt reproved by Angela Cernec's abrupt tone for asking something so obvious. The building was a square, grey block, not un-handsome in its wholly typical way, with a closed black double-doored entrance, big and heavy and yet somehow not grand enough to provide an imposing formal entrance. In front of it stood a blue-uniformed guard, but nobody was coming or going. Monolithic yes, active hardly...

"Why is there no one entering or leaving? The door is shut."

"They enter and leave at the back. That is a ceremonial entrance."

"I see. Does President Ceausescu work there?"

"He works here," she said, whispering, coaxing Tim's voice down to a whisper too, as if the president's name should not be spoken. She nodded towards the older building coming up on their left, the structure of yellowing stone, fronted with bush-filled gardens behind high railings and a sentry in a box; a palace.

"Actually here! Does he live here as well?

"No – He *works* here. He lives somewhere else."

The people passing in these streets, in this square, walked past each other without looking, without speaking. No one lingered; there seemed no easy casualness at all in the way they occupied their city. He and Angela Cernec were walking on a pavement, but on the far side, in front of the Central Committee (no doubt a hive of offices, typewriters and computers if you ever penetrated it) police maintained strict observance of the rules for passers-by. No one could approach the Central Committee, no one stop and look at it, everyone had to pass it quickly and not stop.

He thought he should prepare himself by asking, "Who am I meeting at the Writers' Union?"

"Today I don't know. Sometimes we meet the Secretary, sometimes the official for public relations."

"For public relations?" This sounded very western.

"Yes, for public relations with visitors and with other countries," she said.

"For international relations? For foreign contacts?"

"Yes. I said. And perhaps you will meet publishers, and writers. I don't know. On the left there is a department store."

Was this entire walk a propaganda tour, with his guide careful to point out places of pride and significance and deflect unsuitable questions? And why hadn't Miss Cernec brought him in the car Tillitt had mentioned? They seemed to be about to leave the centre of the city. When – "Here," she said. "I think we are a little early."

She guided him up a very short drive alongside a garden space, ending at a door opening between two challenging stone lions. Inside, the only light came from the windows high above. Tim glanced up and took in a painted ceiling at the top of an extravagant staircase spiralling out of the centre of this concourse. Everything was gold and scarlet and grand. Nothing could be heard when Tim listened for sounds of activity, and nobody was coming or going; except for Angela, who explained, a bit nervously, he thought, that she was going into an office to enquire where they were expected to go. Soon she returned looking reassured.

"No problem, we go here." She took him back to a door on the left just inside the entrance. After the dark of the hall this was bright when they entered it, because it had windows onto the garden, but gloomier when Tim's eyes became accustomed to it. The windows were hung with long dark green curtains, the walls lined with glass-fronted bookcases. Angela switched on the lights.

"We can take off our coats," she instructed. Tim felt that his unsureness about whatever might be allowed or prohibited, must have been miserably clear to her, so that she was issuing elementary, motherly orders. He took off his coat likewise, piled it on top of Angela's, tried to look assured and adult, less like a lost child. Could he endure her company for a fortnight? No, that was a bit brutal. Of course he could, and not only because he realised he had no alternative.

An unobtrusive, silent, anonymous man brought in, on a small tray, coffee in little cups and mineral water bubbling freshly in tumblers. Then the door swung open and someone else entered. This was a man wearing one of the long black leather overcoats people wore in the streets and a black hat, a man with a rough look about him. He had strong eyes, and a hearty, youthful way of greeting Angela (whom he clearly knew) despite being of an age with Tim, even somewhat older.

Tim watched him take her hand at once, lift it up, bow his head with a gesture that said, "I am being just a little ridiculously chivalrous, but you will appreciate it" (which Angela obviously did), and kiss it. Or rather, lower his lips and not quite make contact, the intention and gesture being all. So that was what you did? Angela (charmed by a rogue?), responded to everything with much more warmth and extroversion than she had shown up to this point.

"This –" she said turning to Tim – "is Mr Ioan Ludache." And she looked at Tim in a strangely straight, emphatic way, widening her eyes a little, a look that might have been hinting something. "You will have many things to talk about," said Angela to Tim. "Mr Ludache is a well-known biographer."

Ludache gripped Tim's hand.

– 7 –

But according to Tillitt there were no biographers, except for the writers producing encomia for the President.

"Mr Ludache says you are especially welcome as a fellow archaeologist excavating the remains left behind by the famous." As if he understood English Ludache nodded during Angela's translation; and Tim realised the man still gripped his own hand in heartfelt greeting, smiling in a slightly overbearing way every time Angela completed a phrase. "Mr Ludache says he has been mainly a biographer of past lives, so he is eager to meet someone who concentrates on lives in our century." Tim was about to respond when Ludache started again, volubly, as if he had prepared a long speech in advance and would permit no interruption. "Mr Ludache," Angela interpreted "has ideas he would like to discuss with you some time... He will be pleased to hear about the present task you are working on (on which you are working, sorry!)"

Ludache let go of Tim's hand, gave a wide, rough grin, and stopped. Tim misunderstood, thinking he meant to hear about it in due course, not now.

"Please can you tell Mr Ludache what is the subject of your present work?"

"Oh – well yes, certainly. You won't know about him, but I've been researching the life of an English novelist who died last year." Angela translated, and Ludache said something, and Angela said, "Will you tell him which one. He says three or four English writers died last year."

"He was a friend of mine called Philip Carston."

Ludache was instantly all animation and pleasure.

"But he was my friend too. So that is why they send you here, because you are a friend of Mr Carston!"

Tim could barely speak for astonishment.

"Well – no –"

"Certainly they are sending you because of dear Philip?"

Angela was not translating at all now, because Ludache was speaking in English; and Tim had only just realised.

"You forgive me, please. I was excited. I speak better in Romanian."

Angela returned to her interpreter's role.

"Mr Ludache says he can command a little English – I believe he is being modest – but he can say more things if he speaks in Romanian and I translate. He says it is very important to arrange a special meeting with you to talk about your work on the life of Mr. Carston."

"We can meet any time – I'm free a lot of the time," Tim muttered. "You met Philip –?"

"We will see," Angela said firmly, without translating that for Ludache. "Remember you have many appointments. You are busy. And Mr. Ludache is busy."

"But –" Why was she cancelling his offer?

The door opened again and three more people, not in outdoor coats, walked in; a tall older man, smartly, even exquisitely, dressed in a suit of purplish colour; a younger woman with long black hair, of about Angela's age, carrying a pile of brightly-jacketed books; a man in his middle years in a very correct, clean, ordinary dark blue suit and carrying a file. The last immediately took charge of the occasion. His English gave promise of being excellent.

"Mr. Harker-Jones, welcome! It's extremely good to have you here in Bucharest."

"I am interpreting for Mr. Harker-Jones, if necessary," Angela told him in English, with smiling emphasis, by way of making her presence in the room indubitable and her role effective. He inclined his head to kiss Angela's hand (he too stopped just short of touching it) with a blend of condescending charm and perfunctoriness, not as extravagant as Ludache's performance; putting her in her place.

"Tonaru – Stefan," he told Tim. "I am deputising today for

the Secretary for Public Relations who is ill and unable to join us" – "Am I always to get deputies?" Tim wondered – "but I am not so sad he is incapacitated, because it provides me with the important pleasure of welcoming you myself. And of introducing Dr Mandeliu – Vasile – head of our translation publishing house, and his assistant and talented editor Miss Ciudea – Valeria."

He motioned them ceremoniously to the table as more coffee and more mineral water appeared. Miss Ciudea – why did the name sound familiar to Tim? But yes, of course! he remembered now – spread out her books in front of her so that Tim could see the titles. He took in Flaubert, Chekhov, Thomas Mann, Kafka. She was looking at him with some interest, and a careful smile.

Tim began to speak; to say he knew not what, perhaps just to offer the right noises about his own gladness to be there if he could do that without sounding bewildered. Tonaru, not hearing him, rode robustly over his faltering beginnings.

"On behalf of the Writers' Union, Mr. Harker-Jones, I hope you enjoy your stay in Romania and gain a happy impression of our culture. Naturally you will tell us what you would especially like to do while you are here. But I wish to speak of some of the arrangements we have made." And he opened his file, and began to run through it: magazines to visit, a library, a performance of *Hamlet*. Tim sensed a ritual that had to be performed, something that precluded less formal interchanges. Since most of this was written down in his own programme he let his eyes wander briefly to the other faces in the room: Ludache still grinning affably, Dr Mandeliu beaming, Valeria Ciudea maintaining her intent look, almost implying a familiarity, a renewal of old acquaintance after their exchange on the telephone last night.

Tonaru finished, and before Tim could say anything at all handed over to Dr Vasile Mandeliu. Tonaru lit a cigarette from a packet of Kent, and Valeria Ciudea did the same.

"Dr Mandeliu also welcomes you..." Angela said. "He is the director of the largest publishing house here. He has brought some examples of his most recent books..."

Tim looked at them, in front of Valeria Ciudea, who was now smiling quite openly, and staring at him. He took in the illustrations on the dust-jackets, looked up again at Mandeliu. Then his eyes darted back to the books and he wondered if he was hallucinating.

One of them, with a bright yellow cover had a picture of a girl on it against a neatly-sketched background of the Houses of Parliament, and he could not translate the title but registered that the author's name was Philip Carston and that the girl answered the description of –

"Dr Mandeliu says he is happy to answer one or two questions about the publishing house," Angela was saying. "Mr. Harker-Jones, would you like to ask them?"

Tim appeared to be focusing on the books on the table and not paying attention. Tonaru's right hand rested on his file of papers. His middle finger tapped them lightly, with unconscious impatience.

"Yes..." said Tim. "Yes. I know a novel by my late friend Philip Carston has been translated into your language. Can you tell me which one it is that I can see here?"

Immediately Valeria Ciudea smiled and pushed the book towards him. Everyone looked at him looking at it, and smiled; Ludache smiled longest.

"I am afraid," Tim pleaded, "I cannot translate the title."

"It is not an exact translation for the title in English," Valeria explained. "Philip Carston's English title was *A Time Apart*. We published it last spring."

Now Tim was certain he had been working too hard for the good of his own mind on the biographical project; Philip's last novel was in his thoughts, and in his luggage, and in his dreams last night because he had been re-reading it before falling asleep, and here it was in his hands in a Romanian version with Katrin on the dust-jacket.

"But that is impossible," he heard himself saying, playing

along with his own madness.

Dr Mandeliu smiled very widely and knowingly, and said something.

"Dr Mandeliu says we are very speedy and efficient here in Romania in recognising the best fiction to translate." There was pride but also a little self-mockery in the translated remark that appealed to Tim. "His publishing house brought it out in the spring of the year after it was published in London in the February, so perhaps it was a little slower than you imagine!"

"But how could the translator –" Tim found the name: Carolina Predeanu – Carolina! – "how did Miss Predeanu obtain a copy and work so fast? I mean, how did she lay hands on one? Did Philip Carston come here? And it must have been done at a rate of knots..."

"She is an extremely talented translator," said Valeria. There was failure to understand Tim clearly, perhaps he had spoken too colloquially. "And she was helped by the fact that Katrin is a Romanian girl." Here she gave Tim a very odd little look, severe and humorous.

"She is a Romanian? Specifically a Romanian?"

"He doesn't say it, but she is."

"Can I meet the translator? Carolina –" he looked back at the book, almost trembling – "Carolina Predeanu?"

Immediately Tonaru:

"There will not be time. It is very sad."

"There will not be time?" Obstacles were being placed in his way. "Please, I should very much appreciate the chance of speaking with Miss Predeanu. I am researching into the life of Philip Carston at the moment for a biography, and it would be very interesting – essential! – for me to meet his Romanian translator."

But Tonaru came back with a strong smile and an emphatic negative, as if Tim were a child making a ridiculous, unallowable request, not comprehending adult necessities.

"No. After all, she is only the translator."

Tim heard Angela, beside him, draw in breath sharply at this observation, and saw her sip some mineral water. "And also, she lives a long way out of town, in a city in the provinces. Where do you wish to go at the weekend?"

Tim, emboldened by frustration, was not prepared to be rushed into this one.

"I want time to think," he declared firmly. "Your country is completely new to me and I don't wish to choose too quickly." Suddenly he knew he had to visit Carolina Predeanu in her provincial city.

Suddenly they were all standing up, stubbing out cigarettes, pushing their chairs under the table. The formalities of welcome appeared to be over, Dr Mandeliu was piling the display of books back into Valeria Ciudea's arms. And they were all shaking hands again, and standing back for each other to move out into the dark, warm, beautiful hall with the elaborate staircase leading up, no doubt, to further rooms occupied by laconic editors and suavely-talking cultural officials, and obedient secretaries.

As the six of them strolled towards the front door, Ludache and Angela ahead, chatting, Tim following them with Mandeliu at his side, Tonaru just behind, overwhelmingly attentive and friendly, Tim realised he had left his coat back in the meeting room.

"Oh it is my fault, I am such a poor host," Tonaru exclaimed. "I am too interested in the conversation to remember the essentials of life. I will get."

He ran back, vanishing behind the door of the room which closed behind him. Mandeliu now excused himself and disappeared rapidly up the staircase. Angela and Ioan Ludache, talking together, were already out of the entrance door. In this second Tim felt something changed in the situation, something about the way Valeria Ciudea, who had carefully lowered the books she carried onto a chair, was standing and regarding him, with something in her hand in the lightening gloom.

"Please!" she said in a whisper.

"What –?" Tim was slow.

"Please – Take!"

She was pressing into his hand a twice-folded slip of paper torn out of her writing pad.

"I could not tell you this when I telephoned last night," she murmured. "Carolina's address. Put in your pocket." Wide-eyed he nodded, effusively but covertly. Valeria was picking up her books again, and Stefan Tonaru was back with Tim's coat, helping him into it. Adjusting it round his shoulders Tim turned his back on Valeria for a moment; and when he swung round again to say goodbye she had disappeared.

– 8 –

"They don't bring you a menu, you just ask what there is," Sam Taplin told him as the waiter approached. "Even here at the Athenée Palace, these days." He conversed in fluent, jokey Romanian with the waiter, an old bald man who managed a battered smile. "I assume pork chops are all right by you? Don't suppose you're Jewish, or anything?"

"No. But what do Jews do?"

"Don't come to this restaurant."

"Who does come to this restaurant?"

"That's a story." He spoke with cheerful abruptness, as with most of his answers to Tim's questions. Taplin's astringent manner went with his bristling red hair, his wiriness of feature and physique. When you were accustomed to his style, as Tim was in ten minutes, he seemed a friendly man; but Tim still did not find him particularly expansive. Whereas Nick Tillitt had been expansive in an unhelpful way...

Tim gazed out into the scarlet distances of the Athenée Palace restaurant, the vistas of immaculate tables, the shining glasses and cutlery, the windows with plush curtains, the dead wall-lights. The patrons here seemed, just after noon today, to be mainly a few young men in smart clothes, smoking, wearing grey flannel trousers, jacketed in black leather. But there was a class of older men who came in in long dark overcoats, and Tim saw two groups of unalike persons who might have been transacting business, because they were not eating but keeping to beer or wines, and they huddled together confidentially over their tables. Their waiter set down their pork chops, chips and cucumber salad with cold correctness, his brief opening smile not repeated.

"They get to know you fast," Taplin said. "They know I won't sell them currency. But I can leave them cigarettes as a tip."

He brought a packet of Kent out of his pocket and put it back again.

"How do they get hold of those? They come from the States?" Tim wanted to know.

"Oh *we* bring them in. In quantities!" He laughed. But he had spoken in a quick, confidential way as if he thought his remark indiscreet.

"Does the band ever play?" Tim looked across the spaces, to an unlit, rather forlorn platform where there were lonely seats and music-stands and a microphone.

"Yes. To-night and every night, very, very loudly. Going on as late as nine o'clock. Everything shuts down after that, to save energy."

Tim was almost desperate to find a means of returning to the subject of the slip of paper passed to him by Valeria Ciudea. He had talked about it on the way here in the comparative safety of the street, mentioned Philip and *A Time Apart* and Ludache ("dear Philip") but not had time to broach the subject of any favours Taplin might do him in facilitating arrangements. Taplin had advised him strictly not to use a Romanian name in conversation in the restaurant, as they could be "overheard". There could be listening devices in the walls. They would be directed, most likely, to a corner table kept especially for foreign visitors, where there might be bugs in the lights over their heads, or under the tablecloth, or in a bowl of flowers, or in an ashtray.

And yet they had been guided to a table in the centre of the room. Tim simply had to wring some assistance from Taplin. Surely two discreet sentences of practical advice, a nod or a wink ensuring help, would be possible? As long as he did not utter names.

"See – this is it", Tim said quietly, producing the folded notepad sheet from his pocket and placing it furtively half under the rim of his plate in Taplin's sight. At once Taplin raised a warning forefinger, pointed to his ear, then prodded the side of his own plate with his fork.

"Things in the plates, as well as on them", he murmured. Tim's mouth dropped open. He could not be serious.

Careful not to appear to be reading it, doing it with little downward and sidelong glances, Taplin took in the name and address and phone number scribbled in smudged ballpoint writing. Then he shook his head and shrugged, conveying that the name was not one he knew. He looked at Tim earnestly, with a perplexed look.

Tim had to come clean somehow and demand action. If Carolina Predeanu, whoever she was, had translated the novel so fast, she must have had proofs before publication. Or even the manuscript. And if she had had a manuscript she might have known Philip Carston. There might indeed have been some "illicit travelling" which Alic Paldrey would be interested to hear about.

"Did – did the novelist I was referring to come to Romania ever? Or his translator visit England?"

"Don't know. If so, it was before my time here."

"I want to go to – to this place," Tim went on, pointing to the words 'Târgu Alb' on the slip of paper. "I shall ask to be taken there at the weekend. Is – is the person to whom I made reference –" running his finger along Miss Predeanu's name and trying to avoid easily understandable English words; also lowering his voice – "is the person likely to be someone I could go through the official channels to continue a – a 'consultation' with?"

"Heaven knows!" was the answer conveyed by Taplin's expression. But while Tim was thinking, "Isn't it your business to help me find out?", what Taplin said was, "Well you could try. But it might require a *lot* of asking – a lot of persistence on your part. And if you absolutely failed, then you would find it tricky to continue a 'consultation' by other means, because it would be only too clear you were hell bent on a 'consultation', and measures would be taken to prevent it. So I would strongly advise you against raising the matter at all. I cannot do anything. On the other hand how can I stop you?"

Here Taplin grinned, and shrugged happily. Tim saw in it a grin of encouragement. Accompanied by that sub-diplomatic speech it reminded him of a solicitor hinting that, while he could not openly sanction or approve a client's proposed actions, which he would naturally remain ignorant of, the client would not be blamed for having a go, and good luck to him.

"Therefore you would think it was – so to speak – up to me regarding a 'consultation'?"

"Completely. But first things first: it's a bloody long way away." His finger went to the place-name. "It's way over in Transylvania."

"London to Edinburgh?"

"Less than two-thirds of that. But the trains are slower. You can fly there, but there aren't many flights. Two a week? I don't know."

"Can you – should I start by suggesting it to – to the person you met before lunch?" He meant Angela, who had escorted him to the British embassy compound and delivered him over to Taplin.

Taplin did not take the hint that he himself should do something.

"That's the only one you can suggest it to, isn't it. And you'll have to be extremely persuasive. Say it's utterly crucial for the completion of your work. Bang the table a bit, but nicely. Be politely furious and disappointed. You *might* succeed. No one wants to appear inhospitable. Be prepared for them to come up with somewhere stunning for you to visit at the weekend if they absolutely don't wish you to go to Transylvania. Have objections ready."

"I see."

"The whole of this ball," said Taplin, leaning forward with friendly complicity but also dissociating himself in advance from anything Tim might do, "is totally and utterly in your court. I'm confident –" and Tim expected his own determination to see Carolina Predeanu to be flattered and admired; so that he was genuinely hurt when Taplin ended his sentence, curtly and without smiling now – "that you'll get nowhere whatsoever."

At this put-down, reminding him of his newness and inexperience in a country overwhelmingly strange and unpredictable for him, he could have shed childish tears.

– 9 –

Voltimand and Cornelius were relieved of their swords before they entered Claudius's presence. Claudius was austere, shifty, polished, the inveterate schemer, Gertrude a harrowing monument to her earlier beauty, sunk in uncomprehending grief about her son's condition.

When Hamlet came downstage for 'To be or not to be', two of the absurd company of players parading with drum and trumpet deliberately interrupted him, destroying every expectation of this moment and yet underlining the gravity of the speech when Hamlet could deliver it. As Claudius rose to put an end to the players' performance, Hamlet rose also, to conduct like a maestro, centre-stage, an orchestrated storm of confusion until everyone had fled and he was left in arrogant solitude with the aghast knowledge that the Ghost had spoken true. Ophelia reverted from womanhood to the condition of rejected child, bowed and pitiful, yet luminously beautiful in madness.

At the end, late in the evening despite an early start, the audience stayed on to stand and cheer for a full ten minutes, though the theatre was cold and warmed only by their bodies; then people drifted away along the dark street or across the small park opposite the theatre in thoughtful silence.

"Why was there so much applause at the end?" Tim asked Angela.

"But it was a very good performance. Don't you want to applaud a good performance?"

"It was a *magnificent* performance, even for me – I couldn't understand a word and yet I could understand everything. The only thing puzzling to me was the applause."

"We have wonderful actors in my country. Hamlet is one of our greatest actors, people do applaud Caramitru."

"I can see that. But I thought there might be some particular reason they applauded for so long."

He felt ignorantly persistent. But Taplin had advised persistence. Tim sensed in the darkness that she was embarrassed, and knew he had touched on something not to be openly discussed. Angela made time for herself by guiding him carefully across a rutted roadway. Then she said,

"People go and see these unusual interpretations of Shakespeare, and other plays. And they clap their hands very loudly and think it is so exciting and dangerous. And next morning they forget."

"And *dangerous*?" The word had told Tim more than he had known before about how far Angela was prepared to be frank.

"I would like to make a phone call in the hotel. Will that be easy?"

He felt stared at, in the dark.

"Of course," she said abruptly, defending the normality of her country against this peculiar tendency of foreigners to be paranoiac about everything, or believe that nothing would work. "No problem. But it is late. Who is it you wish to call?"

"I have found a number for Carolina Predeanu – the translator of that novel." He thought he heard her draw in breath in alarm. "In Târgu Alb."

"Oh, it is a long way from Bucharest. It will be an expensive call."

"How much?"

"I don't know. The hotel may want hard currency."

"No problem."

"Are the lines bad?"

"No. It will be very quick. But you cannot –" she spoke quietly – "you understand, there are difficulties here for people talking to foreigners."

"But I am speaking to you," he joked. She ignored the weakness of his answer. "And I must speak to her to tell her I am here. She has never been to England and –"

"Carolina Predeanu has been to England. I don't know her, but people say that."

Angela had fallen into his trap, one he had used before in researching lives: you make a categorical statement and someone in a position to know a truth would unthinkingly deny what you said. He knew now that whatever Angela, or Mr Tonaru, or Sam Taplin maintained, he would persist and get to Târgu Alb. He saw an alluring thread coming into his fingers...

"If she has been to England, I must certainly speak to her, and meet her," he exclaimed with unfeigned eagerness.

When they entered his room in the hotel (she had reluctantly agreed to help him make the call if he couldn't understand what to do) he immediately switched on the television, and turned up the volume even before the vision came through. First there was the announcer's rapid, toneless voice, then a coloured chart: the weather forecast. Tim thought, "We have to drown any conversation I have with Angela in case anyone is listening." He invited her to take an armchair, and opened the personal notebook to which he had transferred Carolina Predeanu's details, and sat on the edge of the bed to examine the English part of the instructions for using the phone, knowing that a phone call would be overheard anyway.

The weather map faded, the presenter said good-night and stared at viewers until his own image faded, then an image of mountains and forests and sunshine glittering round them appeared, while a jaunty signing-off anthem was played. Anything that followed would come, like last night's film he supposed, through the video service of the hotel.

Angela watched him lift the elegantly heavy phone to his ear, giving him a fixed scrutinising stare. He dialled the single digit required.

"Allo!"

"Hullo? Do you speak English?"

There was no answer except a sigh, and the phone at the other end was abandoned for some seconds. Then it was picked up again, and another voice answered in ready, relaxed English.

"Yes. I help you?"

"I want to telephone Târgu Alb. The number? The number is –"

In the video now showing, a group of young girls in peasant dress danced in a circle wielding brooms, coquettishly brushing and sweeping a perfectly polished floor and singing in chorus as an impassive five-man peasant band played in the background.

Tim could imagine the Târgu Alb number being carefully noted down in the exchange. The voice said something he could not understand. "Replace please." "What?" "They are telling you to put your phone down", said Angela. "That means I can't make the call?" he suggested, incompetently. "No. Put it down and they will phone you when they have the line."

The broom-dance, with its exuberant simplicity, was done, the girls giving a triumphant, smiling shout as all their long brooms met in the centre of the circle. Double doors in the scenery in the video opened, and the camera moved into a little arena where – to Tim's surprise because he had expected everything to be as ordinary as the broom girls in their long peasant dresses – five young blondes in tasselled caps and tight blouses and mini-skirts, holding hoops, tripped out and perched themselves cross-legged on high stools. Rapid, westernised rhythms pounded out lightly as each one took her turn to leap down, jump through a hoop held by another and settle herself on the saddle of a single-wheeled cycle which she pedalled round the room: a fetching circus act.

The loud bell of the telephone broke in on Tim's thoughts about this. He looked at Angela; she raised her eyebrows and sat still. He picked up the receiver as if he had never picked up one before, first of all putting the wrong end to his ear.

"Room 410?" a voice said. "Târgu Alb."

A bell was ringing, a voice was answering. It was a quick, calm young woman's voice, clear and close and yet surrounded by telephonic atmosphere which rendered it unmistakeably distant.

"Da? Allo?"

He could only launch helplessly into English. But he decided he was not going to give his name.

"I am a friend of Philip Carston," he said. "I am phoning from Bucharest."

There was an intense telephonic silence at the other end, a few seconds in which sound waves fidgeted and vibrated and rubbed up against one another in the cosmos. When the voice came again it spoke with trembling deliberation, in beautifully enunciated English, slowly but not calmly.

"I am sorry. I do not understand you... This is Predeanu – Carolina, yes?"

"Yes – I am Philip Carston's friend. Tim." He would at least dare the forename.

A further silence. And then –

"Yes. I *see*. Thank you – very much. You *try again*. You try again, yes? *Please*, Mr. Tim. Goodbye."

And this time it was a different quality of silence, the emptiness of a dead line. Carolina Predeanu had rung off.

But she had made it clear that he was speaking to the right

person. And, emphatically, she wanted him to try again. *How*?

A moment later, having put the phone down, with the blonde nymphs still daintily mounting one by one in turn the little cycle and pedalling it round and round with smiles, and busy legs, and hands on hips, he was registering Angela's expression of triumph or resignation ("I expected you would fail") and reaching despairing conclusions. Translators worked hard for their living, the book might now be far from her thoughts. No doubt Carolina Predeanu found the restrictions imposed on meeting foreigners quite a convenient excuse for being dismissive, and ringing off.

And yet; her tone of voice had been far from dismissive. Tim smiled again when Angela, with her fixed, interrogating look (the blonde nymphs all coming to smiling attention on the screen beside her) said, "You had no luck?"

"Oh but I did," he said. "I spoke to her. It was not – convenient at that moment to talk. But I believe she wants me to be in touch with her again."

And oh, he was hungry now. He had forgotten he had had nothing since lunch with Taplin. Since then there had been *Hamlet*, and the walk back from the theatre, and all the enigmas of the telephone. "Do you think the restaurant would be open?"

"It is very strange," she said defensively. "This winter, everything in Bucharest closes at nine."

It was eleven. He thought impatiently, "So she is not hungry herself, and she is actually not prepared to let me find any dinner. *I am not going to get any dinner!*"

"Aren't you hungry?"

"You can use the telephone to order food," she insisted.

"Oh no!" Not the telephone, again.

But he did use it. Rolls and butter and ham came, and cheese, and pots of hot water to make the black Chinese tea, and the waiter readily taking payment in lei.

Food strengthened his will to win.

"I want to go to Târgu Alb this weekend."

Still she came back with excuses; but with a look near to

anguish, as if she wanted him to answer them.

"I would like to go there too. But we will hear it is impossible, there is not time to make the arrangements, other places would be better and more important."

The music from the TV had softened. Angela turned up the volume to ensure it overlay their conversation. The music behind a new troupe of larger, more mature girls was unquestionably western, a twanging synthesizer and a voice singing in broken American-English, perhaps a pirated rock song, a bastard exoticism for Romanian ears:

You're a li – ar
You're my des – i – ah!

Legs crossed themselves, uncrossed themselves, danced and pranced on the screen.

"Do they have publishers we could visit in Târgu Alb? Magazines?"

"Yes. There is a Writers' Union. The magazine *Misiva* is published in Târgu Alb. There is a publishing house for the region. But they are closed at weekends – except Saturday morning."

"We could see the editors in their homes."

"*No!*"

"Is it expensive for Bucharest Writers' Union to send me there?"

"Of course not," with loyal indignation. "Look, I will see."

The music and dancing was over, the TV screen blank, and snowing. Angela rose, and pulled round her the coat she had never taken off.

"I am here at nine to-morrow, as usual." It seemed 'as usual' to Tim also, though to-morrow would be only his second day. "We will take a taxi tour to show you the city."

TWO

– 1 –

Tim was thinking: You devise a metaphor and it transforms into a physical fact. I am in a foreign city, with a thread of cotton or silk in my hand stretching out into the distance at waist level, and it winds around a corner ahead of me. And now, as I turn the corner, it becomes a string. It runs through my fingers smoothly as I follow it, walking through groups of people who smile and watch. I smile back, and reach another street corner – and the string is a thin rope, and I follow it, run my hand along it, taking care not to burn my fingers as I advance to the next corner where —

Somebody or something, before I can turn this corner, has been pulling at the rope, because it's thinning out into a string again, and the string is dwindling back into a thread. Yes, when I turn the corner I am only holding the cotton thread I held at the beginning, although, as I follow it, it is thickening into a string again, so I will go on following it...

That had been at 4.20 a.m., which Tim saw when he had finally found his way along the flex of the bedside lamp and pressed the button to switch on the light. It was now eight-thirty in the hotel restaurant, and he knew all he had to do was shame Angela Cernec into arranging the visit to Târgu Alb by suggesting she or the Writers' Union would be unable to arrange it. It was Târgu Alb or nowhere.

But Angela was late, and when she ran into the hotel restaurant to collect him...

"Quickly, please," she said breathlessly, "the taxi is waiting." A large handbag swung loosely from her arm.

"Where are we going then?"

"A little drive to show you the city..." At this speed? – "And I have – a little call to make."

She began to reel off a guide's standard information. "That is the Intercontinental Hotel, though we have seen that already. And that..."

The Dacia taxi stopped suddenly at a traffic light with brakes wailing, and they were both cast forward onto the backs of the front seats. Angela leaned across and remonstrated with the driver. "We must not lose time, but we must not lose our lives. That is the Heroes' Monument," she pointed out. "With the name of the Party heroes on it."

"Do they change the names when necessary?" Tim asked. "Is it possible to go and look at it?"

"There is no time to go and see," she said, poker-faced. "And you can't go near enough to read very well. That is the parliament building – very quiet this morning." The dignified nineteenth century house at the top of a little hill looked as if it had not been busy for some time. Leaving it, the taxi speeded along wider avenues, turned sharply up a short sloping road towards an open space, and stopped beside a lake.

"Our new reservoir," Angela explained. "It was completed just last year. By our best engineers."

They climbed back into the car, were thrown against each other as the driver charged away. Angela's big handbag fell on the floor and burst open, but nothing fell out. "Why aren't we making this trip in Angela's own car?" Tim wondered.

It was intensely bright, the sky frostily and radiantly blue, a good day for seeing President Ceaușescu's conversion of this quarter of the capital into the kind of city that would reflect his greatness. They saw, first, endless wooden barricades which enclosed construction sites; though Tim noticed little building in progress (because of the winter cold?) and few workmen attending the stationary cranes and diggers. Nearly finished, or so it appeared, the giant task had seemingly come to a stop.

Along a broad avenue stretching far into the distance, its end not visible, shops were ready for occupation at ground level, flats above them. Everything did have a rigorous, absolutely conventional handsomeness; yet most of these structures also looked to have the flimsiness of stage scenery, with their dark red-tiled roofs and pastel fascias, convincing enough to have a spectacle enacted in front of them but not providing spaces in which you live and breathe.

At the near end of this avenue was the summit and climax of the whole undertaking, the presidential palace-to-be, ten times the size of the Central Committee, a square edifice said to be bigger than any other single building in the world, a house of a thousand windows. Their taxi-driver smoked as Tim and Angela sat and looked at it, looking away himself – he had made this journey so many times. On the grass slopes behind the outer walls, on the apparently marble steps in the front, on the balconies, at the windows – no one. No activity that Tim could detect. Huge, impersonal, deserted. A castle of darkness.

How many storeys, how many rooms? Tim thought he might be wrongly trying to imagine separate levels when there was merely a multitude of smaller windows giving onto high halls. But he assumed that the topmost floors were warrens of offices of the kind he imagined in the Central Committee.

"Will the president live there when it's finished?"

"No!" she said curtly, as if the question were peculiarly foolish. "He will work there. He will receive visitors there. He will live in the residence." As if to deny that the president was not so pretentious as to aspire to live inside such a symbol of power. "Have you seen enough?"

Tim nodded, and she gave the driver some lengthy instructions.

Then something unexpected happened. The driver left behind the grandiose and alarming spaces surrounding the palace and drove off fast in a southward direction through a large area of workers' flats, patently a long way from any place of tourist interest. "I have to make this call I mentioned," Angela said. Where they were now, people were living their normal lives. Queues waited at bare food stores, bowed, silently patient, stonefaced.

Angela was pointing now, shouting directions in the driver's ear. She demanded he take a particular route, along a dusty track through a nettle-infested tract of scrubland; to a wire fence and a gate, behind which stood what seemed to be a small factory, a complex of rundown buildings with chimneys or funnels emitting a little dreary smoke or steam. A smell of it penetrated the taxi. Evidently some sort of light engineering went on here.

The driver sighed in resignation as he approached the figure in the wooden hut beside the open gate, who stared out at them through a glassless window. She was wrapped against the cold to the point of invisibility, in coats and shawls and scarves; and was knitting, knitting, with slow red fingers pushing at the heavy wooden needles through the holes in stained woollen mittens. She fixed the driver with a stern gaze equivalent to a spoken question requiring a satisfactory response.

Angela wound down her rear window and said something, naming someone – 'Domnul Ivaneanu' were the last words. The gatekeeper switched her gaze to her for a few hard seconds, the knitting not stopping. Then she nodded, and the car moved on, turning into a small yard with two-storey buildings on three sides.

On a bench half in, half out of one entrance, wearing a short-sleeved shirt, sat a man with one arm, the stump of the other wrapped in a cloth. His grin, when Angela got out and asked him a question was a challenging grimace. "You'll be lucky!" Tim translated it. But he rose, and led her, handbag in hand, inside. The taxi-driver switched off his engine and they waited.

Tim could hear very little going on. There were numerous people inside the workshops, because heads would often pass the windows and occasionally someone would come to a door and look out – always at the taxi, and a bit forbiddingly, Tim thought. Then the one-armed man came back to his bench, not grinning now, and kept an eye on the taxi.

Enclosed by the three sides of this courtyard, sat in the back of this car in a remote industrial suburb of Bucharest, Tim felt trapped, even scared. What if all this were the prelude to a kidnap? Eastern European countries had been known to arrest British visitors on false charges of spying. What if he was about to become a famous hostage? Or a not-so-famous one, because a very moderate biographer, unlike a businessman, was not so desirable a proposition to ransom; or likely to become a reason for freezing diplomatic relations.

But Angela now emerged with her handbag swinging, looking impatient and frustrated. She re-entered the taxi, told the driver something he did not enjoy hearing, and was immediately into a violent argument with him. The man gesticulated, pointed witheringly to the watch on his wrist, and held his ground.

But Angela won. To Tim's relief the man drove fast up the track and out of the factory compound, pausing at the gate while its keeper pushed her head out of the cabin and directed questions solely at him; receiving answers to which she granted a grudging credence. She let him pass through her still-open gate.

Tim expected them to return now to the city centre, perhaps to the hotel. But no. To his amazement they seemed to be, and they *were*, repeating the journey of an hour before; not repeating the stops and the commentary, it was true, but following the same route, with the exception of detours on which the driver, not laconic now but voluble, ironically indicated places of interest to *him*: the Steaua football stadium in particular. Then they had come full circle and were back on the rough track crossing the field of nettles towards the factory gate.

Tim did not know whether to feel more frightened or less the second time. As they went in, the stare of the knitting guardian of the gate, who appeared to expect them, was radiological, but she let them in without more challenges. Tim knew, or just assumed, that there was no intention of taking him prisoner: to leave it to the second visit would show extremely devious ingenuity. But the air of the yard was still menacing. The one-armed man had not moved from his bench in the door, the sun shining on him had not shifted his shadow against the lintel. He nodded without smiling as Angela passed him and once again vanished into the workshops. When she eventually came out again she was walking faster, hugging the handbag to her midriff as if it had suddenly become something to guard and cherish. Back beside Tim, she smiled and closed the rear door with a kind of triumph in her gesture, and balanced the bag on her lap.

This time the gatekeeper was out of the cabin, standing resolutely in the centre of the track, her knitting abandoned. She was determined to do her sworn duty, get to the root of this matter. Her questions to the driver were loud and abrupt. He was ordered out of his own taxi. She peered into the space in front of the vacant passenger seat, felt under that seat and the driver's with mistrustful hands, looked down under the feet of Tim and Angela in the back. Angela stayed impassive; Tim, deeply bewildered, tried to look innocent.

Now they also were ordered out of the vehicle while the gatekeeper scanned under the cushion of the back seat. The driver was then required to lift the bonnet, close it again. She asked him finally to open the boot. It contained an oilcan and an object wrapped in newspaper which turned out to be a pair of shoes. The gatekeeper shook the oilcan. It made no sound. Then she shook her head as if to say, "This time you have fooled me." Her wave of the hand, finally releasing them, spoke frustration and disgust; incredulity. Tim thought she looked crumpled and diminished as she retired to her hut, shut the door, took up the knitting needles in resignation.

When they were well out of her sight, Angela unfolded the handbag with both arms.

"Smugglers!" she declared with glee; but speaking only to Tim, in a wary whisper, with head down. Her eyes shone with mysterious satisfaction. "My distributor. For my car. Now we can drive to places in Bucharest, and not walk everywhere." Probably the whole morning tour, he now saw, paid for by either the British Council or the Romanian Writers' Union, had been set up by Angela in order to collect the item, which someone had been illicitly, and no doubt illegally, and not very quickly, supplying or replacing.

"Perhaps we could drive when we go to Transylvania? And not worry about the train?"

"Now we shall have some lunch," Angela said. "We shall go to the Writers' Union restaurant. We are invited."

Had she not heard him? Yes, she had.

"It is impossible to go to Transylvania, I think," she said. "It is arranged that we go to the Black Sea coast."

"In *winter*?" He was furious at this transparent attempt to prevent the trip he had to make.

"Please understand," she said slowly. "It is not for me to decide where we go. I am very sorry. It is all – all political."

He was about to curse again and ask her what she meant, when he saw a look in her eyes something near to tears. It clearly told him she would be almost as sorry as himself not to visit that city in Transylvania he *must* see, because Carolina lived there, and Carolina was the only person who –

"But, well... We shall see," she said.

– 2 –

*** In the end, after so much thinking about such a small choice, Katrin put on for dinner the very best dress she had, the green, sleeveless velvet one, something suited to a warm early summer evening and a roomful of people. Having done that slowly and carefully, and taken considerable care with her face and with her hair (luckily, if she just brushed and brushed it enough it was all right, it had a natural gloss and softness), she went downstairs. John was out to buy wine, and to keep out of Dora's way while she cooked she sat in an armchair in the dining room reading magazines.

She was intrigued by one coloured journal which seemed to come with one of the Sunday newspapers. She turned over the smooth, slippery pages, her eyes jumped from one disarming image to another and she could not easily interpret what she was seeing.

Here was a double page concerned with members of families reunited after long separation in a Middle Eastern War. Old people were shown embracing in shabby clothes, little cheap hats knocked askew as their furrowed, suffering faces met and kissed, and arms hugged, and tears ran; all of this done in close-up, in vivid colours, not actors in a film but real people in a desert village. Katrin believed the photographer should never have been there to see this, let alone stand close to them and click his little device while they embraced and wept. If he had wanted to take pictures at all he should have stood further away and done it with more sympathy; his camera had been a cold weapon, intrusive, unfeeling.

There was some printed narrative or comment to one side of this big photograph but Katrin did not trouble to read it.

On the next page, and she could not understand these juxtapositions in the least, was a large picture of several young men in full-length dressing-gowns. Nothing indicated that this was in fact an advertisement for night-clothes, but when Katrin did read a little of the print under the picture she realised that was what it was, because the price of every garment and the name of a shop was given at the end of the description.

She dropped the magazine on her lap, mouth open in a gasp of astonishment at the prices. For the cost of one of these dressing-gowns (pounds converted by speedy mental arithmetic) she could live for two or three months in her own country. She could pay her rent for a year!

There were several pages devoted to food and recipes, and because Katrin was beginning to be hungry she looked at them, all the expensive ingredients, all the coy, fastidious instructions, all the coloured displays. She wondered whether you really did add to life, or whether you detracted from it, if you gave so much time and care to food.

Then she realised, when she reached the end of this section and found herself looking, whether she wanted to or not, at a suitcase covered with labels for foreign destinations, brandished at her over a whole page (in bright colours, naturally) by a big grinning girl wearing nothing above her waist – on her legs she wore velvet trousers, on her feet some kind of sporting footwear – Katrin realised that above all she was shocked at the way the female body was used in magazines, the way the women who owned these bodies *let* them be used. To whom would this foolish and shocking advertising picture appeal? Some men, possibly. It did not appeal to Katrin. What was it *for*? What did it *tell* people?

The grin on the girl's face – brazen, cocksure, gratuitously inane – seemed to want to impress on Katrin that here were all the things she knew, didn't she, she was missing in her own country: chances of travel (with the costly suitcase for all her belongings), elaborate clothes (the shoes alone, she read, cost £57), unattainable foods, and some quality of sexual freedom which she did not feel persuaded to acquire. She knew people in her own country, men and women, who would be enthralled by this advertisement, if such it was (advertising and editorial articles were indistinguishable in this magazine), one or two who would delight in it as the quintessence of all they most wanted in the world. Well, perhaps that was a little unfair to them, but they would certainly pin it onto their bedroom wall, if they could have it, as a prized piece of Western exotica.

If anyone here in England mocked, as it was said they might do, at the banal, overweening deadliness of some Marxist-Leninist architecture, she would pick up the picture of the girl with the bare breast displaying the suitcase (one of a luxury set for £79) and ask them to tell her what it meant.

On the edge of the half-laid dining table, just in front of her, she saw a sheet of paper on which Dora had gone to great trouble to work out exactly where everyone should sit at dinner. There seemed nothing private about it if it had been left there, so she supposed she could glance at it.

Dora had done a whole series of little rectangles, scribbling names down the sides and at each end. The problem seemed to be how to separate husbands and wives (though John and herself, no problem, were always at the top and the bottom) while preserving Katrin's place next to Richard Hendleton. In the end, in the only diagram not crossed out (ticked, in fact) one married couple, Jason and Claudine Simmingley, sat side by side. But placing Jason in a centre chair of three opposite Katrin might allow him to converse with Katrin while his wife talked to John and Julian, the husband of Samantha. Unless, of course, everyone joined in one conversation. Katrin looked forward to the intelligent conversation these characteristic English people would provide [...]

– 3 –

The taxi dropped them outside the Writers' Union. Paying the driver off with numerous small lei notes was a question of elaborate discussion, the verification of distances, the demanding of tiny receipts.

Inside the door, in the warm dark, Angela excused herself and Tim waited at the foot of the grand staircase. Again he began to listen to sounds behind the doors opening off the hall. There were voices indeed, behind one door; which now opened and delivered him a figure striding forward and greeting him, grabbing his arm warmly; Ioan Ludache, rough and hearty in a heavy brown suit.

"Mr Harker-Jones, this is a delight! But I knew you were coming here because we have lunch, so it is not a surprise. Are you having an interesting trip to Romania? What is your opinion of our culture?"

To this there was no answer. Tim realised when his mouth opened in automatic courtesy and no sound came out. Ludache grinned, and waited for a response, his face – as Tim's eyes grew used to the dim light – emerging for Tim out of the circumambient gloom like an image in a polaroid snap, Angela had not said who else would be lunching with them. So why Ludache? Had he since yesterday, persisted successfully behind the scenes to obtain a further meeting after all?

Angela was back, to his relief, so Tim had no need to converse. Ludache guided them both through one of the doors out of the hall into the narrowest of corridors where Tim was aware of a hubbub of voices in a further room they were approaching; and the different noise of crockery being washed and stacked up in a kitchen. At one point, as Angela and Tim stepped aside and flattened themselves against walls to let others pass, Ludache ended up ahead of them. He was out of sight round a corner when Angela said, so quietly that Tim thought he could not have heard her correctly – "It is all right for Târgu Alb."

"For *what*?"

"For Târgu Alb. We go on Friday, on the train. It is too far to drive." She was smiling mischievously. He must have looked as surprised and bewildered as he ever had about anything because she exclaimed.

"So you have forgotten – and I have taken all this trouble to arrange it."

"But you said this morning – an hour ago –"

"I did not know for certain then if it *would* be possible."

He could have embraced her, in fact he quite involuntarily took the hand that wasn't carrying the bag. She declined his gesture, raised a finger to her lips, stopped smiling, and led him through a final door into a sudden clamour of voices in a square, high, handsomely-panelled restaurant.

The place was warm, brightly illuminated by the sunshine falling in through high windows, and vibrant with talk going on among animated groups at tables for four or six people. Tim saw food and drink, smoke rising; saw and heard laughter and argument; began to feel for the first time that he had come to a place he really wanted to be; and began to enjoy himself. The news Angela had just given him had raised his spirits.

"What sort of people come here?" he asked her as they moved to a prepared table where Ludache was waiting, in lively converse with other diners.

"All the writers," she said. "Novelists. Poets. Ex-poets." So which was which (and who, and why, particularly the "ex-poets"?) among the grave and humorous and passionate and pompous and frighteningly intelligent faces, men and women, of most ages but mainly older, sitting round the tables, eating, drinking, expostulating, laughing? Were the ex-poets obliged to stop writing poems?

"If you look to your left, at the table next to the door we came through – I didn't see her when we came in – that is Stella Sandoran!" Angela's voice was hushed, as if she did not want Ludache, in full flood of jocularity with the occupants of the adjacent table, to hear. "It is a little – a little daring, that she is eating here." Alone, she sat up straight at her table with a defiantly composed, yet briskly watchful air; she wore an elegantly informal dark yellow dress cut very low at the neck.

Stella Sandoran's name did have a distant familiarity. He tried to see it, in print, in the place from which he had picked it up; downpage in a *Guardian* report on dissident writers? Or was that someone else? A matter of an outspoken play put on for a few nights in a small and normally harmless provincial theatre, perhaps; and then closed down, audiences dispersed by the police? Was that Stella Sandoran? Or someone else? Had that been Romania? Or was it Hungary, or Bulgaria?

A waitress attended them quickly. Tim was noticing that the tales of having to wait endlessly for food in Eastern European restaurants were legends; at least in Romania. Angela interpreted for him.

"You will have some hors d'oeuvres? And salad? And some wine or beer with the meal?"

He would. He was hungry, food and drink would concentrate his mind and stabilise his reactions to unexpected developments. Ludache turned round with apologies to Angela for being sidetracked, he would join their conversation in a moment. Tim seized the chance to ask,

"Why is it so risky for Stella Sandoran to be eating here?"

"Well, it is not risky, not in the least." But Angela had just told him it was daring of her to eat here... He began to recognise a pattern in her behaviour, of speaking with inadvisable candour and then pulling back, denying rumours. "She is still a member," she continued. "She is entitled to come. But she really thinks there is all this nonsense of people listening to everything she says. She thinks women in the room are listening to her through their earrings."

"Through their *earrings*?"

The waitress had set down a bowl of flowers in front of Tim (where had they come from in winter?) and he looked at it warily. The bowl itself was made of thin, delicate glass, clean and clear, shining and transparent.

Ludache rejoined the conversation. Tim thought it would appear suspicious if they stopped talking, but best not to say anything which would reveal the topic.

"I think everything here is very Byzantine," he murmured.

"Yes – we are a Byzantine country," Ludache declared, almost as if he had been listening all the time, to everything. Perhaps he had, Tim thought; then told himself not to catch Stella Sandoran's paranoia. But next he realised that Ludache had just been speaking to him, and had continued to speak, in excellent English, and all his perplexity returned. "We are a Byzantine country," Ludache went on, "a Byzantine, *Greek* country. And we are a Roman country of course. We are a little bit, in some of our folk music, an oriental country. All of those things, and we link with the centre of Europe because we have our Hungarians, and the north of Europe with our Saxons! We love the civilisation of the French, and we wish we had the dignity of the English. And the – the – the soup, do you call it?"

"The stew?" suggested Angela.

"The stew, the stew. Exactly! We are hungry, we think of food metaphors! The stew is a Dadaist stew, with a Romanian flavour you find in no other stew in the world. You know Dada was a Romanian idea?"

It sounded like a prepared speech, one which Tim thought Angela, from her tolerant reaction, might have heard before. All nations were very curious, he suggested, but nations of mixtures were the most fascinating of all. He let Angela translate this off-the-cuff profundity into Romanian for Ludache, who had been so extrovertly delighted with his own remarks that he hadn't listened properly to Tim responding in English.

Hors d'oeuvres had seemingly been abandoned. They were getting the main course, and *this* was Dadaist because – on a bitterly cold day when it surely might have been made into a stew – it was a large plate of several kinds of cold meat, ham, pork, beef. There were rolls, but no butter; there was salt but no pepper or mustard. There was a leaf of lettuce beside the meat. Why give them this when Tim noticed hot food carried to other tables? All the same, he ate well, felt full by the time his plate was empty.

When Angela was drawn into conversation with another table he thought he could try asking Ludache about Philip Carston. He drank some wine, cleared his throat – but Ludache, lowering his head with an air of conspiracy and quietening his strong rough voice to a murmur, began to speak first. Tim lowered his own head to listen. But at once they both raised their heads again: the waitress was setting down in front of them large dishes of strongly-seasoned sausages, lapped by waves of creamed potatoes and a rice-like substance, garnished with small cubes cut from red peppers and accompanied by peas.

"I went yesterday with your – your question, your request to go to Târgu Alb," Ludache murmured, "to Domnul Andrei." He pointed up to the ceiling. Did he mean literally upstairs here, in the Writers' Union? Or to a higher authority altogether, one of the people not mentioned by name, only indicated by signs? The next words clarified matters. "Mr Andrei in the top office here."

Ludache's grin was a man-to-man version of the one he had given him out in the hall. "I know about life," he said. "I write about life, human emotion – love! I said to him, Mr Andrei, you know why Domnul Harker-Jones wants to go to Târgu Alb? He said, no. I said, Domnul Harker-Jones has no interest in politics. He is a man, a writer and artist but first of all a man. It is because of a beautiful woman he wants to go to Târgu Alb. Mr Andrei, *you* are human, *I* am human. Domnisoara Carolina Predeanu is very, very beautiful. So Mr Andrei agree you can go to Târgu Alb."

Tim was astounded. The tale if true, revealed Ludache as possessing ingenuity and perhaps influence. Was he more sinister and significant, therefore more dangerous, than Tim had assumed? And if the forbidden terrain (and the beautiful Miss Predeanu) had suddenly and inexplicably been made available to him, could it be a snare?

Stefan Tonaru now entered the room, moving quickly, smart and suave in his official-looking blue suit, smiled across at them, then paused to speak to Stella Sandoran.

"Please – I should know this, I realise," Tim said resolutely, "but I am ignorant about it because I didn't see Philip Carston in the last years of his life. Did he visit Romania?"

"But of course he visited Romania. He visited Bucharest, he went to Constanta, he was in Târgu Alb like you."

"But when –?"

They were interrupted. Tonaru stood by their table gesturing towards the unoccupied place.

"You are invited to come here by us – by me! – and I am joining you with only my apologies, not favouring you with my company," he said. "Also I am hungry, but life is too hectic for even the necessities, let alone the pleasures. But listen, I have something particular to say. After our meeting yesterday I thought we should try hard to meet your wishes. In the afternoon I contacted the Minister to see what could be arranged, and he understood your reasons completely. You will go to Târgu Alb – Miss Cernec has told you?"

"I have," Angela said.

"Thank you," Tim said.

Tonaru smiled the smile of a stern father or headmaster relenting and bestowing some longed-for relaxation of the rules on a delighted boy. Ludache and Angela smiled equally.

– 4 –

*** Jason Simmingley didn't speak to his wife Claudine, on his right, at all; he talked to Samantha on his left and to Dora, sitting at the top of the table to be near the kitchen door. Claudine talked eagerly across John at the foot of the table, to Julian opposite her. John occasionally intervened, a referee between two people with other partners who seemed more than happy to look at each other at close range and enjoy each other's jokes. Katrin did not think they were lovers – they would have been more circumspect and restrained if they were – but possibly on the brink of becoming lovers. Richard was saying very little to Katrin.

Katrin wondered when a proper conversation would begin. All the rapid talk around the table, about the food (Dora's hors d'oeuvres), about people she could not have known (ignoring her lack of acquaintance with them), about the prices people were paying to buy their houses in Fieldenhurst – it all felt like a preliminary to something.

And then, she thought, I am not a famous person and I do not expect special honours, but perhaps some sort of small welcome, as coming from a very different country, landing among strangers and feeling a little uncertain, would be in order? Then they might feel they could ask me about my country, which they were no doubt shy to do without being given the licence?

But Katrin waited in vain as Dora brought in new plates, and Jason was enlisted to open the bottle and pour the wine (wasn't this a good moment at least to raise glasses to their host?).

Samantha, Jason and Claudine seemed to be discussing a television programme about marriage which Katrin could not have watched, Dora glancing occasionally in her direction to see how she reacted to this talk; not so much anxious lest she was left out of the conversation, just curious as to what she might be thinking.

If Katrin's face revealed confusion, what she felt was surprise – and also disapproval. In her own country, people would discuss marriage, and sexual relations within marriage, and outside marriage, with freedom and openness; but in different and more private circumstances, not in television comedy programmes, not on social occasions like this, in front of strangers, facetiously. And with constant innuendo, with hints and glances and a dangerous edge to the talk; dangerous because Katrin instinctively caught a note of challenge in Claudine's banter with Sam.

"But Sam, didn't you ever do that to Julian? Or anyone?" she grinned. What exactly "that" was Katrin did not know, but it was apparently a kind of sexual activity. And at this question Julian, instead of looking indignant about being brought in on such private matters, or embarrassed that a woman whose company he plainly adored should ask it, only laughed. No one looked uncomfortable, as far as Katrin could see; except perhaps for John, who sat at the end of the table with a fixed smile, saying nothing. Was Claudine wanting an answer, Katrin wondered, or was it a rhetorical challenge?

Samantha's mouth was full of food, she won time by laughing and pretending to choke, she grimaced, chewed, raised her eyebrows, swallowed, moistened her lips. It was coquettish, and displeasing. She picked up her wine and gulped some while everyone waited.

"Julian," she said, "never stays around when there's housework to do."

At this, all these five people, Samantha, Claudine, Julian, Jason and Dora, rocked in their chairs with loud laughter, put their knives and forks down, wiped their mouths, even their eyes. When they had recovered, other hinting remarks flew across the table, references to matters Katrin could not grasp from the vocabulary used to describe them. Katrin looked from face to face, but she did not want to turn her head deliberately and look at Richard Hendleton on her right. She knew that he was not laughing; she realised suddenly that she would not have wanted to find he was smiling and approving.

"We are disgraceful people," Dora eventually said to her when the subject amusing them seemed to be exhausted. "I don't know what you think of us." Katrin had decided what she thought: these particular people bored her. Now that she was actually wishing the meal could end, she had resolved that if no one spoke to her by the time they were drinking coffee she would herself begin to ask questions. She had not come to England to sit in silence as the anonymous, ignored foreign girl who could not possibly appreciate their sophistication.

The coffee was being poured by Dora with much laughter about something and somebody else unknown to her. When it quietened as people received their cups from their hostess Katrin chose her moment.

"There is something I would like to know," she said firmly. "I am a stranger in your country. What is your purpose in life in England?"

Richard Hendleton turned his head to look at her with interest. John stared, but it was a friendly stare. The others gave Katrin and each other disconcerted looks that seemed to question Katrin's sanity. But someone had to produce an answer.

"Say that again?" Julian requested, half-acting a surprised expression.

"People in a country need to have a purpose in their lives. In my country they have one. What is the *meaning* in your lives in England?"

A void had opened up behind their faces. Have they never, Katrin speculated, looked for the keys to unlock their own lives?

"What a very large question!" someone said, almost mockingly. "Now we'll all have to be serious," said another. "I am not sure people think like that in England," Julian offered. "We just live."

"But is it possible just to 'live' if you are an intelligent person? Not to think about *why* you are living? What you are giving to your community? What your community is for?"

Dora, absorbed with the supply of coffee, was not really noticing the change in the atmosphere. But Katrin noticed that John was following her with the utmost fascination, looking from face to face, smiling a little, waiting, silently challenging them almost as much as Katrin herself.

"We are – many people would say we are – trying to make a more *free* society," said Jason unconvincingly.

"What do you *do* for that?" asked Katrin. She came from a country where everyone was expected to have a role, a task; it could be improving the water supply in a village, or increasing the production of petrochemicals, or teaching secondary school pupils their fundamental political knowledge. You asked people, and they told you their job and their philosophy. So now she asked this question innocently of Jason Simmingley, an estate agent, at John and Dora's dinner table, with the intelligentsia of Fieldenhurst listening.

Jason sent her a sharp look across the table. He looked for signs of hostility but saw only innocence. He was unsure how to respond to it, so he answered Katrin in an airy, joking way, as if her question were too ethereal to take seriously.

"I do what everyone does," he replied. "I work, without doing too much of it. I make money, without too much effort. I keep my family fed, and I pay my tax – some of my tax."

"You make the community more free by doing those things?"

John's smile at Katrin's lethal innocence had widened a lot. He was enjoying himself, though he feared the conversation could end with some sort of ungentle scorn or rebuff for Katrin.

Of the others, only Samantha, Julian's wife, rather

unexpectedly seemed to believe that Katrin's questioning merited some response. When Julian made some flippant remark to Claudine in an undertone, as if Katrin were not able to hear it, Samantha heard it and told him to be quiet.

"Please," Sam started, quite gently, "you ask us what we mean by making our country more free. I think you mean that? But you don't tell us about the freedom – or the oppression – in your own country."

"I am very happy to talk about the freedom in my country *later* – after we have decided what we think about the freedom in your country, which is where we started. Can we finish one subject first?"

Dora began to say something, but Sam overrode her.

"But it's the *same* subject. It's the *same* freedom, it seems to me." Then she faltered. "I mean – freedom is freedom wherever you are. Isn't it?"

"Ah, very profound," Jason said. Dora smiled uncomfortably.

"That is why we must have our discussion of your country first," Katrin countered. "Mr. Jason has started it, and we should continue, and decide what your freedom is. Then we can discuss my freedom, and we can compare the freedoms and see if they are the same and if you are right. On the other hand, if you do not wish to discuss freedom, we can speak about some part of English culture, like the drama."

"I," declared Dora, wanting to decide for herself how her party should develop, "prefer to discuss where we should drink the coffee! If you wish to remain at the table we will, but *I* would like us all to move to more comfortable chairs in the lounge."

This conversation needed to be stopped at the start, before it became embarrassing. She hadn't realised what resources of daring and tenacity Katrin had. There had obviously been more thoroughness in her Party education than appeared on first meeting this quiet, old-fashioned young woman. Did she owe this to her father?

Samantha, as well as Katrin, looked pained at this interruption of their conversation; but Dora's tactics succeeded in stopping her. As they all rose and shuffled out, carrying their coffee cups, mostly relieved to be diverted from these serious topics, Richard Hendleton seized a moment when everyone else had gone ahead, when he was standing aside to allow Katrin to go first, to say something to Katrin. He said it in low tones which signified so much more to her than if he had joined impersonally in the brief debate at the table. He said (his "first words" as he described them later),

"I should like to go on talking about all this with you. I'm sorry we've had to stop..." [...]

— 5 —

A big crowd was funnelling through one narrow half of a glass-panelled double door, into the dark station hall of the Gara de Nord, at a quarter to eight in the morning.

Or it was being funnelled, by two hectoring, stocky police who were themselves partly blocking the entrance. Tim and Angela, humping luggage, two large grains in this mass of human sand shifting, being shifted, horizontally forwards towards the trains, had to wait some time before obtaining entry. It was as well they were early.

"Why can't they open the other half of the door?" Tim asked.

"It would let in the cold," Angela assured him. But the hall inside, when they reached it, struck as cold as the station square outside; and as all the platforms were open to the air, and thronged with people who must have arrived there through easier entrances, the obstruction at their own door seemed no more than arbitrary harassment.

Tim had left the hotel too hastily to take breakfast. There

was a station café of sorts, but at this hour the chairs were tilted against the tables on its enclosed forecourt and there were no lights in its interior. He needed a lavatory. Leaving Angela he descended a staircase declaring: *WC: Barbati*, picking his way into deepening darkness, encouraged by the aggravating sound of urinals flushing. In pitch black at the bottom he stumbled into a chair across a gap, behind which a faceless female figure with a mop in one hand and a feeble pocket torch in the other was remonstrating, chiding, telling him that the facility was closed. He climbed back, rejoined Angela, helped carry her case to near the end of the waiting train, finally propelled it up to the damp corridor of a First Class carriage where they identified the numbers of their reserved places.

It was not warm in the corridor. It was very cold in the compartment. But it would warm up when the train started, Tim felt sure. He looked at their fellow travellers, three people already in their seats, and a fourth struggling in behind him and Angela, waiting for Angela to negotiate luggage rack spaces for their belongings by bargaining adjustments of other people's.

Angela finally sat in a corner corridor seat, directed Tim to the one next to her on her left. In the diagonally opposite window seat, her back to the engine, was a woman in a smart but skimpy fawn cardigan and light red skirt, thin stuff for a winter journey. She had a newspaper on her lap, and in one hand a magazine. Tim could read both titles: *Scînteia*, and *Romania Literara*. The second title, he guessed, marked her out as a reader, a thinker. So far she had kept her eyes away from the other passengers, feigning absorption in the nothing happening outside the window.

Two people next to her spoke in low tones, and were together. Yet they seemed unlikely companions, let alone partners. The man, in the corner seat next to the corridor, was very old indeed, seemed frail, could also have been ill. That was Tim's first impression; which modified when this individual leant over with curious agility, dropping the stick he was clutching, and rummaged in a plastic bag set between his woman companion's feet. In a moment he had found a slightly-crushed chocolate cake, conveyed it to his mouth, eaten it, and licked every finger. All this he did with a sly satisfaction, as if defying anyone around him to disapprove. The woman, thirty or even forty years younger, Tim guessed, ostentatiously smart in tweeds and fur coat (which she kept on) – in contrast to the old man's dishevelled gentility – disapproved, and told him.

"*Liviu!*" He was slowly licking the last finger with raw tongue, and did not respond. The name was murmured in a tone of embarrassed reproof, possibly used in vain for years. Liviu enjoyed provoking her indignation, nothing was going to change his behaviour. Tim could see a kind of dignity, even grandeur, in the defiance.

But his clothes, in such inexplicable contrast to the woman's, were not grand, only rough and ordinary: muddy shoes, stained trousers, tatty old coat, and the tie and shirt which looked as if he wore them day and night without change. No one else in the compartment retained their hats when they were seated, only Liviu. It was a fur hat. But what *kind* of fur? It was so run-down and irrecoverable there was no telling.

The fourth stranger took the other window seat. He appeared to know the old man and his companion because his nod and verbal greeting was more than just a formal acknowledgement of their presence. He gave the woman in the cardigan a long look, but neither spoke, as if there was vague recognition but no wish to communicate.

Perhaps they *all* knew each other? This was the only carriage of the train going all the way to Târgu Alb, apparently; the rest of the train would detach at Brasov. Everyone was going to the same town; perhaps they were regular travellers together? Natural as it probably was, to Tim it felt like some kind of conspiracy, an arranged gathering of partners in a scheme, the more sinister for their remarkable variety.

Variety... The tall fourth person was different again: the

sharply-cut brown raincoat (under it a new-looking blue-grey suit) and shining black attaché case implied some official role; everything about him was self-sufficiency, brisk neatness. A sudden smell in the carriage of shaving lotion or a deodorant could only have come from him. Tim thought Liviu's companion regarded this fourth one nervously, taking furtive glances at him when he was not likely to be looking in her direction.

Tannoy fanfares sounded along the platform, a voice enunciated last, clear directions, there were sounds of slamming doors. With a train-long jolt that sent standing passengers in the corridor staggering, they were in motion. Now we are going to Târgu Alb, was Tim's first thought; and soon it will be warmer.

But when he returned from the W.C. and pushed the door of the compartment open it felt even colder than before.

"When does the heating come on?" Tim asked Angela.

"I don't know." Angela shivered. "Probably never."

"But there must be *some* heating? We're going to be five hours on this train."

"Six. We wait at Brasov for one hour." Liviu, opposite, was looking at them with interest.

"Can we get coffee on the train?"

"Not on this train."

He thought he could see on Angela's face an expression which signified, you wanted to go to Târgu Alb, so you must suffer the consequences. Their fellow-passengers, no doubt as the result of hard experience, seemed not to notice the cold.

They were gliding through marshalling yards beside blocks and small towers of grey or light green apartments, some smart and new, some older with their concrete cladding in poor repair, past standing trains badly in need of paint: Vagon Dormit, Vagon Restaurant (how long had they been out of service?). Then they were crossing fields and orchards, passing cottages (outside one of them a man sat in the cold sharpening a scythe – anticipating grass or wheat to cut in the summer?). Long flat stretches followed, with water, and townships of more red-roofed workers' flats. The compartment was silent. Liviu had fallen asleep.

Tim tried to read and interpret the signs on the roofs of the little stations where uniformed stationmasters or – mistresses stood to attention as their train went by, making its passing an event: once again TRAIASCA PARTIDUL COMUNIST ROMAN, or else PRESIDENTELE SI ROMANIA, or CEAUSESCU SI POPORUL, and longer slogans he could make no sense of. Low hills came up, woods; and gaps between the ashes and poplars showed steeper slopes and they were travelling beside a grey, rock-strewn river along a deep valley between thickly-wooded mountains, birches and pines, or following a road travelled by AUTOTRANSPORT lorries or horse-drawn farm carts.

Liviu began to shake weirdly in his sleep, or in waking up, suffering a disconcerting tremor that might have been the prelude to a fit. His wide-awake companion ignored it, and Tim concluded she knew him well enough to know this was a habit, even something deliberate, perhaps done originally to amuse then repeated endlessly to annoy. The old man was shaking himself awake; probably trying to warm himself a bit with a vigorous shiver at the same time. His eyes opened, and they were gazing strangely at Tim, sharp and bright in inquisitive attention.

"You come from America? England?" he asked all at once, in a slow clear voice. In English.

"Yes! From England", Tim answered, in amused surprise and pleasure.

"You travel as a tourist, or on official business?" the old man enquired. Beside him the woman put on a half-resentful, half-anxious face, as if to say, "What a nuisance he is, showing off his English."

"I suppose you could say it's official business, in a sense," Tim replied; then feared that his idiom might not have been understood, he should have been simpler.

"So in *what* sense, exactly?" queried Liviu, in an ancient, precise voice. He had understood fully, his eyes gleamed with curiosity and humour, he would brook no circumlocutions.

"I am a cultural visitor, meeting writers – publishers. You understand?"

"Absolutely I understand. So you are a writer yourself?"

"Yes –"

Over in the opposite window seat the woman in the cardigan was reading a third newspaper she had produced from her bag, something with a title that did not look Romanian at all. She held it up in front of her face, but it looked to Tim as if it was being used as a screen between her and this English conversation. The fourth stranger, the man in the formal, possibly official suit, looked on with more interest and a very slight smile. Was he able to follow the dialogue?

Liviu was into his stride.

"So, a writer from England!" he declared, as if impressed, but not setting out to flatter – he seemed just genuinely pleased at the discovery. "Interesting. *Interesting*. Do you know your Mr Pinter? Or your Mr Golding?"

"Not personally –"

"A pity. We see your Mr Pinter's plays here, in our theatres. And we read Mr Golding's novels, and Miss Murdoch's. In excellent translations. But what do you write? Perhaps *you* write novels?"

"No, I –"

"Did you know your Mr Carston, who so sadly died?"

"My *what*? I mean my *who*?"

"Your Philip Carston, who so sadly left this life last year?"

– 6 –

If the earlier surprise in the Writer's Union had left Tim amazed, what was he now but speechless?

Had all this been arranged?

At some point in the preceding few minutes snow had begun

to fall. Big letters painted on the side of a dusty factory premises (making cement?) said TRAIASCA AL NOSTRU GLORIOS PARTID. Tim had a strong, renewed feeling of a network, a trap. Liviu was persisting, with an expression of some concern.

"But you surely knew your famous English novelist, Mr Philip Carston, if you are a writer from England?"

"Yes – quite well in fact."

"He was not so very old when he died. Not at all old."

"He was fifty-five." Tim felt he had to ask the next question in view of the acquaintance with Philip claimed by Ludache. "Did you by any chance meet him? I think he came to Romania."

"But of course!"

Could his companion understand the conversation? She was bristling with embarrassment, or what might be fear. She did not want this dialogue to have taken place, whether she understood the English or not. She was trying to stop it by fussing at Liviu, picking crumbs from the chocolate cake off his coat, moistening a handkerchief to clean the corners of his mouth. He let her do it passively; and was not to be interrupted. "You have read his books," Tim ventured. "Your English is very good." At once he regretted this remark. What if coincidence had maliciously delivered up a Romanian professor of Tim's own language? Philip Carston had a theory that coincidence was always, by its nature, malicious.

"I am a professor of philology," Liviu murmured quietly and quickly, as if that should have been obvious, even known to Tim already. "I have had the chance to read in Romanian his beautiful book portraying our young Romanian woman."

The woman with the two Romanian newspapers on her knees, and the third – could it be a Hungarian? – newspaper in front of her face, now dropped this screen and looked fiercely at Liviu. Then she deliberately, Tim was certain of it, contorted her face into a scornful expression, by intended, not involuntary, inflation of her cheeks into an imitation (not a genuine) suppressed giggle. She did it by forcing air through her nasal passages to obtain a long, vibrating grunt, pretending that the hiss of air through the lips which it had forced apart was an attempt to hold back a laugh she did not dare release. And she wanted Liviu to hear this scorn, wanted his interlocutor to notice.

"Professor Bobolescu believes it is a – a more Romanian book than some others of us think."

Tim was dazed with bewilderment now. The speaker this time was the fourth stranger, speaking in English also; at first hearing it was almost as accomplished as (if much slower than) *Professor* Liviu's English, and giving the impression of someone enjoying a rare chance to speak and argue in that tongue.

"It is an extremely Romanian book," said Bobolescu with finality. "And I will say it is that because it is true to one young and precious Romanian life. We can call her 'Katrin'."

Was this dadaism, or hallucination, that these Romanian strangers were holding a critical discussion of *A Time Apart*, in English, over Tim's head? Philip's theory now came fully back into Tim's mind: what Philip described as "the malice of coincidence." Most coincidences, Philip would assert, were entertaining, a few were very pleasing. But the hidden forces responsible for *all* of them contained an element of malice (occasionally crude spite).

Of course it was fascinating to think he had arrived in the very country, the one out of eight Eastern European states which Philip Carston had chosen as the place from which Katrin should come; fascinating that his book should have been translated here. But coincidence had behaved spitefully in ensuring that he knew nothing of this connection before setting out, therefore stood to be exposed, and embarrassed.

"The character of the girl – 'Katrin' – *is* the book," the fourth stranger went on emphatically. "That is the part of the book *I* mean to say is *true*. But the rest of it is not something a Romanian could have written. I believe it is a book true to an *English* writer because an *English* writer had to write from a knowledge of *England*."

As if they knew each other well, the woman opposite him began addressing the fourth stranger in Romanian, with vigorous gestures of her hands, eyes flashing towards Bobolescu, whose woman companion was raising her own eyes to heaven. "The worst had to happen," those eyes were saying. "I knew it, he's done it again." – Because Professor Bobolescu and the other two were now conducting something like a quarrel in their own language. Angela joined in calmly, neutrally, or so it seemed. The train sped between high, thickly-forested mountains just visible through the snow flurrying faster outside, almost a blizzard. Finally it drew through industrial suburbs into a large town, a large station where tannoys gave, after sonorous fanfares, loud and clear messages: Brasov; and still the discussion in the compartment continued.

Finally it settled into an exchange of long, uninterrupted, passionate statements, from Angela, the scornful woman, the "official" man. Bobolescu's speech, the last, was the quietest and longest, given with pauses to take breath and to create an effect. During one long pause Tim muttered to Angela, "What is he saying?" "I tell you later," she whispered impatiently. As Bobolescu finished, the others made faces, raised eyebrows, shrugged as if to say, "Well, you could be right, but it's a far-fetched proposition." No one had the energy to contradict him further. There was a glow of victory on the old face. He looked at Tim and seemed to be forgetting for a moment that he could have understood nothing of what had passed.

"But perhaps you can tell us more?" he said.

Tim, about to protest that he couldn't, and in any case was profoundly confused, paused before exposing his ignorance; paused long enough for the man on his left to interpose,

"It would be interesting to read it in English. No one can know until they read this book in its English version." Know what, Tim wondered? What was there to know that translation did not reveal? It was the same book. Wasn't it?

The train was leaving Brasov, crossing a wide plain

surrounded by farther-away hills, clattering steadily north into the very heart of the country and beyond, westwards, into deepest Transylvania. Into the snow.

"'No one can know', our friend thinks," said Bobolescu; repeating the other's words very quietly and ironically. "But *I* know." He leaned across to Tim as he said that, with a profoundly peculiar, sly, furtive look. "All the same," the old man continued to Tim, "do you think, please, you could send me a copy of this book, the English 'original', when you return to England? Georgeta, my wife –" he indicated his companion, and Tim could not help a gasp of surprise – "will write our address for you. Unless we meet you in Târgu Alb."

"There is a copy he could borrow in my luggage on that rack", Tim thought. Then he immediately decided against this generosity. The inscrutable conversation, conducted with such passion, warned him that *A Time Apart*, in its Romanian translation at least, had been a controversial book. If four strangers in a Romanian train, even granted that Romanians appeared to be eager readers, had all read the book and were prepared at a moment's notice to have a heated dispute about it, there must have been a sensitive or dangerous chord – certainly mysterious – struck by Philip's portrayal of that girl.

"What was everyone so passionate about?" Tim murmured to Angela when Bobolescu had fallen asleep once more; keeping his face blank, trying not to be seen turning towards her in conspiracy.

"The book is very interesting to people in Târgu Alb because the translator lives there. And Romanians love to argue about books and music and paintings. I showed you the people queuing to buy books in Bucharest. If people will queue for two hours to buy a book just published they will read it and argue about it."

That seemed to follow from what he had seen and heard on his journey; follow too from the passion to purchase in the first place, join the eager queues which were as long as the queues for tomatoes or lipstick. But it didn't solve the particular puzzle of why these people argued about *A Time Apart*.

"Did they queue up to buy *A Time Apart*?" he asked her.

"It sold out on the afternoon of the same day."

"The day it was *published*?"

"Within five hours, in all the shops."

"In Târgu Alb?"

"Especially in Târgu Alb."

"Could I buy a Romanian copy now?"

"No. I can show you one."

"How many copies does that mean they sold?"

"I don't know. Seventy thousand? A hundred thousand? We can ask Miss Ciudea when we are back in Bucharest."

Bobolescu snored, his wife had not bothered to write down their address. The woman in the corner asked Angela something, received a satisfactory answer, went back to her newspapers. The man read documents.

The approach to Târgu Alb was more appealing than the approach to Brasov. Workers' blocks and industrial sites there were, and large muddy holes gouged out of the embankments, and tracks apparently going nowhere and littered with discarded rolling stock. But there were also impressive white-and-red, faintly Germanic houses, white churches, a river with neat edges and well-made bridges and bright boats, covered in tarpaulin for the winter and locked into the ice.

People had told Tim there was no reason for spending a weekend there, but he thought he could see every conventional reason for coming: it looked picturesque, stately even, certainly better than the prospect of a deserted Black Sea beach resort, with towering tourist hotels, in winter. He concluded again that there had been some good reason for striving to prevent this visit. Something 'political'. The mystery which began with Valeria Ciudea's phone call to the hotel on his first night in Romania (how long ago that seemed!) had taken on several new dimensions. He expected more excuses, procrastinations, barriers. But the pieces now had to be put together and the final picture looked at and understood. Illicit travelling, a beautiful translator, a foreign girl probably drawn from life and apparently drawn from Romania...

It was the end of the line for the train. When Professor Bobolescu was helped up he was a little taller than at first appeared, but bent and shaky. The descent from the train via the steep iron steps to the platform was accomplished by his wife descending first, taking their suitcase from the hands of Tim, then letting the old man lean on her arm and slowly fumble his way down, holding his walking-stick, from step to step.

What was surprising was that when he leant on her arm to walk away Bobolescu picked his way very nimbly across the tracks and the sleepers and the gravel between them to reach the station hall, a sprightly enough figure serene in the assistance other people would invariably provide for him (like that all his life?). Outside, a much younger man, a son perhaps, waited with a car on the forecourt, a Lada with snow chains and lights shining through the falling snow flakes.

There seemed to be no buses here, or taxis. Most of the descending passengers shrank into their coats and paced off resolutely with their belongings on a long road towards the city centre. There were only three other cars, of which two were meeting passengers from Tim and Angela's compartment. The man in the raincoat said "Goodbye!" pointedly, in English, with a broad smile; and the driver of a large Dacia got out to admit him through the front passenger door. With the gesture the man's official status seemed established.

A small Oltcit awaited Angela, and the woman with the newspapers joined Tim in the back; in asking a question of Angela back in the train she had been requesting a lift. The driver who had brought this car, short, bulky, amiable in a reserved way, introduced by Angela as her cousin, kissed her warmly, saw her solicitously into the seat beside him. They began to talk eagerly, continued all the way to the hotel. He held hands with Angela as he drove, and to change gear brought his left hand over with a rapid movement, steadying and turning the steering wheel with his elbow, threading the fingers of his right hand through Angela's. He was plainly very attached to his cousin.

Some five minutes after leaving the station they dropped their extra passenger, addressed by the driver in Hungarian (Angela later confirmed), at the entrance to a block of flats. But before she got out of the car she thrust the copy of *Romania Literara* into Tim's hands as a gift.

She had written something in the margin above the title of the journal, and signed it: Vajna Eva.

"Please *not* believe old man's opinions."

THREE

– 1 –

When Tim finally reached Room 427, he discovered that this Târgu Alb hotel, the Transilvania, was something different altogether.

He had approached it along the same kind of dark corridor, but this was much longer, wider and higher than the one in Bucharest. There was the same groping to read the numbers on the bedroom doors in the gloom, but the keys and locks were altogether grander, much more ornate, and worked without difficulty. His room was splendidly spacious and elegant, except that the huge double bed felt as if the weight of one man (Tim's eleven stones) could break or disconnect one or more of its legs if he came down too heavily; he surmised this when he sprawled across it in complete exhaustion, enjoying the warmth of the room even before opening his suitcase.

Instead of the fitted cupboards with sliding doors there were wardrobes, three of them, as if the individual or couple occupying the bed would have many changes of clothes to store and need all the wooden coat-hangers available. The frayed and discoloured carpet had been a sumptuous purchase in the 1930s, or even the 1920s. The two sofas had the finest upholstery, which had stood up well to many years of insolently affluent use and survived, like the several upright chairs, to contribute an aristocratic dignity of a different age to the Communist dignity of the present.

Who stayed here now? In the next couple of days he rarely saw anyone in the corridors or the lifts, saw no one at all go to the currency exchange counter in the foyer downstairs, full of crimson armchairs and hung with curtains of the same colour. In the early evening the vast restaurant served only Angela and himself with food – well, perhaps there were just one or two other couples – and it was the size of a ballroom, possibly having been that once. Later, of course, between seven and nine, it filled up with drinkers from the town, mostly young men who came in after long, convivial twilight conversations in small groups in the snow-quilted streets, getting together after work and before finally going home to their women. After 9.30 everything was closed and dark, the numerous waiters having energetically cleared it table by table as the customers drifted away, throwing clean tablecloths over them for the morning.

Before he kept his appointment to meet Angela in the foyer to go to dinner, three hours after they had settled in ("You will need a rest, so will I," she had told him) he was determined to have a bath. The bathroom was a high room of dark green tiles stretching up to the ceiling, irregular black tiles on the floor, a heavily beautiful washbasin beginning to detach itself from the wall, a big wall-mirror with flawed glass, and a bath in which he could stretch out his five foot ten inches with space to spare. The water immediately ran scalding hot from gold-plated taps; and when he had cooled it a little, and created bubbles with some of the shampoo he had brought from England, he lay in it happily. Any moment the door might open, the police might enter and ask to inspect his credentials and his luggage, and confiscate *A Time Apart*. But I do have a little time to assemble my thoughts and think out my plans, and I shall ask to see Carolina Predeanu at once, he decided. To-night if possible. It was Friday afternoon, and the fact of the weekend would provide ready excuses for forbidding a meeting...

But after ten minutes of rest and thought in the bath he suddenly jumped out of the warm water and dried himself hastily, knowing exactly what he intended to do while it was still just light, a feeble winter daylight bleached by the snow. When they had arrived, the girl clerk at Reception had hesitantly shown off a little English, had smiled a welcome when he had filled in his form. She might be able to help him. He would dress, go down and pick up a city map from her, look at it in his room, go and find Miss Predeanu's street, Strada Garofitei, for himself. He remembered her tone of voice on the telephone: "*Please* try again."

He was frustrated to see the girl was no longer at her counter, had been replaced by a small and dapper yet formidable man, early middle-aged, her senior perhaps. But then suddenly the girl was back, chatting idly with her colleague. The two had seen him, because observant glances flickered in his direction.

"Excuse me. Do you have a town plan? A map of the city?" he asked airily, as if it was of no importance.

The man produced one from under the counter and set it down in front of Tim.

"Ah yes – that's it! How much?"

"For you? Nothing."

"I am sorry I not speak Romanian", he said, irrelevantly, on the border of pidgin English.

"No problem," the man said unsmilingly. "We are Hungarian." Tim was not sure how this absolved him of his complete ignorance of either tongue.

He re-entered the lift now, and for the first time, as it rose with slow dignity to the fourth floor, he took in what it displayed on its walls. There were scenes of Târgu Alb, its Orthodox Cathedral, its parks, its museums, nothing industrial or even modern. The people in the sepia photographs wore the clothes of forty years before. Here Tim felt that the Romanian Communist Party, working from that huge, dominating hive of a Central Committee building in Bucharest, and numerous smaller hives in provincial centres like this, had still failed to put more than an incongruous cladding of its ideology onto edifices built by nineteenth century history. The Hotel Transilvania was like an old tree, assumed to have died but living its past very happily somewhere inside its century-old trunk.

As if to support this intuition, something caught his eye on the carpeted floor of the lift, something shining at Tim's feet. When the lift door regally opened at the fourth floor he was bending down, with profound curiosity, to pick it up, this coin which somehow did not resemble the light grey, lightweight lei coins he had in a scatter of small change in his pockets.

It was a silver coin, brightly polished, from the period of the monarchy; King Carol II's head and name were on it. And why should he find this bit of dead, irrelevant royalism in a lift in a hotel in Târgu Alb in the third decade of the rule of Nicolae Ceausescu? He slipped it into his pocket, the same pocket as the map of the city.

Entering his room, he closed the door quietly behind him. Although some light still remained, it would not be long before darkness fell, so he had to be quick. He memorised the position of the light switch, crossed to the windows, pulled the curtains across the snow-blanketed streets. Then he returned to the switch, filled the room with dim light from two functioning bulbs out of the eight in a chandelier and wondered where to sit to examine the map.

He chose the dead centre of the room first, then shifted away from it in case it was within range of the mirror and there were hidden cameras... Then he pulled up one of the upright chairs to this spot, sat down, and unfolded the map on his lap.

He had found it! Here it was, Str. Garofitei, a long link between two of the main boulevards, nearer the centre than he had feared but rather obscure, away from anywhere a tourist might stray, or be taken, not far from one patch of green marked *Stadionul Progresul* and another larger patch, a park, labelled *Parcul 1 Mai*.

In the foyer at six Angela greeted him cheerfully, looking refreshed and at ease; there was more colour in her face.

"Did you have a good sleep?" he asked her.

"No. I went to see my cousin." Her smile was radiant. They approached the restaurant door. "And I am hungry," she added.

"So am I. I went to see Carolina Predeanu."

Pleased with himself, he laughed. Angela stopped dead. "I had no answer when I rang the bell, but I left a note under the door to say I'd call on her to-night."

Angela was turning on him a gaze of amazement and consternation, looking very angry and frightened.

"Mr Harker-Jones that was very wrong!" she exclaimed.

Slowly they walked on, across the floor of an enormous room. Waiters were looking up at the sound of her voice. When she lowered it, it became more angry still, a sort of tiger's growl. "You have betrayed my trust." Her eyes were hard with fury, but was there an unexpected moistness in them?

Angela was probably right, he thought; he was letting her down when she stood to suffer much more danger from irregular behaviour than he did. She sighed in resignation, moved them both towards a table, changed her mind, her movements were distracted. Across this huge space on a platform flanked by wide-leaved rubber plants, dusty in their decorated tubs, he saw and heard the members of a small band tuning up: electric violinist, a man at a keyboard, a drummer.

"We will sit close to the band," she said eventually. "Close to the band we can talk." Tim thought the opposite might be true if the music drowned what they were saying; then he realised that her intention was to allow no one else to overhear, even if they were obliged to shout.

"Listen, please Mr Harker-Jones," she resumed, in tones of level reproof. "I am responsible for my guests. I have to answer for them – do you say that? To 'answer for'? It is not right for them to – to –" she wondered how to put this so as not to let her own side down, or disclose too much – "to change the plans arranged. I do not doubt we see Miss Predeanu to-morrow at the Writers' Union here." (That surprised him. Had this just been quietly set up?)

"I am sorry."

"I cannot stop you. But how do you know I did not have something arranged for this evening?"

It took Tim seconds to realise she was conceding he might go to Miss Predeanu's, not forbidding it.

"*Did* you have something arranged?"

"No. Not for us. But I must telephone my cousin."

"Why?"

"Because I could have seen him, and now I am coming with you."

"But I can go by myself. I know where it is now."

"No. I have to come with you because I am your guide."

And how can I blame you, he said to himself? I have stepped out of line, and put you at potential risk, and you have to redeem yourself by following my footsteps and reporting.

The band played very loudly. For centuries bands of musicians had played to assemblies of upper-class people in halls, social gatherings, restaurants, cafés, and never been louder than a background to conversation. Now they have louder instruments, now they can amplify the sound, Tim said to himself, now they can force people to listen and drown their talk, and batter them into submission. In this way they were taking their revenge for aeons of indifference.

"Who in Bucharest gave you Miss Predeanu's address? As well as the phone number? The British Council?"

He could have said Yes to this sudden question. Caught out, he said, "No."

"Someone else. A Romanian?"

He did not answer.

"Valeria Ciudea?"

He nodded, found out, back at school again. There was no band during school lunches, but the feeling he had from Romania *was* predominantly one of being back at school. At a place where there were several levels of authority that could arbitrarily restrict and punish you, from the headmaster downwards: the masters, the prefects, the fifth and fourth form bullies whom the official authorities never seemed to restrain. And all the apparatus of rules, the arbitrary punishments (the detentions), the thefts and punches and insults never righted, all of it going on for the eternity that you lived until you were old enough to rise above it;

or exercise the power for yourself.

"It is all right," Angela said, dropping a whisper into the blessed silence after the band had finished one item and before they started another. "Valeria is all right. Valeria is a friend."

As they passed the blue police, cold in ones and twos in their boxes in every street, "Hunger allows no choice," he was thinking. He had memorised the route, thinking that he might for some reason be obliged to return the map, or suffer its confiscation. Angela let him lead her as they turned the last corner into the Str. Garofitei. It was even darker than all the other streets, though the low lamps in apartment block windows helped them a little along the uneven pavement, allowed them to skirt in safety some of the holes and ruts, where they were visible under the snow or slush.

It was mostly apartment blocks; Tim had imagined decent bourgeois dwellings, part Germanic, part Romanian (Târgu Alb apparently, still had its small German-speaking population), being demolished to make space for them, perhaps in the 1960s – because the blocks were old enough to be crumbling in places, looked jerry-built and sorry for themselves. Inside the faintly-illuminated rooms, though, a little life and warmth was evident: people ate, laughed, read books, tolerated a choir singing on television.

Angela had required him to agree that if anyone was standing outside, or passing, the entrance to Carolina Predeanu's staircase, they would walk on and return later. But at the entrance to the block they did not need to do this. There was nobody at all walking in the whole of Str. Garofitei, certainly no one lurking in the tiny, pitch-black lobby at the bottom of Staircase 4 of Block 5.

There was no seeing where the lift was. When they finally found it, Angela made out a scrawl on a sheet of paper pasted over the button: *Defect*. It had been working when Tim had called earlier, but between then and now it had become *Defect*.

They would need to try the stairs, though to mount them was a case of groping and guessing, feeling for the top step of each flight, feeling or looking for the railing in the faintest effusion of illumination from the city outside that came through the occasional window.

The flats were silent from the landings: no radios, no voices. In the darkness the smell of cooking from somewhere seemed incongruous, and yet hopeful. No number was easily visible. They ascended from the second floor to the third. Angela was tracing with her fingers the cold chromium figures nailed onto the doors. They held hands, leader and led, testing each setting down of a foot for safety, never speaking even in whispers.

When they were convinced they had the right door, Angela established that Tim was standing safely beside her by putting out an arm to draw him close, an intimacy leaving him slightly embarrassed. There was a bell beside this door, one of the very few lighted by a battery; so she pressed it.

It rang weakly inside the flat. Foreignly, not a strident and certain English sound. Tim recognised the sound from four hours before, they had not made a mistake. He shivered from cold, and believed Angela was shivering from fear. Somebody or something moved inside, perhaps an inner door was being opened; but then there was silence again, perhaps the silence of someone listening before they made another move. Angela tried the bell again. Once more it rang; but even more weakly.

Then there were quiet footsteps, the sound of this door being very cautiously unlocked.

– 2 –

When it opened, the immediate interior of the apartment, a narrow corridor about fifteen feet long (Tim's guess) seemed almost as dark as the landing where they had waited. They could only see into it at all because a door at the end on the left was slightly ajar, and light was shining out of it. Music was playing:

opera. The woman opening the door said nothing at all, but stood aside to let them enter first.

When they were safely in, she shut the door and locked it again, negotiated her way past them, and led them into the lighted room, a lounge with very little furniture and bare walls – except for the one where there was a full bookshelf, which caught the eye and gave a centre to this living space. In front of it was a small desk, behind that a chair. There was a sofa, and vases and one or two other straight-backed chairs. The lampshade on a long flex hung down in the middle of the room, only three feet above a low glass-topped table with a book on it.

Carolina Predeanu was more beautiful than Tim could have expected from the general term "a beautiful woman", because her beauty was unconventional. She was very tall, and very slim, at first sight even disturbingly thin; until Tim saw that her height ensured a width of shoulders and hips that gave her more substance, removed any early impression that this narrowness of body was unhealthy, even anorexic.

Her face was unusually long and pale, but had more than a hint of energy in the eyes. She was clothed, he thought, with remarkable style, in a very long, velvety dress, dark green and sleeveless – and Tim then realised that her bare arms were not thin. In fact, most of his original sense of Carolina Predeanu's appearance was changing as he saw her properly. What he had thought was very black hair in the darkness of the hall was in fact dark brown. She had small ears, small lips for her ample features, and a handsomely wide forehead. Her beauty was poised and mature.

She was younger than Tim, and yet older than he expected – thirty-three, thirty-four? She took their coats and stored them in an adjoining room, with a social ease which apologised silently for the cautious, even illicit, way in which she had felt obliged to welcome them. So far she had not said anything at all.

They shook hands – should he have kissed hers? He did not.

She motioned them to sit down; and Tim was aware that

there was something actually *recognisable* about this woman he could never have seen before, could not even have seen in a photograph. Then he knew that Carolina Predeanu was wearing the dress Katrin had worn for dinner with Dora, John and their English guests –

Katrin had never been given a surname in the novel, never accorded a country of origin. Plainly, Philip had not needed to imagine and invent someone resembling Carolina Predeanu because, in appearance, Katrin *was* Carolina. And Carolina had put on the dress for this occasion.

Before she sat down herself, Carolina moved over to the record-player on which the record was turning, put a finger to her lips, and replaced the pick-up arm at the beginning of the side. The music was now almost loud (they would not be overheard), but when they were all three seated together round the low table with the book on it Carolina encouraged them all to lean forward and speak quietly.

"I knew you would eventually come, from four years ago," she said to Tim. What did she mean? "It was only a question of *when* you would come. When it happened" – and "it" was clearly Philip Carston's death – "I knew it would be one day soon; but I had to wait." She gave a sudden smile of excitement. "When last Tuesday you gave me the telephone" – Romanians sometimes said it like this, not "the call" – "I stayed at home every night expecting you. But we have not been introduced."

She indicated Angela, and Tim realised with embarrassment that he had not provided a name for someone whom he assumed Carolina would realise was a guide; and would hope was to be trusted since they had come together.

"Cernec – Angela", Angela said, a little sharply.

"Angela!" Carolina said warmly, and they shook hands again; and now Angela smiled back because they were all in a conspiracy and the best thing to do was to treat each other as agreeable acquaintances and leave it at that. They exchanged remarks about Tim's note forewarning of a visit together, how they found their way up in the dark.

"But you said – 'four years ago'?" Tim needed to explore that extraordinary statement. He took in the fact that the book on the table between them, set down neatly in its exact centre, the sacred subject of this meeting, was Carolina's translation of *A Time Apart*. But now Carolina opened it and took something that looked like a card marking a place; except that it was not a card, it was a photograph.

"Yes. When Philip told me you would be writing about him – and gave me this."

The photograph was of Philip and Tim together, much younger, when they still regularly met; and Tim recognised it well. It had been taken at a publishers' party, an occasion at Ridgbury but before it *was* Ridgbury (and before the Paldreys arrived) and Philip was publishing only his second, or third, novel with them and Tim his first biography. "So you met Philip – a lot?"

Carolina looked surprised, offended, worried – and finally amused.

"Yes. I did meet Philip a lot. But you know that if you are writing his biography?"

"We were not close friends in his last years. He did not tell me very much about that period. Philip never made it clear while he was alive – or never made it *certain* – that he wanted me to write his Life. Though I always knew it was possible."

"Oh it was always more than possible, it was inevitable." But Carolina showed disbelief with her expression, even distress. This was a situation of extraordinary delicacy as well as fascination: it was obvious Philip meant much more to Carolina Predeanu than just the author of a book she had translated. Carolina gave the instant impression of a woman in mourning for Philip Carston, now dead nearly a year, someone to whom Philip was a precious theme, and anyone linked with him – but most particularly the biographer entrusted with writing his Life – was eagerly to be sought out as a way of learning more, of keeping Philip's memory alive, of feeding and nourishing the love –

The love?

"This will need a much longer discussion," Tim said.

"Before we begin the discussion we drink to our meeting – our meeting at last," Carolina said. She left them alone for a moment and then came back with glasses and wine.

"One of the bottles Romanians keep while they wait for special occasions," she proclaimed; and Angela smiled. "This is very special. I am so happy you are here. I thought, when I heard the news that Philip had died, you would come in a day, or a week. But I knew that was hoping too much. I said, 'Mr Harker-Jones will come when his own sorrow is a little less. In a month, perhaps, or two months.' When you did not come, and you did not write, I thought, 'He has come, but it has not been arranged for me to see him, his letters have been lost.' And sometimes I thought, 'He does not want to see me, I am the part of Philip's life he has decided to ignore.' But now I understand you chose your time when not so many people would be watching for you to come, and you came. So we will drink to the fact that you have finally arrived!"

She poured the wine into the delicate glasses with a slightly shaking hand, and Tim was aware that her voice had almost broken with the effort of that speech and that there were tears on her cheeks.

Whatever the nature and depth of Carolina's feelings for Philip Carston they shamed Tim with their strength. The years of neglect reproached him, the years in Philip's life he ought to have known about by maintaining their friendship. He looked at the two smiling young men in the photograph, picked out of a drinking group in a crowded office by some other forgotten person with a camera...

So they drank to his arriving, and implicitly to Philip Carston himself; although Carolina's very failure to use the name at this moment revealed it was too sacred to be quoted as the subject of a toast, even in blessed memory.

When Carolina had taken her first sip of the wine she sat

back and smiled and looked directly at Tim. So did Angela. He sensed that this was a little like the formal meetings in which a statement of welcome would be followed by a silence in which he was expected to say something. Carolina wanted a response.

In his few days here he had learnt that formal replies were not too difficult to make, as long as Angela was interpreting for him: after each sentence he had time to think of what to say next while she was translating. But here he had to think faster, because he could reply directly to Carolina in English without requiring Angela's help.

"I am very moved to be here," he said; this time not being hypocritical as he had been to a cultural official in Bucharest. "You may be able to help me with information – I mean, with more information – about Philip's visits to your country." Carolina looked at him calmly, and just nodded very slightly at this; and he wondered if she found the words condescending. "There are certain profound features of Philip's life and imagination of which I know very little." This was an improvement, and it pleased her. "So far, I have only written some first drafts, some of the earlier chapters. My notes and my researches have only reached as far as 1976."

Carolina smiled with extraordinary pleasure.

"But that is very good! It is very interesting – the *generosity* of coincidence, I think. I met Philip for the first time when he came to Romania in 1977."

"Then you can help me with 1977 onwards," Tim said, sharing her smile. "We must talk about all this." They started to talk about what he had already drafted, about what he needed to know to fill gaps, but only in a general way. They would need much longer than they had. When and where could they –?

But – "I think there will not be time for more meetings," Angela was pronouncing, looking most uncomfortable: her expression had resumed some of the severity and concern he had seen when he told her he had left the note under Carolina's door.

Carolina had an answer to this.

"Of course there is not time today, or to-morrow at the Writers' Union," she said. "And you return to Bucharest on Monday, I believe? But I am coming to Bucharest myself Monday evening. I have arranged for us to have lunch at a restaurant on Tuesday."

Angela's face was all abject amazement and confusion; Carolina's radiant and serene. But why, if Carolina was proposing to meet him so openly, had there been so much conspiracy about meeting in the first place? This country was full of contradictions. Tim knew that if he suggested to Romanians that life here might not be wholly unrestricted – he could walk fairly freely (in most places) in the streets, but did *not* feel able freely to contact and meet the poet X or the critic Y, whom somebody had declared he must be *sure* to meet – the very idea of constraint would be laughingly denied. No one directly admitted it. But ask outright to see poet X, and he or she would be unavailable, there would be a tense embarrassment, a silence.

Well, perhaps X *was* genuinely unavailable: people had families, commitments, deadlines, perhaps did not even want to meet intrusive foreigners. Could he himself automatically meet, at forty-eight hours' notice, a Romanian visitor to London? He knew he would put up barriers, excuses, make out he was away for the weekend.

Yet here was Carolina not only guaranteeing they would meet, but now specifying the place, leaving Angela alarmed and speechless, unable to protest. Later, Angela tried to acquit herself of the confusion by saying, "Miss Predeanu has influence." But for the moment she obviously felt trumped, sidelined even.

"Come on Tuesday at twelve-thirty to the Capsa Restaurant in Calea Victoriei. Angela can tell you where it is. We can talk there."

There was now a glow of triumph in Carolina's eyes; an air of mischief if someone so elegant could show such a small-scale emotion. With the instruction to Angela, which hinted that she should take Tim to the door of the Capsa and leave him there (denying Angela a second lunch in three days!), she was taking charge. And Angela was apparently accepting that she had the power to do so.

Had Carolina, he asked, met a Mr Ioan Ludache, a biographer who belonged to the Writers' Union in Bucharest? Yes, she knew of Mr Ludache, she intimated guardedly; except that she did not think he was really a biographer, surely he was a writer of historical fiction? She did not think he was exceptionally well-known.

She was working on further translations, yes, but it had always to be in her spare time, as she was a full-time editor at the publishing house, in charge of fiction, and criticism, and books for children. No, they published hardly any foreign novel translations themselves though foreign works of other kinds had been translated; her version of *A Time Apart* had been published in Bucharest.

Returning to Philip brought back a gravity into the conversation. They had all drunk more of the wine, but the first flush of relaxation had subsided. Tim began to feel they had better leave deeper matters until Tuesday.

Carolina did not come out of her door, and fell silent as soon as she opened it. Tim and Angela made their way down the stairs again and out into the ghostly white of the deserted, snowy street. There were now few lights in the apartment windows. When Tim almost at once tried to begin a conversation Angela emphatically stopped him. "We *cannot* speak *here*," she whispered firmly. He felt snubbed and foolish for forgetting the rigour of the rules by which he had to play; but accepted the caution; and they walked back to the Hotel Transilvania in silence.

− 3 −

"And this is Miss Predeanu, Carolina," Angela was pronouncing suddenly, in the middle of a long list of the names around the table in the Târgu Alb Writers' Union, given by its President.

The house had much of the dark and haunted grandeur of the building in Bucharest, looking like someone's half-converted bourgeois mansion, in the centre of a large garden or small park, almost too beautiful and large for the purposes it served; could there be so much literary activity in Târgu Alb, Tim asked himself uncharitably? On the other hand, this was a provincial centre with a regional pride which was possibly why a considerable effort was being made to impress, on a Saturday morning. The President of the Writers' Union himself, no substitute, had greeted him at the front door, a man of booming joviality introduced as "poet, philosopher, traveller, friend of culture." He took a seat in the centre of the table when they sat, exactly opposite Tim and Angela, and alongside him was a secretary taking long and rapid notes, even of his formal speech of welcome.

"And next to Miss Predeanu," Angela interpreted, "is Professor Liviu Bobolescu from the university." Bobolescu looked as tatty and crumbling as he had seemed yesterday in the train, but just as artfully bright-eyed. People made space for him to sit down, but he was not greeted warmly. "Professor Bobolescu is a − a −" (this was the President's hesitation and Angela waited tactfully for his chosen word) − "a polymath with a special interest in literary theory and also a − a −" at which point a strange, serious look, an expression almost of warning to Bobolescu as if instructing him not to parade this next preoccupation − "also an interest in the origin of works of literature in terms of the ideas which first inspired them − and the way writers developed those ideas."

Bobolescu gave no sign of having noticed either description

or warning, and gazed down at the table while they were being translated. But Tim saw two people, a man and a woman on the President's right, look at each other significantly.

The list of names continued. Mr Constantinescu was the director of the theatre, Mrs Gasparos was director of the Hungarian theatre in the city, Mr Ilosz – Tamasi – was a Hungarian editor in the publishing house, which had its offices in the city centre. And then the President's formal speech started. It did him credit, Tim thought, that he said it all with a touch of self-parody; his colleagues would know what came next, and certain well-polished, pompous phrases raised smiles and laughter from them.

He found it difficult to stop, Tim thought, because in the moments in which Angela translated a phrase, the President was given time to think of something more to say, another flourish of welcome, another chord of rhetoric.

"And one thing in conclusion," Angela was eventually saying, "you come, Mr Harker-Jones, as someone especially valuable for us to make acquaintance with – because you come as the living representative of Philip Carston. And we are honoured in Târgu Alb to have our own modest connection with the name of Philip Carston in the beautiful guise of his Romanian translator, Miss Predeanu."

Angela rendered this with a smile. More looks were exchanged around the table. Carolina herself did not smile.

"And *lastly*, Mr Harker-Jones, you come as a friend. A new friend. And friendship –"

And he was away on another theme, which would need another peroration, another final, resounding profundity.

But suddenly he had finished, and Tim was vigorously nodding thanks; and about to convey them through Angela when he realised the formalities were still not over. Nearly everyone else apparently had a short prepared statement to make in full.

Most remarkable, Tim thought, was the energy in these speeches. It was as if people were trying to say that everything was normal here under the surface. He thought he heard a message, cloaked or coded in their enthusiasm: the culture flourished, providing a channel for defiance and hope.

So now he broke in, determined not to just sit here and be told things, and asked, "What kind of novels are most popular?" – partly in the hope of stirring a little consternation.

But the answers came readily, with chapter-and-verse detail he could not fully grasp, although he could detect none of the expected Communist clichés in the plots people described. Everything was far more complex and subtle than he had imagined.

"We want to translate your biography of Philip Carston when it is done," Angela was now translating. She was giving him the first words Professor Liviu Bobolescu (polymath interested in the initial inspiration giving rise to works of literature) had spoken. Several people looked at Tim, with what could have been embarrassment, but the President was quick off the mark.

"Exactly what I was intending to say next," Angela translated, smiling, and even laughing a little because the President was laughing. "We believe that is how we shall have the origins of *A Time Apart* fully – fully confirmed for us. We have an excellent publishing house here in Târgu Alb, as I told you. If you and your publisher in England –" Tim thought ruefully of Paldrey, his cluttered office, his chaotic, centreless house – "would accept Romanian lei, we shall be very happy to publish it as soon as it appears in England."

What could Tim say? The proposition seemed unreal, unlikely, even vaguely threatening. But he wished to be polite, even if he could not believe that any of this would ever happen. He smiled therefore, and said through Angela, "I should be greatly honoured."

The President seemed satisfied; since there was a lot of interest in Philip Carston and *A Time Apart* they would hope to bring out the Life in an edition of perhaps seventy thousand copies – Tim's mouth fell open but he was careful to close it again at once, in case his incredulity looked discourteous. When would the book be finished, so they could prepare plans?

"It is very hard to say," he asked Angela to tell them. "A biographer is never sure how much more there is to discover, right to the end."

There were understanding nods. As they talked, and everyone except Carolina and Professor Bobolescu joined in, Tim suddenly remembered, and felt the strength of, the warnings he had been given before his visit. It was as if, by publishing him here, they wanted to draw him in, tempt him to return, make him dependent on them, trap him through his connections with them. And gradually, who knows, his loyalties to the United Kingdom would loosen, he would be prized away by the temptations of acclaim in another country, a dangerous country, people he had been firmly educated against and warned against.

So the sounds he now made were more guarded, more noncommittal. If his biography were ever finished (he gave a self-deprecating smile, at which people looked puzzled) he would need to talk very carefully with his publisher about it being published abroad. Heads nodded courteously, but the faces looked sad; so sad that Tim vowed he would do his best to speed things up. At this, everyone seemed grateful.

Then, for no clear reason, the meeting was breaking up, watches were being consulted, a few people were crowding round him to talk. One of them was Bobolescu, waiting patiently while other conversations went on, waiting as if he had time and reason for waiting.

Another was Carolina. But she did not stop longer than to say quietly, in English, "I will see you on Tuesday", unheard by anyone except Tim and Angela. After a brief and formal handshake she was gone. And "I have tiresome business that cannot wait", Angela translated the words of the President. They were left incongruously alone with Liviu Bobolescu. He guessed the old professor had something to say; but he could not have imagined what it would be.

"I hope you enjoyed your interesting morning," Bobolescu began in English, with a glint of irony in a baleful expression. "And now you and your so kind lady companion will come to lunch with me at my house."

It did not sound like an invitation so much as an order. Angela looked bewildered, exchanged words with him in Romanian, rapidly, then explained to Tim:

"The dining room here is closed, so Professor Bobolescu has invited us."

"If you would give my modest food the pleasure of being eaten," the professor continued, showing relics of old gallantry. His manner suggested, though, that they would do better with him than with anyone else. He was subtly proclaiming himself the most significant person in the room.

Outside, on the steps, looking across the snow-covered lawn Tim and Angela were alone for a few moments.

"This means he has *permission* to invite us?" Tim suggested.

"It is possible he does not *require* it."

In his ancient black fur hat and soiled coat Bobolescu led them along sunlit side streets and across small public gardens, cautioning them against the frequent puddles: the snow had been melting all the morning. If, in the train, he had seemed almost impossibly old and frail, here on his own territory he had become curiously, though precariously, fast and agile.

The streets widened into avenues of sturdy, square, ornate one-storey houses with grand front entrances, fan-shaped canopies of coloured glass shading the doors, wrought-iron railings surrounding the gardens. And in front of one elaborate gate Bobolescu was suddenly all proud, outstretched welcoming arms. With ludicrous ceremony he ushered Angela and Tim up a short path between flowerbeds now desolate with the winter cold, and produced a key for the door.

Immediately they were inside, there came a warm, sociable smell of rich cooking. Lunch had obviously been foreseen; but could it have been planned even before their arrival yesterday in

Târgu Alb? Mrs Bobolescu, in an apron, appeared from the kitchen, more relaxed here in her own house; but under the fulsome welcome Tim thought he could detect an air of embarrassment, as if Liviu might do something for which she had to suffer and apologise. She spoke no English, and Angela said, "Mrs Bobolescu welcomes the rare pleasure of an English visitor in her home."

Liviu guided them first into a dining-room where a table had been laid with special ceremony: silver, little glasses for whiskey or *tuica*, larger glasses for wine, china delicately decorated with what Tim took to be local motifs.

"We can speak here," Bobolescu said. "We can speak here." (About what?) Suddenly he became the eager and solicitous host. From a thick black bottle he poured into the small glasses a colourless liquid. "Now," he continued, his own glass held out to touch the others, "we will raise our glasses!" He looked merry, crafty, mischievous as he paused to let them wonder what the toast would be. Tim guessed it might be their meeting, "literature", or "culture", or even "Anglo-Romanian friendship."

It was none of these.

"We will raise our glasses –" Tim heard glee, triumph, malice, even madness in his voice – "to Miss Carolina Predeanu, author of *A Time Apart*."

– 4 –

"Miss Predeanu is exceedingly modest," Bobolescu was now saying, having drunk half of the drink in his glass at one rapid gulp. "She will never claim the achievement. She is determined it remain a secret, however much you try to persuade her. And I do not wish to take away from the achievements of Mr Philip Carston, whose memory we revere. But Miss Predeanu wrote every word of this book, in her fine original Romanian, which Mr Carston could not understand until she also translated it, with his help, into fine English."

Mrs Bobolescu now returned and invited them to take their places at the table. From nowhere a son appeared, and was introduced: Virgil was tall, with the wiry figure of his father and his vaguely cunning expression, and did not seem to have taken any characteristics from his mother – except perhaps his inability to modify or restrain his father's behaviour in any respect at all. There was some conversation about whether the Professor should have wine, with Virgil attempting to deny or moderate his father's wishes – all in vain because Bobolescu merely grabbed the bottle and poured for himself.

In front of them Mrs Bobolescu set, on top of the dinner plates at each place, bowls of soup, steaming and odorous, rich with rice-grains and slivers of chicken. Undoubtedly she had caught the words "Predeanu" and "Carston": her face registered knowledge that her husband was back to a topic nothing could persuade him to drop, the lunacy of which was evident to everyone except him.

Tim thought he could see the old man's pride in Carolina's talents had unhinged him. He resolved to change the subject, compliment Mrs Bobolescu on her meal. Anything necessary to know he would surely find out from Carolina. But Bobolescu would not give him the opportunity.

"I repeat," Bobolescu went on, spooning soup eagerly, "I do not wish to harm the reputation of your subject, only to assist you. If you should doubt what I say – and I have invited you to lunch to say it, because there is no one else in Târgu Alb will give you the truth – please speak to the famous biographer Mr Ioan Ludache in Bucharest." Tim dropped his spoon. "Mr Ludache will confirm everything I say, and give you the names of other people who will confirm it."

"Are you saying that Miss Predeanu wrote this book entirely out of her own imagination?" he asked, trying not to sound as if he was humouring the insane. "Without ever having visited England?"

"Ah, but of course Carolina went to England. She used her beautiful imagination very powerfully, but she also used her time in England with Mr Carston. 'Mr Hendleton', as he is called. You knew this from Mr Carston, I am sure?"

"Did you meet Philip Carston here in Romania? He came to Târgu Alb?"

"So many times!"

So I shall need also to talk to Bobolescu himself, alone, Tim was thinking. The questions for which he was compelled to seek answers were multiplying, strands in a web into which even Ioan Ludache and Valeria Ciudea had now been firmly woven. He played for a little thinking time, by praising the food Mrs Bobolescu now served: the tenderest slices of beef, carrots in butter, lightly fried potatoes, a sparkling wine, everything cooked and presented with extraordinary delicacy; there was even something about it to suggest a professional hand.

"I enjoyed the meeting this morning," said Tim. It came out as a lame courtesy, an irrelevance. "Meeting you there, and meeting Miss Predeanu."

"Oh not for the first time, surely," Bobolescu said, with infinite mischief, old grey eyebrows raised very high. "But – you know – I had to telephone the President, and the Vice-President of the Committee for Culture, and *insist* that I attend. When I discovered who I had met on the train I naturally thought *they* would telephone *me* with an invitation. But no. I had to tell them that a failure to invite me would indicate that they were frightened of my knowledge – they would be seen as denying Miss Predeanu her just acclaim as a creative artist. I insisted I bring you home to lunch from the meeting, so I would not need to make a statement *in* the meeting!"

Virgil had eaten very quickly. His plate was empty; he excused himself and left the table.

"Mrs Bobolescu wonders 'Are you enjoying our country?'" Angela said, loudly and deliberately.

"Yes. But there is much to understand."

"She says, 'Do not worry there is much to understand for us Romanians also.'" Having said as much, the hostess immediately looked as if she regretted her haste. Tim latched on to the uneasiness. In this small, private group you could surely ask frank questions? "Your political situation intrigues me a lot," Tim ventured. The professor's wife heard the word "political" before Angela translated Tim's statement and who knows whether she did not even tone down the words, to make them a little less suggestive and probing?

But Mrs Bobolescu's look of fear was deep down in her eyes, which stared at him with reproach and warning. Her lips quivered. As she replied, very slowly, she fingered a string of large beads around her neck with obvious agitation, then turned to take cigarettes out of a drawer of the sideboard behind her.

"I don't think – politics – are such an interesting matter to discuss," Angela said; no doubt literally translating this time.

What else would they talk about, then?

He complimented her on the meal again, said what an interesting coincidence it was to have met on the train. He was wondering did she know the other people in the compartment well?

This time she seemed not so much frightened as scornful and guarded at the same time. Oh, Mrs Vajna – Eva – in the corner wearing the cardigan – was a well-known busybody and gossip in Târgu Alb, always ready to argue about anything, a Hungarian of course, as her name suggested. The professor could say a lot more about Mrs Vajna. (In his wallet Tim had her torn-off scrap of paper with the words, "*not* believe old man's opinions"). But Mrs Vajna was talking in Romanian in the train, Tim asked? Yes, why not? Everyone in Târgu Alb spoke both languages, was that surprising? There were nearly 40% of Hungarians in this city, and a few Germans. We live in Transylvania. And the other passenger, the very well-dressed man in the other window corner? That was Mr Radin, Mr Ilie Radin.

(She spoke more slowly.) He works for the – for the government offices, she thought. Yes."

Tim was preparing another question when Virgil reappeared, carrying something; it was cradled in his arms as he pushed through the door; it was trailing wires. It was a video camera, and he also held a lamp to provide extra light for filming in the obscurity of this room on a darkening winter afternoon.

Virgil opened a cabinet in the wall and revealed a recorder. The conversation continued as he worked, as he tested the recorder, as he plugged the lamp into a socket on the wall; and Professor Bobolescu ignored all this as if it was as much part of a lunch at home as his wife's serving up now an extraordinary dessert of fruit, cream and ice-cream decked with spots of syrup and embellished with thin, sweet biscuits.

"My son's favourite toy," Bobolescu eventually said, as Virgil aimed the camera directly and unnervingly, without smiling, at Tim. Light music, incidental music for the video, was playing somewhere in the room, in the background. It was difficult to talk with the glaring strength of the light, which Mrs Bobolescu, having provided her visually handsome dessert, dutifully carried round at her son's instruction; although the professor encouraged them all to go on talking naturally. Tim heard himself muttering empty phrases just so as to be saying *something* when the camera was poked at him. The circulating lamp created shadows out of the wall-cupboards and high furniture in the room, shadows which moved and enlarged and shrank and enlarged again as Mrs Bobolescu shifted around. The entire room was a dizzying study in flickering black and white.

When Virgil had finished they were shown into a large, book-lined study where there was a television and a video-player. It seemed to be the plan that the twenty minutes or so of Virgil's filming should be played back as an accompaniment to coffee. But Mrs Bobolescu had to prepare the coffee first, and the professor to retire for some reason and Angela to excuse herself; and for a minute Tim was left alone.

He could see immediately that Bobolescu's library was extensive, polymathic indeed: rows of bound classic volumes, the bright spines of modern editions, shelf after shelf of austere paperbacks from a large range of countries. There were even translations out of one language into another language not Romanian: James Joyce into French, Tolstoy into German, Proust into English. And almost every book seemed to have its curling and yellowing paper-slips inserted as markers.

Tim took down a handsome Romanian translation of Chaucer and glanced at it; then took down *Swann's Way*, in English, a familiar little blue volume with its crisp thin pages. He opened it casually while Mrs Bobolescu brought in coffee and poured it, found marked the very page where a slip covered with tiny writing in a meticulous hand indicated the moment where the narrator had raised the madeleine to his lips.

Tim wondered what the professor would have wanted to mark in, say, *La Prisonnière*, *The Captive*. A slender, faded marker led him to a page where half a sentence at the end of a paragraph was underlined emphatically in red:

> the 'folly' a man commits by marrying his cook or the mistress of his best friend is as a rule the only poetical action that he performs in the course of his existence.

When the images of their lunch appeared on the television screen, Angela smiled, enjoying the sudden dramatisation of the banal scenes of moments before. And Tim thought that somehow everything said or done at the table, captured by a camera and relayed on a screen where you expected everything to be polished and calculated, did indeed look real and significant. For a time, it could even have been watched as a drama to which you expected an ending. But Tim was appalled to have the discomfort patent in his expressions displayed. And the camera had even found a curious nervous tic of which he was quite unaware: he would pull back the corner of his lips with the muscles of his right cheek when something puzzled him. His face reminded him of nothing grander than a bewildered animal caught out of its habitat in a natural history film, blinking in the headlights or in fierce sunlight, then chewing with perplexed satisfaction (ingesting his hostess's ice-cream) at some titbit thrown down for it so that its eating habits could be noted and analysed.

After the video show Bobolescu suddenly looked tired. He sat in a low armchair with hands clasped, refusing to be drawn out of a melancholic pose. He seemed to have overlooked the fact that the weekend was very short, Tim was only here to-morrow, plans to provide him with any further detail for his biography would have to be made soon. When it seemed tactful to do so, with the coffee exhausted, Tim and Angela offered their thanks and made their farewells, taking directions from Virgil in English as to the quickest route back to the Hotel Transilvania.

In his bedroom, with no further need to feel alert and to think fast, Tim felt the wine rising to his head with delayed strength. He would try to draw some conclusions about their peculiar afternoon before dropping off to sleep.

One possible conclusion, since Bobolescu had not proposed any further meeting, was that he had nothing solid to say. His *idée fixé* was truly that of a madman, his wife's arguing with him in the train (and the other passengers doing so) a way of humouring the insane. Another, more charitable, possibility was that Bobolescu intended him to obtain further information from someone else who could be relied on to support the professor's tale. Well, Ludache had been mentioned; a biographer in his own eyes, and in those of Bobolescu, but a writer of historical novels as far as Carolina knew anything about him.

A third thought came in the shape of a sick dread that he had come upon an insurmountable task: there was a lot more to find out, he had no time to do it, and the only possible provider of information was Carolina, with whom he could expect just one lunch in a very public restaurant. The whole web expanded as he looked at it, stretching ever more thinly over wider areas of air. Far off along a pattern of strands which represented the streets and hotels and restaurants of Bucharest and Târgu Alb, a network glittering like a will of the wisp, rose Carolina's face, smiling in beautiful and pathetic anticipation of what he would write about Philip.

He must have been dreaming that image, because it now flashed luminously and broke before his eyes and he was fumbling for the light of the bedside lamp so as to find, and answer, a telephone which was ringing stridently in his ear. This could only be Angela, but they had agreed (as they had yesterday) that they both deserved a good rest before taking some (light) refreshment in the huge hotel restaurant in the company of the deafening band.

"Mr Harker-Jones, how are you? enquired the male voice, in English of course.

"Very well – but who are you, please?"

"We had the pleasure of meeting on the train yesterday. My name is Radin – Ilie Radin. It would be a pleasure for me to meet you again while you are in town. Perhaps for a little while *now*?"

– 5 –

*** Richard told her he had not spoken what he and she had both begun to call his "first words" out of any protective intention, as Katrin surmised. In fact he had felt decidedly afraid of her directness, as well as attracted to her, and had never thought she might be incapable of standing up for herself. He spoke the 'first words' at that moment because he could not tell, he said, if there would ever in his life be another opportunity to let her know, by implication, what he had begun to feel as soon as she started to question other people at Dora's table. The interval between meeting her and loving her had been very short for

Richard; a different (kind of) interval from hers.

He had been attracted to her immediately, and love started a couple of hours later when he heard himself speak those first words, so quietly and purposefully that they were virtually a confession of love on the spot. He had to contrive some means to see her again, and very quickly.

Katrin smiled at this account and told him she had been fully aware what was meant by his speaking to her. She was at first, for a few seconds, disconcerted and then – bored! She knew about these open statements by men; so this came as just another tedious example which she would have to cope with somehow. Matters were made more difficult by this being the first time it had happened in a foreign country, where the rules and conventions and courtesies might be different.

When he spoke she did not feel the least emotion towards him. That only arrived much later, and took the form of realising after seventy-four hours that Richard Hendleton had come into focus for her as a person in his own right, not just one out of several people at a dinner table.

Much later! Seventy-four hours! For Katrin, every separate hour in England seemed to contain a year's experience. She was going through one of those passages in life when time works with two contradictory speeds. The days, the hours, seem so absorbingly filled with oddity and incident that they go by with unnatural slowness; every excitement occupies less time than it logically needs. And then, when several days have gone by at this pace ("Did I arrive four days ago?" "Did we only meet *three* days ago?"), it is suddenly clear that they have actually passed in an instant. "How can it be a whole fortnight since all this started? It is all so new!"

Later this period of time is like a grand lighted town on a shore that seems, when you have just irrevocably sailed out of it, so close that you could reach out and touch it, you could be there again in a second. Soon, it is farther away, but its lights and excitements are given a coherence by distance which they did not have while you were there among all their wonderful shifts and confusions. The fascination lies in the difference from your routine living; it is a time apart.

Finally these days or weeks resemble a jewel kept in a box or a set of events committed to a diary in a drawer. You can take it out, jewel or book, and scan it lovingly, and recover for a time the sense of most moments in the experience, certainly the most important ones. But – there finally arrives a time when you don't actually remember to take it out at all, or (the same thing) you don't need or *want* to take it out.

Katrin knew almost from her own instant of focusing Richard properly that she would have to fight against the unimaginable day when she would not open the drawer and look at the diary pages. This love was going to be an experience so distinct and clear, so impossible to renew in any future she could plan, that there was a danger of it turning into a remote, unreachable perfection, eventually shining for her no more than one of those grains of sand on a beach which sparkles briefly in the sun and then can't be traced when you look a second time.

To delay that outcome she knew she was going to have to write down as much about it as she could: the diary was a better metaphor than the jewel, and she would keep a real, non-metaphorical diary ...

It was cleverly arranged, that warm afternoon, that Richard should come in his own car, that John and Dora needed to take Samantha and Julian back for some actual or pretended appointment, and that Katrin should be left to do the rest of the sightseeing just with Richard himself.

Katrin identified for him the exact moment in the seventy-fifth hour of their acquaintance when he had become real.

When she and Richard had left the others there had been foolish problems, as there always appeared to be in England, about leaving the car somewhere while they walked the last fifty yards or so to some eventual destination. Katrin asked why people always needed to use their cars? Why shouldn't they walk the whole distance? She was told it was too far to walk. Then why not use a bus?

Had Katrin realised how few buses there were in Fieldenhurst? Certainly none to the centre from where Dora and John lived in a modest, green, bourgeois suburb. But why were more buses not provided? Because they would not pay, Richard explained as they walked along the path through the gardens and up to the Castle Gallery entrance; so many people had cars that buses would be empty.

And therefore, Katrin exclaimed, what people said in her own country was quite correct: if everyone tried to find their own personal answers to such problems life soon became more uncomfortable and more ridiculous. They had spent nearly twenty minutes trying to park Richard's car and had ended up a long way from the Castle, almost ten minutes' walk, in a side street where they had to find a little shop and buy a newspaper to obtain change for a parking meter. If all these people in cars had come to the city centre by bus they would have saved – she made a calculation – at an average of half-an-hour each, a total of three hundred hours of life to spend on other activities. Not to mention the money used on parking meters, and paid to people wearing those smart little uniforms just to check whether drivers had left their cars in one place for too long. It seemed to Katrin that owning a car was not a freedom but a burden.

She thought up this line of argument as she walked with Richard along the path beside the flower-beds under the Castle walls, and she was pleased with it. She soon found that Richard wholly agreed. When, *very* pleased with it, she tried out this approach on Claudine Simmingley the next day, she found her refusing even to listen – superficially agreeing with her, but flatly dismissing the topic.

"Oh, all that's *obvious*," Claudine said quickly. "That's how it is. There's nothing to be done about it."

"But I believe many people feel the same, so why can you

do nothing? It is obvious to me you can do *something*."

"Oh, this is not worth talking about!"

And this exchange had taken place while they had been drinking coffee in the little cafeteria attached to the Fieldenhurst theatre, and during a pause in their talk they had looked out at the solid block of traffic in the street outside. Claudine's abrupt response had left Katrin much more surprised than hurt at being silenced. Why did these English people go around in a state of lazy, frivolous despondency for so much of the time? Why was this subject not worth talking about when, at their dinner a few evenings before, it had apparently been worth talking for some time about – Katrin now admitted this knowledge to herself – sexual stimulation with vacuum cleaners? Katrin did not know how she could engage any of these people on serious subjects; except for Richard.

Some sort of understanding with Richard which she felt she did not have with the other young people at that dinner table was already there in that garden, as they walked, fortuitously in step. Later she remembered the flowers in the flower-beds, the shapes and colours, the labels giving the names, which she stopped to glance at. Then, as they walked on, she suddenly said it herself, said,

"But we are walking in step!"

And Richard turned to look at her, and stopped; so that Katrin walked on a few paces before she realised, then swung round back to him where he stood, smiling.

"Yes. We were. We were walking in step," he replied.

They stood for long seconds looking bemusedly at each other. Then he took her hand and became real ...

"They are all my friends, remember that!" Richard said, laughing, when they were back in the car. "Just as your cousins are my friends."

"Only Dora is supposed to be my cousin," she said, remembering the uneasiness she had felt at passport control at London Airport when she simplified that more distant relationship into elementary cousinhood; something she had explained to Richard in a kind of confession.

"Your 'cousin' and her husband then. They're my particular friends."

"I think that John is a more – more substantial person than my 'cousin' Dora. I think she disappoints him a little."

"*I* think – but you must never say I said this –"

"Of course not" –

"– I think she disappoints him a lot."

"I think he needs more interesting friends than he has. Oh – except for one friend. He has you."

Richard she now counted already as her closest English friend, with whom she could criticise and make fun of other people she had met.

"And he has you while you are staying with them."

She was quiet herself now, thinking about that. Until she resumed and said, too seriously,

"Friendship is a pure and good thing."

"'Say that again'," he said, imitating Jason Simmingley, and they both laughed.

"You are laughing at me for trying to be profound," she said. "And not succeeding to be profound. I mean, *in being* profound."

"I not laugh at you for anything, ever," he said (imitating her lapse from her almost perfect English) ...

"Did you see Dora in that church?" she asked him softly as they followed the others along the street after finishing their sightseeing. "John was interested in the architecture and the monuments. Dora is interested in pretending to pray."

Dora had not sunk to the floor to touch the holy ground, as she might have done in an Orthodox church thirty years before. But she had crossed herself incongruously when she spotted the altar on entering, then confusedly ducked into a pew and sunk her head down on the wooden shelf, Anglican-fashion. John had smiled.

"So you never pray yourself?" Richard asked, half expecting her to deny it.

"Never. I *hope* for people. Hoping is me alone, by myself, more useful than praying to a God who does not exist and more responsible – because I am not placing responsibility on a god to act for me."

"But 'hoping' must be as ineffectual as you consider prayer to be. There is – you say – no God to act in answer to prayer. I suppose I might agree. But if you don't act to fulfil your own hope you are doing no better than a non-existent god. Hoping is easy."

Katrin was very pleased and excited to be corrected with this answer, and grabbed his hand impulsively as they walked, pulling it down and pressing it to her hip, not caring at first whether Dora, or John, or Julian might turn and see her. As Richard synchronised his step with hers, she said,

"It is true, it is true. And there is no hope in acting alone. You can only hope if you act with others."

"I think I believe that," he said. Katrin wanted him to believe it as much as she did herself ...

And now she was laughing, laughing, she couldn't stop laughing; about the thought of these friends of Dora's.

"It is terrible, this laughter," she said. "I thought I would lose it when I ceased to be an adolescent and became an adult. But it goes on."

There was the time, she said, when she had to walk up to receive a diploma from the Party Secretary of the province in an enormous Hall of the Republic in her home city. She had thought she was merely nervous, merely worried, in case her legs should give way on the steps up to the platform, with the huge Party audience ritually applauding her, in a thunderous rhythm of clapping. And half-way up all her trembling certainly vanished. But the laughter returned, for the first time in about a year. Because the Party Secretary was a really small man, an almost abnormally small man, and he had to hand the diploma *up* to this very tall girl.

She went to take it with her right hand, very consciously because (Richard had noticed) she was left-handed and sometimes tried to shake hands, disastrously, with her left. But someone who knew her and who was attending on the Party Secretary in this duty must have considerately told him she was left-handed; so he tried to put the diploma in that hand, and there was a slight confusion and she was giggling over the top of the bald head of this important official with the little pyramid of rolled up diplomas on his desk and beside it (out of sight of the audience) a child's pencil with a Mickey Mouse on it, and a little bag of cough sweets.

Everyone receiving a diploma during this very long afternoon was expected to have a few sentences of conversation with the P.S. (luckily for Katrin out of reach of the microphone on his stand) and the little man's voice was hoarse from a long day's talking, and all Katrin could do was stand and laugh. And he realised, she thought, that it was more than an ordinary shy laughter, he knew it was something actually set off by him, so he frowned severely, and his words came out rather testily. She could make no reply except to giggle and try to keep her face straight; after all, it would be dangerous to offend him. The P.S. was asking her a polite question and she had no polite appropriate answer. She simply stood and shook, helplessly, despairingly. "What was the matter?" friends asked her afterwards. "Nothing. Nothing at *all*," she told them.

And then – believe this, please, she said to her friends, I hope you noticed it if you were looking but please believe it if you were not – the P.S. himself caught the laughter. Katrin thought at first he was just a very good actor; and wanting to not let the audience think this young woman was laughing at him; that he had contrived an excellent performance of the two of them laughing together. But of course it was unheard of for a P.S. to make or receive jokes, and laugh, at a serious Party occasion. So she believed he genuinely could not help it. She assumed she must have awakened the same affliction, long-repressed, in him. The face below the bald head was red and creased with only painfully controlled laughter, the jowls shaking, the moustache twitching.

"Er – good – good luck –" he finally exploded, with a hoarse chuckle; and turned back to pick up the next diploma with tears in his eyes. It took him three attempts to read out the next name accurately.

All this she was telling Richard because she greatly feared, at some point, laughing at one of John's and Dora's friends. It was after they had sat together (though not too obviously close together) at a play at the theatre, and he offered her a lift back, and they had stopped off at his flat.

"You are going to tell me," she said, "that they are generous and kind people. And I am sure it is true. They have given me time, and treats, and friendship. A kind of friendship. But suddenly – I think they are *funny*. And I am ashamed, because you are one of – I mean, because they are your friends also."

Laughing, he said, "You *should* be ashamed!"

"I know."

"They have done their best for you and you do not know how hard they are trying."

"I do realise – all of that," she said. And then she broke down in laughter again, and added: "They are still funny."

He took his arm out from under her shoulders where it was hurting him a little, and tried to find somewhere to rest it on her, or next to her, so that they could still feel their sides touching where they sat [...]

– 6 –

The sun which had melted what remained of the snow shone brilliantly on the wet streets as Tim and Angela brought their bags to the taxi outside the Hotel Transilvania.

"We have plenty of time," Angela was saying. She looked past Tim, still disturbed by his brief disclosure over breakfast. "You can tell me in the taxi. Or in the train, if we have a nice quiet carriage." She clearly meant "a carriage to ourselves." "I will tell this driver we have no need to hurry. He can take us round the park and the river – we have not seen that."

She gave firm instructions to the taxi-driver, including the word "gara" several times, and climbed in beside Tim.

"If Mr Radin telephoned you in your room on Saturday and invited you to meet him it was official – you would not meet him 'unofficially,' you can be sure. But why should he want to see you? I am very interested." Her voice was both wheedling and hard.

He had guessed she would question him, and he had decided to defer telling her until he thought about it long and carefully. The train back to Bucharest seemed a suitable place if they could be sure of some privacy.

This taxi roared away at high speed with the driver – so it sounded – sternly requiring Angela, despite all her instructions, to confirm exactly where it was they wanted to go. They were flung together on the back seat, gripping the arms of their seats with whitened knuckles. This was not some kind of lunatic pride in driving skill; only mere, obdurate recklessness.

"Romanian taxi-drivers!" cursed Angela, leaning forward to remonstrate. It made no difference. She forgot her anger with Tim as the man hurled the vehicle even faster, along cobbled streets past horses drawing farm carts and pedestrians carrying empty plastic bags. "He says he is not going really fast, he can go faster," Angela said in despair.

They arrived at the station half an hour too soon. "I shall tell him he doesn't deserve to be paid" Angela declared.

But she was standing ready, with purse open and a twenty or fifty lei note in her hand, when a man who had been waiting on the station pavement with his family and luggage ran over alone and engaged the driver in desperate dialogue. Something urgent was explained, something beseeched. The driver nodded, opened the door Tim had only just closed, bundled the stranger inside, shouted something at Angela and took her money, threw himself back into his own seat and drove away again.

"I have no receipt," Angela wailed impotently. "I shall never ride in a taxi again. Such people! He was fit only to be a *businessman*, I am sure he was." The word came out with tearful bitterness. Only fury kept back tears.

"But what was that conversation about?" asked Tim.

"The man was at the station with all his family and all his bags – but all his train tickets were at home on the mantelpiece. He was saying to the driver, it is about two kilometres to his house, could he get him there and back to the station to catch his train in ten minutes?"

"What did the driver say?"

"He said he would do his best."

The train came in, with its set of contradictions. The vast square engine with its little curtained windows, rigorously fashioned in the Craiova workshops, spoke of enormous power. It drew a long, line of dark and battered-looking carriages decked with obscure, dusty boards indicating stops on the several-hour slow journey. Inside, the corridors were shabby, the window glass flawed, the doors into the compartments difficult to open or to close against the draughts. And yet despite the wear-and-tear showing in the upholstery, the cushions and head-rests were comfortable, there was plenty of rack room for luggage – and today there was lavish heat.

Angela had ordered greedily at breakfast in the hotel: two eggs boiled hard, a large portion of ham, a second plate of bread.

Then Tim realised she was not eating any of it except a little of the bread with jam. She was wrapping it up in paper napkins for the train.

When the train started he slept, and dreamt. He was already back in Bucharest, at the Writers' Union, lunching with Ioan Ludache in the crowded restaurant but eating Angela's breakfast provision. He must have been telling Ludache about the visit to the Bobolescus'. "Yes a *very* nice son they have. Virgil." Ludache was repeating Radin's words. But then he added: "Did he take a film of you – on a video camera – while you were having lunch?"

"Yes, he did," Tim replied, amazed to think Ludache would know this.

"He always does," Ludache replied, breaking the shell of one of the boiled eggs on the edge of the table. "Then he shows it to the police the next day."

"*He shows it to the –* ?"

"If the police find it interesting, anything his visitors are saying, they keep it. The Bobolescus are very dangerous people. My advice to you is do not believe this old man's opinions –" even in the dream Tim knew that Ludache was simply repeating Mrs Vajna's words – "and do not answer this old man's questions."

Tim woke when Angela suddenly said, as if talking to herself, but probably in order to wake him, "I'm feeling hungry already." She snapped open her big handbag and took out the food, laying it on a seat beside her, passing napkins and the boiled egg and ham out of his dream to Tim opposite her. And he was hungry too.

"I can talk properly if I eat," she said, buttering the slices of bread from a small slab of wrapped butter she certainly had not found in the hotel restaurant. "Mr Harker-Jones!"

"*Tim*," he suggested. So far he had failed in all his efforts at informality, but at least he could try.

"Tim," she said, astonishing him by accepting the correction but with no lightening of her tone. "I have to tell you – I know you will not betray me – everything is not right in my country. Please, I ask you not to say anything about this to any of the people we meet. You will not betray me?"

"Certainly not – never. I –"

Angela looked him directly in the eyes across the carriage, something she hardly ever did.

"I tell you this," she said. "I wish I did not, but I have to write down everything we talk about. I have to write reports about it, do you realise that?" She looked terrified at her own boldness now. "I have to write where we have been, who we have seen also. I have to make sure we have seen all the good places, and I have told you about the achievements. I have to write the name of *everyone* we have seen, and when."

"Will you write about our visit to Carolina Predeanu's flat?"

Angela shook her head to express her dilemma. But then someone passed, outside in the corridor, and looked in, a tall male figure in a very dark blue raincoat and dark glasses. Angela automatically stopped until the shadow passed.

"That's it," she said when it was safely gone. "You cannot believe it, you think we are mad perhaps. But we are afraid of everyone. We don't like to speak in our homes, in the hotel rooms. In the streets – possibly. But I am quite frightened to speak here."

"In a *train*?"

"Yes. In a train. But I will speak and take the chance. Tim, do you understand? In Bucharest someone gave you Carolina's address. *Do I report that*? In Târgu Alb you went in secret to try to meet Carolina and you left her a note. Do I report this also? What will that do for *you*? No one will send you to prison for that, but you may not receive a visa to come to Romania again. That is if I report it. Or if Carolina reports it. But if I don't report it and they find out, there will be no permission for you, and trouble for me. Am I reliable with visitors? And then we go and visit Carolina together. That is a complete secret. I agree to go with you because I must know what you are doing. If I do not report that, it makes me part of a conspiracy. We had no permission to go – so how do I explain it? And now this Mr Radin asks to meet you without approaching me, and you go to meet him without waiting to ask, without telling me for two days!"

She fell silent, trembled with agitation and confusion as she finished this list of his transgressions.

"I think," he said, for something to fill the silence, "you don't have many visitors who are as difficult as me?"

"No, I don't. Never *anyone*," she said emphatically, and was silent.

When she spoke again his stomach was hollow with disappointment at being treated like an erring child.

"You must *not* go to have lunch with Carolina to-morrow," Angela was saying. "It is bad enough for me already. It will be much worse if you go to have lunch with her. I would need to get permission for you, and I would not get it. But you are obstinate and will go despite me – and it will be found out! I have to think of my job."

"I shall not be going there to do anything dangerous to you, I have to write my biography of Philip Carston and ask Carolina about *him*. The 'official' publishers of her translation will understand that."

"It doesn't matter what you are seeing her about. If you are seeing her at all, it is dangerous for me. I shall have to report that I forbade you to talk to her, and you *refused*. Then you will be refused anything else you wish to do here, and not allowed to come back to this country."

"Well, that will mean I *have* to see her this time, to get all the information I can while I have the opportunity."

She ate hungrily and furiously, and thought hard about this reply.

"There is another possibility that is dangerous," she said. "Carolina is able to meet you very openly in a famous restaurant, in the very centre of Bucharest. That probably means she is dangerous herself. Certainly she has influence. She meets you, no problems, where everyone can see you, where everyone – all the waiters, oh yes! – will report on the meeting, where you sit at a table where *they* will listen to everything you say." Angela pointed a finger at the ceiling. "If she can do all of that, an ordinary small town girl from Târgu Alb, she is *allowed* to do it, so that she can report on you – and on me."

Oh no, he was thinking, this is wholly absurd. First Carolina has to let them into her flat in secrecy, set the music playing, talk in low tones and warn them to be careful and covert about everything; she would be in grave danger if anyone knew they had been there. Then she becomes the most dangerous factor in the situation, tempting him to a clandestine meeting so as to spy on him, and shopping his guide for letting him come...

"I believe Carolina is taking a risk in seeing someone close to Philip Carston," Tim replied, beginning to play the same game but fully believing the argument he used. "But she is doing it for Philip's sake. I believe she is doing it openly because to do it secretly and be found out would be infinitely *worse*."

And yet anything you said would be trumped.

"You can be sure she had permission to let us enter her flat, or she would never have opened the door when we rang the bell."

His mouth dropped open.

"Listen!" she continued. "Everyone –" the finger pointing upwards again, indicating high authority – "*everyone* knows about our visit to Carolina on Friday night. You can be sure. Professor Bobolescu knew about it, didn't he? I can tell you the other people at the Writers' Union in Târgu Alb knew about it."

"Is Ioan Ludache a dangerous man?" Tim thought he was going to need to talk to Ludache about Philip if his chance of talking in detail to Carolina vanished.

"Everyone is dangerous. They can be most dangerous of all if they are saving *themselves* from danger. Then, everyone around them is in danger."

He realised she was not answering his question about Ludache, but he pursued the point.

"So where does the threat of danger stop?"

"What do you mean?"

"Is your President free of danger?"

He did not like to use the name.

"I don't know." And she was not going to discuss it.

The train was in Brasov station, where they would wait a long time, as they had on the outward journey. Automatically they fell silent. Angela pretended to take an interest in the bustle and noise of the platforms. The sun came out.

"I will tell you about Mr Radin."

– 7 –

At least this meeting was something of which she had been ignorant. She could possibly make out a case, if she had to, about Tim as a visitor who had been wholly uncontrollable from the start.

"May I suggest," Radin had said on the telephone, "a little restaurant you can reach if you begin by turning left out of your hotel. Then –"

The directions were simple and the short conversation provided no explanation for the call. Tim strode rapidly past the empty Reception desk and, not depositing his key, stepped out into thawing snow.

The restaurant looked as if it might once have been the labyrinthine wine-cellar of a former huge restaurant or hotel: innumerable caves and corners separated by thick walls painted a rich yellow – or perhaps they were naturally yellow, because the place looked as if it had been carved out of bare rock. Tim speculated that this was probably as private as anywhere in Târgu Alb: it would have been difficult to insert microphones or bugs inside such walls; though there were always the tables, the vases, the crockery.

He found Radin easily, recognising him at once at the table in the third alcove on the right. He was sitting alone with – fascinatingly – a copy of the Romanian translation of *A Time Apart* on the table in front of him, resting on a thick, well-used notebook.

The man rose, and greeted him with extreme cordiality in slow, but accomplished, English.

"I did not want to come to the hotel. It is not the most comfortable place to converse."

About what?

"'First things first'," he continued, putting an edge of mockery on his knowledge of the English usage. "You will have a little 'bite' with me?"

"Only a little one," Tim protested, looking ahead to another filling dinner beside the band at the Transilvania, in about two hours' time.

There was no menu, only a vigorous debate with the waiter, including much anxious enquiry and entreaty on Radin's part and many despairing gestures from his interlocutor. Radin turned to Tim.

"He says all we can have is his excellent ghoulash soup, with pieces of chicken, and an even better beefsteak. Will that be sufficient?"

"It will be too much for me," he said. "Does he have any tea, or coffee – a cake perhaps?"

"He says no, there is no tea, or coffee, or any variety of cake."

"Well – does he – does he have an egg? Even an omelette?"

Asked this, the waiter shook his head, once, curtly, and stared into the distance with closed lips.

"He says," Radin explained, "he is sorry, there are regrettably no eggs this afternoon, only the soup and the steak, which he strongly recommends."

"Is it possible just to have the soup?"

"But Mr Harker-Jones, that is not very much to eat?"

"I had lunch only two hours ago."

"It will not be a very large steak, and the soup will not be very bad for your waistline."

"I'd really like just soup."

"I will ask him to make your steak a small one. There is no beer and sadly no wine, but there is some very good local brandy."

"Does he have mineral water?"

"Si *apa minerala*?"

"Nu." The one word, almost angrily from the waiter, as if the lack of it should be obvious without asking.

"He says he is very sorry," Radin translated, taking pleasure in his formal, decorous English, "but there is possibly no mineral water either."

Throughout their interchange, Tim noticed – and it continued throughout this strange encounter – Radin's right leg, trousered in dark blue and jutting out from under the table to Tim's left, shook, and Radin's heel pounded on the floor, partly a tic, partly a deliberate aid to concentration.

The brandy arrived. And raising it,

"Mr Harker-Jones!" Radin exclaimed abruptly. It was a vocative, a fanfare, a preliminary to something. "Romanians like foreigners, and we have very little chance of meeting them. You are only the second English person I have ever met in my life. When I realised in the train you were a distinguished English visitor, I thought I must take this chance or lose it for ever. Do you like my English?"

What was Radin getting at, seeking flattery about his English before coming to the point?

Very large bowls of soup came, and a plate of slices of bread covered with a clean cloth napkin. Tim lifted his spoon, vaguely disturbed the surface of the soup, and considered how to answer.

"I have four years of English at school, but naturally I have never visited England. I have had some private lessons, but not very many. But –" he dropped his voice – "I have listened to the radio and I have tried to read very simple English books. Sadly I read this one in Romanian." He patted his copy of *A Time Apart*; and his leg shook.

From underneath Philip Carston's book he pulled out the

CAIET STUDENTESC, the thick exercise book, and opened it with pride. Proudly he turned over the pages, holding it up in front of Tim's embarrassed eyes, across the soup. Every narrow feint leaf was covered in tiny, neat, single-spaced handwriting: exercises from simple textbooks, English phrases acquired from BBC World Service English lessons, passages from classic English literature.

"Look at it, please," Radin insisted. Tim took the book into his hands with care; it was plainly a precious possession. "You think it is good?"

"I think it is *very* good." He meant it. He flicked through the pages: "Excuse me, can you direct me to a taxi-rank?" "If you *cannot* come to tea on Tuesday, you *may* choose another afternoon."

"And I have *this,* but only this," Radin told him, producing from his pocket an old, very small English-Romanian dictionary and passing it over. Every page was well-thumbed, many entries were underlined in red ballpoint, some words were asterisked and the references amplified at the foot of the page. "It is a good dictionary, I believe? The English words are modern? It would not cause humour to use them?"

Slowly Tim was realising.

"No – of course not. It seems excellent to me."

"Unfortunately it is the only one I have. And it was produced a long time ago, 1948. I have nothing for Romanian-English, which is so important. So it was very important to take this opportunity of some conversation with you."

If disinterested learning still existed anywhere in the world it was in activities like this, among autodidacts like Radin, Tim thought. But when the large steaks came, with chips, and quantities of rice-like vegetable, and sour cabbage, and their glasses were filled with more brandy, he wished more than ever that he had not answered the telephone in his bedroom.

"To our conversation!" Radin toasted, with twinkling eyes in his broad, stern face; and he threw back the brandy in one gulp.

"Perhaps one day I will read this in the English version, with no problems?" He held up Philip's novel.

"Do you think Carolina Predeanu *wrote* the novel?" Tim asked Radin with an incredulous smile.

Radin was about to cut his steak eagerly, but looked up and laughed cheerfully. Tim thought he would be disconcerted, but he seemed to welcome the question.

"No! I am sure Carolina Predeanu did not write the original novel. But I am not a critic. I am not an academic man at all."

"*What* are you?" Tim returned the smiling, and found himself (the brandy?) capable of asking this question directly too. Again Radin did not hesitate; but this time he did not laugh.

"I am to be a lawyer. For a long time I have been a – a kind of official. Offices all day, papers, telephones. But I have studied by correspondence, and I have taken all my tests, and I can now be a lawyer."

"Working for yourself?"

"For the State."

"Oh, yes. I see." Tim found it acutely uncomfortable to try to swallow the food. He tried cutting only tiny pieces off the steak, to try to make it last longer; he hoped that if he was slow enough, some genuine hunger would arrive to cope with it.

"In my opinion," Radin affirmed, eating heartily, "Carolina will one day write books by herself, but she did not write Mr Philip Carston's book for him. 'In my opinion'," he repeated with ironical modesty. "But you can ask when you see her again."

When you see her again? So did Radin know Tim was to meet Carolina in Bucharest?

"Mr Bobolescu – Professor Bobolescu – believes she did write the book."

Again Radin laughed, but this time it was a shorter laugh and followed by a serious expression.

"It is sad. Professor Bobolescu has a different opinion, yes, which he holds very strongly. But you heard all this from him in his house today."

Tim felt as if he was on a progress through a haunted house at a fairground: every turn and corner promised a shock, and the floor would all at once shake and lurch under your feet; though in the end you actually learned to expect something new and shocking all the time and were scarcely surprised by anything at all. And Ludache, Valeria Ciudea, the Bobolescus, the strange Mrs Vajna, Carolina herself and now Ilie Radin – seemed to be inhabitants of the same haunted mansion, with close knowledge of each other.

And was Radin in some way challenging Tim with his knowledge of his whereabouts at lunch time? There was no answer to the challenge if he was, so Tim merely continued: "Professor Bobolescu made his opinion about the book very clear, but he did not explain why he had such an opinion. He told me I should speak to other people about it. There is a Mr Ludache in Bucharest –"

"How can I explain this?" Radin became confidential, lowered his voice. "I will tell you two things about this man, Liviu Bobolescu. The not-so-important thing first. Professor Bobolescu has been very close to Miss Predeanu."

"'Close'?"

"Very close. But you understand me, a little like a father, an uncle, an old friend, who believes he has discovered genius in a most attractive daughter or niece. There is a little in it of what we can call love – even 'sex' as you so much describe it in the West – but he is an old man, of course."

"Of course. And he is married."

"Yes. But that is not a problem for him. This is not the first time."

"Not the – ?"

"Not the first time he was married at all. And not the first beautiful idea he married."

"*Married*?" Tim thought Radin's English had somehow let him down at this point. But Radin repeated the word.

"Married, yes. It is his second marriage, his second *wife*. His fourth or fifth beautiful idea. Your steak will be cold. You must eat while I tell you. The first Mrs Bobolescu is not interesting for us. I begin with *this* Mrs Bobolescu – Georgeta Bobolescu. She is still a woman with great charm, now not so charming as twenty years ago – we all change with time – but really rather beautiful, strong, full of character, when she was young and when he discovered her genius."

"Mrs Bobolescu was – a genius?"

"Professor Bobolescu thought she was a genius. She was a young cook in your hotel restaurant here in Târgu Alb. There is a story that Professor Bobolescu walked into the kitchen to ask about a meal – or perhaps to buy some food to take home – and saw her sitting at a table and writing something instead of cooking. He became interested. Meals were very slow to be served in the Hotel Transilvania in those days, so he had time to talk to her. She told him the kitchen inspired her to write."

"And she published books?"

"One book."

"An interesting book?"

"No."

"But they married?"

"I told you, yes. And a very nice son they have. Virgil. A little more?"

He was so lost in speculation at this moment that he was not noticing what Radin was referring to. Instinctively he dropped his hand on his brandy glass, half-emptied. But the waiter was standing with a dish of further small pieces of meat on a bed of rice and green peppers, and spooning some on to Radin's plate. Radin was accepting it.

"I haven't finished what I have." Tim protested. He had barely begun.

Without heeding his delicate refusal the waiter was making room on Tim's almost full plate and setting down some of the steaming kebabs on it.

"Did you order this?" he asked. "It's someone else's, surely?"

"I asked for a little more. After all, it is not often I get the opportunity of an English conversation with an Englishman."

"You said I am the second Englishman you have met. Who was the first?"

"Mr Harker-Jones, haven't you guessed?"

"I suppose I have."

Tim groaned inwardly with fascination at this knowledge. It was dawning on him that this entire task would have to be followed up by a second visit to Romania before his book could be finished. Next year in the spring possibly?

He told Angela of these thoughts as he finished his story. She had been listening hard and thinking hard while he spoke. Did she conclude that there might, in any case, be no stopping him from meeting all these people again if he returned to Romania for a second visit? Whatever her reason for backing down she now changed her position completely.

"I think – I hope I am not wrong – perhaps it is all right for you to see Carolina for lunch to-morrow," she said. "I will show you the restaurant."

And then, when he looked surprised, she added, "Did you say Mr Radin told you he was a – he was a government official? And he will be a lawyer for the government?"

"He said that, yes."

Angela nodded.

"Yes, I think it is all right," she said. The train was making a slow entrance into the Gara de Nord.

FOUR

– 1 –

Where the narrow side street issued into Calea Victoriei they came to a halt in front of the flat hand of the blue-uniformed policeman. Beyond him everything seemed unusually quiet, the streets free even of the fairly light, normal late-morning traffic. There were few people on the pavements, where at most times there was a steady beat of passengers; they were outnumbered by knots of blue police stationed at intervals and by twos and threes of young men in suits or leather jackets.

"Our President is going home to lunch," Angela said. "We must wait a few minutes."

"Everything stops for the Queen in London," Tim said, pointlessly; at the same time wondering if it was actually so.

The faces of these police, in uniforms or out of them, were impassive. This event was ordinary routine, probably it happened every day, quite likely more than once a day. Their watchful eyes rarely strayed above street level. Were there other eyes scanning from windows and roofs?

From the left came a large grey car, a Mercedes, fast, apparently out of the square where the former Palace and the Central Committee building stood. The police watched it, Tim watched it. It had reached them, it was passing them, he had time to focus the driver (not in uniform) and a large, uniformed figure in the back; and neither of them was, as the television newscaster always fully described him, sometimes five or six times in a bulletin, "Secretary-General of the Romanian Communist Party and President of the Socialist Republic of Romania Comrade Nicolae Ceausescu."

Tim was still following the Mercedes out of sight up Calea Victoriei when he realised a second car, a Dacia, was passing him, had been following the first rather more slowly, as if it was less important, had no need to hurry. And in the front, alongside the driver, sat a small figure in a grey coat and a dark grey fur hat. Below the hat was an old, pinched, sly, recognisable face. Tim had the experience he commonly had when unexpectedly finding himself within yards of a famous, or infamous personage: he thought to himself, "That's a somewhat feeble look-alike of Ceausescu." At this minute, standing where the Strada Cosmonautilor joined Calea Victoriei in Bucharest, he believed he had just seen a passable imitation of the President, someone with a chance resemblance who might have been taken for him at a distance in a poor light.

"Was that him?" he asked Angela immediately. "I think it was?"

"I don't know."

"It looked like him. Does he usually drive in a Dacia?"

"I don't know. I wasn't looking."

As if it was safest not to look.

When the police allowed them, they themselves walked down in the direction from which the cars had come.

"If you continue now, as if you were returning to your hotel," she said, "you will see just before that the Capsa Restaurant on your left. Keep on the left, don't cross over. The restaurant is on the corner and the entrance is *round* the corner. Do you understand me?"

She seemed eager to get away, as if still thoroughly uneasy about allowing him to keep this appointment.

He remembered the fight scene near the end of the television film, set in perhaps 1945 or 1946: the clambering onto and the turning over of tables, the hurling of chairs and glasses, the smashing of mirrors. It was unquestionably the Capsa itself where it had been staged. This street corner was unmistakeable, and so was the shape and (he thought) the atmosphere of the rooms inside, even now in the late 1980s.

Not that it was easy to enter the Capsa. Tim passed the

doorman with a confident half-smile and nod which was not returned, but found himself directed, inside a warm, dim lobby, to a counter where coats and hats were collected.

Here the woman attendant asked him a question he did not understand. He smiled, shrugged amiably, and began to slip out of his coat, but she shook her head and asked the question again, severely. He pointed into the restaurant and said, inanely and nervously, with another smile, "My friend is – Miss Predeanu is waiting – in there." The attendant drummed her fingers on her counter and said nothing more. The doorman joined her. Both of them looked at Tim in silent challenge.

"I am here, in fact," a voice said behind him. The voice brought the temperature and scent of outdoors into the warmth of the lobby on a long black coat, topped by a simple black felt hat, the attractive domed hat worn by so many Romanian women who could afford to appear stylish and smart.

Now they could both leave their coats without problems, and turn into the long, hushed, elegant interior where there were more diners than Tim would have expected. Bowing waiters directed them past a display of rich and delicate confections and down a central aisle to a small table in a corner at the far end. It had a bowl of fresh flowers which Carolina shifted resolutely to one side to get a better view of her guest; he was surprised at her assurance.

Here, unlike anywhere else, large menus, one each, were handed them. Carolina immediately half-hid her face and pretended to discuss their choice from the typed list.

"You realise Philip and I were very important to each other," she said softly, "and there is a lot to tell you. I cannot give you all of the story today." People, in Tim's memory, had talked behind their menus in films, when the message would be, when you get a chance take a look at the man sitting opposite. So Tim looked at the table opposite instead of the menu.

If he had expected only the smartest people in the Capsa he was wrong. The four-place table was occupied only by one young man in a black leather jacket and jeans who was taking just a beer, as he might in any café. He fingered a glass, and gazed confidently into nowhere, and was permitted to do this; that made him interesting. "Today, you understand," Carolina was saying, "is the meeting I am allowed to have. But today is only enough to begin."

They ordered. Only their fourth choice from the list was available: the menu seemed more like a memorial to a past expansiveness than a reality for the present. But the Capsa retained the ancient magnificence in its decor: thickly-carpeted, opulently beautiful, quiet and discreet, with deferential waiters (all loyal and observant Party members?). Tim had the impression that whoever dined here pretended for a couple of hours that this was normal, that the city outside the frosted windows (you could not see the street from inside the Capsa), with the queues you normally had to join for bread or milk or the merest scraps of meat, was the nightmare from which this was a two-hour waking.

"It will help me if I tell you from the beginning, from the first time I met Philip," she went on. "And how it was that *I* met him, and not someone else." Tim could see in her smile that she believed a wonderful luck had delivered Philip Carston to her in the first place; and that in different circumstances none of this would have happened at all, they would not be sitting here today, he would not now be opening the notebook he carried everywhere on his person, never left anywhere (even in his overcoat pocket in a museum cloakroom while looking at the exhibits) in case it was read by someone else.

"But you must put that away!" Carolina told him in a severe whisper. "It looks bad to be writing things here."

– 2 –

I had never heard the name "Philip Carston" before the letter arrived, I have to confess that. But perhaps there was no reason why I *should*. The reputations of foreign writers arrive first in Bucharest, they take time to reach more distant places. And I was only just graduated from the university, on a course which stopped short of the *most* modern literature, though we studied D.H. Lawrence and Virginia Woolf and we read James Joyce. (Because original copies of his books were extremely rare, we waited and waited for the Romanian translation of *Ulysses* – yes, *Ulysses* – to appear, and queued for it when they finally published it. Yes, I have a copy at home. Yes, of course completely uncensored and uncut. And yes, the suitable equivalent for every word.)

My best university friend in Târgu Alb – Valeria, of course – was the daughter of a high official at the Council for Culture and Socialist Education in Bucharest, in the Casa Scînteii. So when the guide who had been allocated to a visiting English writer fell ill, she recommended me to her mother and I received the official communication. It was almost a command. I was working in a publishing house and would know about modern English fiction!

I could have refused? Yes, if I had a good reason for refusing. But why refuse? It would be a chance to work in Bucharest, and if I could do the job well, perhaps I would be invited on other occasions and have the chance to visit one of the visitors in their own country. Except that I didn't want to change my first job, in the publishing house, for the job of an interpreter – which by itself is badly paid. It is impossible just to live as an interpreter and guide. And interpreters are not an organised group, they do not have their own collective.

In the publishing house in Târgu Alb – yes, the same one, I have worked there all the time since graduating – they said I would be given some very important instructions before they released me to take charge of my visitor: to keep up-to-date with my written reports on what we did, and the conversations the visitor had with our hosts at the various meetings, and to report anything exceptional by telephone; to draw attention to the achievements of the Socialist Republic, but to be natural about it and not boring; to be efficient about the arrangements and report any inefficiencies in other people; and to try to find out what my visitor had been doing when he took time off on his own.

But so much of this was overlooked, and not followed up as strictly as I expected it to be, because of the event which put normal routines out of everyone's mind.

Philip was due to come on 30th March 1977. On Friday 4th March 1977 the worst earthquake in living memory happened in our country, you will know about that. We felt the tremors in Târgu Alb, although there was no serious damage there. It's like when a passing truck has caused all your walls and windows to vibrate, except that it's continuous, for many seconds, and you realise there is no truck passing and the vibration is coming out of the ground itself, and shaking the buildings from the foundations upwards. So you just leave everything and run out of the house, and hope you are out before the buildings are shaken down.

But none of the buildings fell in Târgu Alb. We escaped that. And no one died, only some ceilings fell and people had very light injuries. The earthquake was much stronger in Brasov, and worst of all in Bucharest, where thousands of people died. In the first days afterwards there were hundreds of earthquake stories: of the cats that cried and cried to be let out of houses ten minutes before the tremor started; of the man who left a party to check he had turned off his lights when he parked his car, and everyone in the party died; of the old woman who survived nine days under the ruins of a block of flats where they believed everyone was dead. Everyone had holes in their ceilings and walls where the earthquake had cracked the plaster.

Then came the black humour, about prostitutes saying to men in the streets, Come up and see my cavity, the people leaving their top floor flat and saying, Shall we take the lift – or go down with the building?

And I believed Mr Philip Carston would not want to come in these conditions, and perhaps the Council for Culture would not let him come, and I would not go to Bucharest. But I was wrong, because the Council for Culture insisted he *must* come if he was still willing. He would observe the reconstruction work that was taking place, he would see how the Socialist Republic was rebuilding itself after this disaster. Our President had ordered that every resource should be given to the repair of Bucharest in particular.

I was not at all familiar with Bucharest. I had to be prepared to learn the geography of the city, find out where the museums and monuments and theatres were, before I showed them to a visitor. I went there for a few days before Philip arrived, to learn my way around. For some reason I could only go by a night train which arrived in Bucharest at dawn. Because I had come on official work they were kind enough to send a car for me at the Gara de Nord, the North Station. I arrived exactly as the sun was rising.

We drove through a city of ruins and dust, yellowed by the sunlight which struck through the terrible gaps in the streets. Because, although there were places where whole boulevards or districts were badly devastated, in many avenues in the centre of the city *alternate* buildings, or terraces of buildings, or blocks, had gone down. Or just two or three buildings here and there. Or just one. Some of the oldest buildings remained unharmed, some were piles of shattered stones. Occasionally, where shops or restaurants had been carved out of the ground floors of older buildings, supporting walls or pillars had been taken down and the structures of the strongest had been gravely weakened, so that they fell. Of course some flimsy modern buildings went down, but most stronger modern buildings stood.

At street level all or most of the ruins had been cleared away and the traffic could pass (remember this was four weeks after it happened). It was a warm and sunny spring. In every ruin were the little groups of candles lighted in memory of the ones who had died in that place, the flames calmly burning in the still bright daylight, the small crowds standing alongside. The word you heard most in crowds was always *Cutremur*, *Cutremur*: earthquake. It had overwhelmed the consciousness of the people, they could think of nothing beyond the disaster and what it had done to their lives.

And I had to find my way about Bucharest, and try to learn the city, in the midst of all this devastation and grief; as well as try to prepare myself for my visitor. At the library at the British Embassy they found me a copy of one of the early novels – *The Winter Book* – which I read, and some mentions in directories of modern writers; but they had no reference works giving me detailed information. There was a youthful photograph of Philip on the back of the novel. I learnt something about his age and education, and I read a few favourable comments by critics on his writings. I gauged that he had considerable critical status. Nothing gave me any clues as to why they sent him to Romania. I realised that he would be a 'reliable' visitor in the eyes of the British government, of course, but I couldn't predict how many questions he would ask or calculate what I would be expected to tell him. They did see me at the Council for Culture; but I think they were too preoccupied with the aftermath of the earthquake to instruct me very vigorously.

It was so strange entering that vast building, the Casa Scînteii, which we had been taught to despise as an example of Stalinist architecture: the decorative enormousness, hard ornateness, you see in pictures of ceremonial Soviet, or Polish buildings raised in the first years after the people's revolutions. It was common to make excuses for it as 'a giant Stalinist wedding–cake' – in Romania we had come out of the Stalinism a long time before. But it had stood up well – externally at least – to the earthquake; it was one of the great survivors among our public buildings.

A protocol official sat in on my interview with the cultural people, but he didn't seem specially interested in what a young graduate might reveal to an English writer of whom he (like the young graduate herself!) had not heard. Mr Philip Carston was evidently not a politician, or a businessman, or a journalist; or even a professor of modern history – the kind of people he might be anxious about – so what I did with him did not matter greatly as long as I filled in the forms. What he did tell me was that I should report to the Casa Scînteii on the day of Philip's arrival and another official car would take me to the airport to meet his plane and take us on to his hotel.

I had a letter of permission to go past the customs tables in the outer halls at the international airport, Otopeni, and into the area just beyond it, where the luggage carousel operates. I had never before stood and watched luggage coming up out of the depths of the earth, as it seemed to me, and rotating on the moving belt until one by one every piece was collected and dragged away by its owner. Every piece except for the one, or two, that nobody seemed to remember or want, continuing on round and round, neglected, forlorn, rather suspicious. Were they deliberately forgotten?

I was early, so I had plenty of time to look at everything. I saw all the luggage opened and crazily ransacked at the customs tables, with questions asked about separate objects, each suitcase requiring about ten minutes. People had to open presents, which friends abroad had carefully wrapped for them, and sometimes give part of the present to the customs official to get the rest of their luggage past. It was like the scenes at the airport at Târgu Alb, but on a much huger scale.

One consignment of suitcases, except for those stray, unclaimed ones, finished its trip around the carousel, and the luggage hall was left empty, except for one or other favoured and privileged guides waiting for other visitors.

Please remember I was new, and didn't know any of these guides, and was too shy to speak to them and ask questions. I can recall the faces of those few strangers even now, and the British names on the cards they were holding up for the visitors soon to arrive: Mrs WALKER, Professor PATTERSON, Mr Clive DEANLEY, Mr STENNETT. I stood a little way apart from them with the card I had written myself, in red ink letters: Mr PHILIP CARSTON. I had the book from the British library in my other hand, and the photograph to refer to. People began to trickle through very slowly from the barriers where they examined passports at the little windows, and made notes on them and on their owners.

Remember that I had come out from a city littered with painful ruins, on the long sunny road to the great airport I had never before seen, had walked out of the car in the warm spring sunshine into the dark cavern of the customs hall and the baggage reclamation area, to meet the first English person I had ever met, from a different universe altogether. And he was talented and famous in his own country. I wanted Philip to resemble the photograph on the book – and *not* resemble it. I wanted him to be superior to the photograph, and different; and yet I wanted the good features of the photograph to be true: the strong but friendly eyes, the shy yet slightly humorous set of the lips.

Of course I can see Philip coming towards me now, out of the passport control – the single most important moment of my life, a turning-point. But I mostly remember that I was desperately anxious not to make a mistake and identify the wrong person, only to have him walk coldly past my card to someone holding up a different name. I recognised Philip immediately, but I had forgotten that a photograph of a face doesn't prepare you for someone's *height*. I am tall, but Philip – you will realise – was even taller. He had to peer down at the card quite closely, as he was so very short-sighted.

And I had never seen anyone who looked so monumentally ordinary. If it is not a contradiction, Philip made ordinariness of appearance into an art. You could not help noticing, and you could not help admiring, how every plain uninteresting feature was 'writ large,' as he puts it. There was the huge, balding head, the wide spectacles for the weak eyes – which were really very powerful eyes when they looked straight at you – and then the large ears.

I must have been staring at him hard, card-in-hand, because, "I think you've *probably* spotted the right person," Philip said. The voice was slow, gloomy and clear – and the most ordinary feature of all.

"Mr Philip Carston?"
"You have."

– 3 –

"Please!"

Tim had no wish to break the flow of Carolina's story, but – They had reached the coffee and he knew that there was no hope at all of her finishing it today. She had talked about an opportunity to continue it elsewhere. "I think we can't wrap it up now – I mean *you* can't. I mean – we can't reach the whole point of the thing," he said; meaning the information he needed for his book. He had been drinking too much while listening to her, and spoke colloquially. Carolina had been pouring wine for him from a first bottle, from a second. She had not been emptying her glass. He had been filling his own for himself.

"Can we go over to my hotel?" he proposed, absurdly.

"No!" She shook her head hard, as if the idea of talking in the quiet of a bugged hotel room was something so crazy he should never have dreamt of it. "I have arranged something," she added.

Suddenly things were happening. The first and least important was that Tim had seen, approaching him with insolent speed, the borderline which he would cross from the last moment in which he was provably sober to the first moments in which he was incontestably not sober any more. He hoped Carolina would not appreciate that he was soon to be, purely and simply, drunk.

He could see the coffee cups, and an empty ashtray made of glass, transparent, ostensibly bug-less, and he could see their wine-glasses, also empty, and the sugar-bowl and his hands resting on the tablecloth, and the vase of fresh flowers, he could see all these objects with such clarity! He could count them, one by one, and distinguish between them if required to. Indeed, any action like speaking that last sentence to Carolina, or like rising from his chair soon now if he had to, could be undertaken with a slow and perfect precision; inconceivable when he hadn't been drinking.

"Well – can we meet somewhere else completely different – later on?" He had formulated that utterance with truly immaculate care, but Carolina did not reply, was not even looking at him because a second thing was happening now: Valeria Ciudea, in a long yellow coat, was all at once standing beside them having appeared from nowhere at all as they sat in this table at the Capsa. Carolina and she were talking in rapid Romanian.

They ignored Tim's weak protests about the bill, and his offers to contribute, and guided him solicitously through the lobby (where he somehow re-acquired his coat and hat) out into the street. And there the third thing occurred, the most unbelievable and farcical thing today. Instead of letting Tim turn right when they emerged through the modest front door of the Capsa, and face in the direction of his hotel, they steered him to the left, round another corner, and into the arms of Professor Liviu Bobolescu.

Literally into the arms of Bobolescu, who greeted him as a lifelong friend, worthy of aged embraces and kisses on both cheeks. "I hope you enjoyed your lunch and had some help with your researches?" he was saying. "This isn't the way to my hotel," Tim exclaimed; they seemed to be shifting him along inscrutably in the opposite direction. "You want to talk, you take a walk," Bobolescu said, a sly murmur in his ear as they moved along rapidly through busy side streets at first, then across a wide thoroughfare – Tim acknowledged through an uneasy haze the big bulk of the Intercontinental Hotel, the highest building in the city, and nodded bemusedly at it – and into altogether quieter streets lined with villas and gardens. "Mr Ludache cannot see you today," he heard the Professor murmuring. "He will see what he can do to-morrow." Oh yes, there was Ludache...

As they walked, more slowly now, Valeria was pausing every so often to write something in a notebook and always concealing it under her coat as they moved on; looking round circumspectly. Then she appeared to be drawing a rudimentary sketch map of somewhere. Tim concentrated on crossing these narrow streets with care: the cobbles were uneven and tricky to negotiate, the tar surfaces of the pavements, which would probably melt in summer weather, surged and spread and broke up into hard ruts.

Carolina was saying something to him with her head down, very quietly, at his side.

"Can you meet to-morrow? Any time after ten-thirty in the morning, I have until six. Come to Valeria's house, near Piata Unirii Metro station."

"I should love to come," he said, also in a low voice but with a rather too exuberant eagerness. Valeria – again! – was slipping a piece of paper into his hand and putting the hand firmly into his overcoat pocket. He tried to apply the precision he had given to numbering the articles on the restaurant table to the act of walking: he could get everything right, he was sure of it, avoiding that tree-root which forced up the concrete, stepping over that pot-hole in the cobbled carriageway.

"You will need at least forty minutes to get there from the hotel," Valeria said. "You have put the details away carefully? We can find you again if you lose it, but it would be better if *you* found *us*."

"Oh yes, I've got them," Tim said. He felt for the slip of paper in his pocket and it was undoubtedly there. All three of them looked at him with concern

Then the next unforeseen thing occurred. I, Tim Harker-Jones, he thought, am walking with superb accuracy along an uneven pavement in Bucharest, capital city of the Socialist Republic of Romania, in confidential conversation with Philip Carston's friend and/or lover Carolina Predeanu, and with Valeria Ciudea from a leading Romanian publishing house, and – for some inexplicable reason – with Professor Bobolescu whom I have not yet defined but whom I find, alternately, thoroughly absorbing and deeply suspicious. And I can see that three yards, or should I say a little short of three *metres* ahead of me, is an open man-hole. Yes, its lid is off, and it presents to me a round, black, modest, and yet conclusive abyss. I am talking to my companions, nodding, understanding most of what they are saying, but needing to take a simple, sensible initiative very soon now.

"I understand that," he said in reply to a quick remark from Carolina which he had not caught. He took in the dusty lid of the man-hole lying on the pavement beside it. He smiled, there was a distant confusion of warning voices, and then he was falling down towards the centre of the earth.

In no longer than an eternity, a brief and yet so clear and detailed an age, Tim had vanished, going down, plunging dexterously down into foreign, Romanian darkness, whimsically curious as to how far he would fall in that cool cavity.

He expected to drop to where the street above him was no more than a patch of wintry sky, half blue and half clouded; but in the end he did not fall so far. How absorbing, he thought! I have fallen four, perhaps five feet. I feel none the worse for it, except that there *is* a slight pain forming in my right ankle. I am standing with relief on a pipe or cable under the pavement, my fall less jarring because the said instrument is covered by some softer, cladding substance, where I could be content to remain for the rest of the afternoon, conducting any further conversation from here, my shoulders at pavement level.

But then there was a riot of words around him, and hands

stretching down. He put out one of his own hands gratefully, shook a hand offered him in a warm and friendly way, and released it. If hands could assume facial expressions, that hand did. It signified that Tim Harker-Jones had done the Wrong Thing by shaking it. It repeated its original offer with angry desperation. It was also a strong, insistent female hand. It was joined by a counterpart hand of the same shade of pink, its partner, indicating the same helpful purpose. These two hands, and several voices, entreated co-operation with their efforts.

He took pity on the two hands and held them, and they were vigorous in assisting him. With the help of other hands attaching themselves to his forearms and elbows, they lifted him. He felt himself raising his good foot off the cable and scraping for support with his toes on the wall of the shaft. And indeed there was, most conveniently, a jutting brick which gave him a step to rest his foot on, and another, and these helpful devices continued right up to the level of the pavement.

Standing there again he was dusted down by innumerable hands, singly or in pairs, more than he expected, because a small crowd of people had arrived from somewhere to witness the whole proceeding. He began to answer concerned questions about his condition with absolute clarity and ease and – the first sign of returning sobriety – a touch of embarrassment. Gradually the anxious strangers left them, he was alone again with Carolina and Valeria and Bobolescu, the Professor smiling anciently with a cunning look as if he might even have contrived Tim's descent into the hole.

The ankle hurt him just enough for him to limp a little.

"I think I should go back to my hotel and rest," he suggested.

"We are taking you there. And you still have my address?" Valeria asked. He supposed he could have lost it in the turmoil; but he produced it with pride. Immediately her hand grabbed his and once again stuffed it back into his pocket.

They appeared to have walked in a circle, because here they

were again under the Intercontinental Hotel with the vast Ceausescu-classical facade of the National Theatre beyond it; and retracing their steps across this wide boulevard towards the Capsa.

"If we now leave you here," Carolina proposed. "Will you know where your hotel is? How is your foot? Will it need treatment?"

"No, it won't," Tim later remembered saying. Later he remembered thinking also that all the same it would get a good soak in a hot bath. The hotel room had begun to seem like a haven to him, a place relatively free of the confusions of meeting people and adapting to their codes. Unless its telephone rang.

"I'm fine now. Absolutely fine," he declared, staring across at the revolving door of the Hotel Vidraru.

But when he swivelled round humbly to address this final reassurance to the others they had all vanished.

– 4 –

*** When Katrin set out to write down as much of the experience as possible so as to preserve it, she decided not to include any detailed description of Richard Hendleton's physical appearance, or to record his 'character,' however you defined that.

She made that decision for various reasons. One was, she thought such descriptions would be impossible for her to accomplish. Before that moment when she had fallen in love with Richard – when they had suddenly discovered they were "walking in step" – she could have seen him then, distantly enough to put him into words. She could have easily written down "ordinary in appearance, but *so* ordinary he achieves a kind of personality through it," "nearly bald, and with spectacles, and weak eyes which were much more penetrating than you expected when you looked into them." She would probably have written him off as likely to be a dull individual who was proposing to bother her with laborious attentions. Now she would have to do him justice; and she doubted whether she could convert his essence into words.

Another reason was more complicated. Katrin firmly believed that any elaborate detail about Richard, his curious physical appearance in particular, would fix him much too rigidly in time and place. If you made a physical being too real and clear for yourself, in the words you thought suitable at that moment, you gave it over to the action of time, and time would weaken it and destroy the true nature of it in your recollection. And that would be the opposite of what she intended. So she was fighting against the arrival of the future day when she might not think to take the diary out of the drawer.

She had hit upon a tantalising paradox! To keep the experience of loving Richard Hendleton and his loving her luminous and compelling, she needed to keep Richard vague and shadowy when she wrote him down. [...]

– 5 –

Next morning.

This is his travelling clock ringing now, its insolent bleeps (so effective in dipping down into his sleeping self and dragging his consciousness up to the surface) made more strident by echoing in a high-ceilinged Romanian hotel bedroom.

No, it wasn't. He had forgotten to set it last night after his bath. This noise was the bedside telephone. He had overslept, badly, with Angela due to meet him after breakfast in the foyer at nine. And Angela was not half-an-hour away at home, but downstairs waiting at Reception already, asking him sternly, "Did you have a good lunch yesterday?"

"Angela, I've overslept – and I've hurt my ankle." He tried

to put pleasure into his greeting, and felt guilty about setting out to deceive her. "Can you give me ten minutes? I've had no breakfast..."

"I *have*." There was nothing like a difficulty to put Angela back into her severe mood.

When he had nominally washed and shaved and dressed he opened his door onto the quiet corridor and practised a hobble as he walked towards the lift. The ankle was a little weak and uncomfortable, but it wasn't really hurting. A good limp might have been easier to contrive if his ankle had been perfectly sound: all he had was something to prevent him taking a long walk up a mountain.

When the lift doors opened he did genuinely stumble on the three marble steps down to the Reception area, where Angela sat in an armchair looking worried and impatient.

"I did this yesterday afternoon," he said, wincing. "It hurts me to walk."

"I have my car," said Angela. "It is one of the days the law allows me to drive."

"But I can hardly walk at all. Or I don't *dare* to. It often happens, and I know what I have to do."

"*What* do you have to do?"

"If I rest it for a day – two days – it will be all right. Otherwise I might have to go to bed for a fortnight."

"But you can rest it this afternoon? Or to-morrow?" She looked despairing. "This morning we have a meeting."

"Immediate rest is vital," he insisted.

"I have my car on the other side of the street. You can walk to it slowly. You walked to the lift. You can walk into the Writers' Union from my car."

Tim rotated his foot as if he was considering this plan, and winced again.

"We are meeting Mr Ludache," Angela said.

He put his foot down and momentarily forgot it.

"I see," he said.

"He says Professor Bobolescu telephoned him to suggest it. He could not manage any time except now."

"Well –"

This was a dilemma. If he went to the Writers' Union and saw Ioan Ludache the meeting might lengthen into lunch, and he might never reach Valeria's house... While thinking, he rubbed his ankle with his hand. Was it the acting or the obstinacy which won Angela over?

"I have an idea," she suggested. "I will drive to the Writers' Union and bring Mr Ludache here. He can have some breakfast with you, and you can rest your ankle when he is gone. I have so many things to do..."

Ludache, a polished-looking leather hat pulled well down over his forehead, came bounding through the revolving door of the hotel in under a quarter of an hour, followed uncertainly by Angela. Today his English was rapid and virtually perfect.

"'We meet again', as they say in the novels," he exclaimed briskly, shaking Tim's hand with alarming warmth, converting the restaurant into an arena in which he could play the munificent host, guiding Tim and Angela to a table.

"You may sit in the sun or out of the sun as you choose," he exclaimed. Angela chose the shade. With a passable hangover, Tim saw with alarm that he had to opt for the sunshine; but shifted his chair to sit with his back to it. "I believe you have not had your breakfast?" Ludache asked. "Nor have I." He slung his coat over the fourth chair, put the hat down on the table beside his place.

"Mr Ludache speaks good English so you are in good hands," Angela assured him. "I will telephone you this afternoon."

"I shall sleep this afternoon," Tim insisted.

"Mr Harker-Jones!" Ludache began abruptly the moment Angela had left them. Before he went on he looked around him, but it was all a humorous performance. He came back to Tim with a smile.

"We can talk as biographers?" he asked. Did this mean "as

researcher to researcher"? Or even "as man to man"? The question filled Tim with apprehension. "I hear you had a very interesting weekend in Târgu Alb," Ludache continued knowingly. "You had a pleasant lunch with Professor Bobolescu – and a meeting with Miss Predeanu."

Tim winced, but not because of his ankle.

"She is in a very fascinating situation to tell you facts about the subject of your biography," Ludache went on, when he had ordered omelettes and coffee for both of them. "She is a famous lady. But I want to tell you, it is not necessary to believe *all* her facts. Or Professor Bobolescu's facts, though he is my friend and a wonderful scholar. But we *can* talk as biographers, I hope?" It now did seem to mean, "Can we talk *confidentially*?"

Ludache was not beginning his omelette. Disregard for the food on your plate, rare in this country, invariably threw Tim. He had had no dinner last night after the large meal in the Capsa, he had overslept, he was hungry, but a taught childhood courtesy told him he could not start eating until Ludache did. But Ludache would not start.

"In my country," he said, "we know about fear." He spoke with a peculiar smile. "Some of us also *perform* fear. You look surprised. Many Romanians would disagree with me. But I think some of us dispel fear by *acting* fear and *enjoying* fear. We have real things to fear, but we also enjoy having fiction things to fear. 'Fictitious', do I mean? We enjoy to live by romantic inventions."

Tim did not understand.

"Miss Predeanu is a woman," Ludache continued. That was incontestable, Tim supposed. "She likes to live a little not by political fear but by romantic inventions."

"Has she written – a book, herself?"

"If you have the correct answer to that question, Mr Harker-Jones, everyone in Târgu Alb and many people here in Bucharest will want to know. If you discover the answer, tell me first. I only know that Miss Predeanu has invented a romantic legend to make herself immortal. Perhaps she will tell it to you. Who knows if some of it is *true*? This is the task of we biographers, to answer these questions for our readers."

At the word 'true' Ludache spread his hands and raised his shoulders in an almost Gallic shrug, and knocked the leather hat onto the carpet, where it rolled past two tables and came to rest under a third. Tim leapt up, ran across and retrieved it for him.

"Your ankle is feeling better?"

"No," said Tim abjectly; trapped. "She has found an immortal love," Ludache went on. "And the question is, was it returned to her? You will know Mr Carston's feelings. You will know how much of Miss Predeanu's story to believe?"

The omelettes were cold, but Tim began to eat his, and play for time. He all at once disliked Ludache, and his imputation that Carolina's veneration for Philip – love for Philip? – was "invented." And Ludache seemed to infer from his silence that the matter needed explaining more fully.

"I am saying," he declared, "was Mr Carston equally in love with *her*? Or was he *not* in love with her, and was she deluding herself? Performing the fiction, to lighten her life and make herself interesting in this grey country of ours?"

This is a denigration of everything I see in Carolina, Tim said to himself. But I cannot answer you. I cannot tell you the truth – yet. If I knew, I – well, *would* he tell Ludache without requiring Ludache to tell him what he wanted the knowledge *for*? The political caution instilled in him in London flooded back. Tim couldn't believe that the sceptical, rational, ultra-English Philip would get himself into a romantic tangle with a girl twenty-five years his junior in a Communist country.

"Mr Ludache, why do you want to know this?"

Ludache attacked his own omelette, looking down hard at it, but did not hesitate with an answer.

"Because one day we might have a similar task," he said. "A similar biographical task."

"What do you mean?"

"To explain it is unpleasant," Ludache said. "Do you believe in casting horoscopes, Mr Harker-Jones?"

"Er –no."

"You will forgive me, then, if I believe in it a little myself. When every other kind of prediction in the world – the economist's prediction, the meteorologists's, the sporting journalist's – is correct no more often than the astrologer's prediction, why should we not believe the astrologer as much?"

Tim was silent.

"We are very quiet about the astrologer's predictions in Romania," Ludache said, dropping his voice as if to prove it. "But sometimes we listen to him. In Bucharest here there is a very good astrologer who has cast Miss Predeanu's horoscope for me. It is a remarkable horoscope, and it will frighten you. I have not told it to Miss Predeanu.

"You have? I mean, you haven't?"

"I haven't. I am sorry your ankle hurts you. It might be a good idea to go for a walk and visit this man."

Ludache saw Tim was reluctant to move, so he glanced round at the empty restaurant, then whispered almost inaudibly,

"Miss Predeanu will be in great danger of her life in a time of profound political disturbance in this country before she is forty years old."

Tim was astounded.

"But how old is she now?"

"Miss Predeanu is probably thirty-five years old, that is my calculation."

"That means it could be five years before there is – "

Before what?

"It can be *before* she is forty years old, we think. Therefore it could be sooner."

"You believe this?" Tim asked; and received a nod. "Why is it so important then?"

"Mr Harker-Jones, I am a biographer too. I am thinking of the future. At sometime in the future when biographers in my country may write whatever we wish..." He shook his head in patent disbelief that Mr Harker-Jones had failed to grasp the point.

"You in your country write and publish whatever you wish. You have your publisher begging you to write a life of Mr Philip Carston." Tim remembered the take-away meal with the Paldreys. "We don't have such conditions in my country. But when I can write what I like –"

"You mean – you want to write Philip Carston's life yourself, from the Romanian side?"

"No, no, no! I am writing in the future perhaps a book about the tragic Miss Predeanu when, alas, she is dead. In five years or less. And there is a legend of the love between her and Mr Carston. When you have found it, Mr Harker-Jones, it costs you nothing at all to tell me the truth."

– 6 –

When he left the Hotel Vidraru around mid-day he looked, carefully, out of habit now, in both directions along the busy street. He could make out no one in the least suspicious taking any interest in him or preparing to take it. Unless the occasional young man in a smart leather overcoat strolling slowly past... He wondered if on one point he might not agree with Ludache: it was possible to slip into a ritual of performing a fear so as to *exorcise* a fear.

He cut quickly through from Calea Victoriei to the broad avenue under the Intercontinental Hotel which he could now identify as the Bulevard Balcescu; and turned right towards the 'M' sign of the Metro. He had Valeria's slip of paper safely in an inside pocket, slipped tightly into the notebook he always kept on his person, but he had also memorised the address and the sketch map of the route from the Piata Unirii station so that he would not need to take it out.

Now he was descending the steps (the escalator was not working) into a dark, wide concourse, walking past a seller of Party newspapers, looking round for ticket machines and directions for the platforms. But he saw no such devices in the walls of this gloomy, chilly concourse. Alarmed, determined not to seem conspicuous, he walked to and fro with the crowds as if he had a purpose, and watched what people were doing. Some were walking off down long corridors towards other exits, some were checking out the few bare shops in this arena. Others appeared to be making off into deeper and darker regions with the purpose of travelling. Tim joined this last group, walking with moderate speed down some steps; and came to a second, smaller concourse or hall where there were more escalators, and waist-level metal barriers not dissimilar to those in inner London. But no one seemed to have found any machines, no one carried tickets in their hands, no one was inserting them in the metal barriers in the little mechanical ritual you had to go through in London. People seemed just to be slipping coins – or tokens? – into slots and passing through; wonderfully elementary, and for Tim confusing.

He looked at one barrier to see if he could grasp the rules. A voice spoke to him, and he jumped, and smiled awkwardly and nodded. He had been noticed, he had drawn attention to himself, the last thing he wanted. The stranger was pointing at a coin slot in the barrier which was labelled '1 leu', and pointing back to a window in the wall which Tim saw for the first time, at which people were receiving change. Too nervous to try to fathom in the near-darkness whether the loose change in his pocket included a one leu coin, he complied with the advice, got away from this observant individual, and joined the short queue.

He saw the man in the grey cap for the first time when he turned from the window. He knew he had never seen him before, but he looked the kind of man he *might* have seen operating in some official capacity, because his face resembled someone else's. He could have been present, watchfully, on the fringes of a group or deputation welcoming him in a meeting, keeping tabs on everyone in the room, making punctilious notes.

Tim slipped a single leu coin into a barrier and its turnstile loosened itself to admit him. Inside – feeling committed, even trapped – he let the escalator take him at its own speed down to two open platforms. But which to choose? Which offered trains going north, which south? 'Pipera' was the ultimate destination of northbound trains, so he would need to take a train in the opposite direction.

It said nothing at all on the front of this first train, so he dared to project the question "Piata Unirii?" at a fellow passenger. He received a vigorous nod. As he entered and sat down on a hard red plastic seat with a wide space between him and the seats opposite (no dogged pushing to get out as in London), he saw the man in the grey cap enter behind him, look at him, and take up a standing position (though there were several vacant seats) holding onto a rail and leaning against the automatic doors.

It was if he knew Tim's journey was short, and therefore did not bother to sit down. When Tim rose at Piata Unirii and made for a door, deliberately a farther-off door, he followed him out onto the smooth grey platform.

He was of medium height, or a little taller (it was hard to tell how much the cap added), austere-looking, with vigilant eyes, probably in his late fifties. To look like an ordinary shopper he carried a plastic bag, but it appeared to have nothing in it, it hung down loose. His short coat (or long outdoor jacket) looked studiedly rough and informal, as if he was trying to blend in with the crowd.

Should I quicken my pace, Tim wondered? Even run? Should I double back in the crowd, wait behind some concrete column, take another train onwards for a few stations, then return? No, that would make him all the more conspicuous, waiting and skulking aimlessly on the platform. So he walked quickly up the steps to the exit doors, where there was no barrier, nothing to pay. At this point he thought he might have lost the man until he glanced round, saw him turn away from a stand carrying a magazine, saw him following.

Tim resolved to face the challenge head-on, stride ahead, let him follow if he wished, then run and give him the slip – thereby openly showing he knew he was being tracked and would not put up with it. In one direction he could see the shops and apartments, the future lawns and fountains along the Avenue of the Victory of Socialism. But he didn't have to take that direction, he remembered that, and he walked in the opposite direction as quickly as he could, after losing a minute or two in this bewilderment.

His memory of the map directed him across a wide road at a certain point, and into an area of narrower, unpaved, rather muddy streets, lined with agreeable villas. Here he did run, for perhaps fifty yards; but when he dared to look round for the first time since leaving the Metro station, he saw the man gamely striding after him, the only visible figure, now in blatant pursuit.

Now he felt incriminated, experienced a guilty fear and pity for the people he was visiting, believed also that the purpose of his trip to Valeria's house was already defeated. He would never have the audacity to turn into the street and find the house and knock at the door while his pursuer was in sight. Surely he would have to turn back.

Suddenly he clearly saw the name of the street, Str. Rozmarin, on a sign, and there was no escaping it. (He supposed he could walk past the house, go in a circle, return to it. But what if the man in the grey cap contrived to follow him throughout his detour?)

What he decided to do was walk along Strada Rozmarin, identify the house, and resolve to come back another time, by a different route. The man duly turned into the street also. Still they were the only two people walking in the sunny cold of a winter day along the uneven pavement of this street of handsome, vaguely run-down houses; comfortable, he imagined, behind walls which would be covered by creepers and other climbing-plants in the summer months. When he reached Valeria Ciudea's door, he went on past it, offering the house not even a glance of interest in case his pursuer observed that.

He was appalled to hear that the footsteps had halted behind him, that the man was not following him any more. He seemed to have stopped somewhere near to his own intended destination. Tim slowed a little, intensely, desperately anxious. Had he tired the man out? Was he just pausing to rest?

The street curved; and if there was no audible indication of his still following, Tim might now safely look round? If there was no sign of him at all, perhaps he could venture to walk back after ten minutes or so, and approach Valeria's door after all?

What he did see when he turned, alarmed him more than anything else this afternoon, this fortnight. The street had not curved sharply enough to put Valeria's door out of sight. The man was still there, about fifty yards behind Tim, he had stopped actually at Valeria's gate, resting a hand on it, and was looking in Tim's direction. At first Tim thought, He knows, – he *even* knows – the exact address for which I was making. And how would he know so much? Well of course, this was a police state, some people would know everything.

And then, to Tim's gulping amazement, the man was waving – to *him*. He was, yes, undoubtedly waving, but – couldn't he be waving to someone else?

But the street was deserted and quiet, no one stood in the gardens, there was no one at any window, and even at this fifty yards' distance Tim could see that the man was smiling in triumph, as if to say, You needn't pretend Mr Harker-Jones, I knew you were coming here, I knew what you were coming *for*, you need not walk on any farther.

So Tim turned back in shame and despair, the betrayer of his friends, the destroyer of his own ambition to find out the facts about Carolina Predeanu and Philip Carston, for a biography that could never be adequately finished. But that was a later problem, and Tim had to face this one first.

When he reached Valeria's gate the man in the grey cap looked behind and around himself, then put out a hand to greet him. At the end of a short path beyond the gate, the door of the house was open, and a head, Valeria's, was looking round it; cautiously, that was true, but with a smile. The man said something in Romanian with his face towards Valeria as Tim weakly shook the hand, and Valeria nodded.

"My father says you were walking past the house, we might have lost you. He knew you were coming this afternoon. There are not many obvious English people in Bucharest at the moment, certainly not getting out of a Metro station at Piata Unirii. But he did not like to offer help and walk with you in case he was mistaken – he speaks no English."

They went in through a small dark hall with a grandfather clock in it, and into a room that looked as if it was furnished in a style Valeria's parents had inherited from her grandparents. Valeria explained proudly: this house had been theirs since before the war, and stayed in the family through all the upheavals and changes of the post-war years. (Were all those paintings of uniformed figures family portraits?) One surviving grandparent still lived here, both of Valeria's parents, Valeria and her younger brother and of course Valeria's husband. There were, as yet, no children to form a further generation. It was not a large house for such a considerable family. But Valeria had found a room in which Tim and Carolina could sit alone – 'our visitors' room' she called it.

Carolina was already sitting in it, an empty coffee cup in front of her, smoking a cigarette. The air of privacy and discretion in these surroundings was complete. Carolina smiled.

"You found the house without too much trouble?"

– 7 –

*** "... That's the first promise," Richard said, turning her round to face the view from this vantage point.

"It is all that you said it was," Katrin replied eventually. She had needed to absorb it and think about it first, before turning to face him. As soon as she gazed down the valley over the tops of the trees she knew she would want to take the view into her mind gradually, and fix it there, and write it down later.

"And *can* you hear anything from here?" he asked her, as they climbed, after a moment or two, into denser and denser woodland on the other side of the path which brought them here. The shade was a relief from the glare of the sun. "My second promise?"

Again Katrin was silent, while they walked on and reached a place where the ground levelled out and there was rather more light; though not enough space between the branches above them to let in the full sun of their unusual heatwave afternoon.

"Yes, you *have* kept both promises," she said. This was too small to be called a clearing, was no more than a hidden space of grass under the trees; away from any path, and Katrin doubted whether they would even hear anyone walking past them, down below. No one would come up here.

"I can't hear anything at all," she said, smiling at her exaggeration because there *was* birdsong, there *might* be a distant aircraft, the daytime outdoors could never be entirely without sounds, anywhere, even though the 'silences' were indefinably different.

"I think we are making a third promise," he said. "Both of us."

"What do you mean?"

"We can't always be together, but we shall never walk out of step."

"I think we are making that promise," she told him.

They were prolonging the hesitation, looking directly at each other, smiling, threading fingers.

"You think so?"
"I think so." ...

He raised his head a little and drew his front teeth back over the tip of his tongue, leaving it momentarily dry and raw. Then he dropped his head again over her breast, touched it with the tip of his tongue so that she shivered. She stroked his hair and gave herself to this.

How long had they been lying here? Half-an-hour, one hour, two? When the impulse to pull him closer subsided, she let it, she released him, because she knew it would return even more strongly at some unexpected thought, and she was going to leave the question of time to him ...

"Oh find me, please! Oh help –" he said; laughing with the ridiculous desperation of this. She was laughing too, with pure nerves, she pushed her hand down between their two bodies, caught it in clothes, drew in her stomach and exhaled breath, tightened her lips, kissed him across the face and in the mouth again, found him, lost him, laughed again, all in seconds.

"There – now."
"No – it's not."
"Yes. Try. *Try*!"
"Ye–e–es."

"Please, something for my head! I'm lying on a rock, or something, I can't –" She was lifting her head from the grass in discomfort, even in pain, she *had* to have something to rest her head on.

He had nothing. He had left his jacket in the car. He held her shoulders, eased both bodies a few degrees round from the spot where the painful stone was, not losing her, never losing the deep, conclusive certainty of it. But in the new place her head sank too far back into a small hollow in the ground: patches of grass formed by nature in woods were not as regular as lawns. They both laughed.

"I know," she said. "I know what to do." She used both hands to pull and unbutton his shirt, push it back over his shoulders while he propped himself up on his hands, eased his arms out of the sleeves one at a time, shook it out and folded it behind his back into a slim cotton cushion, pressed it with her right hand down under her neck and dropped her head onto it. And it worked, it was sufficient, it was even comfortable. It was so restful. Nothing had stopped, any of the time she was doing this ...

"When you do not have this it is *so* important," he said. "When you *do* have it, it is – not important."

It seemed so many days later. They had to remind themselves that all this had happened to them within one narrow week.

"It is *not* important?" Katrin complained. "Oh, I am disappointed. I must try to make it *more* important." But she knew what he meant, and continued more quietly. "To me it feels the *natural* thing, different from all the unnatural ones. Nothing else can be as easy as this."

"You mean – you mean when you are doing it, you wonder why you ever did anything else?"

"That is it, yes."

And minutes later, after one of their serious silences,

"This is my idea for eternal life," he said. "To be only ever doing this with you."

"And never eating?"

"No. Never even eating. Eternal life is an idea which presupposes any kind of unlikely condition you choose. There would be no need to eat, no need to sleep –"

" – No need to speak!" But in a moment she went on speaking. "Unfortunately it is not eternal life. Or not yet. I leave in three days."

This was unanswerable, and he did not want to consider it, and was quiet again. So Katrin spoke next.

"Beds have as many problems as the open air," she decided.

"So where do I put this pillow? If I keep it, my head is too high for you. If I throw it on the floor my head is too low. The ground in the country doesn't make noises like the springs of a bed. The ground doesn't have neighbours who might hear you."

"The ground is less flexible than a bed. It doesn't give you the *option* of a pillow."

"Next time we will take a pillow into the country."

"It would get very wet. *We* would get very wet."

They lay talking happily on his single bed in the flat itself, talking about the room, as the rain dropped outside and they watched it battering against the window.

"Of course Dora guesses I am here," she said. "At first she said she would arrange so *much* for me to do in the afternoons. But now, you know, she has stopped. And she says, 'I suppose you may see Richard in the town. Will you tell him *this*, and tell him *that* –?'"

"Oh God!" he exclaimed, in a moment of feigned remorse. "I am forgetting. She is responsible for you."

Katrin pushed herself up on one elbow and stared down at him with equally feigned indignation.

"But I am responsible for myself!" she insisted. "I am not in my own country, but I am a woman with my own life and I am twenty-five years old. Dora is having me to stay, and she is being very kind to me and spending a lot of money. But she knows she must allow me my freedom of action."

"They are not – jealous?"

"No." But in truth she had never considered that.

"How do you know John is content for us to meet?"

"Well – I don't know. But he doesn't complain if I want to do something else, and not with Dora."

"He doesn't realise you are doing *this*?"

"*No*!" But again she had never thought about it. She rather believed Dora, as a woman, would realise, but John would be genial and incurious about such matters.

At this second she thought, I am politically mature, and yet emotionally uncertain. Then she thought of Dora's friends and modified her reaction. No, by comparison with them I am emotionally sensible, she decided.

He broke into her brief silence with, "You could have moved in with me, here, on your first day. *Eleven* days ago!" He was smiling.

"I could have moved in." Repeating what he was suggesting to her, and thinking about it. She lay back again, crumpling his offending pillow to prop up her head, frowning rather, feeling for his hand and finding it, moving it along her thigh towards her hair, but just to have it rest there. "I enter your life. I could have moved into your flat." Then she saw the nonsense of that. "No. It was impossible!" Of course, it was inconceivable, for every reason; she was just playing his game with him. "Impossible. If I move into your flat, I am nearly moving into your country."

"Someone in *your* country would know, and there would be danger?" he asked.

In numerous conversations she had avoided the playful challenges and reproaches.

"No. There would be no trouble. It is a personal question." But she did not feel sure of this argument, and was glad he was not going to press her on it.

"I like your flat, because I like home to be simple," she said.

"Is your home simple?"

"Yes. There is no need for anything more than simple things."

"Describe it please."

She did. And ended up saying,

"I like Dora, she is very kind. But you know, she has become an English bourgeoise. On the first day I liked her house, it was so different from my little workers' flat. But now I've been to other houses, and I see it's a typical bourgeois home like the others. She is older, and they bought their things thirty years ago, but it makes no difference. Whether they are old homes with lace curtains or new homes with posters and rock records, they are all English bourgeois."

"There must be something you don't like in *this* flat?"

"I would not keep all the pictures."

"But I only have two – *three* pictures. Wouldn't you keep any of them? You don't like reproductions?"

"I like them, but not here. I would keep the one picture I really needed to see, and not the pictures I would never notice."

"But the walls would be bare."

"Yes, and a picture you never notice on a wall is just the same as a bare wall."

"What picture do you have on the wall at home now?"

"None. Nothing."

"What picture would you want?"

She thought, and smiled.

"No picture for the moment. Do you have a good photograph you can give me? Of you?" ...

Whatever has happened in life, she realised, starts receding – at once – at a much faster rate then you imagine.

It started to accelerate for her the moment she stepped into the cool interior of the plane and met the vigilant smiles of the cabin crew. But inside the bag she carried was the full account she had written of her visit to England, to prevent it speeding away for ever. She had written it in her own hand and she left nothing out, with one exception: the appearance and voice and mannerisms of Richard himself (though not where they went, and what they did, and their conversations) she carried in her head. She trusted her memory of him much more than she would have trusted the words she could have used to write down the living man. Words were victims of the action of time [...]

FIVE

– 1 –

"I am Carolina Predeanu, I am to be your guide in Romania, and I will interpret for you, I have been engaged by the Council for Culture," I said rapidly, using every phrase I had carefully prepared. Did I see a curious flicker of distaste – and humour – pass across his lips? Whatever reaction he had to my speech he disguised it quickly and courteously, and smiled.

"Ah, I am sorry for you," he said.

"Why?" I was naively amazed.

"Because you have to guide an ignorant and reluctant person like me."

He smiled again, and stared down, shyly and myopically, at the bags and haversacks and suitcases now beginning to circulate on the slow-moving belt, as if his luggage were the only secure object in a bewildering world. How could he be 'ignorant,' when he had written a novel I had read, *The Winter Book*, and several others?

And why 'reluctant'?

"I have never guided any other people," I said. "You are my first visitor." I would be the ignorant one.

"What a ghastly start!"

I had never experienced the famous, self-deprecating modesty of the English in the flesh before.

"I hope I can help to make it a pleasure for you," I said, looking up at Philip cautiously, and smiling; or trying to look up, because he suddenly bent down with unexpected vigour and pulled two heavy black suitcases out of the mass of luggage moving slowly and doggedly past our feet.

"Now we have the customs," I explained. "But I hope it will not be long. I have a letter I can show to say you are an official visitor and guest of the Writers' Union."

"I'm a *what*?" At that moment Philip looked almost ready to drop his suitcases and turn back.

"A guest of the Writers' Union."

"But I'm here through the British Council. I think?"

"It is true. But your visit is approved by the Council for Culture and the Writers' Union also."

"Ha!"

It was a curious, alarmed, cynical, resigned sort of exclamation. Perhaps all these arrangements sounded complicated and had never been made clear to him? Later Philip said the knowledge that he was partly a guest of the Council for Culture and the Writers' Union "felt like steel jaws closing on him," and that he "felt a very long way from home." And much later he told me it was only my "extreme sex appeal" that prevented him calling up a taxi to the British Embassy and asking "to be extradited forthwith."

He would not have known how difficult it was becoming to obtain a taxi at Otopeni. At some of the large stations, particularly in the provinces, you might find a state taxi if you were prepared to wait a long time; and you could probably spot a taxi driven by an unlicensed 'businessman,' as we called them – 'cowboys' was the word Philip suggested – which would be three times the price and one tenth as reliable. But not at Otopeni. So it was essential to have the official car.

Philip held on to his English umbrella and looked around him with something between terror and resignation as he climbed into the back of the car beside me. Another thing he told me later was that he said to himself at that moment, "Well, I am on my way to my fate, and Death is a lovely woman after all." And about our driver, that "he looked like the kind of bodyguard who would turn his gun on the bastard he was overpaid to protect." I was aware, to express this very mildly, that my first (and only?) assignment as a guide and interpreter was with someone who felt no sympathy at all with our socialist revolution here in Romania!

And yet I knew by instinct, at once, that I was going to like him. It would take time, of course, to adjust to his humour and his absolute Englishness (and something quite near to xenophobia).

What Philip actually said in the car on the way to the Hotel Vidraru (yes, the Council uses it for a lot of our foreign visitors) was very polite and pleasant.

"Please don't misunderstand me," he began. "It's just that I'm not the kind of man who cadges foreign trips. I'm a rather unwilling traveller doing it to oblige." He said that the British authorities appeared to be rather short of 'representative' writers to visit Eastern European countries at that time, and he was 'between novels' and able to go. "It really is very bad luck for you to get me as your first job. Wouldn't you have preferred a pop poet?"

"What is a 'pop' poet?"

"Ah, you don't know what a pop poet is? How lucky you are in Romania! Such innocence... I'm sorry, I'm just thinking I might be rather a boring old – old prospect to take round the collective farms."

"You will not bore me, I am sure of that," I laughed. "And I do not think there are plans to see any farms."

Philip smiled back when I smiled; but he soon became rather reserved again. The road from Otopeni, as you know, takes you past the Casa Scînteii, which I think must be impressive enough when you first see it to deserve a comment or a question. Philip said nothing. But when we were past the Arc de Triomphe, which he *did* notice and remark upon rather favourably (though he pretended afterwards that he loathed everything inspired by the French), and entering the top of Calea Victoriei, he asked me about the earthquake for the first time and began to stare, appalled, at the destruction, the heaps of masonry, the roped-off areas where no one could walk because it was still unsafe, the small crowds gathered round the pale candles in the evening sunshine. I had heard awful rumours that there were still dead bodies to be taken from some of the wreckage; but I did not say this to Philip.

"You are too young to have seen anything like this in a war," he exclaimed suddenly, pointing at one entirely demolished street. "It reminds me of the British cities in 1940, 1941 – London, Coventry where I was born. At least it's not going to happen again in another air raid to-night, or to-morrow night."

In fact, in the second week of Philip's first visit there was a tremor strong enough to shake buildings and crack windows, but not with enough force to cause destruction or injury. It happened between nine and ten one night, during a thunderstorm over Bucharest, and Philip noticed the storm but not the earthquake – or thought it was *only* a storm.

In the hotel I asked him how long he needed to settle in before we had dinner.

"Several hours, to adjust," he replied. "One hour to fathom how the taps and the toilet work, another to discover how I get into the bed in case I'm too drunk to work it out later, another to master the light switches and the window catches. Call it – twenty minutes." When we entered the restaurant after exactly that time he was changed from his nearly black suit into a lighter jacket and grey trousers, and seemed prepared to relax.

But the restaurant puzzled him completely, especially the pianist who pounded at the grand piano with a clumsiness which regular patrons, judging by their enthusiastic and slightly ironic applause, seemed to recognise and enjoy. When we had finished our pork chops and starting our ice-cream desserts the pianist gave way to a trio of brightly-dressed musicians including a violinist who circulated among the tables – the hotel had pretensions of that kind in those days – and Philip said, "I've only ever seen this in films, and I've never found out – do I tip him anything? How much?"

I was too shy to say it was my own first time in a city restaurant, and I simply did not know myself. Tip, or pay, the violinist, undoubtedly. But pay him what? I guessed. "I think you are expected to give them at least 50 lei." "*What*? Nearly three pounds?" Philip's voice was full of exasperated shock, and he went through a mime, while the violinist stood there and played, of not being able to locate any money. Eventually the man bowed gracefully, and went on to another table despairing of these unsophisticated foreigners.

"So how many weeks have I been here already?" Philip asked me over coffee. He was more than a little drunk by then, on the good wine, the Murfatlar you could still find in the restaurants; and more than a little sleepy, I thought. I saw him to the door of his room.

"I shall speak very slowly in these meetings," he assured me as he wavered on the threshold. "Very slowly – and deliberately – because I shall not have the f – f– faintest notion what to say." At that very second, I wondered whether the ordinariness was really a long-cultivated performance or disguise. Because he was not ordinary at all, but *extra*ordinary.

When it came to it he talked both slowly and intelligently, of course. As to the people we were seeing – some proceeded slowly and waited for me, others talked so *fast*. There was invariably one person from Protocol there, or someone with Protocol responsibilities, often a member of the staff of the publishing house or magazine we were visiting, but occasionally an outsider, a roughly-dressed individual who looked out of his depth with cultural concerns. Philip got into the habit, when we were alone again after a meeting, of saying, "Well, who was the goon this time?" Or, "I reckon it was the old girl with the auburn wig" (someone in fact very proud of her special hair, still a natural deep chestnut colour in her late fifties). Or "Why was that shark-faced character writing everything down?" I could try to answer that one. "He was keeping a record of the meeting," I said. He would want to keep a record of a discussion like that with an important visitor." "Would he hell!" Philip said. "Yes, he would!" I smiled, but I began to feel rather patriotic. Philip in this mood was being deliberately negative and refusing to understand how life worked in my country, as if any country different from his own was wrong. We were human beings, we had normal hard-working lives, we ate and slept, we were not spies, we were simply *not* frozen with terror just to walk down the street. We enjoyed life, especially the young people. "If only I was important in England," Philip said jokingly. "No one ever wants to make notes on me there." Or, "I've never, never, in my whole life, been so deferentially received by *publishers*."

People eagerly wanted to see copies of his novels. He had not brought any himself, the British Council had asked his publishers but they had not responded fast enough. So he made careful note of names to whom books would be sent by his agent, or by himself, as soon as he returned to England. In four or five days he had unexpectedly mellowed. "Seeing that this trip is inevitable, I shall – as we say in England – relax and enjoy it," he said.

"I was watching TV last night, until it stopped at about nine-seventeen," he said one day. (An exaggeration: you could see programmes until well after ten o'clock.) "I noticed something rather remarkable. For the first time since I've been here the newsreader on *Telejurnal* did *not* begin with the same words. Something like: 'Secretary-General of the Romanian Communist Party and President of the Socialist Republic of Romania Comrade Nicolae Ceausescu.' Is that it? Well, last night he *didn't* begin with those words. Do you think that is significant? There wouldn't have been a *coup*, would there?"

"Why must that be significant? Probably the President was not doing anything important yesterday." I had to be more cautious in talking to a foreigner than I would with friends.

"He seems to do something important most days," Philip said.

"He is the head of our government."

"They don't get a chance to forget it, do they! Is he popular?"

"You must be popular with the people to be President."

"Do you elect the President?"

"There is a vote of all the people."

"And they elect the same President every time?"

This conversation was going on in one of the most public places in Bucharest, the famous Carul cu Bere, the "Beer Cart" tavern and restaurant, a huge, high, round room with handsome wooden galleries and hundreds of tables for the diners. It was very crowded, and no one *appeared* to be paying attention to us, but how could I tell? I was learning quite fast. I had to stop Philip talking like this in this kind of place, he didn't appreciate how tactless it was.

"What would happen if someone overheard us having the wrong kind of conversation?" he asked me when we were alone the next day in the park.

"People might think it is not fair for visitors to criticise," I explained. "It doesn't matter to *me*, but if other people hear *you*..."

"But that means it would be allowed for you or your friends to criticise? What if a Romanian stood up in that bandstand over there and shouted, 'The President is a bloody fool'?"

"A policeman would come and stop him and arrest him. It is not right to swear, and abuse people – abuse anyone in a public place. If an Englishman was in your St. James's Park in London and said your Queen was – what you said, a policeman would stop him there?"

"Yes. I suppose so. But –"

"So it is the same. But in most ways I think our systems are different. You have a lot to discover before you understand our democracy here, I would have a lot to find out in your country."

"Do you support your own system?"

I was watching a man who had been aimlessly strolling up and down the path in front of us, reaching the little café that juts out over the water, with the tables where people sit and take coffee and cakes and ices in the summer, reaching it and turning back, approaching it and turning back again, passing us without looking. Then he came closer. So I did not try to answer Philip's question.

There was room on this bench in the beautiful Cisnigiu Park in spring for more than two people (sitting not so far apart), and the pacing stranger stopped and sat down beside us. You are anxious now every time this happens, and it was beginning then, in 1977. I was anxious that day because Philip was a foreigner. This time he was tactful, and he changed the subject himself.

"What exactly are we to do this weekend? We're taking a trip somewhere, I believe?"

"I meant to say, yes, it's all arranged – we go to Constanta."

– 2 –

I felt guilty about dragging Philip, who was over forty years old, on that long trek down from the station at Constanta to the hotel on the seafront. But there was no state taxi waiting at the station, only a few "businessmen". I could not claim the extra for a businessman's car, so we walked.

In hot weather (or any weather), that is a long walk with your baggage. For the first time Philip was openly irritated. He showed it by stopping repeatedly, partly to rest but sometimes, I am sure, to show his disapproval of having to walk at all. "I shall walk about as far as the length of a cricket pitch – and no farther," he said at one point, when we had about half a kilometre left.

"How long shall we need before we meet here for some lunch?" I asked him at the door of the lift in the hotel.

"The rest of the weekend," he said.

Our rooms were on different floors, and he was two floors above me. I told him to come down and call at my room on the way when he was ready for lunch, so that I would not have to wait in the dark reception hall by myself: sometimes odd and sinister people cluster in hotel foyers, all men, all apparently intent on some deal or other, or just watching whoever passes, alert for "exchange."

Philip was strange about the people who offered illicit currency deals. Apparently he took a walk alone on the second day he was in Bucharest, in the rain; and everyone who offered to sell him Romanian currency mentioned pounds sterling. Never dollars. "How did they know not to ask for dollars?" he asked me. "I thought it was incredibly perceptive," he said. He hadn't been talking to anyone so that his accent had been overheard. He had just been strolling along looking at the sights with his umbrella up. I laughed and agreed, yes it was extraordinarily perceptive; Philip had no idea how English, absolutely English, he looked with his umbrella and suit, like the director of a bank in one of those old English film comedies.

Quickly I changed out of the clothes I had worn in the train from Bucharest, and sat looking out at the esplanade. And suddenly one of those unforgettably defining moments occurred, when, for no reason you can describe, life seems enhanced and significant and precious, more *real* than before; you feel you are on the brink of something that will change you forever.

Somewhere along the corridor a radio was playing while the cleaners unwound the leads of their vacuum cleaners along the red carpets and set about cleaning the rooms. And the door of the room where the radio played stood wide open, so that the loud sound of an orchestra and singers came out. A resonant, deep bass-baritone soared out of that opened room, a voice in a nineteenth century romantic opera I did not recognise. Not a well-known opera, not Verdi or Mascagni. Bellini? Flotow? It was a voice of confidence and hope, singing in my own language words I could not catch. I looked out over the esplanade in the radiance of the early afternoon and gazed at the endless calm of the Black Sea, indeed a dark sea, telling of deep and inscrutable distance: you can stand there and feel you are gazing out into Asia.

Next minute my eyes dropped to the level of the concrete esplanade itself, and the closer mystery of mortality was added to the unfathomable mystery of distance. First I looked at a grass slope to my left which fell steeply down to the water. Then I noticed a dog lying asleep on the esplanade itself, with a man, two men, standing over it, one of them carrying something in his hand.

I forgot the dog and turned to the mirror. I hoped I looked

respectable enough for the restaurant. I sat down to wait. But realising something just in time I jumped up and opened wide the door of my own room. The opera had stopped; the cleaners' voices had died out at the far end of the corridor, but it would not be right to be seen (by anyone) opening the door to a foreigner's knock, a foreign man especially.

When he did come (dreading to be 'compromised' he told me later!) he stood back shyly from the open gap and tapped very courteously before crossing the threshold. When he entered, he still held the door with one hand as if uncertain what to do with it. "Please leave it open, it is best," I said. He did, and came in, and looked all the way round the room at everything as if he was going to find something here completely different from his own room.

"You face the same way – did you see that dog down on the promenade?" he asked me.

"Yes – I didn't know if it was asleep or –"

We both went to the window.

"It's gone. It was just asleep," he said.

"I don't know. Look there." I pointed.

"Well it's possible," Philip said, thinking what I was thinking. "But I don't know that they are the same men. And there are four of them now."

There might, among the group of four men walking away on our extreme right, have been the two men who had been standing over the sleeping animal moments before. But one of the four was now carrying something, a sack, as if the dog had not been sleeping – and what else except dead? I wanted to look harder and longer and see the dog trotting away beyond the men in the distance. But I couldn't. And in another few seconds the men themselves had all disappeared.

"Could you hear the music?"

"I could hear the music."

We were silent for a moment, looking at each other.

"I have a better armchair than you," Philip said. My

armchair was broken, one of its very short legs having separated itself from the rest of the structure. It didn't look as if you could sit on it safely and I hadn't tried. "You must come up and see it."

"Do you think you *can* help me?" I had the courage to ask him that evening. I had been trying to make up my mind to say it for most of the afternoon, when we strolled through the port area, and went into the aquarium, and saw the Roman mosaic, all for the sake of my guide's report. My days with Philip did not cause my office work to disappear. What I required help with was a short piece of scholarly prose translation, Romanian into English, for my publishing house – yes, we did, and we still do, publish some books in English, and people are very eager to buy them.

We were still at the restaurant table after dinner, and a loud band was playing (for whom, except themselves. I didn't know: we were the only diners; but our very chairs were vibrating with the din).

"Do you have it with you?" he asked; a little resignedly, I thought, as if there was no using excuses now for escaping this obligation – though he spoke with perfect courtesy.

"I have it here. It will only take a few minutes."

"Well, 'let's get on with it', as they say at the end of that terrible French play," he murmured in a melancholy tone. We had been discussing plays we liked and plays we hated, but I was surprised when he said that. Because *Huis Clos* is a classic concerned with the nature of hell. I know he was joking, but was my piece of translation work going to be so hell-like for him?

"We shall have to go to the room," I said before very long. This restaurant was much too noisy.

"'The room'," he said, echoing me with a grin. "With the door open. We shall not want to escape." He was referring to *Huis Clos* again. "My door or yours? I have two splendid armchairs, better than your one armchair. There isn't much of a table."

I chose his room because I thought I could always leave it; that is, it would give me the decision when to leave, and how much conversation we should have when my work was finished. Was I not in a hotel, in a city where I had only been once in my life before, with a distinguished foreign man, unmarried, friendly, full of ironical humour but wholly out of his element in a Black Sea resort? I had to be prepared to handle the fact that he *was* a man.

It is enough to say that as I entered Philip's room in the hotel in Constanta that evening I knew that I could trust him, and close the door (it would have been absurd to leave it open at night time). And I knew also that I only kept the other door open at lunch time because I had sensed that I was attracted to him too much.

We sat down side by side in his two armchairs with a rather faint table lamp between us, and I produced from my handbag the sheets of paper on which I drafted the translation.

"Mr Carston," I began.

"These courtesy titles!" he exclaimed, banging the arm of his chair. "'Domnul Carston,' all the week. In meetings and out of meetings. It's too grand and godlike ... I see I don't get Comrade Carston from anyone."

"No one uses that now."

"Thank God they don't. You have my consent to use 'Philip'."

"I can use that when it is time."

"When it's *time*? When on earth is that?"

"When I can *feel* it's time." I had realised I was unconsciously transforming it into a big step...

"I think I see. Do I wait until then before I use 'Carolina'?"

"Part of me wants to be the reader in a distant country who admires you through the books. That part says 'Mr Carston.'"

"Don't let it get the upper hand."

"I'm sorry. You mean – ?"

"I mean I am not just the writer of the books, and I am not in my distant country during this fortnight. *And* I have admirable attributes apart from the writing."

Sitting solidly in his armchair, hunched up, with a mischievous expression... we were silent for a few moments, our second strange silence at least, in these past few hours. Silence can be as ambiguous as any talk. Why did I not break it by unfolding the papers on my lap and passing them over to him at once?

"And now you are thinking: He is inviting me to question him about his other qualities," he said.

The answer to that was easy.

"Oh, but I have been questioning you about yourself every day for one week," I said laughing. "I have no questions left, except did you enjoy this afternoon's walk? You have never told me."

"I like the aquarium."

"Now that is very odd indeed, because I was thinking about the aquarium. I was thinking about how the eels in that enormous tank looked at us."

"I remember the eels."

"They were saying, 'Please we all want to get out, can't you help us?'"

"Can't you give us passports?"

I ignored his implication with – I think – a blank-faced look.

"I think perhaps when I have a passport to visit more foreign countries I shall come to England – and ask very tactless questions about capitalism."

"Will your work give you a chance to come some time?"

"I don't know."

"You enjoy your work?"

"But of course!"

And then I was – and why should I have been, I don't know why to this day? – I was crying helplessly and saying, "I am sorry, I am very sorry... This is nothing to do with anything we are talking about, it's other things. It's more important things, that are personal."

That was how I said it. Imagine – I was only twenty-two, twenty-three? An age when time begins to go *so* fast, you will be twenty-five and thirty before you know, and never seventeen or eighteen, never at school or university studying again. You are an adult, and working for ever, that is what you suddenly feel, and so many of the chances in life are already out of reach. And it was late in this strange place, and I was tired, and I was nearly telling a foreign stranger twenty years older than me all about this.

Nearly? I did tell him. I just assumed he would listen. He did listen. How irreversibly embarrassing it could have been if he had not sympathised. If he had not stretched out a hand from his chair, and held mine, and listened. I apologised tearfully for revealing so much.

"The only difference between us is that I've spent twenty years keeping the cork in the bottle until I was ready to pour it out on the printed page," he said at the end. "You'd have a lot to write down if you tried." He said that because I had told him things I had never told anyone. "Have you ever thought about it?"

Did he know what he was starting in me with this encouragement?

"I think we must think about this translation," I said.

It wasn't just fifteen minutes. It was nearly four hours.

– 3 –

I woke up and I was in Târgu Alb. No, I was not back in Târgu Alb, it was my hotel bedroom over the esplanade facing the sea at Constanta, the bed happened to be in the same position in relation to the window as it was at home. And *I* was in the same position, my feet dropping off the end of the bed as I lay on my stomach, with my soles facing the curtains, the dawn light directly in front of them.

No, I was without doubt back in Târgu Alb, and dawn was earlier because it was now well on into the summer of that same year, 1977. This was my bedroom in my parents' house, and that was the small line of Philip's books, the ones he had sent me, on the shelf over there on my right.

He had naturally kept his promise. The books had come to me singly in a series of packets, every one of them, nothing lost or stolen, between two weeks and five weeks after he returned to England early that April. And he had kept his undertaking to send books to other people. Philip's – or his agent's – wrapping and tying of the books was immaculate; and impenetrable. As we agreed, no letters or notes inside.

It is quite possible to post things freely between our two countries, but it was not a good thing to be receiving a lot of private mail in Târgu Alb, so everything had to come to me at the publishing house. When I sent Philip postcards (only postcards at the beginning) I tried to mail them from somewhere else and alter my usual writing just a little, though not so much as to leave it looking a deliberate disguise. I sent him warm and elaborate good wishes in our own style, no English restraint.

All the same, when Philip's first letter came, he sent me nothing better than a few paragraphs of remote formality. It was neatly typed, dry, factual, chilly. In my country he had said he actually enjoyed letter-writing – but to enjoy writing a letter like that! Immediately I wrote back on a postcard and said it was a deep pleasure, a joy, for me to have his letter; but there was nothing of his true feelings in it, it was so *cold* for a letter between friends. What he must do, I said, was write me a proper letter that was full of himself and his genuine emotions, not a frosty disappointing letter like the one I had just received. I used a post office at the other end of town, and insisted on taking the stamp away and affixing it myself, not letting them take it and post-mark it there and then and perhaps drop it onto a shelf for inquisitive eyes to look at.

But I had taken a risk with Philip by expressing myself so frankly. It could have greatly embarrassed him. Yet I had to know what he was thinking. If he never did reply to this communication (assuming he received it) I should know for certain that he had been shocked into silence and had no wish to perpetuate the friendship.

A reply did come. It was still guarded and cautious, but such an improvement on the first letter! Philip even allowed some of his humour into it, and referred to some of the private jokes we had had during his visit. "I am well into a new novel," he said. "Nothing about Romania in it, I'm sorry to say – perhaps that's for the future – but plenty of slippery characters in it, milling around like eels in a tank, unable to get out of the tangle into which I have got them. If I had a *deus ex machina* I could smash the glass and all the little beggars could wriggle free. But where could they go? Freedom might be worse suffering. Why *do* I create people and then have to struggle to find some reason, use, and future for them? It's like having children, something I at least avoided in life. If I had your clear mind here, you could sort it out for me." Such flattery of a twenty-two year old from an important writer with more talent than I would ever have! "Only the clear-minded should ever write novels, 'oh dear me yes'! (to misquote one of your favourite English literary men.)"

But I am leaping ahead... I was posting my postcard which evoked this reply, purposely choosing the other end of town to do it, when I turned round and the person waiting to post a letter of her own was Mrs Vajna, Eva Vajna.

"You are a long way from home," she said, much too sweetly, wheedling an explanation.

"I have an aunt I visit," I said, which was true except that she was a *great*-aunt. I had already seen her and was carrying the empty bag in which I had brought garden vegetables and sugar (for some reason in short supply).

"Now that I've *caught* you," she exclaimed (and to meet her was usually to be "caught"), "I wonder if you could say a word about something to Tamasi for me?" Tamasi Ilosz was the chief of our small department publishing Hungarian books in the publishing house. His scale of activity was limited, and I knew he was not going to welcome any word from Eva. As their names suggest, he and she were both Hungarians.

I saw Tamasi every day in the office. I liked Tamasi. But I tried to avoid him because he was a notorious office flirt. Now I had to be Eva Vajna's messenger to him. Yes, I had to – she might remember to gossip about my posting something in an out-of-the-way district if I refused.

"It's about the manuscript of mine he has."

We stood under the grey facade of this post office on this very warm, dry and dusty day in early July. It had been so dry – one of our drought years – that there were already yellowed leaves from the trees in a garden opposite blowing round our feet; and it was also a windy day. Dust from demolition and construction work in this quarter of the city was blowing and rising around us. Somehow all of this focused Mrs Vajna for me more clearly than she had ever been before. Eva worked for the hospital administration but she had no family – yet; she was then in her early thirties, I would guess – she lived for the novels she tried to write. The first had nearly been published by us, but in the end the Editor-in-Chief – and ultimately it had to be the Director, Dr Mandeliu – refused to give in to all the pressure she put on him. Dr Mandeliu was – in the last resort – honourable, and had standards: he deserved the promotion to Bucharest they gave him later. Mrs Vajna's book remained in manuscript, postponed "for later consideration" because of paper shortages. I was sorry for her because I would not have wanted any manuscript of my own, should I ever write one, to be so treated.

Eva Vajna's second and third books were similarly read with sympathy and postponed with sorrow. It was not very long before even Professor Bobolescu began to lose interest in – in his protegé! *And you can imagine how, all this time, Georgeta Bobolescu, his wife, felt?* She needed a patience beyond human power, a saintliness even. Remember that it was back in the early 1970s Eva started writing, when she was still very young and beautiful (even then she was married, but that did not matter to the Professor.)

By the time I was having this conversation with Eva outside that post office, Georgeta was used to anything and prepared for anything her husband did. But it would still have been humiliating for her. She was having to recover from the disappointment of discovering she was not a genius herself, she was just a very good cook who had become the second wife of a middle-aged scholar and borne his child. I suppose she *is* a saint, because she learnt to tolerate it all, and did not hate Eva, and would greet her in the street. In the same way she tolerated what happened to me.

I lived dutifully. I conveyed Mrs Vajna's message to Tamasi Ilosz, trying to do it in the plainest, quickest way possible. I ran up the stairs and walked straight into his office next day, before I'd even been to my own room, and I said,

"I met Eva Vajna in the Piata Stefan cel Mare yesterday afternoon." (That was my lie, of course. It had not been anywhere so central.) "She wants to give you some improvements to the new manuscript of hers you have been considering. I promised to ask you if she could bring them in."

Tamasi had that perpetually, I have to say attractively, melancholy look so many Hungarian men have: the sad, troubled, distant eyes, the pale face fringed with thick black hair, the black moustache drooping downwards at the corners of the mouth (Philip said, "I think the melancholy Magyars have got it right about life: it *is* as miserable as that, why try to look cheerful?"). Tamasi's look of melancholy deepened when he heard Mrs Vajna's name.

"You promised to have a glass of wine with me at the Transilvania a month ago, and you never have," he said.

"Tamasi, don't try and change the subject," I said. "Mrs Vajna –"

"Why do you keep this promise to Mrs Vajna and not your promise to me?"

But Tamasi didn't expect an answer. He sighed, stretched, moved a thick notebook on his desk along the stained wooden surface, opened it, closed it immediately.

"Yes, we are considering the novel... Do you see her very often? She's not a neighbour or anything? Good. Tell her the next time, *not* before then, that she can send the extra material, but she will not get a quick decision. *Don't* tell her that it's impossible to publish it because it is so bad. Tell her anything kind. Tell her it's a political judgment, if *that's* kind. You understand?"

I didn't know why Tamasi was giving the task to me; and then I realised he was not serious, or had softened his attitude.

"But if you like, I can offer to tell her myself," he said. "She telephones me about once a week. I was just thinking you could tell her more kindly than me. But – do you ever see Professor Liviu Bobolescu? Now *that's* an idea! Tell him *he* ought to break the news to Mrs Vajna, and help her. He started it, after all." I didn't respond to that, because I hardly ever encountered Professor Bobolescu and Tamasi realised that. I turned to leave.

"Are you writing about your English visitor for *Misiva* – or for us?" By "us" he meant the monthly Hungarian cultural paper. I certainly could have written it in Hungarian. I am bilingual, like most people of my generation in Târgu Alb, and write reasonably well in that language.

"*Misiva*," I told him; our Romanian journal: *The Message*.

"Bring Mr Carston to Târgu Alb next time," he said. "Bring him to me. But come and have a glass of wine with me before that."

I left without giving Tamasi any such undertaking. And ran on up to my own office, three floors up, six short flights of stairs. I was conscious that I was a little late, and Dr Mandeliu in particular had a custom of arriving very early. And I was out of breath from hurrying. So I was less than well prepared for the encounter at the door of the Director's office, at the top of the last flight of carpeted stone steps.

The two men standing there were laughing together as if they had just finished a meeting that had been going on amicably for some time – this at eight-ten in the morning! The visitor must have arrived very early indeed. Dr Mandeliu was putting out a hand to the other, younger man in comradely farewell. The visitor taking it, I was soon to learn, was Mr Ilie Radin. But when they saw me, and the Director said, "Oh, but here she is!" they both simultaneously turned to greet me.

"Yes, now I can put the name and the face together," said Mr Radin, when introductions were made. They both smiled with the happy warmth of two adults who can give a pleasant gift to a deserving child: the two beaming faces made me *feel* a child again.

"I think we should go back into the office," Radin said, too genially.

Dr Mandeliu was opening the door very widely, ushering us both in – I went into the Director's office very rarely, and with awe and uneasiness. Dr Mandeliu was pulling out his own imposing chair for Mr Radin to sit in, pushing one of the two low armchairs in the room over towards the desk, so that I could sit down immediately in front of him. But he didn't shift a second chair, and it was clear that he himself was not staying. He was full of good humour as he retreated.

The first thing I noticed when I sat down facing Mr Radin was that he had some physical resemblances to the President of the Socialist Republic. Dr Mandeliu had the President's picture, a large, framed, tinted photograph, on the wall above his desk. It was now exactly above Mr Radin's head, and he unquestionably copied its haircut. More than that, his skin was – in its natural colour – the same as President Ceausescu's tinted cheeks in the picture. Mr Radin also had a smart bluish-grey suit.

The disconcerting element in this comparison was my knowledge, everyone's private knowledge, that President Ceausescu no longer looked this debonair model of youthful middle age. He was now in his late fifties, and if anything looking somewhat older than that already. But Mr Radin could only have been in his late thirties. He was one of the many men in the employ of the authorities who wanted to look like what the President of the Republic *hoped* he still looked like.

"I have had extremely good reports on your fortnight working as a guide to the Englishman," he began. "From Bucharest – and also from Constanta." (But we had met no one officially in Constanta! He was obviously pretending. Wasn't he?)

"You handled the visit well. Your own reports on the time you spent with him were *excellent*."

I really *was* back at school. I was receiving praise from behind the school director's desk, the only difference being that I was sitting down in a low chair to hear it – a position that enabled Mr Radin to use his higher chair to advantage. Could I guess what all that praise implied? Of course I could. Mr Radin would probably know it was the second time something like this had happened to me, although the party, more naturally, raised matters the first time (just before I took my degree exams at the university). He might know that I had declined the invitation then, by simply promising to think carefully about it. What would I say this time? It was a very direct approach at the beginning.

"You made a very good impression on a foreign visitor. You made him begin to realise that our country was not what he had been told it was. We know that for a fact."

I was frightened. He spoke almost as if he could have read the report Philip himself was giving to his own authorities in London, in which he promised, to my embarrassment, to praise me. "We are very happy with you."

"Then I am happy," I heard myself saying nervously. It was true. Who would not have been flattered to be praised knowing it was for something harmless and good, even if the voice professing the praise was certainly no tone I would have chosen. The voice went on with blunt directness.

"Have you considered further the possibility of joining the Party, and working for it? It is not really my job to invite you, but with these excellent reports... Well, as a good friend of Dr Mandeliu, I have yielded to his suggestion that I do just that."

And there it was.

I knew that if you joined in the eagerness to progress in life you might be absorbed into the Party. I looked at Mr Radin across the table and did not know what to say. He simply sat there under the President's picture smiling confidently, waiting for me to respond.

I noticed he had a curious little nervous, unconscious habit. As he spoke (and while he waited) he drummed his right heel on the floor – I heard it before I saw it, the fast, steady, tap-tap-tap of his foot under Dr Mandeliu's chair, like a chattering of teeth in the cold. I smiled and said nothing.

Suddenly he said, "I envy you. I envy you more than I can admit."

I looked up in surprise.

"Shall I tell you something?" he said. "I have wanted to speak English well since I was a young man seeing English films of Shakespeare on television. I have a little book at home for learning English – I bought it in the second-hand bookshop near the Giulesti Theatre in Bucharest. I did not go to university, but I learnt some English, a little, at school – when we were not learning Russian. Nowadays I sit with this book and try to learn English words and phrases. It is a small passion."

He smiled, yet he seemed intensely serious, as if confessing some strong, strange emotion for the first time. How complex and unpredictable – or ingenious? – people could be.

"It's a lovely language," I assured him, ridiculously, for something to say when he paused.

"I say to myself," he continued, "'will I ever use these phrases with English people?'" He turned his head aside and continued on a subject that seemed so inexplicable I wondered whether he was altogether sane. Tap-tap-tap. "I have a friend in Medias," he went on, "who is a very good carpenter. Where he lives is nowhere near the sea, or a lake. But he bought in a second-hand shop a set of plans for building a small boat. Really no more than a large rowing-boat, but he could fit an outboard motor on to it if he had one. When he can obtain the timber he works on constructing this boat, in his own cellar under the house. Do you understand me? *In his cellar*. He is half-way finished, but he will never get that boat out of his cellar-door and up the cellar stairs – they are too narrow. You think it's all for nothing? *He* doesn't. No. It's for the love of building a boat he will never use unless he pulls his house down to take it out. Or an earthquake knocks it down."

We were both silent for a moment, at the thought of the earthquake in the spring.

"I am learning English I can never use," he continued. "For the pleasure of learning English and reading English for myself. You studied philology at university. One day you might be able to take your boat out and sail it to England."

To England, and Philip Carston, I thought.

– 4 –

I walked home very slowly and reflectively after work that day. I delayed going home because I wanted to think, and the circumstances offered me the chance of being late: I joined a long queue for some mineral water (very long: past the grocery, the pharmacy and the record shop and right round the corner) and succeeded in buying two bottles. Walking home hugging them, I continued to think about what I had finally said to Mr Radin, and why I said it. I had been struck by the plaintiveness of his boat metaphor; drawn from life, it seemed. I had been an unusually easy convert. What did this tell me about myself?

I told my parents nothing about it that evening. They didn't ask me about my day when they saw the mineral water, which was very desirable to have in the increasing summer heat. We had the usual kind of evening at home. I read. I telephoned Ioana for a chat. I came out of my bedroom for the news on television, *Telejurnal*, in case it revealed anything new. It didn't. We heard what Philip called "that jaunty little tune that closes television transmissions", while the screen shows the image of the sun over Romanian mountains; and then we went to bed.

But how could I sleep? The next day was my birthday. I was twenty-*three* years old. I had not been aware, when I allowed myself to make that decision with Mr Radin, that my birthday falling on the very next day would leave me feeling I had made some kind of new beginning. My sudden decision left me feeling both an older person and a changed person. Should I see myself in the mirror in different clothes – some severely cut, expensive style perhaps – and with new, stern lines on my face?

When the telephone rang so early next morning – I was up, and dressed – the line was not clear. And it sounded as if the voice came from very far away. It was very indistinct.

"Mr Carston, how are you?" I was saying, with stupefied pleasure.

"Miss Predeanu, I am well!" he said. "This is to wish you a happy birthday, provided I have the right day."

"You *have* the right day," I said, laughing with joy. "You have a good memory."

"I have a meticulous mind," he insisted. "Anyway, very happy birthday."

We were then both at a loss as to how to go on. I was aware how much this call would be costing, and that took away all power of speech.

"This is the cheapest time to phone," he said, as if reading my mind.

"It is before five o'clock for you?"

"Ten to five. It's just getting light round the edges of the curtains. I've been awake for an hour. I think I drank too much last night... What will you be doing today?"

"Some friends will bring some wine, and some food. We will have a small party, that's all."

"I wish I could be there. It would be more fun than working here."

"It would for me... I cannot think how you remembered my birthday..."

"*I* can."

When I put down the phone I did remember. I had told him and asked him his own in Constanta.

"Why do you ask? If I tell you, are you going to say I'm a

bloody *Pisces* or something?"

Contemptuous italics. I laughed.

"No. It's just that the last four times I have asked people's birthdays it has always been the same month – November. It would be such a coincidence if –"

"Bad luck. April. That proves something I believe in very deeply: the fallibility of coincidence. Most coincidences are malicious, but many more coincidences don't happen than do happen."

He went on to explain: there were unlimited possibilities of coincidence every time someone left his or her house. But it would have taken gigantic efforts on the part of destiny to cause more than one in a million coincidences. All the time we are narrowly *missing* each other in the streets, in the lifts, in the corridors. The telephones are ringing in empty rooms because people who just chanced to be there for that one hour in the year had in fact just left. Coincidence is an inaccurate marksman.

I told my parents who it was had telephoned; but I so wanted to tell a friend. It was still early, and I had no special need to be at the office before eight. So when I left the house at seven-twenty I turned left instead of right, crossed the Avenue of the Pioneers near the tram depot, and went on down Strada Sinaia until it widened out and became 1848 Boulevard and ended in the Piata Stefan cel Mare.

The small Museum of the Romanian Communist Party, the only one outside Bucharest, stood on the far side. It's never easy to cross the road there at that time of the morning, the buses and trams are taking thousands of people out to work in the industrial suburbs. But my excitement sent me scurrying dangerously across and running up the sloping approach to the Museum. Only when I was inside and halfway along the gallery leading to Ioana's office did I realise how much I was going to reveal.

And how much I was going to confirm for myself: Because to reveal out loud to someone, suddenly, what is on your mind about a third person clarifies your feeling by placing it on record.

From that moment it is irremovable from someone else's memory, and it is engraved on your own behaviour.

I knocked as I entered Ioana's room, and saw her at that second as a colleague or stranger would see her, sitting down at her desk to begin the day with a sheaf of papers in front of her, looking very officially correct and cold. Ioana relaxed and smiled, though, when she saw me smiling; and I closed the door firmly behind me.

"Philip Carston telephoned me an hour ago to wish me a happy birthday – from England," I said.

Now she smiled more warmly, with an amused look.

"And you have fallen in love with him?"

"Why do you say that?" I really was shocked, though I was still smiling and trembling with delight.

"Because you have talked about no one else for months," Ioana said. "Well – I congratulate you. And happy birthday, by the way."

"Yes," I said. "And yesterday I joined the Communist Party."

"Well done!" Ioana said; and laughed. "Then my guided tour was not a waste of time."

– 5 –

The Party Museum had been open for just a year, and Ioana's job was multifarious: assistant curator with care of exhibits, translator of materials received in French and Hungarian (her mother was an ethnic Hungarian), guide for visitors. I had been at school with her, and at university we overlapped for two years (she being two years older than me). She thought the best way of showing me what her job was like – I often asked – was to show me round one day with some foreign visitors.

They were French Communists with their guide, man and

wife, quick-witted, sceptical, not very appreciative of Ioana's efforts. Ioana came out to meet them – and me – in the square front hall with its drapery of banners and the mural of several centuries of Romanian history up to the present, with Nicolae and Elena Ceausescu evident in the foreground, the President bearing a sceptre. The French couple seemed used to guided tours like this and walked on too fast for Ioana's prepared patter – "and this – and this" – she pointed out breathlessly, as she struggled to keep up with their incurious stares. It was not until she reached the 1930s and 1940s that she suddenly held their attention.

Suddenly her own account of events became more confident, even passionate. The visitors looked with interest on pictures of their own Communist leaders – Thorez, Duclos – in Romanian newspapers of the period, yellowing in glass cases. They listened with courtesy when Ioana spoke of the fascist Iron Guard and their murder of fifty liberal opponents in their homes in one night. All this she had learnt at her father's knee: Ion Guranu had been as faithful a Communist fighter in the pre-Ceausescu days as you could find.

Did I suspect something of her father's private views when Ioana reached the Ceausescu exhibits? Here the French Communist visitors paused for longer than anywhere else, as if wanting to check the appropriateness of admitting our President to the pantheon of Communist immortals. They asked questions about his village birth and early life which Ioana answered only dutifully. When they put awkward supplementary enquiries to her she hesitated, tended to go back over the same ground as if she knew nothing more. I knew she was the daughter of someone who *believed*, but had never risen beyond the rank of respected Party official in the provincial city of his birth; while unbelievers who hitched themselves shamelessly to Ceausescu's wagon had done far better. The Guranus had their villa in a tree-lined street; but it was a small house with rooms of inconvenient shape and size. When later Mr Guranu retired, its too large kitchen filled with bottles of his home-made wine.

The French passed the display, under glass, of books written about President Ceausescu by foreign authors, and published by foreign publishing houses like Mr Maxwell's, and turned to look at the small array of photographs of the President in his early years: the young man in a group on a balcony, in a crowd near his wife to be, among young Communists on the back of a lorry. And there he was at the back of a committee photograph of important Communist figures in – about 1940? Or *was* he? That young figure didn't seem to be looking either fixedly at the camera or heedlessly away from it.

"Is that really your President?" the French woman enquired sharply.

"Of course," Ioana replied. "He was a very young man when that photograph was taken."

"I can see that," said the visitor. "I can also see that he arrived a little too late to be in the original photograph and had to be included later."

Ioana said nothing at all, and led us all away to the last rooms in the Museum.

"We are nearly finished now," she said. "These rooms represent the epoch of Ceausescu." Almost indifferently she indicated the big coloured pictures, the clean factories and sunny cornfields. The French acknowledged with casual smiles, made no more sceptical remarks, thanked her rather briefly at the door, and disappeared with their guide into the street.

That had been in the previous autumn, and around then Mr Guranu had started to make me regular gifts of his wine. So today, on my birthday, I called back at the museum after work to collect a promised "bottle or two of the best" on the way home. Ion Guranu grew grapes, apricots, peaches and mulberries in quantities in the garden behind their house, which was a sunny tangle of fruit-laden bushes in the summer. The wine was brewed in his garden shed, but the shed had overflowed and the kitchen was beginning to be a wine-cellar and bottle store. Ilona Guranu, Ioana's mother, despaired.

Of course Mr Guranu was a drinker. When sober he was given to a rough, sometimes even obscene, humour which you learned to live with if you spent any time in his company. But after drinking his mood changed: he became solemn and earnest and indiscreet, a strange fire came into his eyes that spoke of an idealism still alive in his mind yet increasingly frustrated. In that year, 1977, I remember him saying – I can see him sitting on the one bench in the overgrown garden, a short, solidly-built, badly-shaven figure (his dark beard grew quickly and he never had enough razor blades, even as a Party official) – that no, things were not quite as good as in the hopeful early years of Nicolae Ceausescu, but they were better than in the horrifying period before that, there were hardly any food queues, the restaurants functioned, the trams didn't stop because of power cuts. There was culture on television. He did not like to see the portrait of the President appearing in more and more places, newspapers making it an obligation to print it on the front page. But given time, things would come right. The memories of the young could only be short: how could you expect them to feel what their parents and grandparents had experienced in the 1920s and 1930s, before there was modern industry and transport? A New Man would slowly be created as society became more civilised and less selfish; but it would take time, and the West would spare no effort to prevent it and pull us back into greed and violence. Such was Ion Guranu's case, expounded with more passion the more his own mulberry wine warmed him to it.

On that birthday Ioana and I sat after work in the strong, serene late afternoon sunshine on the garden bench, with full wine glasses on the wooden table in front of us – "a little drop while you're waiting," Mr Guranu said, while he went into the shed and the house to find some bottles for me to carry away for my birthday party. We smelt the scents of the garden, saw the sunshine on the shifting leaves and branches. We could hear distant laughter in other gardens, we were young people with work and with hopes – well, with vague hopes – and in a socialist country, Ion Guranu insisted; and we were content. We had the freedom security allows. We tried the wine. It was good; and in the sunshine, time would not pass. I remember Ioana saying how surprised she had been to see me enter her office early in the morning; but not for a second anxious because I was smiling so ecstatically.

"You knew your feelings before today?"

"No. Well – at least – I never *said* it to myself."

"You never said it to *Philip* in Bucharest – or Constanta?"

"*No*. Never *anything*."

"Are you sure you *know* what you feel?"

Can you believe this? I had spent almost all the day at work trying to define the nature of the feeling I had, if I had it, and I believed I had been successful; but when Ioana faced me with that question – the older, wiser student talking to the younger one – I realised I had no clear answer at all.

"I know – I know that I feel –"

I waited, because Ioana's father was walking across, within earshot, from the shed to the kitchen. Ioana waited.

"I feel that I have formed a spiritual love."

"What you mean is a deep *friendship*?"

"I would call it a *very* deep friendship," I replied.

What Ioana thought she saw was someone experiencing love but unwilling to admit it to herself until she was sure. And because even spiritual love, or very deep friendship, is only complete if the other person is able to respond, Ioana then said,

"Did Philip express any feelings towards you?"

For a moment it reduced me to feeling ridiculous. I had seen how some women could be so pathetically hopeful in this situation, clutching at straws in men's words or gestures or casual undertakings.

"Yes. Several things he said and did. And he writes to me. And he *telephoned*!"

She nodded firmly and reassuringly, smiling.

"Is he planning to come back to Romania?"

"When he left he said he really hoped so." But I had told her this more than once.

"Here you are! You can drink to your country – and your birthday," Mr Guranu declared, banging down on the table six of his best bottles, concealed in brown paper in a wicker basket. The wine in my glass swayed and spilt. The droplets on the table glistened. I picked up the glass, and raised it in thanks to Ion Guranu; and Ioana and I smiled vividly and knowingly at each other, having information Mr Guranu did not possess. This was my twenty-third birthday. I was happy.

– 6 –

I did not blame Tamasi for shirking his responsibility over Eva Vajna's manuscript; but I did resent Dr Mandeliu's sleight of hand in passing the problem on to me – because he could not persuade Tamasi to solve it.

He had been all smiles and warmth towards me in the weeks after my birthday. I had still to come to terms with this relaxation of his normal severity, and with subtle changes in the attitudes of others after my recruitment to the Party. Dr Mandeliu let me see, genially, that he was trusting me with more responsibility. This allowed him to enter my room one afternoon early that winter – December, or late November, I think – in a friendly and yet sheepish manner, exclaiming loudly, perhaps even nervously,

"I have Mrs Eva Vajna in my office. She should be talking to the Hungarian section, but she insists on coming to me. I really am too busy to talk to *her* for the rest of the morning! Can you see her, please, about her manuscript?

I had forgotten about Mrs Vajna all that time. I assumed Tamasi had settled the problem. I was amazed this task was coming to me as a non-Hungarian, and rather alarmed.

"This is the *same* novel – ? But I haven't read it."

"Neither has Tamasi Ilosz," Dr Mandeliu declared with an

angry sigh, raising his hands in the air. "That is the problem. Tell her – tell her it has been passed to you, there have been delays, but you *will* read it and give her a report."

I was horrified. Was I so responsible now that I had to take on deeply embarrassing tasks that other people could not face? Have to see Mrs Vajna and make excuses? Invent reasons of paper shortages, or hint that her book was not quite correct, politically?

"Tamasi Ilosz *should* have read it," I said, rather angrily. "Why isn't he seeing her?"

"She came straight up to my office!" complained Dr Mandeliu, as if he hadn't been able to keep her out.

"Tamasi could see her anyway. Surely *he* should report on a Hungarian book?"

"Mrs Vajna refuses to *let* him report on the book." He dropped his voice. "She says he is prejudiced against her because he is a member of the Party."

But this was farcical. The Director himself was a senior Party member, Mrs Vajna could have been sure of that. I imagined that she was simply going over Tamasi's head to higher authority, in the hope of spiting Tamasi and obtaining some action.

"I will go and see Tamasi now," I said.

"It will be no use. *You* see her. You can put off a decision a bit longer."

He brought Mrs Vajna down. As she entered my room I could not help reflecting that what I felt about Philip had unconsciously – yet not *so* unconsciously – swayed me to accept Mr Radin's proposition; and that accepting it had led to my having to see Eva Vajna; and that seeing Mrs Vajna might require my needing to go and see Professor Bobolescu, since Tamasi obviously would not. I had brought these problems on myself. All these events do relate to Philip in very curious ways...

Eva Vajna had dressed well, even attractively, for this venture into our office. I wondered where she had bought (or who had made her a gift of) the extremely clean and smart denim skirt, the white blouse, the very dark blue cardigan. I had half-expected that she would come nervously, even tearfully. I was wrong. She presented an image of the utmost assurance and resolve, hanging her coat on my coat-stand without invitation and sitting down at once, pointedly repositioning the chair exactly where she preferred it. Then she clasped her hands together on her lap, looked at me with head erect, and smiled. Eva was letting me know that she could have spoken first if she had chosen to, but she was prepared to let me begin.

"Dr Mandeliu says you've come about your novel," I began tentatively in Hungarian; and she nodded. "It needs to have more than just one reader before we can decide on it. I'm afraid we have been taking a long time with it –"

"Since April. In eight months – *nine* months – *ten* people could have read it." But she still smiled, with amiable assurance, with no anger in her voice.

"I have to give you our apologies," I continued. "I also have to say that I am at the beginning, because I have only just been asked to be one of the readers."

"How long will it take you to read it?"

"Ten days, perhaps. A fortnight."

"I hope you will read it thoroughly – and carefully," she said. "Tamasi Ilosz is not a careful reader. He does not read between the lines."

"I will read it," I said, feeling very selfless and responsible.

"Your Hungarian is good?"

"I read Hungarian. My grandmother is Hungarian."

Mrs Vajna smiled.

"And I will see about reporting to you fairly soon," I said; feeling arrogantly efficient. I was not going to talk about the many other books waiting to be published, all the other excuses; and I believe she appreciated that. But Eva was not going to let me off lightly.

"Here is my phone number," she said, leaning over and writing it on the top sheet of her latest revisions.

As I talked with Eva I resolved that I would shame Tamasi for shirking this task – and refer the problem to Professor Bobolescu myself. If the book was as unpublishable as Tamasi believed, Bobolescu would have to admit that, and be prepared to break the news to Eva for us. It would require courage, and tact, to approach him, but I felt confident that I had it.

I escorted Mrs Vajna downstairs and along the cold corridor to the front door. As I opened the door for her I experienced a strange moment of strength and elation. The city looked fresh and neat under the snow. Low lights were on in the shops and offices, light traffic moved slowly to and fro across this stage set, its sounds hushed and at the same time resonant in the clear air. Naturally I had seen magazine and television pictures of the colourful, glowing cities of the West – even those of Hungary and Yugoslavia – and they made me avid to see them. I had asked Philip about London ("I go there as rarely as possible!") But Târgu Alb in a good winter (snowy and clear, and without dangerously low temperatures) seemed to me to be the more beautiful. For one thing, you could see the shapes of the buildings which bright lighting (including neon advertisements) would have concealed with its own uniformity of colour.

I collected Eva Vajna's manuscript and took it home to read that evening.

I think – I dare to hope! – that I make quite a good publisher in Eastern European terms. I knew as a matter of course that I could read a manuscript looking for enduring quality rather than twists of saleable oddity or sensation. Our authors do not understand the motives of Western authors in seeking to sell their books with "newness" or "sexiness" for its own sake. If a novel or a book of poems is good, with or without such attributes, it will sell very well in this country. Our readers are intelligent: remember they do not have pornography shops, there is no commercial television. Therefore I could read Mrs Vajna's novel without asking myself if it would sell enough to make "a decent profit." I could read it and make a wholly literary judgement. It did not need to be on the level of Tolstoy, or George Eliot, or Joyce, or Virginia Woolf, or E.M.Forster – as long as it was well–constructed and readable in its own right.

In fact it was appallingly bad. It was a love story, set in an historical past without an exact date and in a locality I could not place. At one moment it could not have been *before* the 1848 revolutions, in another chapter it had to be *after*. It contained a town which resembled a much smaller nineteenth century Târgu Alb, but it was not clear whether Eva intended the place to be, at that point, in distant Hungary or what was to become Romania. The action was over-vigorous, melodramatically romantic; and yet the love scenes were slow and wooden.

But if I was going to dare to hint at all this to Professor Bobolescu, I had to know what he had said when he had commended the novel to Tamasi Ilosz in the first place – his third attempt with a book of Eva's. I had to talk to Tamasi before I went to see the professor. But it was nearly office closing time before I could meet him alone.

"All right. Get your coat," he said to me, almost curtly. "We'll talk about this somewhere else."

"Where?"

We walked out into the snow, getting our feet wet as it had begun to melt into a grey slush. We crossed the square, not heading towards the restaurant of the Hotel Transilvania but stopping at the cellar restaurant, which was quiet at this time on a midwinter afternoon. I was finally keeping my non-existent promise to drink some wine with Tamasi Ilosz.

It was Tamasi's curt, abstracted air that deceived me, or so I say now. I thought he only wished to talk briefly about the matter of Eva Vajna's book – certainly all I wanted was some quick information from him. I started even before the wine arrived.

"You have *read* the novel?"

"Not all of it."

"I have read all of it. You are going to have to turn it down, aren't you!"

"Someone has to," he said.

"Dr Mandeliu doesn't deal with such matters himself."

We were sitting in one of the cavernous alcoves of the restaurant; out of sight of anyone else, if indeed there was anyone else at all in the place. As Tamasi said "Exactly," he placed his hand on mine, almost as a spontaneous gesture of emphasis. But not just that, because he did not take it away again.

It was a transparent tactic; but it worked, because I had not expected it from his earlier manner. Was I surprised into letting him leave it there? He lifted my hand from the table and looked at it while apparently considering how to reply. Then he interlocked the fingers of his own hand with my fingers, and smiled as if he had settled something. Which I suppose he had. And I felt guilty, and uneasy. What he suggested next was not the only thing he had settled. Still holding my hand tightly, he said,

"One of us is going to have to ask a different person to break it to Eva. Isn't she!"

And I *could* have taken my hand away, but I didn't. I could have disentangled it quite politely, and folded my arms, or picked up my wine glass while he went on talking. And given the responsibility for visiting Professor Bobolescu firmly back to him. I had been walking past Tamasi's hinting smiles on the stairs, or in the lunch room, or in the corridor, for months – and the first time he contrives a serious approach to me I do not resist it. Why? I had theories. One was that it was an act of rebellion against the correct (middle-aged?) behaviour expected of me when I joined the Party. Another was that with Philip, a man showing, albeit in his very English way, a kind of affection towards me – perhaps (that phone call) turning into something more – I had realised I was a person who could be loved; and I could not be sure I would ever see Philip again...

How to arrange my crucial appeal to Professor Bobolescu? I thought I knew *what* to do: appeal to his wisdom as a scholar. I decided to make it ostensibly a social call, go as a young worker in the publishing house sitting at his feet and asking for the benefit of his knowledge and experience in literary matters. Among those matters would be Eva Vajna's unpublishable book.

How could I know this would alter all my relations with Philip Carston?

Liviu Bobolescu arranged to invite me to his home three days later. He came alone to the grand door of his large villa in a quiet avenue, kissed my hand gracefully, took my coat and my heavy carrier bag, and showed me into his study where we sat by ourselves, in two facing armchairs. There was coffee in a pot, and chilled mineral water, and a plate of cakes, and the faintest smell of cooking from somewhere in the house; but no sign of other people, no sounds.

I took one cake when he perfunctorily offered them, but was too nervous to eat it. He ate all the others avidly, listening to my prepared speech, all attention, even though he would occasionally rise from his chair and gaze thoughtfully along a row of volumes on a shelf.

I lied a little. I said various people had recommended I speak to him, in general terms, about the kinds of books a lively state publishing house should be producing. Professor Bobolescu reacted without surprise, rather as if he would naturally expect young graduates working for the publishing house to consult him. When I had finished, he started questioning me. Question *after* question.

What had I read? What did I most enjoy reading? Who were the Romanian classic authors who meant most to me? Eminescu? Caragiale? Arghezi? What foreign authors had made most impression? So I had studied English at the university? He switched to fluent English. Did I love Shakespeare? Which plays? Which women? Did I like Rosalind and Portia? Viola? Or did I sympathise more with Cordelia? Did I admire Perdita in *The Winter's Tale*? He would so like to know.

"I – I don't know," I said. I could remember little about *The Winter's Tale*. I wished I had never come. All my brave resolution about my persuading him to return Eva Vajna's novel – in the carrier bag beside my chair – had vanished.

"Perdita is a spirit of beauty surviving in a region of rude manners and peasant ignorance," he declared. "'What she does still betters what is done'," he quoted, still in English. I did not understand him; my confusion was deep and desperate. "Her guardian, you can almost say, is a *nouveau riche*, he becomes a *bourgeois* shepherd." He smiled at his own notion. "But Perdita remains an example of untouched purity. She is an inspiration to all around her. Yes."

For a moment he was apparently lost in incoherent reflection, and fell into silence. This gave me time to recover something of my dispersed courage.

"There is a particular thing I wish to ask you, Professor Bobolescu," I said in a rush. "I have read the manuscript of a novel by Mrs Eva Vajna, which I am told you have also seen. We have a problem with it. We admire what Mrs Vajna is trying to do, but we do not think the book is good enough to publish. Some people think there are political problems."

His reaction was immediate, and impatient.

"But there are not political problems with that book. I know it very well and I do *not* admire it. You are being too generous – compassionate, perhaps. Give it to me – I will make sure Mrs Vajna has it back."

"You mean – ?"

"Do you have it in that bag? Yes? Give it here, please. It is a very bad novel. It was a mistake."

What was a "mistake"?

"She will be very disappointed."

"Mrs Vajna will not be so disappointed if it is returned by me as she would if someone at the publishing house were returning it. Can we forget about it? I am sure you did not come here only to talk about that? I am quite sure you write yourself?"

"No, but –"

"But what?"

"I should like to translate something. Before I –"

"Before you what? Before you write anything?"

"Yes. But that doesn't mean I *want* to write anything. Or can." I was rehearsing my vaguest student illusions about translating or writing books, and Liviu Bobolescu was latching on to them.

"If you translated a novel and *then* tried to write a novel," he said, expounding, "you would find nothing in the novel you translated would help you at all. Because the length, and structure and the pace of your own novel must come out of *you* and your own *voice*. You will have to listen first to your own *voice*. Then after that you can learn from translating."

I was silent. It sounded true.

"I am listening," he said. "I am waiting."

What did he mean?

"Go on," he said. "Speak. In your own voice. I am waiting and listening to see if it is a writer's voice."

He was sitting stock still and smiling, his hands resting on his knees. I said nothing.

"Well, I know it is not easy for you just to speak like that," he reassured me. "We can talk about other things. We can talk a little more about Proust."

Which was strange; because he had not spoken of Proust at all. Then the professor realised his mistake. "I mean of Shakespeare," he said. He seemed embarrassed by something, and he frowned; and got up again, and did not know what to say next. After a few moments he began talking about Shakespeare again, and I listened as he spoke and watched me. And then,

"Come back soon," he said all at once. "I don't have many interesting conversations. I knew when I first saw you at the Writers' Union that you had a writer's voice in the way you spoke. You will make your mark as a writer. Come back to–morrow afternoon."

At least twice in his life Liviu Bobolescu had discovered writing talents in much younger women. In the case of his wife, Georgeta, one novel, ordinary yet in some respects quite accomplished, had gone to publication. And he had married her, they had a child of nine. I had expected him to defend the novel which his second or third discovery, Eva Vajna, had delivered to us through him. Eva was a married woman; perhaps the Professor was thinking to change wife and family and move on in his late fifties to a second (at *least* a second) female genius? If so, I had thought, he would defend the book with passion and I would reply with cool reason and require him to return it; he could sort out the matter himself.

But there had been no such passion, only dismissiveness. That afternoon, I gradually came to realise, Professor Liviu Bobolescu had impulsively decided to cast aside the hopeless task of championing Eva Vajna's romantic novels, and transfer all his cunning energies into cultivating me.

SIX

– 1 –

"I've got something very tiresome to tell you," the dry, droll voice told me across space. "They're sending me on another visit to your country. And it's only three years since the last time!"

"I will be your interpreter!" Of course I did not know how I could contrive to be Philip's interpreter. "And if I am not your interpreter, we will have an official meeting in Târgu Alb."

"Why do you think I might be visiting Târgu Alb?"

"Well – it is obvious, I think? Last time you were in Bucharest and Constanta – this time you must go to other centres. Târgu Alb will be the best place."

"Yes, I am sure it will, but –"

"I will arrange it," I said; although at that moment I did not know how I could. But if Philip was actually coming back, nothing seemed impossible.

Until then there had been the very occasional letter, three cards annually, arriving fastidiously just before the appropriate day, five telephone calls in all.

He would ring on my birthday itself, and on my name day. It was on my name day that he was now telephoning to tell me about his visit.

I would have missed these calls, and been profoundly anxious if they had ever stopped. Philip was a connection, not my only one but my most interesting one, with the world beyond my own country. And yet I knew, and Ioana Guranu knew – and probably my lover Tamasi Ilosz sensed – that it went far beyond that.

Did Ioana know about Tamasi? I supposed that a lot of people knew about Tamasi and me. But I never talked about it with Ioana. Some women like to involve their friends fully in the dismal complexity of their emotional lives, their dreams, adventures and compromises. I did not. I remembered so clearly the bright morning I entered Ioana's office in the Party museum and told her about Philip's first phone call. I had no inclination to repeat (and parody?) my actions with a similar but much more uncertain revelation about Tamasi.

I had moved, incidentally. I was very, very lucky, seeing that my parents lived in Târgu Alb, to be given a very small flat for myself. There were new blocks being built, and I had the chance (through circumstances too complicated to explain) of taking my own flat while it was new. Soon it didn't look or feel very new; but it was mine to make my own, and this call was Philip's third to the apartment.

"I don't know *why* they preferred me to more creative and flamboyant people," he went on. "There are shoals of young novelists and poets who would do it much better. Not to mention sculptors – and 'folk groups'."

He said the last two words, with a peculiar contempt. If I had not grown used to Philip's self-deprecating tone during that previous visit, I would have taken him seriously. I knew, though, that he was concealing a pride in being invited, even an eagerness to come; although what I would have liked from him was a hint that he was especially eager to see *me*.

"Mr Carston, I have one thing to tell you that is new," I said very nervously. "I have started writing."

"You *have*?"

"I will tell you about it when you come."

"Do."

"Of course I haven't published anything," I continued in stupid pride, "but I will try to translate a little to show you."

"Hallo?"

"I'm still here," he said. "I – I don't promise to be a very useful critic."

But I had never expected Philip to offer criticism. I was shocked to think he imagined I wanted him to do anything more than just read something I had written and share my pleasure in writing it.

I did manage to secure leave from work to be Philip Carston's guide and interpreter a second time. I don't know who Dr Mandeliu spoke to in Bucharest; nevertheless, it all happened, more simply than I dared to believe. Of course there was the agony of waiting before it was confirmed. But there was the reassurance that *when* something is at last officially sanctioned in Romania, nothing in the world will ever reverse it.

So this time I was there in my own room in the Hotel Vidraru, unpacking my suitcase on the day before I was due to meet Philip at Otopeni. On the spare bed I laid out my clothes, my few cosmetics, the schedule for the first few days of Philip's visit as arranged by the Writers' Union – and my first few pages of manuscript.

I wanted Philip to know that my writing was only and wholly for him. Yes, I was writing to *conciliate* Professor Bobolescu; but I was writing *for* Philip Carston. I was using what the Professor liked to call "my voice" to speak to Philip through the barriers of geography and politics, of physical distance and apartness.

After I had written a first few pages descriptive of things and experiences, descriptive of feelings about them – all prose, obviously, as Philip wrote in prose – I wrote a kind of preface or prelude to my writings, for Philip to read if, or when, the time came, to read alone and even in a prescribed place and at a prescribed time of day. It was in the form of a letter.

"Now I have given you this," it said, "I shall know you are receiving and reading it as a true friend. I shall have asked you to keep it until you have some uninterrupted time when you are alone and warm and calm, in the evening preferably, and when you have music to listen to. Something we both know? In my mind it will be the Beethoven Opus 132, the A Minor – your old box of 78s you told me about?

"I have never seen your room and can only imagine it. But I

can describe my room for you."

I described it, and continued what was to be a secret letter, put in a secret place until the time when it could be handed over, or sent, with its revelatory date at the top; and Philip Carston could know what I had been feeling and writing months before, even years before.

As to Professor Bobolescu: it was sadly, dangerously true that in one afternoon he had chosen me to replace the disappointing Eva Vajna. I did not go back to his house as soon as possible, in the way he demanded – but when I did not, he began his pursuit of me. He would turn up at the office with messages to impart to Dr Mandeliu. If he caught me by myself he pressed on me invitations to private meetings, to lunches, to walks even, so that we could discuss the conversion of my wonderful voice into written words. At first I resolved to tell him I was never going to be a writer, that I never really desired to write anything at all. But since this was wrong, I thought that if I assured him I was slowly writing *something*, then delayed showing it to him almost indefinitely, it might keep him away until he tired of the obsession; or transferred it to someone else.

And then there was Tamasi and my relationship with him, a different kind of problem. I had not really thought of any of this when I as good as insisted that Philip be sent to my home city during his second visit. Unpacking in the hotel I began to see that there were enough potential embarrassments in Târgu Alb to put me in some apprehension about the "official" days we should spend there.

My bedside telephone rang. Methodically, Mrs Oltean from the Writers' Union told me that the Council for Culture had indeed confirmed my visit with Mr Carston to Târgu Alb. I would need no hotel accommodation because I lived in the city myself (I knew that!) and Mr Carston would stay in the Hotel Transilvania, who had notice of the reservation for Wednesday, Thursday and Friday nights in the following week. All the details firmly set out.

Nothing at all had changed at Otopeni itself; unless the movement of people through passport control and customs had become slower. The experience of waiting at a station or an airport for someone I haven't seen for a long time has begun to hold a special kind of unease for me. But I didn't have it on that April day in 1980 when I was simply, greedily eager to meet Philip again. Certainly I was three years older and my life had taken different directions, but I was exactly the same in myself, and Philip would be no different at all.

And yes, he came out of passport control into the baggage reclaim area with the same lost, perplexed air as before, immaculately dressed in his formal English clothes, wholly unchanged in appearance (except that he did not have his English umbrella with him this time.)

The one change was in his attitude to me. Philip greeted me with the relief you show when you realise a friend has come to the rescue in some difficult or hazardous situation.

"Carolina! No one in London knew who would be meeting me. I can't *tell* you what it means to find you here."

"I told you I would be your interpreter."

"But that was months ago. How was I to know they wouldn't forbid you – ?"

"Who would forbid me?" I said.

"You are no different. But I am feeling ten years older. You aren't – married, or anything?"

"I am not married, Philip. I mean *Mr Carston*." It was the mistake you make when you have whispered a name to yourself a thousand times.

"Are we going to – wherever it is you live?"

I knew enough of his offhand English manner not to be disturbed by this pretence that he had forgotten the name of Târgu Alb.

I told him when. The suitcases arrived on the carousel and we trundled them out somehow through the crowd to the Customs. I told a tall, truculent official that Philip was a guest of the Council for Culture and the Writers' Union, and showed letters, but he still insisted Philip open his larger case.

Everything was packed with characteristic neatness: suits, a toilet bag, tablets, a little box of shoe-cleaning equipment – and several large notepads. Having gone this far, the Customs man felt obliged to ask a question about something. He picked up one of these notepads and asked what it was. He riffled through the blank pages, did this with a second, and a third. He asked for Philip's passport, saw the word "Author", and seemed to be placated when I translated that for him. But then he asked if Philip was a journalist. I told him he was not.

Under the notepads he found a book; as it turned out, the only book Philip had brought with him: *Tess of the d'Urbervilles*, by Thomas Hardy. The official opened it with duteous curiosity: it was a new paperback edition with a glamorous illustration of Tess on the cover. He asked whether it was pornography. Philip caught the word and smiled. "Ninety years ago it was," he said.

"Are you hoping to write something while you are here?" I asked him in the bus to the city centre (I was now considered too experienced to need a car, which would also be expensive).

"I don't know," he said, cagily. "I haven't written anything for some time."

"But why did you bring so many writing pads?"

"I do know that. I was wondering whether I could set myself at a distance from England – from Britain – while I was abroad, and write something about it. I certainly *feel* distant already." He gazed out of the window. "Are there more of these than before? It seems to me there are." He was pointing out roadside signs with messages like TRAIASCA PARTIDUL COMUNIST ROMAN.

The surprises for Philip began at Reception. On hearing his name, even before asking for his passport and pushing across a form to fill in, the blonde receptionist smiled and presented him with a letter. Philip's astonishment was virtually terror, as if someone dangerous was already on his track.

"What is this?" he exclaimed. "Marked 'Personal'?"

"Many people know you are here," I said, covering up. I had not expected this approach so soon. "You are very popular in Romania." I said it half as a joke, half seriously, with a touch of pride also. Philip held the letter as if it was likely to explode. The receptionist was waiting for her form to be filled, holding Philip's room key in one hand, tapping it on the palm of the other. Philip put the letter down. It was marked 'By hand', and I saw without undue surprise that it was in a handwriting I knew, Liviu Bobolescu's.

Surely Philip was going to open it at once, out of pure curiosity? No, he wasn't. When we finally bundled his suitcases into the lift he still held the letter unopened in his hand. When we went down to eat together in the restaurant, with the same circulating violinist as last time playing, I expected him to produce it from his pocket. He didn't. I gave him his first allowance of lei, which he received with much eagerness; and this time he tipped the violinist, ten lei, the man receiving it with a profound bow which stopped just, only just, short of profound irony. I noticed that Philip was drinking much more than before.

And then he did take the letter out of his pocket. It consisted of two sheets, closely and yet clearly written, and Philip folded them so that at first only the signature at the end of the letter was visible.

"What should I know about this chap?" he asked. I played for time.

"That is the letter you had from the Reception?"

"Yes. Did you know about it?"

"No."

"I didn't think you did."

He seemed almost overwhelmingly embarrassed, lost for his next sentence. The band now struck up violently, a strident, brutal, smothering noise.

"I do not know why Professor Bobolescu wrote to you. I cannot understand –" I was having to shout to be heard above the rock music they had started on. That probably made me sound almost hysterical. Philip took another gulp of the wine; but he smiled at last.

"Right!" he said. "I think you'd better read it and we'll get it over with," he said.

The letter was written throughout in (so I judged) faultless English. It began with courtesies about Philip's novels that might have had a flattering effect on a vulnerable reader. It showed unexpected knowledge of some of the books. It hoped there might soon be an opportunity to translate something into Romanian. That led him, it said, to his principal reason for writing.

Miss Carolina Predeanu was a young woman of prodigious abilities. His experience in researching the origins and the fulfilment of literary inspiration (thinking of Georgeta, and of Eva Vajna, I gaped at these words!) led him to believe that when Miss Predeanu gave her writings to the world everyone would recognise their originality (I could have cried with embarrassment and shame). In this process he believed Mr Carston had an important part to play. He asked two favours of Mr Carston.

One was that he encourage Miss Predeanu to release some of her manuscripts for others to see. The second was that Mr Carston allow Miss Predeanu the privilege of translating a suitable novel of his own, perhaps something recent or new, so that her own abilities might be affirmed and strengthened by that close contact with the work of a major living writer which only the labour of translation can afford.

This letter, dropped into Philip's hand now (had Professor Bobolescu been here and left it himself?), meant that it had to be discussed with me before we both went to Târgu Alb. There we would certainly be confronted by Liviu Bobolescu himself. The only reason for not discussing it would be if Philip concluded that the letter-writer was mad. I was sickened to think what I was forced to think at once: that Liviu Bobolescu might come between Philip Carston and myself (not Tamasi, but Liviu!) and compromise our friendship. Was this even part of his devious intention? It was intolerable, humiliating. Now I *was* weeping, and having to turn my head away.

Eventually I fought away the tears and found the strength to say, "Professor Bobolescu has no right to say any of this. It is presumptuous. I am very, very angry and very embarrassed. And you – I think you want to go home again?"

"No. I *don't* want to go home again."

Philip's denial and smile left me overjoyed.

"But we are going to have to talk about it," he continued. "These Romanian offers are very touching – as long as they come to nothing. It's very pleasing to think they want to translate me – as long as no one tries it."

"I don't understand you."

"Well firstly, I am not translatable – my language and tone is much too English for that. Secondly, there's nothing remotely of interest to Romanians in anything I've written. My books include cricket matches! Thirdly – and most important – I should feel deeply guilty if anyone actually burdened you, of all people, with the underpaid job of translating me."

"The payment is nothing."

"I'm sure it's nothing. It would be nothing in England."

"I don't mean it's no *money*. I mean the being paid is not important. We don't consider everything in terms of money in my country."

"Don't you? We do in my country. But in any case I wouldn't have you do it for love."

I gasped.

"Do it for – ?"

I hadn't understood the phrase. I thought he was saying I must not do it out of love for him.

"For free," he said. "For no payment whatsoever. For love of doing it and nothing else." And then he added, quickly, "About your own abilities: I don't doubt those. I would just feel guilty if they gave you the burden of translating me."

"None of that about my abilities is true," I said, laying my hand flat on the letter on the table.

"Let's go. I've heard enough Balkan rock for one night."

As he said it, and we rose from our chairs, he put his hand round my waist to guide me away.

– 2 –

When we arrived at the Writers' Union next day there was another surprise.

Someone I had never met before, whose work as a writer I did not know, said a lot during the formal proceedings. This was an official of the Council for Culture, whose exact role in it I never discovered: Stefan Tonaru. Someone said, in a deferential aside when poetry was mentioned, that Mr Tonaru was a poet: he smiled, and accepted the flattery. At the last of all our subsequent meetings he presented Philip with a small volume of verse, and Philip stored it with several similar gifts in a special corner of his suitcase.

All our meetings... Philip and I were to have few daylight hours alone until just before we left for Târgu Alb; because Stefan Tonaru jocularly attached himself to us from the moment when we met him in that dark and haunting room with the green curtains in the Writers' Union where honoured guests were received, and there was no shaking him off. Was he deputed by someone to follow us around Bucharest on our official assignments, to make sure nothing irregular was happening? Day by day he mentioned a tiring burden of work of an unspecified kind, but each day he was back, sometimes as early as breakfast in the hotel, always in time for our first meeting. Philip would say he was exhausted by lunch time, so after lunch Stefan would say, well, let us find a park to relax in. One day we sat in the gardens in front of the Bulandra Theatre, and Philip complained of a mild headache. Stefan offered to find a doctor! He said he knew of an excellent one who lived only five minutes away, in the Strada

Batistei. "Oh, for Christ's sake, it's only a headache," Philip protested. Stefan turned fulsomely apologetic, offered to escort us back to the hotel. Philip tried saying he was perfectly content to sit here in the shade, if he could only do that in peace. But finally he said yes, he would return and take a rest in his room.

We walked back past a bookshop where a long line of people waited at the door.

"What are they waiting for? Food it can't be, if that *is* a bookshop," Philip remarked.

"It is not bread," Stefan said, smiling broadly, when he returned. "It will be a bad time when we are queuing for food in Romania: remember we are a 'most favoured' nation, the West pats us on the back. We are a good dog. No, they are queuing for a new novel."

"*For-a-new-novel?*" Every one of Philip's words was italicised with amazement.

"For a new novel which is rumoured to be critical of some aspects of our system. And of some people."

"They will queue up to buy a *book*?"

"They will have to queue for it if they want a copy. Every copy will be sold by to-morrow. Or by to-night."

"I do think I'm in need of a rest," Philip said.

Standing in the entrance to the full and noisy restaurant, shifting aside to let people pass through the swing doors, Stefan looked strangely despairing for a moment, as if he himself needed our company.

Next morning he had arranged a taxi tour of the city for us, not listening when I told him Philip and I had seen all the sights and monuments on a similar tour last time. Abruptly, near the top of the Bulevard Republicii, when we had only driven for ten minutes or so, he stopped the taxi, paid off the driver, marched us across the Cismigiu Park, and led us to that pavilion by the waterside where we could sit at a table, and watch the swans, and eat ice cream.

All the time he had seemed fidgety and uneasy. Stefan had

been an inexplicable nuisance for several days, almost spoiling the visit, certainly leaving me with so much less time alone with Philip in Bucharest, but now, all at once: "I have to tell you both something which I wish you to regard as confidential," he said. "*I am not so happy at some of the things happening in our country. Now who can I tell but two friends like you?* Mr Carston, you have no part in our affairs in Romania, but I implore you to keep a secret and not refer to me among your friends you speak about, in the British Embassy." In fact we had not been to the Embassy, though Philip had twice asked me if I knew anyone there. "And you, Miss Predeanu, are young, and from a city where things are at least a little different. I take a risk with you, but I know you will not let me down."

"I shall say nothing to anyone at all," Philip assured him, with a look of consternation which said, "I have come to a bizarre and frightening country where anything might happen."

I believe that at that moment I made an important decision for myself. I was obliged, as a Party member, to reveal any information I received which might relate to activities detrimental to the Party, or denigratory of the Party. In theory I could be punished for not revealing it; though now, in 1980, with President Ceausescu in control of things, it did not seem nearly so serious a possibility as it had been under his predecessor. But that day in Cismigiu Park I suddenly and instinctively defined *for myself* the boundaries of my loyalty to the Party. I would report, but not inform.

Stefan Tonaru now gave me my escape clause.

"Regard anything I say as not having been said, not having been heard by you. *I will never have said it.* I have written some criticism of recent productions in the theatres of Bucharest in a long article for the magazine *Stralucire*" – I suppose you could translate that as "radiance", or "bright light" – "and there are attacks on the cultural policy of the Socialist Republic. I think this could bring me serious trouble."

Stefan appeared exhausted by these revelations, drained,

deeply unhappy, and yet relieved to be able to mention them to someone. But why had he prefaced this confession with several days of his attentions, at his own expense? To gain our confidence first, to enlist friends for the future?

Naturally I could discuss none of this with Philip. I was still thinking and worrying about it, keeping the anxiety to myself, when we were driven to Baneasa, the domestic flights airport, by Valeria Ciudea two days later. She was representing her publishing house, officially, but I thought she had arranged the lift for other reasons. Normally she spoke in English all the time in Philip's presence; that day she wanted to talk to me only, in Romanian, even a rather complicated Romanian of which Philip would grasp less than nothing.

"Did you see our acquaintance from the Council for Culture again. I hear he was giving you a lot of time?"

"He was with us *all* the time. I can't understand why."

"I can't either, Carolina."

She was silent for a moment. And then,

"Have you seen today's *Stralucire*?"

I could not show foreknowledge of Stefan Tonaru's article. I said I had not seen the magazine.

"He's written something. Something quite long."

"Has he? What does it say?" I was alarmed that people were once again having to talk cautiously about matters like this, as they had, so they told me, in the first post-war years: President Ceausescu's early years had been so much freer.

"You will read it. What he's done is very risky. Or so it appears. I've even heard that *she* is asking to see him for a talk."

Could this really be true? That the President's wife, who liked to watch cultural matters closely, would actually call in a writer to question him about unorthodox opinions?

"Is he so important?"

"The magazine is important."

"Will she want to see Vladeanu?" Vladeanu was the editor of *Stralucire*.

"I don't know. Perhaps this article has been approved?" Valeria speculated.

When we had unloaded our luggage at Baneasa, Valeria turned to Philip with a smile.

"I am sorry we were talking what you call 'shop', I believe? Perhaps you would like to both come to dinner with me one evening when you come back to Bucharest?"

"I should like that very much," Philip said quickly, with some of the most genuine pleasure he had yet shown on a frustrating visit. He looked at me as he said it. He had taken the point too, realising the risk Valeria was taking in inviting a foreigner to her home without official permission. That is, *if* she had no official permission.

One short conversation, in the car that day, ten minutes' guarded talk with all its unelaborated hints and nuances, had been a milestone in my adult relations with Valeria. We had been close and confiding friends as students in university. Valeria was the friend I spoke to in term time, in the same way I spoke to Ioana Guranu in the holidays. But graduating from university, getting employed, moving in different circles, all this separated us. We had grown up. I could not be sure I was still in the same relation of trust with her. Our exchanges that day in the car seemed to me – seemed – to prove that we were.

– 3 –

Before the days in Târgu Alb I was stricken with the fear that I would never get a single hour in which to talk to Philip alone, settle his doubts about Professor Bobolescu's letter. I had expected so very much from this visit, and time was wasting away with nothing said. I felt we were being prevented by circumstances from making the same personal contact we had made in Constanta three years before.

The first face I saw at the airport was that of Georgeta Bobolescu. She had pushed to the front of the little waiting crowd, and Liviu was just behind – but just behind *him* was Eva Vajna! After seeing these three I expected to see almost anyone or everyone else I could name from among my colleagues or Party acquaintances; except that you could not say this was an official delegation. The most "official" was the fourth, and he was equally unexpected: Tamasi.

Later I heard that Bobolescu had come to follow up his letter to Philip, and Georgeta had brought him, mainly because he couldn't drive, but also to interfere with any plan he might be implementing in respect of me. Tamasi had come (he said) because he thought Philip should be aware that the Hungarian culture was the most vital culture in the region; but his arrival fitted in with his wish to observe any relationship between Philip and myself. Eva had come because she had turned up in the office as he was leaving to meet us. She too had a dual motive, as became clear a long time after: the notion had entered her mind that she might find, by meeting Philip, openings to publish in the West the novels of hers which had been rejected in Romania...

It was a deeply odd and fulsome and embarrassing occasion. Philip assumed that any people coming to greet him were cultural dignitaries of whom he should take note. I had to make introductions and explain. I introduced Tamasi first, as the nearest to an official host and because I wanted to hold back Professor Bobolescu and not let him take command of Philip. Tamasi said, "I can tell you what you would like to know about Hungarian writers in this region." Philip told me that this beginning weighed down on him very hard, because he was still far from grasping what the Romanian culture was all about.

As we milled around in the late afternoon light on the forecourt of the terminal building, Tamasi took me aside and told me that this curious confluence of people was accidental, he hadn't been able to foresee it. And it was while we were speaking that I saw Professor Bobolescu engage Philip in some quiet, rapid conversation. I could only catch Philip's face in profile, listening – "in sufferance", he said later – and nodding. When Philip finally murmured some remark to terminate the conversation the Professor gave a radiantly artful smile, as if he had won a victory.

Philip drew away from Liviu with some such formula as "We can discuss this later," came back to where I was standing with Tamasi, and readily allowed himself to be manoeuvred into Tamasi's Dacia. He chatted agreeably with Tamasi (whose English is good) on the way into town, and warmed to him. "The only sane character in the group," he said later; another surprise. He even asked whether Tamasi had used his excellent English with other English visitors. I sat silently with Eva Vajna in the back, and the Bobolescus followed on in their Oltcit by themselves.

The entire group reassembled ridiculously in the foyer of the Hotel Transilvania, dropping Philip's belongings onto the small, square, hard armchairs that you see in most hotel vestibules; where Reception had no information about a room reserved for 'Mr Philip'. Everyone was insistently helpful, angry with the Hungarian clerks behind the counter who rattled off grievances into their telephones in vain, Tamasi arguing with them in Hungarian, Liviu in Hungarian *and* Romanian, Liviu apologising constantly to Philip in English.

"When I eventually *do* have a room," Philip said to me softly, "I will take a brief rest to recover and then call you, in Reception – if you can wait?"

They finally named a room, and produced a key, and he retired with his luggage, looking relieved and exhausted. His welcoming party dispersed, apparently content that for now it had done its duty by Philip Carston and Târgu Alb. I waited, and Philip's call came in five minutes.

"Are you alone down there?" he asked.
"Yes."
"What the hell is going on?"

"Shall I come up and tell you?" I had lost any fear that it would not seem correct.

"Can you come now?"

When I knocked at Philip's door at the end of the empty and dark corridor, he was there ready, and opened it so quickly that I jumped with fear. Closing the door, he put one of his writing pads in my hand, open where he had written in pencil: "Is it all right to talk here?"

He tried to give me the pencil for a written reply, but I said aloud, "Why shouldn't we talk? No one will be interested here." At once I realised I had given away a suspicion that in some places they *might* be interested. "We are not talking business secrets," I added quickly.

My manuscript translated by me into English was on the table between the two beds where we relaxed and smoked. "Hadn't I better read it?" he said. I nodded before I could have second thoughts. I watched every single movement of his face as he did that, fearful to the point of terror. I dreaded most of all that he would read through to the end giving no sign of what he thought – and then deliver some faint praise by way of consolation.

Instead, Philip Carston raised his eyebrows two or three times as he read, smiled once, nodded, pursed his lips emphatically as he reached the last sentence, then picked up the several pages and collected them together, pausing to look back over one or two passages.

"In my opinion," he said – I trembled – "you have a little way to go. But it could be worse. In fact, I am impressed." And then he began to ask questions. To me that was praise enough for me to believe that I *could* write and should continue.

And then we talked through everything he needed to have explained about Liviu Bobolescu and his letter, and the deputation that had arrived at the airport. Now I believed everything was back on the level of understanding we had known three years before; or a deeper level. Philip heard the whole story: about my certainty that Liviu Bobolescu would have tried to turn me into his mistress (and wife?) if he had been ten years younger, but that even encouraging me from a distance in the way he did made him hardly less of a nuisance; and about his regarding Philip as a potential instrument in starting my literary career.

"At the airport," Philip said, "when I was introduced, could you hear what was going on with the Professor? You couldn't! It was about my giving him a novel of mine for you to translate. He says you're keen to translate something now you have begun to write yourself."

"What did you tell him?"

"What I told you. Nothing I'd written would be suitable. If ever I *did* write something suitable then he could see it. I have a kind-of idea I might develop..."

"You said *that*? What did he say then?"

"He said he would regard it as a promise. I made an excuse and dropped the subject."

"But you have given him an opportunity," I said.

"What sort of opportunity?"

"You will see," I said resignedly.

"Would he assume I know the things you've just told me – about his wife, and Mrs Vajna, and *their* novels?"

"No, *no*." I shook my head very hard. "But he will assume that we are collaborating about him. 'Working together'. That is, *if* we are working together?"

The idea of "working together" was such an intriguing thought...

"Yes, we could possibly be working together," Philip added. "And we need some tactics" – putting out a hand which I grasped with relief and delight. He pressed it.

"We need a policy," I said. He looked at me smiling, and let my hand fall.

"Yes. It is different," he said. "Tactics come first, policy later. I'll try to let you know whether I have a policy before I return to England."

I was fairly sure he was saying that if he did develop this idea for writing the "suitable" book I could translate, he would tell me. And if he wanted to begin it while he was in my country he had enough writing pads to work with!

"The tactic for to-morrow, or whenever we next meet him," he explained, "is to play it coolly. A little courteously and distantly."

"English people are very good at that."

"How many do you know?"

"You. And you are very good at it."

"Sometimes I don't think so." He picked up my hand again and looked at the palm.

"You are a palm-reader? What can you see?"

"God almighty, no!" he exclaimed, and let the hand fall as if it was infected. "Look, I might as well tell you, though I hardly ever talk about my plans in case nothing comes of them. I abandoned the book I'd been writing before I first came to Romania. I haven't written anything for a long time. But – I told you – I did have this feeling that I could write something about England if I distanced myself from it – it's partly why I accepted the invitation to come here again. Something your Professor said to me at the airport gave flesh to the notion. And now reading your manuscript..."

What he elaborated there and then, gave me a hope and a happiness I could not begin to describe. It concentrated our alliance. And it made all my previous yearnings for the development of this friendship seem cloudy and primitive.

– 4 –

Next day came the full official welcome in the Writers' Union with everyone present, with the President of the Union, and the Vice-President, and Dr Mandeliu, all at their smartest and most decorous. And then there was lunch to follow, given in our celebrated cellar Restaurant, where everyone who visits has to be taken.

The next day we were invited to the university, where we did *not* meet Liviu, for some unknown reason; and we were taken out for lunch in the other good restaurant of the city, the sumptuous banquet room of the Hotel Triumf. This lunch was extending dangerously towards dinner time when Dr Mandeliu appeared in the restaurant, just after four-thirty, to announce that the evening (Philip's rest evening) would be given to a concert visit in the Philharmonic Centre. I gave Philip credit for lasting so well. He was miraculously patient, courteous right up to the moment when Tamasi – who had come to the concert – insisted on escorting him all the way back to the hotel, leaving us no chance of talking.

The third day, until the evening, really was a day for resting and relaxing, for "seeing the sights" as our programme stated. This was my city, and the sights could be my choice. Philip had no special zest for museums, but as the Peasant Museum was on the opposite side of town from where we might accidentally meet any of our friends, and had a park beside the river where we might sit, the weather having suddenly turned exceptionally warm, we went there and gave the exhibits half-an-hour (to my surprise Philip later recalled more than I expected) and then sat on a bench.

"This park," Philip suddenly said, after we had walked round it for several minutes to find an empty seat in the sun, "is a microcosm of your country. The weather is dry, and you probably need some rain. But it's much fresher and pleasanter to be in than you would imagine if someone who disliked your country was describing it. The people –" some were hurrying by, looking at us with interest when they heard a foreign language – "are unexpectedly friendly, and unbelievably cautious. The grass is certainly not trimmed as severely as I was told it would be under Communism. Something has painted a sheen of dandelions on it, which would never be allowed in the municipal gardens in

Harrogate. Over there a large girl of about thirteen – what is she doing out of school? – is wearing a wreath of dandelions on her head, and no section leader from the Pioneers has yet told her to take it off. Where are the compulsory floral displays depicting the genial features of your President?"

"Please! Even here –" I exclaimed.

"And the paths. When we were walking round just now I noticed something. There are three footbridges over the river to the road and the houses on the other side. But when you enter the park from the Museum side, none of the paths leads directly to them. The place is a maze. In the photos in the hotel it looks very severe and regular, but in reality it's a free and uncontrollable surrealist contraption. If I were your President I would not trust it. But then, he is a kind of surrealist contraption as well. Ultimately he is a little like a small, sinister, bourgeois figure in a painting by Magritte, or Max Ernst. He would probably feel at home here, sitting perched in the air above that empty fountain."

I was simply horrified in case anyone nearby heard even one syllable of all this.

I already knew what we would do with the afternoon. First we found lunch in a tiny restaurant near the Museum, then I guided us both to the bus station. For half-an-hour we bumped along roads which were alternately rutted and very smooth. There was no logic in this, and I began to see my own country with Philip's eyes; that is, with more humour and more interest.

"You'll have to come to England, that is vital," Philip said, referring back to our conversation about plans to "collaborate", which had begun to take shape in these last few days. We shall have to get an invitation. You'll have to come so that I can observe your reactions in the way you've observed mine."

"Why do you say I'm doing that?"

"Because you can't help it. And having done some of it rather well in that manuscript of yours you showed me – oh yes, you know you did! – you'd be eager to do it again. Where are you taking me?"

"It is a surprise," I told him. "It is not very far from the city, but you can see and hear *nothing* of the city."

"Yes. I am *most* impressed," Philip said about forty minutes later when I turned him to face the view. I believe he meant it. "'The mountains have all opened out themselves'," he continued. "I am quoting, naturally. I couldn't have written that myself. Especially in these shoes."

He looked down at his staid English town footwear, dusty after the climb. He seemed impressed enough by the view to produce an extremely sophisticated small camera from his pocket and take a photograph of it. I did not realise he carried a camera... Then he turned and photographed me against that background. Finally he said, disconcertingly,

"After all this talking, I think we have a deal, don't you think?"

I pretended innocence, and he smiled again.

"I meant that I go ahead and write the book, starting as soon as I can. And as soon as I have done some, you translate it. And give me some assistance."

"How do I receive what you have written?"

"I send it to you."

"There are difficulties," I said. "It may get lost in the mail."

"I can keep copies, and send replacements. You can tell me when you receive instalments."

"Will you come to Romania again?"

"Oh, I think so. I think we are making – a policy of that? Do you think you *can* come to England? I can talk to people, and ask. I can't promise anything."

"I think it is easier for you to come here?"

"It feels easy to be where you are simply *because* you are there. You forget how hard it was to reach that place in the beginning. We are looking down over the top of the fir trees at the top of a valley in Transylvania. At the bottom, on the right, completely hidden and silent, is the city of Târgu Alb. There are rocks and stones sticking out of the dusty soil. Here the grass is a little thin and scanty, but further up under the trees it is quite long and lush. It seems so simple to *be* here. I could be here any day by turning left out of my pub at home, instead of right."

"You will *try* to turn left again soon?"

Now Philip hesitated again.

"I think so. Yes, I will. But shouldn't we do some more 'talking' before I answer definitely. Now?"

He was holding my hand.

"Yes."

"Here? Or higher up?"

"Anywhere."

Thus the afternoon was the pivot on which all my subsequent life turned. The evening sent it spinning round even faster. Liviu Bobolescu had put word round that all the most important persons involved in receiving Philip in Târgu Alb should come to dinner at his house, late, after dark, that night. At that time of year it meant 9 o'clock, by which time it was fully dark and people arriving would not be so noticeable; these precautions despite his arranging an official, or semi-official, invitation.

So there in his handsome villa, sitting uneasily around that book-lined study before we were led in by Georgeta for dinner at a candlelit table were: Liviu and Georgeta, Dr Vasile Mandeliu as the most senior and influential guest from the publishing house, who would no doubt be pressed to publish any translation of a book of Philip's which I made; Mrs Mandeliu, who, unlike her husband, spoke just a little English; Ilie Radin, to whom literature – I thought – was a closed book, but whose (and Securitate's?) presence regularised the proceedings; Tamasi, who had to be invited because he accidentally heard about it; Philip Carston; and myself.

This table arrangement was subtle. Liviu took the head place, obviously, and his wife faced him at the bottom of the table. He insisted that Philip sit at his right hand, and that I sit on his left. On my left came Dr Mandeliu, and beyond him Tamasi.

On the other side, next to Philip, sat Ilie Radin, and then, Mrs Mandeliu next to Georgeta at the bottom end. By this artful design Philip was – and I am sure Liviu calculated this – insulated from anyone who spoke English; or so Liviu imagined. Tamasi spoke English well, and Mrs Mandeliu falteringly, but they could not easily share Philip's conversation. Liviu had been ignorant of something known to me: that Mr Radin had been privately, almost secretly, learning English for a long time.

You will know Chekhov's *Cherry Orchard* very well. Ilie Radin, I came to realise that evening, was our Communist version of Lopakhin, who buys the orchard to build an estate of private houses. Inside Radin, the cold and dutiful, even cruel official, was a deep yearning, as in Lopakhin, for things his day-to-day life could not provide: for learning, even for the arts, and for all the mysteries and insights that went with them. Perhaps he also envied the respect – and fear – that Communist society managed to accord to the learned and the artistic but not to its own bureaucrats and functionaries, whom it just expected to be unimaginative and efficient. But if he had a private passion for English, Radin was also learning it in an obscure hope of enhanced status.

I confess I respected Mr Radin for his sitting there so uncomfortably, attending the dinner out of duty, the "cultural committee" official out of his element in a cultural gathering, where the conversation started on music (was very late Schubert as good as late Beethoven? Were the young atonal composers in Romania the equal of better-known Western contemporaries?). He came in the "official" suit he always wore, now rather shiny and shabby but well-preserved and clean. But he was not being arrogant; if anything, he seemed prepared to be humble, and deferential.

And he was determined to practise his English. This led, through no fault at all of his, to the first uneasy note of the evening. In a no more than momentary silence towards the end of our soups, he turned to Philip and quietly said, "Did you meet some of our writers in Bucharest?"

Philip gave the first name that came to mind, possibly because at the moment he couldn't think of others.

"We met a writer call Stefan Tonaru. And –"

Immediately there was a cold uneasiness on every face. Liviu and Tamasi just nodded. Ilie himself looked discomfited and embarrassed to think his polite enquiry had elicited such an unsuitable answer. In those few seconds it was clear to me that if people had not actually read Stefan's article in *Stralucire*, news of it had already reached Târgu Alb.

Ilie had asked the question. How should he respond to the answer? He began to say something – who knows what? – when our host, Liviu, butted in to redeem the situation.

"I think he is not one of our best writers," he said calmly.

Philip, oblivious of the undertones of the conversation, sailed on.

"I found him an interesting man. What kind of thing does he write? I can't judge it – he gave me his book of poems but I don't know any Romanian."

Perplexity descended on the table. At last Tamasi said,

"He has written some very – very *interesting* things – but insulting to people's feelings – about some of our actors and theatre directors. Mr Tonaru is a kind of critic."

Tamasi spoke with such emphasis that Philip did now understand he could go no further. To finish the topic, he said, "He was very pleasant to us when we met him."

"Oh he can be a very agreeable man to individuals," Liviu declared. "We don't deny that. Do you like this beef? It is done to a special recipe of my wife's. I married her because of this recipe."

That was the second uneasy moment! Everyone round that table knew that it had not been only for love of her recipes that Liviu had married Georgeta.

It was enough to turn the conversation away from Stefan Tonaru, which is what Liviu intended.

I played my own part by asking Philip for his small camera and taking photographs of the company as they all sat and ate; but only a few, because the film in the camera was nearly finished.

"I have another here," Philip said. I rewound the first film and took it out, slipped it into my handbag for safe keeping, and handed the camera back to Philip who now realised he did *not* have another film.

The atmosphere had become easier and Philip was making complimentary noises, of the most perfunctory sort, about the meal, when Ilie Radin felt emboldened to resume his English practice with another topic.

"Mr Carston. You had an opportunity to see our Romanian culture on your last visit, and in one week here now. What is your opinion of it?"

For a second I thought Philip was unwell. He was having trouble in swallowing a mouthful of Georgeta's delicately-cooked vegetables. He virtually choked, he set down his knife and fork and coughed, wiped his mouth with the paper napkin put at the side of his plate. I am glad he only told me later how difficult it was for him not to fall into hysterical laughter.

"I need more than two or three weeks to answer that," he said. "Ask me at the end of my *next* visit."

Ilie seemed gratified by this response.

"So you will come again? Soon?"

Philip looked at me. The table seemed to wait with fascination for his answer. Or did I imagine it? Philip opened his mouth to make some hesitantly polite reply, but –

"Mr Carston and I have a little secret plan," Liviu said. "We do not spread around the good news everywhere, but Mr Carston is already at work on a new novel which Miss Predeanu will translate."

I was too infuriated and scared to listen. And Liviu was not just speaking, but delivering an address. His face creased and wrinkled in a glowing smile of triumph. Every face around the table except mine and Philip Carston's was turned towards him, registering his announcement with varieties of respect, or surprise, or interest. I am wrong! Georgeta Bobolescu sat hearing her husband out with saintly patience.

"We do not know yet how far Mr Carston has progressed with it. But he tells me it will include a Romanian character travelling as a visitor to his own country with the eye of innocence."

Mrs Mandeliu, with difficulty, was conveying the gist of all this to her husband, who was taking an intense and approving interest. Philip's stare in my direction was beyond describing. As for me, as soon as we were again alone together he told me that I had looked to him both frightened and suspicious. For a moment of terrible fear in which I saw all Philip's friendship and trust crumbling away, I thought that he suspected me of promising firmly to Liviu, on his behalf, things Philip himself had not firmly agreed before the afternoon of this day. Nothing had been sealed before our hours in the forest; and he thought I had promised other things to Liviu *before* our agreements there.

"Well – hang on a moment," Philip now said, in a tone which I, knowing him, could already tell was his English way of issuing a total disclaimer. "Nothing's even been *started*."

Liviu Bobolescu chose to hear it all as English modesty. To all his Romanian listeners, whatever denials Philip issued, news was news. Philip had planned a novel primarily with a Romanian theme. As he was a famous author it would be published in England, and in me he had a translator who would work with him. No one in the room, in the candlelight, faces reflected in the shining table, would imagine Liviu had been manoeuvring Philip and myself into this commitment. But then, of course, since that afternoon, an idea conceived in friendship had actually existed.

So in this way Professor Liviu Bobolescu was, in a sense, the progenitor of *A Time Apart*.

The table was now pouring congratulations on Philip; even Georgeta was smiling, probably happy to think that another man, not her husband, was to be primarily involved in the endeavour.

The Mandelius were fervently flattered. Mr Radin smiled; he could no doubt tell himself he would keep an eye on the translation. "How very fascinating for us," he said. "I think we should raise our glasses to this creative alliance. To Peace, and to Cultural Friendship," he said, in English.

Liviu, radiant with success, raised his own glass again – "to Mr Carston and Miss Predeanu. *Domnul Carston si Domnisoara Predeanu*!" As Philip ruefully described it afterwards, "We were 'the happy pair'."

What could Philip and I do except *not* raise our glasses and accept the tribute?

It was midnight before we left. Tamasi had walked. Ilie Radin had come by car, as had the Mandelius. Who would offer us a lift? Both did. It seemed more convenient for the Mandelius, who lived between the hotel and my flat. Philip and I crammed into the back. I asked to be dropped with him at the street corner nearest to the Hotel Transilvania, as we had things to settle about our arrangements for the next day.

"I can't come upstairs at this hour," I said to Philip when we were absolutely alone in the street, not even a patrolling policeman in sight. "Do you have your room-key?" "I do." "Come to my flat. We will walk half-way to it, then say good-night – then you follow me." These were normal precautions: would not a girl in the West prefer not to be seen returning late at night to her flat in the company of a man?

About half-an-hour later: "You didn't tell me there were no lights on the stairs," Philip complained. I apologised. There was dust on his face – and oil, from the oiled edge of the entrance door, which creaked. His glasses were sticking out of his top pocket, as he had taken them off from fear of banging into something and smashing them. I had listened with my door open, and heard the muffled blundering and fumbling and cursing down below. I put some music on the record-player – deliberately and symbolically the final side of the Beethoven Op.132 – but I had to play it softly. We sat down close together to talk in low tones about the evening.

"I want to see you without them," I said, when he went to replace his glasses.

"You could see *me*. But I couldn't see *you*. I'd have to communicate by touch."

"You are doing that already."

"But I can't do *everything* by touch."

"I can *hear* you as well."

"Look, I wouldn't mind seeing where I *am*," he said. And he put the spectacles on again, and looked all round my room with feigned surprise.

"You only need the umbrella to be the Englishman at the airport in 1977."

"My umbrella is safe at home in England. *Carolina* – please, I've got to use the name –"

"Mr Carston, we have an *official* relationship."

But we were both laughing, almost unable to *stop* laughing.

"What more has to happen for us to be *un*official?"

"That is a little unworthy of you, I think."

I was thinking I had to make certain we used this time and this place for our principal purpose: checking what we had decided.

"Mr Carston. Philip. You are going to write a book about a beautiful young intelligent Romanian girl."

"I am?"

"Who lives in a beautiful city in – perhaps – Transylvania."

"Called?"

"Târgu Alb. No – something else in the novel. Or not named at all. An unnamed country even. She receives an invitation –"

Now I changed my tone again, to become completely serious. We *had* to settle what to do about Liviu Bobolescu's schemes.

"If I were to write nothing at all Bobolescu would probably forget," Philip suggested.

I shook my head wildly.

"*No*. Not true. I know him. He will *never* forget. He will be writing to you every week. And asking me every day."

On the record the musicians were moving on from that slow, flowing yet frail theme which opens the last movement, through those transitional passages of doubt and even discord before they can reach the affirmation of the great final melody. Uncertainty to certainty. Precarious certainty.

In the end, very softly, "Carolina," Philip said. "In one way or another, it looks as if I've got this commission, doesn't it! Or we've got it jointly."

"It does. Philip."

I felt I now knew him so well that a heavy, unignorable misery began to overcome me at the thought that it could be two, three, six, ten years before there was a possibility of meeting again. If he wrote the book and it was due to be published in England he would have reason for coming to Romania again and – somehow – contriving to bring it. But if he did not manage to write it, he could not bring it... There would be no reason for coming, every reason for staying away.

He *had* to write it, he *had* to finish it. I had to help and encourage him in any way I could.

We didn't take the plane back to Bucharest, or make the long train journey either. It so happened that Mr Guranu had to visit the capital on Party concerns. He did not have a car of his own, but was allowed by the Party to use one of theirs. Why shouldn't we take the advantage, two days later, of an offer to take us all the way back by car?

I had never been to Bucharest this way myself. So both Philip and I admired as strangers the view of the mountains, the pine-trees growing to the very tops of these 2000-metre peaks, where I thought no trees *could* grow – rather like the drawing of a child who has filled every space with trees.

"I didn't know this part of your country existed," Philip said, by way of conversation for Mr Guranu, who nodded when I translated. Because he had no prescribed assignment to sound out Philip and note his answers (though he had to report formally on their meeting and what they talked about) he only asked questions out of pure interest. And because news of the discussion at the Bobolescu's table had reached him from me via Ioana, he was extremely interested to hear about Philip's planned novel.

"Is it to be about Romania?"

"It is supposed to be *going* to be about Romania." (How to translate all the hesitancy and conditionality in Philip's answer?) "But nothing – nothing at all – has been written. I have no story. Only one character. Can you *please* convey that to Mr Guranu somehow?"

Mr Guranu picked it up without further explanation when I translated. Philip was impressed by his answer.

"Everyone – not only writers – should be cautious about their hopes in case they do not happen," Mr Guranu said. Ioana must have conveyed my fears about Philip's "writer's block" to her father; hence his tactful reticence and encouragement.

Outside the Hotel Vidraru in Bucharest – "Home again!" Philip remarked – Mr Guranu unloaded our suitcases, then reached into the loaded depths of the boot and opened a bundle which we had heard jangling and clinking throughout the journey. Into our arms he put no fewer than four bottles of home-made wine, leaving about three times that number in his parcel.

"Mr Guranu says he has come well-equipped for long Party meetings, but he can spare a little for us," I told Philip, who laughed. As we waved him away Philip said, "He seems rather a good chap despite his Party leanings." "He is more than 'leaning' towards the Party," I assured Philip. "He is very important in Târgu Alb."

Philip was thinking it out.

"More important than Mr Radin?"

"Really I do not know that. I think – I think Mr Radin has a different kind of work."

Three days later Mr Guranu was free to take us to Otopeni airport for Philip's return flight. How understanding and sensible he was to leave us to move alone to the check-in, making his own farewells to Philip in a rough yet cordial way in the car park.

I returned to the car unable to speak, not even able to look at Mr Guranu when I had guided Philip in. He did not disturb this silence until we were back at the hotel, where I had to start putting my belongings together and preparing to catch the evening train which would return me to Târgu Alb early next morning.

"You know what I said to Ioana?" he asked me just before we said goodbye. "About this book old Bobolescu dreams about."

"No?"

"If your Englishman doesn't produce anything you would be capable of writing it very well yourself. You could write *some* of it for him anyway."

I laughed; how perceptive he was.

SEVEN

– 1 –

I stood looking at my belongings in that hotel bedroom and I knew and felt, in a sudden moment of illumination and faith, that Philip *would* come back.

We had a kind of joke code to be used in letters or telephone conversations. "I've begun to help out my poor aunt with her living costs – I gave her £20 for a start," would mean he had begun the novel and written the equivalent of twenty typed pages. Any subsequent references to Aunt Mary's finances would be self-explanatory – once he wrote, "I've been too hard up to give Aunt Mary more than five pounds this month." I longed for him to write, marvellously, "I'm planning to come to your country soon, having saved a total of three hundred pounds I *should* have used to help Auntie." But he didn't.

Of course we did not really need this elaborate system of concealment. We could have written or talked quite openly about his novel. But Philip, not at all superstitious in any usual way, thought it brought bad luck, or weakened resolution, to be explicit about his writing; so I suppose these subterfuges had their purpose.

"I've only been able to scrape together a few paltry pence for my aunt's birthday – nothing like the present she deserves," he said when he telephoned on my name day. Modesty, caution, I hoped. I needed to be so patient.

Rather in the way I had imagined Philip reading my secret letter to him in his room, I tried to see him in my imagination in England among acquaintances he had told me about. I tried also to think of myself arriving in England – all the unfamiliar sensations of a Western country – and being with these same people, "observing" them as Philip maintained I observed him. I even imagined our alliance deepening there... Visiting a forest, away from a city?... I started to write down some of this, as I had written that letter (still not shown to him), and with the same purpose.

I went to stay with Valeria Ciudea in Bucharest occasionally, always a chance to exchange news of people we knew.

"Is Liviu Bobolescu still calling in at the office?" she said one night, in the street outside the Little Theatre, where we were standing to breathe some air in the interval of *The Master and Margarita*.

"Oh yes," I said. "But I didn't tell you the main news – you may know already – Dr Mandeliu is moving to Bucharest. He will be your boss."

"I see... So the famous translation will be published in Bucharest?"

We were friends enough for me to be certain that this was a completely friendly joke. I smiled.

"If so, it will be a long time in the future."

"If Philip comes to Bucharest again, and it's summer, remember we are all at Mamaia a lot of the time." By 'we' Valeria meant her grandfather, the parents, her brother and herself (she wasn't married then) – all at the Black Sea resort.

"So we shan't see you if Philip comes at a bad time?" I said, being really a little slow.

"It's a good time for the house to be available," Valeria replied, smiling. And then I blushed with embarrassment, even a slight resentment because I believed Valeria was trying to find out how far my relationship with Philip went. I could hardly speak, except to say something like, "Oh, he could not go to your house!"

For my next birthday both a phone call and a postcard arrived. Philip sounded reserved and cautious on the appallingly bad early morning line, and said nothing I could hear as referring to the novel. "Work for money is a bit slow at the moment. A couple of radio programmes – they won't make me rich." But the card seemed to bear better news: "Would you believe my aunt's rent is up to one hundred and fifty pounds already!" There was an ambiguous P.S. which left me feeling flattered, and curious: "How much do your relations have to find?" – as if he was hoping I had written something myself, and wishing to know.

That winter Liviu was looking ill. His visits to the office became rarer, and he had less excuse for calling in when Dr Mandeliu – an old acquaintance – had moved to Bucharest. One day Mrs Bobolescu actually telephoned to ask me to come and see *him*, an indication that anxiety for his spirits outweighed any jealousy. There was a power cut, and Liviu sat with a thick, shabby blanket over his knees in his study, an array of pills and syrups on a table beside him. At first he didn't say anything at all about Philip's novel, or Philip, or the subject of translation. He just wanted to talk to me about literature. About women in literature, true, which bore some relation to the project; but so much of the old resilience seemed to have gone. Professor Bobolescu now looked like an ordinary old, ailing invalid, fingers fidgeting at the edge of his blanket. As I rose to go, he gazed up sadly from his chair and remarked,

"Please will you show me a *little* of what you *yourself* are writing? Next time you come? I would be so interested..."

And in sorrow for him, I thought: there *are* some things, as as long as I choose carefully what to show him, why should I *not*? Before I left his chilly, gloomy study he had closed his eyes in sleep.

"How is Professor Bobolescu?" I asked Georgeta when I met her in a queue about a week later (can you believe it? There was a shortage of *cheese* at that time.) She shook her head first, then smiled bravely.

"He is down – and he is up," she said. "But better than he was. Better." She didn't ask me to visit again, and I never at that point did show Liviu anything I had written. His visits to the office resumed; but whatever illness he had seemed to have slowed him, taken away some of his enthusiasm, and mania. For a while, at least.

I attended the meetings. I began to take the courses in socialist economics, and ideology. I was reading, reading. But if you are an intellectual, most particularly a writer, you are a puzzling animal to Party officials. They can understand, or believe they understand, the mind and motives and needs of a factory or farm worker, even an office worker. Their efforts can be monitored, production figures can be scrutinised, instructions and exhortations issued. The publisher (granted paper supplies) can say he has produced thirty thousand copies of a book of poems and sold them, and this proves that he is helping culture to flourish. But what does selling all those poems *mean*? Party officials would not know what answers to give to that question.

Philip was astounded to think so many books were sold in my country. "If they are books of sufficiently high quality they will sell here," I said. "You don't mean "of sufficiently *low* quality," do you?" he asked, almost seriously. I can remember the conversation so well. It happened towards the end of his third visit, not in a park or a forest but, rather riskily, in a café in Bucharest. (Yes, I am leaping ahead, to his third, very brief, private arrival in my country; but I will follow to the end of this thread now I have started.) Our writers' freedom, I was saying, is to be published and read as long as they are talented, and not because of any other reason. Certainly not because they prostitute themselves and appeal only to very simple, or very crude, minds which have been fed on crudities all their lives – and make profits for their publishers.

"But don't they have to write about what they are told to? Things such as the delights of the National Day Demonstrations?" Philip had come during August, in the very week of our National Day. In the café, a television showed our President and Mrs Ceausescu receiving the acclaim of huge crowds in Bucharest the day before; and similar vast demonstrations happening all over the country: Galati, Brasov, Sfintu Gheorge, Târgu Mures, Cluj...

"Our writers may write about anything they wish as long as they write well."

"So a writer could publish a brilliantly-written satire on the Socialist Republic of Romania and its President?"

"No – ."

"And you and I can't even talk freely in the hotels without putting on the radio. Or in people's houses"

I needed to think before answering, because I did take these precautions. But the next moment I heard myself giving, with a smile, answers I had learnt in those ideological sessions, to see how Philip could respond."

"It is a habit. You do not easily lose a habit... Are you never anxious about being overheard in your country? You never hold back your political opinions so that someone else shall not know them, and place you in a difficult position?"

"No one is going to report them to someone else."

"*No* one? No one is going to say, "Be careful, he will tell the boss and the boss is a fanatical Conservative', or, 'We have a report from his last employer, this man has been a *Communist*?'"

"Carolina!" Philip almost shouted. I put my hand on his knee under the table to stop him talking too loud and drawing attention to himself, even in a foreign language most listeners would not understand. Or especially in a foreign language.

"Carolina," more quietly, "no one in my country is going to be taken away by the police and held without trial for his opinions. And murdered."

"Never? Never your Irish people?"

"Look – Carolina, *please* – how can I explain this to you?"

"You explain another time." Heads were noticeably turning.

"So," Philip eventually said, at last speaking very quietly, "if or when we do finish this novel we shall have to be just a little bit cautious about what it says about your country? Out of habit."

I smiled and said nothing.

"It can't make uncomplimentary references to your President?" Philip was looking up at the figure on the television screen, rising from his seat to be applauded, and sitting down, rising and sitting down. The massed squares of children waved flags in patterned unison in the sunshine.

"No, it can't," I said helplessly. But I have leapt far ahead, and now have to go back and explain why. All mention of his gifts, or loans, or payments to or for his aunt had ceased, for several months. Then there suddenly came an unexpected phone call, nothing to do with my birthday or name day.

"Are you likely to be in Bucharest in August? Between 21st and 28th, say?" he asked me, immediately. I knew instantly that he was wanting me to be there. Without even thinking, and with one of those flashes of happiness that strikes people in love, I just said,

"Yes! I am." I would arrange it, guarantee it, somehow.

"I plan to arrive by Tarom on 21st August. Can you be there to meet me? Is that possible for you? I shall be a tourist," he said.

"I shall be your interpreter again," I said, laughing with pleasure. Somehow I *had* to arrange that, so that I could officially meet him. I was confident I could do that, even if I had to obtain Party help; or even solicit Professor Bobolescu's influence. "Where will you stay?"

He didn't know. I told him I would arrange for the same Bucharest hotel as before to take both of us. He agreed. I thought, we shall go back, nostalgically, to the gloomy corridors and elegant rooms, the wheedling violinist in the restaurant.

Philip looked tired at Otopeni. I saw him before he saw me, so I had the chance to notice that with concern before he could break into a genuine smile of relief and pleasure at noticing me. Passport control had been very slow (why did it become slower *and* slower, I wondered?) and I put his look of exhaustion down to that.

"We are 'official'," I said. "I can see you through the Customs without problems. We will visit the Writers' Union, but there are not many people for meetings in August – they are all on holiday."

"Good."

I made a very formal, cool matter of Philip's registration at the desk in the Hotel Vidraru standing aside from him as if he was still very much the foreign stranger and I was his guide (therefore there could be nothing wrong about helping him find his room before I found my own.) As soon as the door of his room was safely closed we were embracing just behind it with the suitcase dropped on the floor.

"Why have you come?" I whispered.

He stood back a little, pointed around the room at the walls, at the ceiling, at the telephone. I went across and put a pillow over the telephone, and switched on the television: choirs were singing.

"Because I can't write this thing without seeing you. Or I can't try to write any more of it. It's lunatic. I thought I could do it without coming back. But – " He gave a grimace of despair, and held me to him again, tightly. "I thought the need to see you would diminish in two years – *three* – and I could create a different character. But it didn't, and I couldn't. I needed to meet."

"And see me for no other reason?"

"See you for every other reason too." I could not see it, but I could hear the choir on the television screen singing the President's name. "And you *must* visit England. It's essential."

He leant down and picked up his suitcase, swung it onto the bed, snapped it open.

"A good thing the Customs man didn't look," he said. "I've got about a couple of hundred written – *re*-written – pages in this. He drew a thick pad of thin sheets out of a clean shirt ironed and folded neatly and wrapped in cellophane paper by a laundry. "I hoped no one would want to look at my shirts. You can read this, if you are quick – we have six days."

He said it again next day as we sat smoking his Kent cigarettes, here in Valeria's house. I had accepted her offer: everyone was indeed down at the Black Sea, and it felt safer to have our talks there than spend long hours in one or other of our hotel rooms (though even here we switched on the radio.)

He said: "You *have* to come to England. I can't afford to pay for your trip, but I am making approaches about an invitation. If you agree?"

"I will come, please. And then you can watch me and write about me in England."

"Not only for that."

The pages of the manuscript, written in pencil, were on the floor between us, and I had begun to read, just longing to be able to study it without the noise of the radio. I had brought nothing of what *I* had done, so Philip had to sit and watch me, apprehensively, while I read. Probably my nervousness produced his defensive questions.

"*Is* that you I'm writing about? It isn't really *you*, is it?"

"Some of it is."

He suddenly looked agonised, and very tired again, though it was only mid-afternoon.

"*I have to see you in England*. Would you be able to come soon? I want to finish this before I die."

"Philip, why say you will die?" I was shocked. He had never spoken like this before.

"Who knows *what* will happen? I want to finish it anyway." He relaxed, stretched out a hand and pulled me down beside him, muddling the papers we had carefully arranged on the carpet. "If you come, I shall be meeting you for a change, at *our* airport, in the rain. But not having to write reports about you."

"No," I said. "You will only be writing a novel about me."

I went on reading the manuscript.

There was no question of Philip visiting Târgu Alb this time. Liviu Bobolescu knew that he was coming, but said he did not feel well enough to come to Bucharest himself; he instructed me to tell him everything about the progress of the book. Dr Mandeliu, now in Bucharest, had helped to get permission from his successor as director at the publishing house, Sorin Micu, allowing me to escort Philip during his week's stay.

That first afternoon I read no more than half of Philip's

pages, stopping to ask him questions so as to clarify his meaning, hear him explain things about England I would not understand. But there were much larger matters than those to consider. How much did Philip want me to be exactly myself in his narrative? How far should I let him invent me? His woman character seemed to me more bold and forthright than I was. It was all uncannily fascinating! There I was, landing in England full of imaginable uncertainty, being met and taken to a typical English home as set up by an emigré couple... I had never seen an English bourgeois residence. What Philip described had its equivalents in provincial Romania, and yet... I was meeting, and reacting to, slightly absurd English people, and I had only ever met Philip, not one other English person.

How much could I leave to Philip of what was beginning to happen, might rapidly develop, between myself and his main male character, the young Richard Hendleton? That night, after dinner in the hotel, I had taken the half of the manuscript I had not read back to my own room. As this aspect of Philip's plot began to evolve, I forgot time and read on. Fortunately his handwriting, in this neatly re-written draft, was very clear. I could read quickly, transferring sheets from quilt to bedside table as I scanned them one by one under the lamp, eagerly, apprehensively – and finally with alarm. With alarm on the last neat page... Because Philip's story broke off on the brink of what was clearly going to be – *was going to be a consummated love relationship between these two people.*

I recoiled from the implications! Recoiled especially from the knowledge that this was where Philip had come to, he had told me, to a dead stop some months before, because he "could not write about what had not happened in life." He had not said in words what it was that had not happened in life – he was letting me read the implication in his unfinished manuscript.

Do not ask me to say more at the moment. Reflecting on this in the very house, the very room, to which I brought Philip five years ago, and then on his final visit, I do not feel I can say more about what particular words I use about our relationship. I shall continue my story.

The next day we had an appointment at the Writers' Union. I forewarned Philip after breakfast about one probability. It was unlikely we would be seeing Stefan Tonaru, our overwhelming host of four years before. Yes, he was all right, but for a long time now he had been having to spend his day at home, and he did not come to official gatherings.

We walked up Calea Victoriei in silence, past the corner bookshop on the left where Philip stopped us for a moment to stare at the window display of the books of our President and his wife, and their photograph portraits. It was a hot day, a day of dry heat and oppressive clouds that hid the sun, and the atmosphere slowed us down. There was a slight wind that raised dust clouds from the surface of the wide roadway between the old royal palace and the Central Committee. Few vehicles crossed this square at this, or any, time of day. The usual flow of passers-by walked across it to the right, keeping strictly to the unmarked corridor guarded by the police, a long strip between the pavement outside the Athenée Palace Hotel and the corner where the University Library stands. Philip and I walked up the other side, on the path past the palace guards, along by the back wing of the National Museum of Art, across the narrow road which enters the square at that point, up past the folk ornaments shop on the corner, on beyond the smaller stores in the narrower upper reaches of the street, past the closed Enescu Museum. I believe he had guessed I had read to the end of his manuscript. Each of us was waiting for the other to speak first. There were now only four days left of his visit, really very few hours in which the future of this book could be fully settled; few hours in which we could be alone and talk about it. Perhaps we could find somewhere to lunch today, then go back to the hotel where I could collect the second half of the manuscript (slipped in the lining of my locked suitcase in a wardrobe for safety) and return separately to Valeria's, where I had left the first half under a mattress in a bedroom?

We turned into the little leafy area, part garden and part courtyard, in front of the Union, and Philip glanced at the statuary: the nude nymphs on pedestals, the stone lions set in the front of the house. As we came up to the handsome but narrow entrance, I stood aside to let someone emerge. He did not focus on me at first, but he saw and recognised Philip. "Mr Carston, this is an enormous pleasure."

In returning the greeting, Philip managed to mix a tone of pleasure with his obvious surprise very skilfully. I was too surprised to say anything at all; not surprised that Ilie Radin should have known everything, but very shocked that he was here.

He began to talk fast to me in Romanian, after a brief apology to an uneasy-looking Philip ("little matters to discuss"). "I just happened to be in Bucharest at this time – let me know quickly how everything goes, please – especially in regard to progress with the book." (I swallowed.) "Have been speaking to Dr Mandeliu – he says *of course* the translation, when you are finished, must be published here in Bucharest – he says Mr Sorin Micu in Târgu Alb will not mind – some of the honour will go to Târgu Alb and to his publishing house because you work there – Mr Micu will make sure his magazine *Misiva* prints articles and interviews."

And then he switched to his English – which I have to admire him for: all the time it was improving and extending – and continued, almost as if Philip had understood everything else so far: "Although I do not have very much time to read, I look forward to reading your book – perhaps even in English first! But with Miss Predeanu's excellent translation in my other hand to help me."

At that point he made his farewells, giving me a not-very-believable assurance that he would not trouble me again. He had left Philip looking disquieted and almost sullen: the look remained with him throughout our brief meeting with the few Union officials still working in late August (Dr Mandeliu was away.) And when we left the building and went off in search of lunch, I was in dread that Philip's feelings about the novel had regressed into an obstinate lack of confidence again.

"I feel like abandoning it," he said. "I feel people are watching me everywhere, I feel *caught*. It won't be finished – unless you can really help me with it. When are we going back to Valeria's place? After lunch, or now? Half my work of the last three years is under that mattress. It's all I have to show. If I lose that..." His words trailed away in gloomy confusion.

"You do have a copy?" I asked.

"No – actually I don't. I didn't have time to get to a copier. Can we make one here?"

"*No*! Impossible. Or very, very difficult. I can copy it by hand."

"You'll *never* have time for that!"

"Yes, I will. We will go back to the hotel, and then I will go to Valeria's. You follow, in an hour. Can you remember the way?"

– 2 –

Tim Harker-Jones had occasionally interrupted Carolina's story (with hesitation) to ask for a name to be spelt or a detail to be checked. At this point he wanted to revert to a topic she had seemed about to take up – and had then dropped. This was the question of whether she had been to England or not. He sensed that England was the subject that would enable him to find out if she and Philip had become "lovers".

He finished noting down what she had just told him, prepared his question and looked up – to find she was weeping. Carolina's voice had been relatively controlled as she hinted at Philip's desire to complete the novel by "completing" their relationship. Now, as she sped on past that point (on which Alic Paldrey, for one, would want a very clear answer) to the moment when she said goodbye to Philip again at the airport at the end of his week, tears ran down her face. Tim knew he could not interrupt her at such a time with delicate questions. He had to let her get as far as she could in the time left today, his last chance to talk to her.

I told Tamasi Ilosz (she said) that he was not to come to my apartment any more; and since we had mainly been meeting there, it was telling him that our liaison was over. I had been preparing him for this for a long time, so he could not be surprised. And he could not come to me and say, because it had happened at just this moment, that it was all due to Philip Carston.

I had given enormous thought to my small living room, to the possessions it was essential to have and how I would obtain them. My parents helped with furniture, wanted to help *too* much, discard things they had no use for themselves. I acquired the record-player second hand, after saving and saving; it still has the sapphire needle the previous owner started with. Records, when you can find good ones (I was constantly in the shops in Calea Victoriei when I was in Bucharest) are not so expensive: I bought operas, chamber music (Beethoven especially). The only shelf in the room was one narrow mantelpiece and I decided I would put no ornaments on it. It would remain clear and austere, and above it just one picture, the only one in the room. It would not be an icon.

It had been hardest of all to contrive the bookshelves, which had to be the focus of the room, the justification *for* the room and its inhabitant. Perhaps one day a book I had written would stand on my shelf.

You could not buy planks of wood in the stores then (you can buy it even less now.) But at least this is a region of the timber industry. I had to see if I could obtain some wood, and some supports, and some nails and some glue by private means; but I had no friends in the timber yards, nor did my friends have friends.

Then I thought of Ion Guranu. After all, he had shelves

enough in his garden shed and in his kitchen, for his bottles of wine – he now had them in the corridors as well. Ioana had bookshelves in her bedroom, I had seen those. Would her father know how to find some wood?

Mr Guranu arrived in the lift with the planks the next Saturday afternoon, determined to install them himself.

"But how much did these cost?"

He banged them down on the floor of the room.

"Are they very expensive?"

He said nothing, and went downstairs again to the friend in the small van who had brought him, to collect tools, nails, supports, glue, even an electric drill. When he returned,

"How much money will this be?"

He made a rough mental calculation, took a folding ruler out of his pocket, measured, marked the plank with a pencil, dropped the plank again and turned to me.

"It will be *no* money," he said. "Listen. This embarrasses me, very much. I know as a Party man where to get wood for shelving. I know where and how to get sausages, and butter, and even a typewriter. Occasionally. But I don't often *use* my knowledge."

"Some people do. I think many do."

"I can't say that openly."

I said, "Can't you say it in Party meetings? That these transactions go on all the time?" I was relatively new, no one had yet said anything about this in any meeting I had attended.

"I think that's about 1.5 metres. Would you agree?" he said.

He had received the wood for my bookshelves through a 'contact'. But he had paid the necessary price for it, "no less – and no *more*." But neither Mr Guranu nor his daughter would accept the money from me. I had benefited from "a favour". But Mr Guranu had made it the least tainted favour possible; paying the right rate for the wood and making it a gift to me had salved his conscience.

I think the first books to occupy the shelves were much less expensive to me than the planks were to Mr Guranu. At exactly head height, and immediately behind me (when I sat down at my working table) I arranged the most needed classics, the Shakespeares, Goethes and Dantes (the last two only in Romanian), the volumes of Eminescu and Arghezi and Blaga. These books are so magisterial that they reinforce you. True greatness never browbeats or discourages. (All the same, I placed the novels of Tolstoy and Zola and George Eliot and Conrad further away: I wanted to write prose myself, and I didn't want the greatest prose so near me.) Almost any modern novel I put where I could not see it except by looking hard; and any novel by a living author – Nicolae Breban, Augustin Buzura – I left farther away still. They were much too close in time. I feared the temptation to look at them and make comparisons of method, paragraph by paragraph. That would only reveal to me an indefinable skill to which I could not aspire. (I had tried seeing how individual passages in novels by E.M. Forster and Constantin Toiu were constructed, and I knew!) As for Philip's gifts of novels of his own – I had a mantelpiece of books in my bedroom, and they went there.

Now, with all of two hundred books on the shelves (with such marvellous plenty of space for more!) I began my most serious work.

I had heard indirectly that Liviu Bobolescu was ill again; every winter now he seemed weaker. Irresponsibly, because tactless talk about illness does no one – sufferer, relatives, friends – any good, Sorin Micu one day said aloud, in front of some visitors to the office, "I suspect Bobolescu is not long for this world." I found Mr Micu a cold man, no sort of worthy successor to Vasile Mandeliu as director of the publishing house: well-informed, but no scholar or genuine lover of literature, a Party man interested only in his own advancement with no heart for any cause beyond his own. I sense that this curt, chilly little man with the trim moustache was unpopular generally, but especially with the non-Party people on his staff.

If what he said about Professor Bobolescu was true (I had no news at all from Liviu, and the silence – usually welcome – was suddenly distressing) I believed I should go and see him.

I went, by telephone arrangement with Georgeta, one freezing November weekend. He was in bed, and the bedroom, which had one of those huge, tiled wood-burning stoves you find in the larger houses, was overwhelmingly hot. Georgeta brought him hot drinks I could not identify (and his beloved cakes, which he ate with greedy eagerness) and gave me coffee.

"And how is the book proceeding?"

"I am writing when I have time. Mr Carston passed me some more chapters through a friend of his who visited Bucharest." Not quite true, of course.

"You have only been – translating?"

"I have been translating."

"But you have been working also for yourself?"

"Yes." I did not wish to say any more than that.

"One day when I am better," he continued, "I will ask you to bring me everything you have done so far, so that we can read it together, just ourselves."

"Professor Bobolescu is going to have an operation in a month, a big operation, but one which the hospital does well," Georgeta said.

"At my age, I have only a little time to get better, and I intend to get better," Liviu said. He dug his elbows into his pillows and propelled himself up into a sitting position. "Tell me some more about this work," he said to me. So I was not going to get away very quickly.

Philip's letters sent further encouraging news of Aunt Mary; but began hinting that his health was not good. One letter said it only too clearly. "My health (or whatever you call it in my case): they've found nothing particularly wrong yet, but they go on trying." This was during that winter. "I am going into the hospital here 'for a few tests' later this month. I shall keep you informed."

I would occasionally read some of Liviu's recommended

passages from Shakespeare (from *The Winter's Tale*, say or *The Tempest*), from the handsome books in which the Dutescu translations faced the original speeches. Or I would take the ritual short walk up and down my room to keep warm, and start the kettle slowly, so slowly, warming up on the gas ring to make some coffee – while I put something on the record-player to listen to as I drank it. I had a record of *The Magic Flute* which I played repeatedly; but quite often it was the late Beethoven again, the Op.132.

Sometimes you could not keep warm in my block. In the daytimes at the weekends I would pause in my work and go to stand at the window watching rain or snow falling and seeing the unloved areas around these new apartments, where children played in warm weather, growing muddier and more untidy. Sometimes it was so cold I retreated to my parents' house, where at least there were more of us in the room to provide warmth. Or it would feel better to snatch up a bag and go out in search of a queue. A queue for anything, for food and drink obviously, but also for books or magazines.

One day I went out and found myself in a queue for tins of Russian sardines – strictly only two tins per person – behind Eva Vajna. We stood in the freezing cold, backs turned against the wind, edging forward mechanically towards the open window in the wall of the grocery where we could see the small yellow pyramid of tins shrinking gradually and the stern-faced shop assistants counting out notes and coins in change. I wondered – everyone near us wondered, and was doing calculations – whether the last of the tins would disappear before we reached the head of the queue.

"I am writing another novel," she declared. "It will be very *different*. It will be very modern. It will all happen in Romania *now*. People want to read about reality," Eva said, briefly gesturing at the queue with one open hand. I recalled that her turned-down novel had had nothing of "reality" in it. "And if they cannot read about it now, there will come a time when they *will*," she said confidently. Only as I walked home (with my two tins of sardines) did I appreciate that Eva Vajna thought her novel would be politically very daring and outspoken.

"I hear that Liviu Bobolescu is very ill," she said, rather neutrally, when we parted. "His operation did not go very well."

"So he has *had* the operation?"

"Two weeks ago."

"And it didn't succeed?"

"No, I think not. But I thought you saw him all the time? Surely you are a very particular friend of his?"

I did not rise to this remark. Did Eva Vajna feel as sad as I did for old Liviu? She did not show it.

– 3 –

Three weeks later I was hurrying, not to be late somewhere, on an equally cold day, profoundly shaken and cast down.

I was a little late even so. I joined in the funeral procession with Ioana just at the end of the Guranus' street. We were walking just behind the large, black-overcoated group of Party officials following on immediately behind the slow hearse. I did not know what to say, and Ioana realised that. She put out a hand to me first, took my hand as we walked, and I began to weep; the tears seemed even less adequate because of the ease with which they ran in the extreme cold. Suddenly I noticed Ilie Radin in the crowd just in front of me, seemingly trying hard not to shiver in a coat too thin for the time of year – though at least his shoes looked solid enough to keep out the snow under our feet.

From here it was a long way to the cemetery – or a long way for a walking procession, about a kilometre I suppose. Strangers who did not feel entitled to join the funeral line stopped reverently at the side of the road, and I felt public, and exposed, when they looked at us. I was sure very many of them would have known whom we were burying. I had never before looked out on people from a funeral parade; it was my first time.

This long line of slowly-walking people stopped the cars in the streets; drivers switched off their engines and switched on their headlights. The uncanny pale shine of the lamps under a grey sky full of snow – giving light supposed to assist the dead one on his or her journey into darkness – was something he might have appreciated as a gesture, if not as a superstition. We walked on in silence. I remembered that he had come from peasant stock, and grown up in a village, but I was certain he would not have wanted the traditional keening and weeping by mourners, hired or unhired – nor was there any, you did not see it now in Târgu Alb.

The line halted, then turned from a line into a black, silent crowd at the bottleneck of the cemetery entrance as the coffin was slowly driven in. Some of those waiting mingled with us, nodding to friends, but I kept my head down, thus did not see who had entered the crowd behind me. I felt a gloved hand on my right shoulder, gripping me from behind with a consolatory touch. In the first second when I turned I saw that its owner had lightly rested his other hand, which also carried a stick, on Ioana's shoulder. And then I was almost frightened to realise that the hands were Liviu Bobolescu's.

I was astonished to see him out in such weather. I had been reluctant, or afraid, to contact Georgeta Bobolescu to enquire about Liviu after Mrs Vajna's words in that queue. If there were very bad news it would reach me soon enough, I thought. When I heard nothing at all I assumed there was nothing worse to learn; and then Mr Guranu's dreadfully sudden illness and death put everything else out of my mind.

Liviu in fact looked healthier and smarter than he had for a long time: the black fur hat (increasing his height) and the black coat and gloves all looked new, his face, though pale, no longer looked pinched and despairing. His eyes looked bright – and curiously artful again.

"It is appallingly sad for you," he said to Ioana with some

grace and delicacy. "For you *both*." Mrs Guranu was by Ioana's side, and he hugged her in sympathy, gravely and gently. I wondered how often the two of them had met. What would have brought them together? Liviu's bright eyes softened with respect. He believed in what he was saying; even if dread of death may have driven him to say it.

"You are feeling better now, Professor Bobolescu?" I asked, thinking it was almost a disgrace to be discussing anyone's health at a funeral.

"I had my operation, yes, and I am better," he said, nodding; tactfully brief about his own improvement... Dr Mandeliu, clearly up from Bucharest for the funeral, was suddenly alongside us, with Sorin Micu close behind him. I imagined that all of these people, whom I would not have associated with him, had kept Party connections with Mr Guranu through the years, and would be expected to come, would wish to be there. Vasile Mandeliu was more upset than I thought he would be.

"Your father," he proclaimed hoarsely to Ioana, who wept with pride and grief, "was a *good* man. A good Romanian, a good *man*." You cannot predict how people will react. Dr Mandeliu's voice was breaking, he was sobbing. He could not control his emotions, and he tried to do so by continuing to talk. "He made such good wine, Ion Guranu," he said. "So many bottles." Then he hid his face in a handkerchief in embarrassment, and was relieved when Ilie Radin, who had appeared at his side and sensed a difficulty, pulled him away with the pretence of some matter they had to talk about. But I noticed little Sorin Micu looking up at them with a cold, impatient expression.

There were orations, tributes, words written in Bucharest and delivered by unknown officials reading them from scripts, speeches prepared in formal fashion in Târgu Alb. I wished that something in all of it had touched more intimately on the man himself, his hopes and doubts, his honesty, his generosity. We needed him in these harsh years, and he had gone.

All this is important to tell because that unexpected death

gave me a premonition of someone else's. I find it so hard to speak of it, but I have to.

I had been watching Philip during that third visit. Apart from a few wry remarks about life in general, the same as he usually made, he actually said nothing about his health. But occasionally he exercised his shoulders awkwardly and painfully, rubbed his side, frowned – as if he sensed something might be wrong. What gave me most concern were his remarks about writing the novel "while he was still alive." In retrospect they appear to have been his way of telling me he was dying.

When he came to Romania for the last time, one year later, he moved slowly; and seemed to be estimating the effort involved in any slightly rigorous physical action before he undertook it. He had a long, long wait before passport formalities were concluded, and he walked out to the luggage hall with *such* an exhausted air. He did not try to pick up his smallish suitcase from the carousel when it moved a little too fast for him; and I held the bag I was carrying very tightly while we waited. The next time it came round I stepped in and picked it up myself.

By an eerie chance the room I had reserved for him, in the same hotel again, was the one he had had on his first visit, so many years before. "And makes me end where I begun," he intoned; and laughed for the first time. I had to ask him to name the poet and identify the quotation, which I only half recognised. The laugh briefly rounded out his drawn face.

Out of the case he took a heavy-looking winter suit on a coat-hanger, wrapped in a kind of transparent plastic film, as if it was newly bought. Carefully he removed this flimsy, tearable covering, felt inside the suspiciously bulky seat of the trousers – and drew out something flat and large, wrapped and taped up in brown paper. It had been clipped or fastened to the inside of the trousers so that it would not have fallen out even if Philip had had to hold them up and shake them.

"We have a week. Well, six days. When can you look at this?"

I was overwhelmed with joy. My fear had been that nothing

would ever come of this book because of Philip's diffidence. Now he was literally putting it in my hands as a finished work. I began to try to unwrap it, to pick at the edges of the sticky tape which sealed it. He stopped me, produced a small pair of scissors, stood the parcel upright on the bed and began to cut scrupulously along the top edge. "I have some more tape, we can seal it up again," he said. He slid the manuscript out, thick in a black plastic folder, and laid it on the bed; at the same time leaving something else in the wrapping. "There's a second copy here in case this is ever mislaid," he told me. "But do you have –?" I asked. "I have two more copies in England," he reassured me.

"But you read it. Please," Philip said, holding me close to him, the manuscript laid on his lap as we sat on the bed. The television, behind us, had started loudly on the final news, *Telejurnal*, already; I hadn't realised, overlooking the long delay at the airport, that it was as late as that. "Read it, and tell me quickly what you feel," he went on. "You can do whatever you like with it. Really."

Philip said that in a tone of joking despair, of ultimate modesty about his achievement in finishing the book. I tried to begin reading there and then but he would not let me. He turned to me and kissed me, and I allowed the balance to be easily tipped away from the manuscript and towards love for those moments. In this evening hotel room, before dinner, my lost world with Philip had come back to me again.

But after a while I stretched over to where I had left my own bag on a table, under a mirror. I saw myself grabbing at it, overbalancing on the bed in the reflection, regaining the sheer joy of having the contents of the bag ready to give to him.

Philip had lain back on the bed, rubbing his eyes, his glasses in his hand. *Telejurnal* was finishing on the screen. The solemn, penetrating eyes of the woman newsreader continued to stare into the eyes of the viewer at the fade-out. Then the concluding anthem struck up, jaunty and cracked in its old recording, behind the image of forest and mountain and the silhouette of Romania sprouting spokes of sunshine.

I waited for Philip to fix his glasses on his face with his usual care, and then I took my own, much smaller manuscript out of the plastic camera bag and set it on his lap. He smiled and laughed, with amazement.

"You mean – ? We have it all? And in English?"

I nodded and laughed; and kissed him.

– 4 –

I am sure I shall not be betrayed if I say – in confidence – that the situation in our country has deteriorated badly in recent years. Existence has become a question of working out how to supply yourself with food, and heat, and light for the next few days of your life and making sure that those close to you are supplied.

We all have our routines. In my family my mother continues to queue for meat, my father for bread and for cheese (butter has been difficult to find in the shops). I look for vegetables in the markets, for mineral water, for anything rarer like decent coffee or tea. Whenever I have found vegetables, or any "luxury" items, I take some home to my parents' house and exchange them for whatever my parents have been able to buy.

But you must not forget that we have not been an industrialised country for very long; so that our connections, through relations and friends, with the countryside and its products are still very close. This means that actual hunger has been rare, and starvation – despite what is said in the West – does *not* happen. But we *have* needed to work out our own devices, and in the atmosphere of suspicion in which we live – there, I have confessed that! – we sometimes need to conceal our expedients from other people.

I do not wish to be misunderstood. We did have these

problems with day-to-day living which people – or the fortunate people – do not have in England. But my life, and the life of most of my friends (unless they were unhappy for quite different reasons) was a happy life because I could rely on having what really mattered: books, music, culture generally. To a woman, clothes have been a problem, certainly. So many times I have looked with despair on the few garments I had which I could actually wear with comfort and pride. But if you have few clothes in the shops, you are forced back on your own skill, or your friends' skill, in mending and altering and varying what you have. When I look round at my friends I see they are all smartly dressed – a fetching necklace here, a smart, simple hat there – and probably better off for not having to chase fashion.

I took no holiday. I managed somehow to remain in my flat through long, hot, dusty summer weeks, often even without mineral water (and certainly without coffee), working. Working against time, working to fulfil my promise to Philip to have the completed novel ready so that it could be published in Romania almost as soon as it appeared in England.

I knew I could not avoid letting Liviu Bobolescu know that a book conceived by Philip Carston *was* taking shape in Romanian. He would know about it eventually so he might as well know immediately. Then he could continue to back up my plan to have it published – as everyone had come to expect – through Dr Mandeliu's state publishing house in Bucharest. Liviu really did seem to wield some influence.

I had made two typed copies of my work but pretended I only had one, and therefore could not lend Professor Bobolescu another to read for himself. He insisted I give him an outline of the story but could not require me to leave a whole manuscript with him to study. I had to take it to Bucharest as soon as possible. I stayed with Valeria. I took the manuscript in to Dr Mandeliu's office, and he received it warmly, promising to read it right away and saying how proud he was that "one of his own students" in publishing had given him the opportunity to bring out a completely new novel by Philip Carston.

But then, on a Friday morning only three weeks later something happened which I had – foolishly, I now think – not allowed myself to expect. I was called in to answer for my own part in all these proceedings.

You wake up in the morning, and you immediately think of how you are going to manage the day. That Friday I was calculating, in my waking thoughts, what food I had and how long it would last, wondering how much I needed to be up early and hurry to the market for vegetables next day. I had bread, there were jars of peaches and beans, tins of fish and two bottles of wine from those Ioana had given me, out of her of father's store, still not exhausted. If Ioana were bringing me in some vegetables from the country on Sunday evening I could live on what I had. You develop a philosophy about these things which is really a very sound philosophy for living in a world which is mostly poor: a sufficiency of material things is more than the Third World countries have, so you are lucky to be able to live on them quite adequately; you are lucky in what you lack, because an abundance would be a distraction from living properly.

But problems concerning the book were soon to drive any other issue into the background.

That day I was punctually at work at eight, in the office – to find word had already gone round that Sorin Micu wished to see me the minute I arrived. Mr Micu was a literary man of sorts, but mainly one of those forty-year old career officials who was determined to use all the power he could find and enjoy all the privileges. Everyone (undoubtedly Dr Mandeliu) had always been ingratiating towards Ilie Radin as our outside "supervisor". But Mr Micu grovelled, and sought favours, and also set about constructing a small private fortune out of his position.

You could, if you looked for them, find numerous people, in different areas of employment, perhaps most of all in "secret" employment, who turned the system to their private advantage. But you didn't often see them in my country in publishing; so Mr

Micu must have been clever.

"He wants to speak to you about the manuscript," the secretary said while I waited in the outer office. "It came up from Bucharest and he gave it to Mrs Lagean to read." Silvia Lagean was a retired professor from our university, quite high in the Party in the past.

"There are a lot of questions about this book," Mr Micu was saying almost as soon as I had closed the door. He was sighing as he said it. "The Council for Culture in Bucharest is asking some, and I have others."

"Even if you have nothing to do with publishing it?" I felt like saying. But that would have been silly and hostile, and I sensed that it might be harmful to the book to say anything at all. Mr Micu hated to be contradicted.

"This book, you say, is to be published in England next year?" I nodded. "I have had a report on it from Mrs Lagean," he continued. "As far as I can see, there is no problem from the political point of view. A girl goes to England from an unnamed socialist country. It would be embarrassing if there were criticisms of the political system of her country, which could apply to our own country. But I am told there is nothing. The people in England who criticise the girl's country do that from ignorance and they are represented as ignorant people. And the book is almost wholly about England, or about this girl looking at England. Now the first important question I ask is – and the readers will ask it – who *is* this girl?"

Of course I had evolved an answer to that!

"I believe she is not so much a real girl as a creative spirit out of one of our countries – or all of them."

"So – a 'symbolic' girl?"

"Yes."

"But a 'symbolic girl' who is not a real girl may have a passionate physical love affair with a man in a Western country? Will not someone say she is not just 'symbolic', that she is rather human and lifelike? You are not famous, Miss Predeanu, but publishing a translation of this novel might not be the best way of making your name?"

"Mr Micu, if you want reassurance that the girl in the book has had experiences which are – are different from my own, I can give it. And I hardly think unknown readers will link the girl in the book with its translator."

I hoped to disconcert Mr Micu with my frankness, knowing him to be a prudish and formal individual. He did look embarrassed, and seemed ready to accept my reassurance; although that did not deter him from making his next and more important point.

"But I have also," he said, "to ask you – because people at the Council for Culture in Bucharest wish to know – how the original manuscript was obtained. I know that Dr Mandeliu – and others – encouraged Mr Carston in his work. But how did the book come to Romania?"

I tried to look mystified that he should ask such a question.

"Well – Mr Carston gave it to me when he visited for that purpose – in the spring."

"No one else who could read English saw it?"

"No."

"He didn't show it to anyone else here who could read English? To get an opinion on its suitability for translation?"

"No. He knew that after it was translated the important people would give an opinion about publishing it – people who would read it in Romanian. At the Council for Culture probably."

He acknowledged that, and he passed over my risky hint that the last word rested not with him but with his seniors. But now,

"In the course of making your translation – did you make many alterations?" he asked.

"I *altered* nothing at all that Philip Carston wrote." This covered my omitting one or two sentences.

"But you see, Miss Predeanu, there are people who are saying exactly that."

"What do you mean?"

"There are people already saying you altered nothing that Mr Carston wrote – because you yourself *wrote* the entire novel. With Mr Carston's help, possibly."

During our conversation we had not sat down, simply stood and faced each other across his office, under the smiling picture of the President; but now, without being invited to, I sat down suddenly and furiously in the very deep and comfortable armchair set squarely in front of Sorin Micu's.

Mr Micu remained standing up.

"Where are people saying that?"

I meant to say, "What people are saying that?" and the wrong words came out. But the mistake was useful.

"Here in Târgu Alb." So not in Bucharest.

"*Who?*"

"I think you might guess. And I should say I have no view at all myself on the possibility. But you are aware how serious that would be? It would mean you were publishing a book under Mr Carston's name which was not his."

"It is madness to say that!"

"And also it would mean that you had sent a manuscript out of this country, entirely without permission, to be translated into English and published in the West."

"But they don't even know what the book is about."

"Miss Predeanu, you have given a person we don't name an outline of the story."

I was consumed with fury – and despair – at the thought that everything should have been put in jeopardy by Liviu Bobolescu's indiscretions. But I forced myself to smile, and dismiss the idea as nonsense. Mr Micu now retired behind his desk and sat down.

"Why has Bucharest sent the book to you?" I asked. If the Council for Culture had doubts, I faced big difficulties. If the Council had no objections, Mr Micu's opinion would not matter. He opened a drawer and produced a bulky manuscript – bound in yellow card.

"They sent me a xerox copy. As a courtesy, so that I should read it as your Director."

"Have you read it?"

"No. I have not read it. But I told you, Mrs Lagean has read it."

Mr Micu had a reputation for not reading so much as he might, in or out of the office. I had caught him out. He was defensive. We talked further, and after about twenty minutes, he did accept all my assurances; even apologised before releasing me.

"Keep the second copy somewhere safe," Philip had said. "It's sealed in a separate packet inside the parcel. It's a photocopy of this one, and when you know your excellent translation is going to be published for sure, please open it up. In fact, don't open it *until* then, but do open it then."

When I had drawn the curtains in my flat that evening I took out all of my stock of spare china from the bottom compartment of the kitchen cupboard, lifted up the ten-layer lining of newspaper placed in it, and took out Philip's second copy.

I had one wild, sudden, extraordinary vision of finding a second, completely different novel sealed in the shiny brown paper. But it was simply a second copy as Philip had told me, the first page – and all the pages – beginning with the same words. And I found a sealed envelope marking a place about half-way through, slipped between pages at a particular point in the narrative. This envelope contained a letter. My curiosity was so great that I could not wait until I was absolutely certain of my work being published before I read it – as I knew Philip had wished.

I had never given Philip the letter I wrote for him to read by himself in his room in England, all those years before (and now he can never receive it). I still had it, and although I did not dare to re-read something I wrote when very young – I was twenty-two then, had passed thirty now – I had no desire to destroy it, or lose it. And now Philip had written to me in exactly the same way;

sent me a letter I could open only when he was far away from me.

I will try now to read the appropriate parts of this letter out loud. I shall not read all of it; and hope that will be understood.

– 5 –

My very dear Carolina,

I am assuming that you will not be reading this until you know for certain that the novel is to be published in Romania. Therefore I congratulate you on your achievement in enhancing even further, by your creative ingenuity in translation, a work of such outstanding merit! (So far it was the ironical, gently self-mocking Philip I had come to expect. Then the mood altered.)

But truly – I am (shall be) very moved to know that you have succeeded in having the book accepted in your country. It has been so long in the writing, and I was so fearful of letting you down (and letting myself down) by producing nothing at all, that I could weep with relief to know that this work is going to appear. I *believe* that it will come out in England next year. It's with Ridgbury now – which means it's mainly in the smooth hands of that trendy, power-crazy bastard I've told you about, Dominick Paldrey, "and his fiend-like queen", but the reactions are favourable and a contract should be drawn up soon. As with all novels, I shall actually believe it's going to be published when I see it in the shops.

Carolina, I long for the chance to see you again – there, or here, or anywhere... I remember, daily, everything...

But the point is, I do wonder just when our next meeting will happen. Or *whether* it will happen. I want to tell you something, as calmly as possible, so as not to alarm you or dip myself even deeper into terminal pessimism and melancholia. I am *not* well these days, and I began to wonder whether this novel hasn't been finished just in time.

The doctors here have taken a gloomy view of the entrails. Not sheep's entrails, or any entrails except my very own long-cherished and much-abused entrails...

A specialist I saw a week before I left for Romania started to tell me what he *thought* might be the problem, though of course there would have to be further tests and no one could be absolutely sure and in any case the prognoses in these circumstances weren't *uniformly* unfavourable – at that point I stopped him and said, "I don't want to be told what's wrong with me and I don't propose even to ask you, just get on with whatever's necessary in terms of *treatment*."

I've only wanted you to know all this stuff when you were happy in the certainty that the fruits of your toil would be published. It's not wanting, God knows, to spoil your happiness – it's just wanting to feel you had good news to counter my bad news. If the worst comes to the worst (the Titanic and the iceberg), I really do – unlike many writers – wish a biography of me to be written; I *am* as vain as that. And I want you, and all you mean to me, to be in that book, indeed the climax of the book. I don't intend *anybody* to be given the job of writing it. So I am leaving word – how macabre all this is, I could be alive for years yet! – that one particular reliable friend, Tim Harker-Jones, should have the task.

I thought long and hard about wishing this job on him (though he is not compelled to do it). And I concluded he was the most suitable choice, for a number of reasons. Tim is only a year or two younger than me, so really of my generation (we overlapped for a year at university, which is where we met). We were close friends in our earlier years, then met less often – and I haven't seen Tim now for some time. That means he was not too close to me in my later years to do a scrupulous, impartial job uninfluenced by friends. Another advantage of Tim is that we share publishers – yes, he suffers from Ridgbury too! It would make sense for a Ridgbury author to have his Life done by a

Ridgbury author. Lastly: I have a feeling that if the idea of a Life occurred to Dominick Paldrey he would not be inclined to offer it to someone of the very first rank who would need to be paid in gold ingots. Tim is a good and honest biographer, but would not command a huge advance – he would probably need whatever money Paldrey suggested and willingly undertake the research. Which means that one day you will no doubt be meeting him.

I'm enclosing with this letter an unflattering, over-large photo of the two of us together at a publisher's party in our extreme youth, plus one or two smaller ones of myself alone, as you've often said you'd like a photograph...

Returning to Tim Harker-Jones. If I know Tim, he will not be prying or inquisitorial. In fact, he does not always prove *supremely* effective in teasing out all the details, and the implications of the details, in someone's life – this makes him a good biographer in my view, because he doesn't always *find*, or find out, the material he can use to make shabby disclosures about someone's private affairs! *That means you, Carolina, can tell him just as much as you like and no more.* It will be your decision. I don't think the dead have an eternal right to their secrets, but if they are good and beautiful secrets and the living would think it right to disclose some of them, eventually, then the living may do as they wish. Or as *she* wishes, because you are "the living" in this case.

Tell him, please, exactly what *you* wish to tell him about yourself, ourselves – and the book...

And I love you to the last.

Philip

A LITTLE LATER

EIGHT

– 1 –

From Simon Stonehurst
Theatre Director

Dear Dominick Paldrey,

I can now at last enclose the complete script for the project we have been corresponding about during the last year.

You will see that the extracts from *A Time Apart* are a little longer than I first planned. I hope you can manage to keep copyright fees to the same level we agreed when we were last discussing that aspect?

I have been trying to meet Tim Harker-Jones. He was quite forthcoming at first, but recently I seem to have encountered a brick wall. He insists he is shutting himself away to get on with the biography, and having to revisit Romania soon to check on some final points. All this is very frustrating to me, as I really just wanted to get from him a few basic facts about Carolina's background, and friends, and the places Philip Carston went with her – nothing that would involve disclosing any substantial elements of his book before publication. Harker-Jones has not answered my last letter requesting a short meeting in London. I pointed out that it was in *his* interests (and Philip Carston's posthumously) to get all the facts in a play about Philip and Carolina *right*. The author of the script, Nick Tillitt, can supply valuable Romanian colour from his own experience, and knows about Philip and Carolina from gossip that passed around British circles in Bucharest. But Harker-Jones has actually met Carolina and people connected with her, and could be of invaluable help to me.

May I thus ask you if you could do something to help? If there was a chance, for example, of bringing me in on a meeting –

or lunch – with him, when I could ask him a few things quite informally? I cannot tell you how grateful I would be if you could contrive that. Or suggest any other way I could meet him? I am sure that a short letter or telephone call from you would solve the entire problem in an instant.

I hope you can help me. All the best.

Yours ever,

Simon Stonehurst

– 2 –

"All right, all right. But did he fuck her?" Alic Paldrey had asked.

Once again Tim Harker-Jones was on a Tarom flight on his way to Bucharest, remembering a lunch meeting with the Paldreys. It had happened on a weekday this time, and had been a better meal than the take-away eaten on their knees the year before. They were in a restaurant, for one thing; and for another, Dominick had made it clear that there were few questions at Ridgbury about the completed draft of nearly all the biography.

Besides, Alic Paldrey had just joined them in the restaurant, with a casual air – grinning at lunching acquaintances as she made her way towards the table – but Alic did nothing casually, and her presence made the publication of the biography a serious proposition. Alic would be saying to herself that the book just needed her own touch of flair, her sense of what would make it sellable.

"We like the book," Dominick said.

"But we'd like to know about the sex side," Alic continued. "Readers will want to know if they had it." Philip and Carolina of course. About other, earlier relationships in Philip's life Tim had left no doubt.

"I think they were in love," Tim began. "And –"

"Yes, you make that *clear*." Almost as if she meant *boringly* clear, when Tim had striven to make those passages, a culmination of his biography as Philip had wished, as moving as possible. "But you have to have *all* of it. You do *know* whether they had sex? Don't you?"

No. Tim Harker-Jones did not know that. Nor did he know the answer to another all-important question: had Carolina Predeanu made a visit to England? She had evaded the point, declined to the last even to give him a simple yes or no answer. This left him believing that she had, but was not prepared to discuss it as the connection between any visit and Katrin's trip in the novel was potentially very sensitive.

"Carolina – the 'Katrin' in Philip's novel" he began, "is still very much alive. She gave me, at great risk, before the revolution, the story of her meetings with Philip and how the idea for the final novel originated. I've got to be sensitive with her, and discreet."

The second adjective had a bad effect on Alic Paldrey. She gave him a look of almost pitying impatience.

"Romania's a much freer country now," Dominick said banally. "You can ask things when you are there which you could not ask before."

All of this conversation had taken place with the main course of their meal landing on the table in front of them. Tim sensed that they had to conclude this subject before they put to use the knives and forks already raised in their hands. Out of their home, and on expenses, the Paldreys were eager eaters, so Tim believed they would want to settle matters quickly, before the first mouthful.

"It's a much freer country since Christmas, and for that very reason I have to be careful not to misrepresent Carolina in case she sees an opening for the lawyers," he said.

This registered quite effectively with Alic, who dropped to the horizontal the knife that had been pointing up at Tim at about forty degrees. She nodded; and they got on with their eating.

When they finally rose to leave, Dominick searched in his pockets for something.

"This chap has written to us again," he said, holding out a folded and crumpled letter: on bright light-blue paper with a word-processed letterhead. "Simon Stonehurst. I've taken a copy of it, but I haven't replied, I'm afraid. I hoped *you* might like to deal with it."

He laughed as he said that.

So once again, too, a Simon Stonehurst letter was among Tim's belongings as he flew east.

He had a room booked for him in Bucharest by a holiday concern in London, this time in a more expensive hotel, the Vidraru being temporarily closed, he was told, for refurbishment. He thought of how he would be showing Carolina Predeanu the last chapters of his draft in a hotel bedroom in the same way Philip Carston had shown the manuscript of a novel... Then he decided not to show them; keep the sequence of events clear in his mind, and remember where there were gaps he might be able to fill, but not show them.

He expected change and revelation from this visit, in the late May of 1990. People who had been guarded and reticent and frightened the first time would now be able to speak. He had seen on television the crowd breaking into the Central Committee building on 22nd December. And that six-storey monument to Party power, surmounted by its triumphant message, TRAIASCA PARTIDUL COMUNIST ROMAN, the monolith he had supposed to be full of computers and filing cabinets, inhabited by dedicated, unsmiling officials, had proved to be little more than an empty shell. Behind the heavy façade there were mainly elegant concourses and large ceremonial rooms, not nearly so many offices as he imagined, not so many workers, fewer corridors of rooms where work went on, much empty grandeur to impress the privileged, while from outside its sternness symbolised strength and implacability.

And the crowds had defied it, broken into it, defaced the portraits of the President and his consort in the ceremonial books, turned over the furniture, occupied the grand rooms with committees of the revolution.

But when he, later on this day, in the evening, walked over to stand outside the black, brass-studded front door of the Central Committee – this had been forbidden under pain of arrest before – and gazed up, standing five yards from it, at the face of that building, he noticed something strange which the television images had not conveyed. When Nicolae Ceausescu went out on the balcony to address his supposedly faithful multitudes for the very last time, and the crowd had responded with a defiant mind of its own, the President had not been standing on a remote, elevated level far above the people. The balcony was only a little higher than the first floor of an English terrace house. The small figure at the microphone would have been audible through his public address system to thousands far back in the crowd. And just visible, from the middle of the mass that filled the square, above the heads of those in front. But President Ceausescu would have been on virtually the same level as everyone else. When the crowd began to shout abuse and defiance, it was not seeking to tear down a tyrant who at that moment towered over them on high – but destroying a small man who had contrived to win power over his fellows and serve them (as they thought) well in the early years, and then, slowly at first but in those last years ever more inexorably indulged his own vanity and imposed his own fear.

Carolina knew that Tim was coming. Immediately after the revolution he had written to her promising to telephone, and then had telephoned three weeks after posting the letter. Yes, she would see him, she said, whenever he came. And yes, she was certainly able to be in Bucharest, and could probably also accompany him to Târgu Alb if he wished to go there. Had he finished his Life of Philip, and would he be bringing the manuscript? There would be no problem about bringing it into the country, she reassured him. And yet there was something cool and cautious in her voice, a distant sound. He noticed that she did not raise the possibility of translating the biography, although she had been very eager to ask about it before.

The May weather had been cool in England. It was hot when he landed at Otopeni. In the downstairs hall, where the security inspection of luggage went on, he noticed that there were many more people lining up than in the past. More flights? Proceedings went faster here than they used to; so did they at passport control. In the baggage reclaim area, too, there was more activity, much more luggage.

He could see a gathering of many faces at the exit beyond the customs tables. Should he look for Carolina Predeanu among them? She had not said she would actually meet him and he did not presume to request her to do that. If she was not there, should he wait? No, he had told her which hotel he was at, she could trace him. He had Valeria Ciudea's address and phone number in Bucharest, and of course Carolina's in Târgu Alb.

Here among the crowds waiting for their baggage he listened. Did he merely *imagine* the voices raised around him in this dark, low-ceilinged luggage hall were more confident, more informal, than they had been last time? Probably; because he remembered several occasions when Romanian crowds had been noisy, vocal in impatience and complaint. And yet was he hearing one important difference? Yes, he was. He could hear on people's lips, openly, for the first time, the word 'Ceausescu'. The former President's name could now be casually used by people in public places, the dead man could be invoked and discussed in a way the live one never was.

The noisy, creaking carousel would every now and again stop, and sighs of frustration would pass around the crowd. An airport official would leap across it to break a crazy, crammed bottleneck of suitcases where they arrived at the top of the slope rising from the vault below. Finally his own bag came round, comfortingly familiar like a face in a waiting crowd.

Young men and women at customs looked only once at the suitcase when he lifted it onto their tables; and nodded him on. He made his way to the exit. Would there be a familiar human face waiting in this tightly-packed assembly of persons outside this narrow door, the parents and families and friends, the officials with neatly-lettered cards?

There was not. He scanned the crowd carefully. None of them showed him "Harker-Jones." Tim steered his bag through a gap and went out into bright light and dusty heat, stepping down with a bump onto a roadway where persistent men offered him "Taxi," "Taxi," quoting him prices in dollars – fifteen, twelve, ten – and asking him if he wanted the Hotel Intercontinental. He ignored them, lugged his suitcase on past them with difficulty, looked around him for a bus, could not see a bus.

He reckoned he could now fill in the physical detail of Otopeni airport well enough, in his paragraph about Philip Carston's arrival there on his various visits. He was sure from Carolina's description of it and his own vivid memories from last time (when Tillitt's eager British face had hauled him out of the queue at the passport window) that he could describe it quite well.

Today it had not changed much, or so he thought at first. But outside the terminal there were bullet-holes in the walls and some shattered windows still boarded up after the fighting around this strategic point; also an indefinable sense of relaxation – and disorder.

"*Taxi?*"

"How much?" he asked in English. "To the Hotel Bucuresti?" He had to get to his destination somehow.

"Twelve dollars."

"How much in pounds?"

Puzzlement, embarrassment, as if the pound were an obscure, dubious currency.

"How much in pounds *sterling*?" he persisted.

The extra word produced a flicker of recognition but did not clear the confusion.

"One pound," he enunciated clearly, "is, at present, one dollar and seventy."

"One dollar one pound?"

"Nearer two. Between the two. One dollar and *seventy*."

"Ten pounds sterling Hotel Bucuresti?"

"Oh all right." He capitulated in exhaustion, in relief, at striking some sort of a deal with this "businessman," at the hope that he would be where he was supposed to be, with time and space to drop his suitcase, lie down on a bed, think calmly what he might do next.

The taxi drove off at something less than the usual speed. The driver, who had showed him – almost bullied him – into the front seat, was talkative, and Tim understood nothing. He seemed to be asking questions which Tim could not answer. The only words he grasped – spoken in English – were "change dollars?" He had no dollars. Weakly he said, "I only have pounds." He took out the brown ten pound note with which he proposed to pay. The driver glanced at it, took in the fact that it was not a green dollar note, gave up for the time being.

Down the long wide highway from the airport, past the brown, red and cream model apartments built late in the Ceausescu days to replace a village, Tim noticed the sudden, the obvious, absence of roadside signs proclaiming patriotically the power of the President and the pre-eminence of the Romanian Communist Party. A few indicators of something different had already arrived: Agfa, Rank Xerox. If he now noticed the removal of the Ceausescu slogans, then he had observed them well enough last time to describe them adequately in the book. Good.

"No Ceausescu," he said, pointing at the empty roadside.

The driver swept the very memory aside with a contemptuous gesture of the right hand and arm. "*Ceausescu!*" he growled. "Ceausescu. Ceausescu." Then more quietly, as if the bitterness went too deep to articulate, "State, state, state," he muttered.

Tim believed he had understood.

"This taxi –" He circled a forefinger in air to indicate the interior of the vehicle, then tapped the top of the dashboard. "This taxi – you?"

"Da da, da da! Yes. *Privatizare. Particular.* Taxi – *me.*" He pointed to himself. "*Privat, Privat!*"

He shot up to the entrance of Tim's hotel, the Bucuresti in Calea Victoriei, between rows of favoured cars parked in front of it; but a uniformed commissionaire angrily waved him away. He pleaded, protested, through his wound-down window. The man yielded as far as to allow him to stop a few yards further on, and unload Tim's belongings. "Twelve pounds sterling," he declared.

"But we said *ten* pounds sterling." Tim showed him the brown note which had made so little impression.

"One pound per dollar," the driver insisted.

"We said *ten* pounds sterling. One pound is one dollar *seventy*." Tim found new energy to flash seven fingers several times.

"*Privat!*"

"I shall never take another private taxi," Tim said to himself when the man refused two one-pound coins and would only accept, in a surly, doubting way, a green five-pound note along with the ten. Fifteen pounds!

At Reception he noticed that the form he filled in was less than half the length of documents he had previously complied with in Bucharest and Târgu Alb. No, there were no letters or messages for him, he was told. He crossed the wide foyer under high wall-clocks which gave the time in London, Moscow, New York, Tokyo and Peking. A baggage porter carried his suitcase. Inside the lift the man set them on course for the fourth floor; faint rock music buzzed and rattled out from somewhere. Then he asked him in English if he would like to change some money; but accepted refusal with a certain grace.

Inside his room, at nearly the end of a long dim, calm corridor walled and carpeted in a brownish orange, with sets of heavy leather armchairs grouped in alcoves at intervals, he waited for the telephone to ring. Or something to happen. Something which would prove his presence here. He did not feel hungry yet. And he wanted to settle matters before he ate, know whether he could meet Carolina, or meet anyone, to-night. When he found courage and energy to try a call, the phone rang noisily on Valeria Ciudea's number, but the older woman's voice answering it spoke no English and he could not understand the information she was giving. He sought the switchboard, gave Carolina's Târgu Alb number, replaced his receiver and waited: five, ten, fifteen minutes. When it rang the operator told him there was no answer in Târgu Alb. He switched on the television.

The screen was flooded with flowers, and music played. A female figure in a flowing dress walked out of a mist and simpered at the camera. A young man in evening clothes appeared camera left, kissed her hand, and they simpered at the camera together. With a shock he realised he had been looking at a commercial. This interval ended, some kind of interview programme commenced, a man behind a desk questioned a man in an armchair – and that man he recognised. It was Stefan Tonaru.

The interviewer was being deferential, ingratiating. Tonaru was immaculately dressed, in what looked like a brand-new light grey suit, his eyes were bright and vivacious, he spread his hands with a confident smile. This was how he had been when Tim had met him, far from the mysteriously controversial figure who, in Carolina's account, had clung on to her and Philip shortly before he was driven off the scene by his indiscretions.

Tonaru was invited to rise from his chair in the television studio and cross to a map on the studio wall, the Pacific Basin: mainland China, Taiwan, South-East Asia and the South Pacific, at the top the Koreas and Japan, over on the right the Western coast of the United States, everything tapped with a stick and named by the interviewer. Whatever all this implied for Tonaru it seemed clear that the revolution had enhanced his fortunes.

He switched off the television. It was no use waiting, he still did not feel like eating, he would go out. He left his key at Reception, turned right, and almost immediately came upon the large open square where the former royal palace stood on one side and the monolithic hulk of the Central Committee of the Romanian Communist Party on the other.

Bullet-holes marked the side of the Athenée Palace Hotel, but the domed Atheneul looked untouched. A small but elaborate redbrick house between the two seemed to have been half destroyed by gunfire, something larger than rifle bullets. Fences surrounded the scarred walls of the University Library; fences plastered with posters screened off an area of the roadway, and cars were parked everywhere, many more than he had ever seen here on his previous visit.

He walked down the pavement alongside the palace, a path to tread with circumspection on his strolls with Angela Cernec. From the upper windows of the palace flowed huge versions of the new tricolour flag, the one with the national emblem symbolising the Ceausescu era cut out of the centre leaving a round hole: a gesture of eradication begging the question of what was to fill the vacant space.

He remembered by heart, without understanding it, the words of the sign on the roof of the telecommunications centre: TRAIASCA SCUMPA NOASTRA PATRIE REPUBLICA SOCIALISTA ROMANIA. They were no longer there. He crossed the road and passed a newspaper and magazine stall he recalled from the last time. The names of most of the publications had changed. *Romania Literara* and *Contemporanul* were still there, but *Informatia* and *Scînteia* had gone; instead he saw *Adevarul* and *Romania Libera*. Something extraordinary: a magazine with a cover in pale pastel shades showed a woman with bare breasts and pudenda. Its title was *Westporn*.

Crossing over and turning left at the busy intersection, remembering that he could find his way back to Calea Victoriei by simply turning left, and left again, he found the broad stretch of road which ended at the roundabout below University Square and under the Intercontinental Hotel. The square itself was closed to all traffic except for two narrow lanes kept nominally open by police holding back thronging crowds. Nearly five months after the revolution this was still named, he saw, the "Communist-free Zone." To-night, in the warm May twilight, the crowds were not massing for any purpose, just assembling to talk and argue.

The atmosphere seemed as uncertain and explosive now as it had seemed subdued and inarticulately resentful in the past. He discreetly joined the fringes of arguing groups, understanding nothing, trying to seem unnoticeable in case someone addressed a question to him. One pugnacious individual in a black felt hat seemed to be outnumbered, even alone, in whatever opinions he was voicing, battering the air with clenched fist as if beating at a closed door. The group around him derided his words, he dropped his fist in despair, walked away; they followed him for several yards calling "Jos Comunismul!" shaking their fists and laughing dangerously. On the façades of the university buildings the hammer-and-sickle were set up ironically alongside the faces of the six-month post-revolution government.

Now he left the crowds, found his way through a side street of small shops which brought him out to the back of the Central Committee building, then out into that square with the Athenée Palace Hotel on the right, and on to his own hotel.

People milled around this Reception counter of the Hotel Bucuresti, but with a different kind of discontent. He realised he was among the new business visitors flooding into this hotel, probably also into the Athenée Palace, certainly into the Intercontinental (though there persons from 'the media' often outnumbered everyone else.) They were plump, suited men, casual and blasé, indifferent as to where they might be as long as the inhabitants were malleable and it made money for them – or they were paid well for making it on behalf of someone else. They expected to be noticed immediately. Tim did not expect that, consequently was not seen. He looked up helplessly at the row of clocks above the marble staircase: here in Bucharest it was

9.45, in London it was 7.45... He could see his key lying in his pigeon-hole behind the counter, but there was no way of entering the clerks' enclosure and picking it up himself. He could also see that there was still no letter or note awaiting him there.

There was an argument at the end of the counter which distracted his attention, something about a bill, or a charge on a bill. A big man in a black suit gesticulated, bellowed in bad English, slammed a black dispatch-case on the counter and beat on it with the flat of his hands. The clerks watched and listened patiently.

"It is not our problem, sir," said one. "Sir, please, it is your problem."

Somebody accidentally nudged against, or touched, Tim's arm in the press of bodies at the counter, and instinctively he tried to move aside. But he had no space to do that, and whoever it was repeated the touch, and when he turned he saw it was Carolina.

– 3 –

In the time since they had last met, she had completely changed. Then she had worn, each time they met, the clothes in which Philip Carston had dressed Katrin in *A Time Apart*. Now her clothes were hard, tweedy and formal, severe. At first glance, with her hair taken up, scraped back, leaving her face thin and diminished, the change seemed to have aged her. But Tim soon saw that her face when she spoke to him was still clear and radiant.

"You're here!" he exclaimed with enormous pleasure and relief.

"I arrived at the station half-an-hour ago," she said.

At her signal, one of the Reception staff who had detached himself from the dispute at the end of the counter ignored other waiting guests and came to see what she wanted; he seemed to recognise her, she gave instructions.

"You are important here," Tim said wonderingly.

"No – just known here, before. They will help Romanian guests, especially women."

"And you are staying here too?"

"I am staying here."

"Not with Valeria Ciudea?"

"No." Rather flatly, in a curiously final way. "It is a little difficult now."

"Why?"

Carolina gave no answer for the moment, let him carry her suitcase over to the lifts. In the lift, where they were alone with the distant tap-tapping of music, she suddenly said,

"Valeria is no longer a friend. In times of 'freedom' you know who was really your friend in the past, and who was *not* your friend."

"But Valeria was your friend all the time from university onwards... Wasn't she?"

Carolina was silent, and he felt obliged to change the subject.

"It is very pleasant in this hotel, but very expensive for you?"

"*Very* expensive for Romanians. But when you have no other place – no friends in this city – you must stay where you can. It is most convenient to stay where *you* stay. We can talk a little before we go to Târgu Alb – you say you want to go there again, to describe it in your book?" He nodded. He wanted to see the place in the forest above the town, in particular. "I think you are my friend?" she said, with something like fright and doubt in her eyes, her brow furrowed as she asked. Tim saw that for some reason she sought and needed reassurance.

"Of course I am your friend."

"I have not so many. Ioana Guranu will always be a friend. And – it is strange – Tamasi Ilosz has been a good friend in these days."

The lift door opened at her floor. He helped her along the

endless corridor, quiet and deserted, a hundred doors and no sound from behind any of them, the wall lights dimmed almost to darkness. When they entered her room she offered him a chair as if she had always inhabited it, not just seen it for the first time in her life. Then she took the photograph of Philip Carston and Tim together out of her handbag.

"My dead friend," she said. "And my living friend." Then she sat down and seemed to want to say nothing more. He felt he had to say something; to break a strange silence.

"How is Professor Bobolescu?"

Carolina smiled and at once began talking volubly.

"He has not changed!" She even laughed at the thought. "There is nothing that will ever change him. He was always the same despite Ceausescu, and now he is the same with Iliescu. He is very old and frail and cunning, and he is indestructible... But Mrs Vajna is an enemy – you remember Eva Vajna? Dr Mandeliu has had problems, but he tries to be a good friend. But Mr Micu–"

"You told me about him. I didn't meet him."

"No, that's right. Well, he is an enemy."

"I saw Mr Stefan Tonaru on television."

Carolina was laughing, a very vigorous laugh, a forced laugh, making switchback motions with her right hand.

"I told you about him. Philip and I were his confidants when he was in trouble the first time. When you met him he was back in favour and very powerful. Then he was in trouble the second time, a few months before the revolution. Now the tide has turned and he is important again, very important. In two days he goes to be Cultural Attaché to – to – I forget which country, it is one of the little countries on the Pacific."

"I haven't had dinner yet. Have you?" Tim hoped that a meal and some wine might clear his mind of some of the confusions. "I will treat us both," he added, unnecessarily.

The lifts seemed unwilling to arrive, so they set out down the marble stairs, two slippery flights for each level, past foyer after foyer of leather chairs and sofas and spotless chandeliers, huge clusters of bulbs like grapes. She seemed so tensely quiet; he had spent the time in which he had not seen her thinking about a Carolina who had behaved with a luminous assurance which had mostly disappeared.

"When do you wish to go to Târgu Alb?"

"Friday? Saturday?"

"We will go on Friday. To-morrow we will go together for lunch at the Writers' Union," she said. It was almost a command. "I am a member now," she continued. "I was made a member in the autumn before the revolution so I have every right to be there."

The doorman in the hotel restaurant, who made a speciality of smiling welcome, waved them in and they passed along a thickly-carpeted approach to the large lighted spaces of the restaurant, as impressive in its vistas as the restaurant of the Athenée Palace opposite. Carolina led the way to a small table far from the band, which had struck up 'Over the Rainbow' noisily, in an only vaguely Romanised arrangement.

It was in a setting exactly like this, after an excellent meal with wine, that Tim had been thinking he would bluntly yet politely ask Carolina Predeanu, with the perfect choice of words, whether she had ever had a profound physical relationship with Philip Carston. If Carolina answered him directly on that point, there would surely be no problem about asking her at once whether she altered, or even wrote, *A Time Apart*. And certainly no problem on the question of whether Carolina had actually visited England.

But Carolina wanted to speak first.

"I will explain everything," she said. "It is like this. You know there was some foolish argument about who wrote this book? Before our revolution this was only a literary argument," she explained. "Now it is a political argument." Tim looked perplexed. "You do not understand. Listen. A book is published, here in Romania, which is about a very intelligent, very innocent Romanian girl visiting England. She stays with a Romanian couple who have emigrated to England. The husband is a good man with nostalgia for Romania, the wife is kind but foolish. She is a bourgeoise, she would be a bourgeoise anywhere in the world. Plant her anywhere, she would grow and grow like a little fat lettuce with no taste."

"But the girl and the couple are *not* Romanian in the original novel," Tim interrupted.

Did Carolina hesitate?

"Romanian readers *understand* the girl is Romanian. So: this Romanian girl sees your country in the 1980s through the people she meets and the places she visits, as a foolish, selfish, ridiculous place, yes?" This was to represent Philip's gentle satire rather strongly. But he nodded tentative agreement. "It is about your greedy, cruel, uncultured, Mrs Thatcher kind of society. And this Katrin is a member of the Romanian Communist Party?"

"Well, sort of –"

"You might also think that since Katrin travelled to England she was privileged, she was *allowed* to travel."

"English readers don't make all those assumptions – they wouldn't know they *could*." He wondered why Carolina was saying all this, where it was leading.

Wine was being poured for them, and Carolina made time by raising her glass in a toast, with something of the awe but none of the conspiracy she had shown in her dark apartment in Târgu Alb so long ago.

"To your Life of Philip!" she said firmly, sipped the Murfatlar thoughtfully, and put the glass down. "I am talking about some Romanian intellectuals. They believed this book to be an attack on Western bourgeois values. Do you understand? I was a member of the Party, I had succeeded in making a big English writer write and publish a novel about the folly of England, and, by implication, the virtues of President Ceausescu's Romania. I was made a member of the Union of Writers. You understand me? Before the revolution I had some honour for what I did. I had friends. Then – it changed. I was with my parents the day before

Christmas, and Christmas itself. We were watching all of that happen on television. The bodies of the President and Elena. On the day after Christmas I went to my apartment for half an hour. When I was putting my key in my door, my neighbour on the same landing came out and said, 'Your telephone has been ringing and ringing. I thought there was some emergency. It was ringing all last night. And today.'

Then suddenly it rang as I stood talking with her on the landing. When I picked it up a strange man's voice said, 'So your two friends are dead?' I was terrified. No friends I knew were dead. I could say nothing. Then he said, 'Your two friends, Nicolae and Elena.' 'My friends Nicolae and –?' Still I didn't understand. Then – 'They shot your two friends Nicolae and Elena, I saw it on television,' he said. 'Nicolae and Elena Ceausescu – your two old friends. You will miss them.' I put down the phone in horror. My neighbour was waiting at the door. She could see me holding the phone down with my hand, as if it might leap up into my face again the moment I let go. She is a very good, kind person, a Hungarian, our block is half and half, Hungarian and Romanian. I told her it was no emergency. She looked very unsure, and asked me if I was all right.

I didn't tell my parents. When I went back to the flat the next day it happened two or three times again, so I took the phone off for long periods, especially at night. Gradually it stopped. Once a week perhaps, then nothing. But after that the problems began at work."

Carolina's story entered a labyrinth of detail, internal politics of the Târgu Alb Writers' Union and its publishing house which Tim could not follow. But the general drift of the story was distressingly clear. Within the last five months the majority of the most dedicated Party stalwarts had been voted out of the publishing house or demoted. Dr Vasile Mandeliu was safe in Bucharest, where he had not been so conspicuous a Party man as he had been in Târgu Alb, but Carolina heard rumours that he had told someone his arm had been twisted to oblige him to publish *A*

Time Apart. Mr Sorin Micu, Dr Mandeliu's successor as director, had been sacked after a vote of the editors and workers. Tamasi Ilosz had declared himself a supporter of the U.D.M.R., the ethnic Hungarian party contesting the elections, so that the Hungarians generally stood by him and his future was not put to a vote. Carolina herself...

There had been people jealous of her success. She was only an ordinary young editor in the organisation, yet – they said – she had managed to arrange for herself this task which had (she laughed ironically as she told Tim this, it was so absurd) made her well-off, and famous, and had given her membership of the Writers' Union with all its freedoms and privileges.

And some people were saying that was not all. Carolina had not just translated *A Time Apart*. She had altered it, to make it more unfavourable to the West, and more favourable to the regime (a few people had been hinting this even before the revolution.) Other people were maintaining that she had been guilty of deception and written all of it herself, with Philip Carston supplying English background detail – he had been to see her in Romania several times. So the entire novel was a piece of Ceausist propaganda. That original dispute on Tim's train journey with Angela Cernec to Târgu Alb came back to him.

"But Ceausescu is never mentioned in the novel," Tim said incredulously. "Is he?" He began himself to wonder, almost, whether what appeared in the Romanian translation and what he had read in the original was point for point the same, or whether...

"You *know* Ceausescu is never mentioned," Carolina said sternly. "Not one word about Ceausescu, not the *name* Ceausescu. There are people accusing me who have never read the book, who would not understand the book if they had read it."

In the end it came to a vote on Carolina's future also; a farce, a humiliation, trial by jealous persons, she said. Tamasi abandoned any least resentment of the way she had broken off their love affair. It took courage because Tamasi had only narrowly escaped censure himself, and there he was, an ethnic Hungarian, defending a Romanian. He made a brave speech. People in Romania, he said, were now free to write, or sing, or act anything they wanted. They had the freedoms of the West. One of the freedoms of the West was the right to criticise your own political system. Mr Philip Carston had used that freedom in England, and Carolina Predeanu had translated his novel, and therefore many Romanians had seen that a writer in England was free to make fun of the values of his own society. So why should Romanians not have that freedom? Very subservient and boring propaganda literature had never sold well in the era of Ceausescu. Who bought the books Nicolae Ceausescu had 'written', unless they were obliged to buy them? But Carolina's translation had sold in thousands, it had sold out two days after it was published. If they allowed Carolina to keep her job they were acknowledging the quality and popularity of her work, and showing the tolerance that went with freedom of expression. And of course she had not written the novel herself! She had simply translated it, and why should she be condemned for translating what someone else had written.

Carolina feared, as she listened, that this was too clever, too over-subtle an argument for envious and determined people at the publishing house meeting. It reminded her a little of Tamasi and herself arguing about 'personal' versus 'political' philosophies – Jean-Jacques Rousseau, John Stuart Mill, Bentham, Karl Marx. But people had suffered intolerance for so long that they seemed afraid, when they realised how many different political opinions had surfaced in the office, lest their own opinion should be held against them some time in the future. So, to her surprise, the argument worked; up to a point. They voted to continue her salary, though without any rises for the time being.

And now, mysteriously, the most important editing work in the publishing house ceased to come her way. Silent jealousies worked against her now, friends became unfriendly, opportunities evaporated. Her work was menial, she had been quietly and subtly and thoroughly humiliated.

"It *is* humiliating," Tim agreed. "I am truly sorry." He did not really know how to respond. "Do you have enough money to stay in this hotel?"

"I saved a little from the payment for the book. I saved it for this purpose alone. I have enough for two nights. Not three. We can go to Târgu Alb on Friday. I have a very inexpensive hotel for you there."

"Will we meet enemies if we go to the Writers' Union here for lunch?"

"I told you. I am a member of the Union now. I have a right to go there, and you will come as my guest. Our enemies will see us there and it will show them we are not afraid."

"We"? Tim wondered how he was to be part of Carolina's defiance. If he needed to defend Philip's reputation, he would do that. But he could not do it in any language other than his own. He wished he had Angela Cernec, with all her diplomacy, to help him.

"Do you see Angela Cernec? My interpreter?"

"Angela is good. She is strong and true, and doesn't have two or three faces. We will see if we can meet her to-morrow." He was to be Carolina's guest at the Writers' Union and in her care in Târgu Alb; she was organising his second visit as Angela had organised the first. And suddenly her eyes lit up with an idea. "She has been showing her foreign visitors the House of the Republic. Perhaps she can take us there."

"You mean it's open now? We could go *inside* it?"

"It is open just for this month. Yes, we can see inside it. Angela can tell us all about it if she is free to come."

They parted, with Tim's large questions unasked, when the lift reached Carolina's floor, agreeing to meet at breakfast. Back in his own room Tim realised he had not even unlocked his suitcase. He began to look around for somewhere obscure to hide the draft manuscript of the final chapters of the Life. Then he decided it was no longer necessary; and simply left it under the pile of his clean shirts, in the wall cupboard with the sliding doors. He also decided he need not avoid walking across in the front of the mirror with the manuscript in his hand.

– 4 –

Turning right outside the Hotel Bucuresti they walked down the side of the square along the pavement, then down the length of Calea Victoriei to the point where it met the Bulevardul Republicii, then over into the narrower stretch where it passed the Militia headquarters (painted in light brown) and the Museum of the History of Bucharest, then out onto the Piata Unirii. In minutes they were in the huge cleared space where every avenue and walkway led to the largest building in the world. It now stood grand and mediocre and empty, with a future use no one could decide or imagine.

Outside the gate by which they were to enter the vast enclosure Angela Cernec waited.

She presented the same trim image, and Tim was certain now that she was a little younger than Carolina. She looked as neat and well-groomed as before, in a smart suit and with highlights sparkling in her short hair. When she greeted them it was with the same cool, impersonal efficiency.

So vivid was she in Tim's memory that he greeted her enthusiastically, half-expecting all kinds of immediate exchanges about their experiences together the last time they met. But Angela just smiled as he shook her hand; warmly enough, and yet – he suddenly realised – treating him just as one of many visitors, someone (it was true) happening to come back a second time, but in no way special or remarkable.

"You like our country, to come back to it?" she asked.

"I do," he said; and began to explain his other reasons for returning. But although Angela smiled and nodded as they walked up the approach road to the great edifice she did not respond to his words; and at the first opportunity she turned and spoke quickly and rapidly to Carolina. Their conversation, in Romanian, personal-sounding, continued up to the door of the Casa Republicii.

When the three of them entered the front door – the chill of the interior caused them all to shiver – Tim and Carolina stood silenced by the alarming scale of the place; then began to adjust to it.

In the first vast hall they saw a counter, no more than two tables, with people gathered around it.

"Postcards," Angela explained. "We can see them later. And sign the book. And *I* can guide you," she said when an official guide approached them and offered a tour.

They mounted a wide staircase under the dizzyingly high, plaster-embellished ceilings, turned into something that was too huge for a corridor, too unfocused for a hall, just a large and pointless indoor space with white columns in solid marble interrupting the line of vision. Or what appeared to be solid marble; they saw that on several columns the smooth facings of marble had not yet been set in place, and a thick core of grey concrete stood exposed.

"These chandeliers, they tell me," said Angela pointing upwards – heavily ornate, giant versions of what Tim had seen in hotels and the grander offices, they were all brilliantly alight – "are made of one hundred and twenty carat gold."

"I didn't know you could go above twenty-two carat."

"And the elevators," Angela went on, " are large enough for limousines."

Further along they stood among schoolgirls gazing down into an unfinished, steeply-raked assembly hall with tiers of seats facing a platform and a podium. Wires ran everywhere, trailed down from holes in the plaster of the ceiling. The indoor lighting here (no windows) was low, but allowed them to see everything.

"For the Grand National Assembly," Angela explained.

"Which will not now meet?" Tim reflected.

"Which will not now meet."

They came to a very large double door. Inside was a room that would have seemed large anywhere else but was small for this place, no bigger than the floor area of a medium-sized church in England. Two further doors opened out of it, to the right and to the left.

"This is the outer office, the ante-room to the two presidential offices. One for him, one for her."

Tim looked sidelong at Carolina to watch her reaction to all this. She was impassive, taking in everything, but betraying no feelings.

A guide accompanying schoolgirls stepped past them, beckoned to Tim and Carolina to follow, and opened the doors on each side for them. Tim had glimpses of wide, square, eerily vacant spaces, this time with high windows looking out over the city and up the long, long avenue with its shops and flats and fountains.

"May we go in?"

"They say *this* would have been Elena Ceaucescu's room," Angela told them. "She would have looked out at that house over there. It was to have been the House of Science, her particular house." They returned to the endless halls with the chandeliers, the plasterwork, the marble, the industrial gold, the wires leaking out of uncovered panels in the walls. Angela had dropped behind, now caught them up.

"I have been curious," She said. "I asked that guide why there are no mirrors – or where they were planning to put the mirrors. She says there were to be no mirrors. Ceaucescu did not *like* mirrors."

And then Tim realised why, in this last hour, he had heard no distinct echoes. It was because the House of the Republic was nothing *but* echoes. The spaces carried away and repeated everything you said. Could it ever have been filled with enough inflated averageness – oak desks and tables, characterless panelling, padding and carpeting, chairs of real or bogus leather – to make normal, unresonant converse possible? Tim deliberately wandered some yards away from Carolina and Angela. "Can you hear me from here?" he said quietly when they looked at him. Shrill chatter from the groups of girls drowned the words. He tried again, from a few steps further on still. "I can hear you," Carolina replied. Their words went out to the farthest walls, came back.

Downstairs again, on the way out, they looked at the postcards. They cost ten lei each, which seemed expensive to Tim by Romanian standards (almost twenty-five pence in London, so the same as most English prices.) They looked at the visitors' book, with its spaces for names, addresses – and a column for suggestions as to the future of the building. Opposite the signature and address of someone from Detroit, Michigan were the words: *A wonderful place for a great new bank*! Carolina took a pen from her handbag, and wrote something, in Romanian, in a fast and flowing hand.

"What did you write?" Tim asked her. "'Give it to some public purpose which will benefit *everyone*'," she said. "'A university, a hospital, a world library'."

"I will buy some postcards," Tim said. He paid out the 100 lei for ten different views: the standard view from outside, the halls and spaces, the chandeliers. "You don't want any? I can get you some as a present?"

"I have plenty," she said. "They were sent to me by the voice on the telephone. With threats of death."

Outside they realised how humid and oppressive the day had become; the heat of the sun physically weighed on them from behind low clouds. Here Angela gave at least some sign that she remembered him as somebody different from other visitors.

"So. You have come back to collect all the information you could not find out last time?" she began. He wondered if Carolina had told her about his secret visits to Valeria Ciudea's home to hear her story.

"I *hope* I can collect it," he said.

"And Carolina says you go up to Târgu Alb to-morrow?"

"I do. You know – I remember so many things from our visit there. It was all so strange –"

"It will be the same. Not different yet. Nothing is different yet," she said enigmatically.

"It would be nice to meet and have a talk when I come back to Bucharest."

"I don't know." She grimaced her regret. "I have so little time next week... Perhaps you will be a regular visitor to Romania? We can meet on the next occasion?"

That reply sounded no more than a courtesy. Tim felt that the months and the events that had fallen between – and Angela's other visitors – had separated them. Without the prospect of a fortnight in Angela's care, the appointments to keep, the interpreting to be done, the trains and the taxis, there was no chance of their coming closely together again. Probably last time was now only a distant memory for her, for all the problems Tim had produced for her.

"How is your car? Still running well on its new distributor?"

For a few moments she looked puzzled; and then she laughed.

"Oh yes. it runs very well now. But it needs new tyres..."

They were back at the gate, and it was obvious from Carolina's manner that she was preparing to say goodbye to Angela for today and carry Tim off to lunch by himself. He tried one more reminiscent remark as they shook hands a bit stiffly in farewell – neither thought of a kiss.

"You said I was probably your most difficult visitor," he reminded her.

"Did I?" Angela said. And then thought. "Oh yes, I remember. I did, Yes, you *were*."

– 5 –

What Tim saw and heard as they entered the dark entrance hall of the Writers' Union now, in May 1990, was certainly no different. He remembered at once the three-cornered, cushioned seat in front of him, and beyond it the marble staircase, more modest in scale than the one in the House of the Republic and more genuine; thus more magisterial and authoritative. He felt and smelt the coolness of the house after the heavy heat of the cloudy morning outside in Calea Victoriei. He heard again the very distant, subdued murmur of voices in offices, downstairs and upstairs. He felt a nostalgia for the room – the bugged and eavesdropped room? – on the left of the front entrance, the one with the green curtains, the packed glass-fronted bookcases and the big stove. That was where he had first been welcomed by official Romania, first seen the translation of *A Time Apart* among Dr Mandeliu's display of books on the table, first heard the name of Carolina Predeanu.

At this spot where he paused now, with Carolina urging him towards their lunch, he had been given her address and phone number covertly by Valeria Ciudea, while someone – yes, Stefan Tonaru, no less – had doubled back to gather up his forgotten overcoat. He wanted to tell Carolina about all this, indulge his clear memories of the moment, but she was hurrying him on.

They went along the oddly narrow corridor to the restaurant entrance, aware of welcome food smells and of voices chattering loudly and rattling crockery somewhere out of sight in a kitchen. In the restaurant itself – the dark panelling, the flowers on the close-together tables – there seemed to be as many people as in the past. Tim liked to think he remembered faces well; but he saw no one familiar to him from his last lunch here.

Carolina firmly indicated a chair for him at a table laid for four, where already a man and a woman ate steadily, doggedly in silence. Carolina's manner, in surveying the room with a comprehensive gaze before she sat down, was bold and defiant; as if she dared anyone who might know her to come over and talk.

The first person Tim did recognise was Valeria herself, suddenly entering and greeting acquaintances at a table near the door. He could see them more clearly across the room now because the two people at their own table had risen to leave.

"That's Valeria Ciudea," he could not help exclaiming. She

hasn't seen us."

"She has seen us."

"No she hasn't – I'll go and say hallo."

"No!" Carolina dropped a hand on his wrist. "Never!"

Valeria looked over towards their table, looked past it. It was as if she was seeing only strangers' faces. A waitress came for instructions."Why is Valeria no longer a friend?"

"She had *permission* to let you meet me at her home." Carolina said it quietly, ominously. Everything I said to you was recorded. *Everything!*"

Tim stared at her.

"Somebody knew I was meeting Philip there on his last visits. They asked Valeria to explain. She could not explain. Because she could not, they required her to report *in detail* any more meetings with foreigners in her house. She reported you were going there to talk with me, and the Securitate made sure it was all recorded."

"You are saying that – that all our conversations were –?– your whole story –?"

Now Tim Harker-Jones was shocked into speechlessness. What had he said on those occasions that compromised or incriminated *him*? Or put Carolina Predeanu in any danger? What had Carolina herself said? But then, why should he – why should Carolina – be fearing anything now, nearly six months after the revolution, in a free Romania, with a free election campaign in progress, the file opened?

"How do you know this?"

"You know the revolutionaries, the students, broke into the secret records of the Securitate? Someone from Târgu Alb was in Bucharest during the revolution – well, he is a student in the University here. He found a file about people living in that sector of the city – and by chance he saw my name in some pages of information about foreigners. I was visiting Valeria's house with a foreigner – you! What I said was written there."

Tim needed time to think...

"Were there things about Philip seeing you there?" The peculiar possibility that he would need to look at a Securitate file to discover the ultimate truth about Philip and Carolina left him almost breathless with amazement and alarm.

"No, thank God no, only the *fact* that we went there is known, nothing is on the records. Only my visits there with you." *Only* those, he thought!

"Was there anything likely to get you into trouble in anything we said? *You* said?"

"No, nothing. Or very little. No great revelations. I spoke like a loyal Party woman. I was always careful to do that. But that is not the point at all. The point is that my 'friend' was passing the information back."

"Perhaps she had to?"

"Oh yes. Everyone had to. But not everyone *did*."

Over at the table, with her companions, Valeria laughed. It was not more than twenty feet away. The crowd in the restaurant thinned out. Tim wondered what would happen if the only people left were Valeria and her friends at one table, Carolina and himself at another. But soon more diners entered to make up the numbers.

"Have you seen this file? Can you prove this?"

"I didn't see it. But I believe the person who told me. It is Liviu Bobolescu's son, Virgil. I trust him."

"Have you *asked* Valeria?"

"If I see her I do not speak to her. Her manner tells me she realises I have found out. She makes no attempt to speak to *me*. She is making no attempt now."

This was true. But could it not, all the same, be a mutual mistake? The light shone into the labyrinths after the revolution had not dispersed the paranoia, perhaps even compounded it.

"Do you think they expected *me* to reveal anything interesting?" Tim asked. That there might be a Securitate file devoted exclusively to *him* seemed ludicrous.

"No, I am sure they did not expect that." Tim was slightly

disappointed. "You see, if someone is in Valeria's position, a very clever girl and she wants promotion... In Ceausescu's time, she had to be useful if there was a chance of reporting on foreign visitors. When she knew Philip was invited to Romania she thought, 'What a good idea if my mother – Valeria's mother was very important at the Council for Culture – if my mother asked my student friend Carolina to interpret for him, because Carolina will tell me everything they do and everything they talk about.' You know every time Philip was here she was asking questions, questions, questions."

"But did she arrange for Philip to meet you at her house so as to –?"

"No, I don't believe that. Because Virgil Bobolescu saw no records of meetings there with Philip. But someone *saw* Philip going there, I told you that, and from then onwards she had to work to give them more information about foreigners because she had been secret about Philip. She was *not* secret about you. And those visits were allowed so that the Securitate could listen."

Two more strangers filled the vacant places at their table and Carolina fell silent again. Generous plates of ham arrived, bread without butter, *apa minerala* and wine. They ate. From out of the crowd of diners a woman arrived to chat to the newcomers, very tall, very thin, rather jerky in her movements, with a naturally fierce and observant expression which she relaxed when she spoke to someone.

And where could Tim have seen her if not here, because he certainly associated her with this room? And suddenly the name came to him; and the story, without needing to turn to Carolina and ask (impossible while the woman was standing at their table.) This was Stella Sandoran, dissident playwright, author of a play with religious overtones, staged in a small theatre a long way from Bucharest, and successful with audiences – until the run was arbitrarily ended.

She was in intense and animated conversation; perhaps, if it was interesting, Carolina would have eavesdropped and could translate later? Tim watched Stella as she talked. He remembered the low-cut dress – but today she wore, as well, a necklace, consisting of a string of coins which lay flat on the skin below her neck. When she bent over and rested a hand on the table, her tall body tilting markedly out of the vertical, the coins detached themselves from the tanned and mottled skin on which they lay flat when she stood up straight, and Tim could see what they were. They were polished silver coins, lei minted during the reign of King Carol II, before the Second World War. They all resembled the stray monarchist coin Tim had discovered on the floor of the hotel lift in Târgu Alb...

"But this is Mr Harker-Jones, yes?"

Standing alongside Stella Sandoran, obviously with her, was Ioan Ludache.

And Ludache, like Stefan Tonaru and Stella Sandoran, seemed to have drawn new confidence and verve from the revolution. He did not greet Carolina but stood smiling warmly, rather too warmly, at Tim himself, dropping a bag he carried and launching out a hand to be shaken. Tim shook it; he did not imagine his response was very heartening, yet Ludache seemed well pleased.

"You have met Mademoiselle Stella? Stella Sandoran?" he asked. Introductions were made, Tim half standing up to shake (not kiss) Stella's hand while she remained bending over the table, the necklace suspended in mid-air. Still Carolina was not included in the exchanges – but she was now in separate conversation with the two strangers at their table. Sausages and side salads came.

Stella greeted Tim with curious warmth, perhaps that of someone overcoming a reluctance to meet him.

"*Vous êtes bien connu ici. Extrêmement bien connu!*"

Tim did not enjoy the sound of that information. And did she mean well-known just in the Writers' Union, or in Romania generally?

"*Vous avez fini votre grand livre?*"

"*Non.*" He had not really finished his biography, had he... In slow, exact French he began to explain, but had the impression that Stella was not willing to listen. Angela Cernec's forgetting about him a little when she had perhaps twenty visitors a year he could understand; but he put down Stella as someone with no particular interest in others, merely an ability to think of polite questions.

Ludache, whose English had always been better than he made out, now seemed to have an easy command of Tim's language. He pulled up two chairs for Stella and himself – away from Carolina, Tim noticed – but Stella declined the offer. She had to go. She stood up straight, and the silver monarchist coins fell back coolly onto her bare skin. Her handshake was that dismissive kind which declared, I am finishing this conversation, good-bye, I am glad to be rid of you.

"Do you see differences in our country?" Ludache asked him.

"I do – and I don't," Tim replied. "But I suppose you are much more free to write biographies now?"

Ludache gave him an odd, superior, tolerant smile.

"Yes, it is possible," he said. "But 'biographies' – I do not write them."

Not even a biography of Carolina Predeanu, Tim speculated in silence? Even if Carolina had disobligingly not died yet, despite the "period of political upheaval" through which the country had passed, the prediction quoted by Ludache all those months ago.

"My activities are different now," the man went on. He reached down eagerly into his bag, and Tim saw it contained several copies of a magazine. Tim now had one pushed into his hands. He could not understand the title; its plain black-and-white cover consisted of signs of the zodiac. As he looked at it he was aware of Valeria Ciudea rising from her table, looking around the room, not greeting Carolina or himself, leaving.

"For you!" Ludache proclaimed. "I am editor-in-chief."

"You are? It is a literary magazine?"

"No!" Ludache shook his head as if nothing could have been more ridiculous. "It is a horoscope magazine."

"*Horoscopes*? Just – horoscopes?"

"Yes. Just horoscopes. You remember I told you about horoscopes?" He said this lamely, as if suddenly realising that his predictions about Carolina had been wrong.

"And is this your job now – for a salary?"

"For a good salary. Eight thousand lei a month." He seemed inordinately pleased with himself.

"And you have no plans to write a – a biographical work?"

"Nothing at all at the moment." His smile was complacency itself. Now Stella had gone he seemed eager to leave also. When he had gone, Carolina turned back to Tim.

"This lady and this gentleman do not speak any English," she said indicating the others. "So I can say what I think."

"What *do* you think?"

"I could not speak to that – that man. You understand that!" She was trembling with anger, but also bright-eyed with triumph.

"Yes," Tim agreed, uncertainly.

"And I will never speak to Stella Sandoran – never. You notice they do not speak to me in this house. But I have come here – and I have stayed until they all left. Valeria Ciudea has left. And I am still here."

And she drank off the wine in her glass.

NINE

– 1 –

Since his first visit here Tim had not nearly so often experienced that alarming sense of the need to piece himself together when he woke in the morning. He had come to the interesting conclusion that piecing together Philip Carston's early and middle life had proved a substitute for that. But when he began work on Philip's last years the old sensations of disintegration frequently returned. And now, back in Romania, in particular today, lying in bed in Târgu Alb, they took a different form. He had a nightmare.

Usually his rare nightmares would strike Tim at about three or four in the morning. He would sit up in bed afterwards, shake his head hard to put it out of mind – and go back to sleep. But on this occasion he did not wake up – he just dreamed repeatedly that he was already awake and utterly unable to make anything in his prostrate body connect and work. He saw himself, literally saw the familiar body of Tim Harker-Jones waking up in relief, shaking his head vigorously – and then he would find he was back ineluctably into the horror, as if condemned to an eternal existence inside this phantasm.

And Tim's body, which would *not* be put together, so that it could move, limb by limb and muscle by muscle, with terrible physical and intellectual effort, was really the later life of Philip Carston. The body had had a pleasant, tranquil, explicable time until near the end of its night's rest – no problem. Then it reached the point where it was all unconnectable pieces. No metaphor Tim's brain could employ seemed to be of any use: putting a child's building blocks together, fitting a light bulb, laboriously assembling an electric plug, none of it would avail. Nor could he use his formerly strong elbows to lift his torso into life and pull his limbs after it: he couldn't find firm spots on which to rest those elbows, they contacted only sand, mud, air.

So he eventually woke up in this eerie, empty 'hotel' in a secluded avenue in Târgu Alb utterly exhausted, fully realising what his nightmare meant.

"I have been working all night," he said aloud, "working, working, working, fruitlessly and in confusion".

He had arrived with Carolina by train the night before, Carolina, like Angela Cernec, had contrived to bring food for the journey, so they had not gone hungry. As they talked, Tim had tried to lead up to his unanswered questions by enquiring what things people Philip had met would be doing now. He knew a little about Tamasi Ilosz's fortunes and Dr Mandeliu's, but what about Ilie Radin? And Eva Vajna?

"Is Mr Radin able to use his English these days?" he asked, thinking of the drafted page in his biography where he related (from Carolina's description) the intriguing account of Philip, always the correct and decent Englishman, courteously allowing a self-taught Securitate officer to practise his English with him over a dinner table in Târgu Alb.

"He is still learning it, but no he is not able to use it," she told him.

"He is not still working for the – the police?"

"No, he is not. At first people wanted to arrest him. But after the first month they left him alone. And they allowed him a job. He is employed in small courts in the country. Around Târgu Alb. You did not know he was studying law and taking examinations all the time he was working for the Securitate? He has all the qualifications to be a full lawyer now."

But the English? That really was a boat built in a cellar, an accomplishment that made no sense.

"And Mrs Vajna?"

"That enemy! Eva Vajna is making her name at last. With a *book*."

"You mean she's to *publish* a book?"

"She is publishing a book. A novel she has been working on for several years – her modern novel she told me about years ago. It is in the form of her diary she pretends to have written – many people are wanting to publish their secret diaries of the Ceausescu years, but this is fiction. She pretends that we refused to publish her work for political reasons, and now she can reveal to the world that her novels were too daring."

"Is the new novel good?"

"I haven't read it. Tamasi Ilosz has read it."

"Does he want to publish it?"

"No."

Outside the station in Târgu Alb they had taken a private taxi operated by a "businessman", and Tim paid for it, not sure whether he had been overcharged or not. It left them at a modest, virtually anonymous, hotel entrance, alongside which the plaque announcing a previous name had been painted over.

"It is an old Party hotel," Carolina said. "It is to be for forestry scientists now."

Tim was surprised that it wasn't larger and more pompous. They pushed through swing doors on which (presumably) a name or a Party symbol had been obliterated in readiness for something different, and arrived in an empty foyer. Tapping loudly on the high Reception counter eventually brought a clerk who greeted Carolina familiarly and knew about the booking.

The whole building was silent, seemingly unoccupied at the moment by anyone else at all. Carolina left her bag in reception and they walked to the second floor, where the scanty floor-covering changed from crimson to fawn and the yellow walls were as bare as anywhere else. Tim looked along them for signs of pictures or posters having been removed. There were none. The place had apparently always been like this, austerely decorated, no distractions. What would Tim's room be like?

It had a plain, institutional door faced with painted hardboard, numbered 29. The key opened it readily, and they were through a dark lobby where the overhead light did not work and into a bedroom that felt agreeably cool on this warm day in late May. Instinctively Tim looked at all the facilities, doubling back to see the bathroom had no bath, just a shower with green plastic curtains – and he hated showers.

The coverlet on the single bed was serviceable but drab, the pillows gave promise of unmanageable foam rubber. There was no ceiling light, just a lamp on the small bedside cabinet; but there was the largest television set Tim had ever found in a hotel. Pushing a button produced a grainy black-and-white picture of imaginary voters in the coming elections presenting identity cards at a polling station and receiving large booklets containing lists of candidates.

"You will be all right here?" Carolina asked him, a little anxiously.

"Yes. It's – excellent. But I'm surprised a Party hotel isn't luxurious," Tim ventured.

"There is a problem here now it is *not* a Party hotel – there will be no food here," she told him.

"No *food*?"

He was not yet hungry, but he soon might be. And yet he would prefer to sort out his plans alone this evening rather than dine once more with Carolina and shout out delicate questions above the amplified racket of a restaurant band.

"I think I will rest," he said. "And it's quite late."

She showed a little reluctance to leave him alone; but he assured her he would not come to harm and they agreed to meet again downstairs at ten in the morning (without breakfast, he reflected.)

When she left he began to unpack, half watching the television. The slow, methodical explanation of polling procedures was continuing. A polling official, a tall, silently beautiful girl, stood behind her desk while her superior explained to the camera what she would do. She would stamp identity cards and voting booklets, and people would pass on to the polling booths where they could mark their preferences in secrecy.

Then the picture changed and a long, long list of very old or very new political parties slowly slid up the screen. Tim counted over fifty. He reflected deeply on the strangeness of sitting in what once had been a Romanian Communist Party hotel, ambiguous symbol of a monolithic one-party state, watching the procedures of a free election elaborately recounted on television.

At the end a voice-over announced something else. This was a party election broadcast, probably on behalf of a small party because the presentation consisted of statements read earnestly from scripts held by four dour men at a plain wooden table. When it finished there was a brief, unannounced intermission during which spring flowers filled the screen in silence. And suddenly there came a brief neo-surrealist (or dadaist?) performance with puppets and droll music, asking votes (Carolina later translated) for "Liber Schimbist," the Party of Free Exchange: the new Romanian politics had some appealingly curious corners.

The major parties were more conventional: the Peasants' leader appealed magisterially, face-to-camera; the Liberals provided a symbol of recrudescence and hope, the sun rising over mountains (how strange that it partly resembled the symbol cut out of the flag); the National Salvation Front came on with whirling graphics and loud fanfares in a fully-fledged western-style party political broadcast. This was the climax and the end of the parties' television parade for the evening. After one misty commercial and another spring flower came the news, which Tim was unable to understand. He switched off the set, looked at his unopened manuscript, lay on his bed, realised he was not sleepy but beginning to be hungry, and resolved to have a shower and go out.

Always, in a shower, he realised how very much he loathed them. In no shower in the world does the plastic curtain wholly screen off the rest of the room, but at least Romania seemed to guarantee sloping tiled floors which let escaping water run away down a drain. In no showerbath anywhere is the fixed shower-rose set at an ideal angle for everyone's height. Here in the Party hotel it was set exactly at Tim's head level, just too low for him to stand under it, experience a suitably strong spray, and turn his body round to get everything satisfactorily drenched. He was obliged to take it off its hook. But when you do that, and hold it, you can't obtain a lather from the soap one-handed, you have to try to rest the instrument on a ledge, where it falls off, or on the floor, where it bucks and twists like a trapped snake. All of which is only the beginning: there is how to secure the right temperature of water, the right strength of the jet... Tim had never in his life come out of a shower feeling other than scalded (or chilled), demoralised, and inadequately washed.

It was just after eight-thirty, still pleasantly light, cooler. He would stroll into the centre and dine at the Transilvania, where both he and Philip had dined separately in the past. When he arrived the restaurant looked almost full. The vast room was magnified and extended by the reflections of hundreds of drinkers and diners in the large oval wall-mirrors with their floral decorations wrought into the glass around the edges. On every table was a pot of African violets cased in silver paper. The band was playing vigorously; here at least it was back to (or it had never left) the music of the country, possibly even the music of the region: to-night it was led by a gipsy electric violin. The clientele at the tables, mainly just drinkers, sang along noisily to boisterous or maudlin melodies. There were no empty tables. Tim thought it best to join a table where some dining as well as imbibing was taking place.

His two companions were young men eating with contented concentration; one of them – fair-haired, clean-shaven, affable, with humorous eyes – nodded as Tim took a seat, and addressed him in Romanian. Tim put on his best look of vulnerable, genial bewilderment, and the young man tried another tongue, perhaps Hungarian, Tim couldn't tell. The third attempt was in German, and in that language Tim could at least say he did not speak it. He tried English.

"English? Good! Good!"

The fair young man shook his hand warmly. The second,

with downturned lips and a long black moustache, black close-cropped hair, blue eyes and a sad expression, put out a hand more tentatively but put it out all the same, saying something to his companion.

"My friend is sorry he speaks only Hungarian. He is visiting from Hungary."

"But *you* speak Romanian *and* Hungarian – I think?" Tim asked.

"I speak Romanian first, then Hungarian, then German a little. I live in Târgu Alb, he is from Debreczen in Hungary. I speak English also – from the university."

They were sitting not far from a wide entrance to the kitchen, two broad swing doors. Above it was a notice strictly forbidding any strangers to enter the kitchen – *strict interzis* – but people from the tables seemed to be constantly passing in and out. A woman brandishing a bag of national lottery tickets stopped at their table.

"I will buy you a ticket," declared Tim's new acquaintance. He gave a few lei to the seller, who insisted Tim accept a sealed number from her store. He looked at it with embarrassment not knowing what to do.

"The English have good luck. A good government and good luck with it," the fair-haired man proclaimed. "Open it. You tear it."

Tim tore it open, failed to understand what it meant, showed it the seller. All three of the others laughed with delight.

"I told you, the English have good luck! You have won twenty lei!" The seller counted out four five lei coins into Tim's hand. "Alexandru," the young man announced, pointing to himself. "Imre," pointing to his friend. "Tim," said Tim. "I will buy you a drink," he suggested.

"We will buy *you* a drink." Alexandru insisted. Immediately he found a waitress and gave orders as she cleared away their empty plates. Tim, almost desperately hungry now, caught her arm. The usual exchanges began. "What food?" "No food." "But –" Intervention from the helpful strangers. "They have soup, salad, schnitzel," Alexandru informed him. "I will have all of those. Please." The waitress readily agreed when Alexandru translated, apparently also agreed to bring wine, because the two men also pointed to their empty glasses, asked for a glass for Tim.

Famished, Tim parried questions at first, then relented genially when dry bread and thick bean soup came; and told them he was here to write a book. Imre poured him wine. They toasted each other. "You will bring us luck," Alexandru said. "Why?" Tim said. "English and Americans bring us luck." "Why English more than – Russians?" "Russians? Never! *Bad* luck." "I hope you have luck without needing to meet English people – not many come here," said Tim. "But you," Alexandru wished to know, "do you have luck so far with this book you write? Do you have ideas?"

"I wish I knew," Tim told them doubtfully.

Out of the corner of his eye, far away across the room, he suddenly saw, arriving alone at a small table and taking his seat, a solid, unmistakeable figure: Ilie Radin, wearing the same kind of smart, official blue suit; but a newer one.

"What kind of book is this?"

"The life of someone. A biography."

"A Romanian?"

"No. An Englishman who knew a Romanian and visited Târgu Alb."

"A Romanian *girl*?"

"Yes –"

"This is Mr Carston you write about?"

- 2 -

Tim gaped.

"You have *guessed*... Do *you* know about Mr Carston?"

"*Everyone* who reads books in Târgu Alb knows the name of Mr Carston. He has made our town famous in England." Alexandru laughed loudly, signifying that this was patent exaggeration. He poured Tim more wine.

"He was a friend of someone called Carolina Predeanu." Tim thought it best to declare his own connection. "She has kindly brought me to Târgu Alb and is helping me."

"Ah!" There was mischief, or flattery, in the young man's broad smile. Tim felt the wine taking effect, sensed also that he was about to place a sort of lunatic trust in this stranger and ask him direct questions which might not be answered fully (or truly?) by other people whom he knew a little – even if that seemed unfair, improper, intruding on Carolina's privacy from a distance.

"I believe Mr Carston was deeply in love with Miss Predeanu," he observed.

"Sure he was, it is well-known," came the answer, as if Tim must be the last person on earth to discover that.

"Do you know Miss Predeanu?"

"No, not at all. I have never met her. But, you know, she is a legend here, everyone knows her story. And –" for some reason he glanced round the restaurant, seeing someone he waved to and focusing someone else, a face over there in Radin's direction – "it is not a good story."

"Why?"

"Everyone knows she and her friend worked for the Securitate –"

"Her *friend*?"

Although Imre was patently understanding nothing and seemed bored, Alexandru put a hand on his arm as if to reassure him that he had no ill-feeling towards Hungarians in themselves. "Her Hungarian lover. Tamasi Ilosz."

"I see."

"They had instructions – and an old professor had instructions – to lure Mr Carston into writing the book. Then they 'translated' the book together – and miracle! – it is a different book. You cannot speak – read – Romanian?"

"No."

"In Romanian it is another book."

"Have you seen the English version? In my room I have –"

Alexandru laughed.

"There are no copies of the English novel in shops in our country even now. They do not wish the people who can read English to compare."

"So how do you know there is a difference?"

Alexandru smiled patiently.

"When any novel was translated in the era of Ceausescu some small things had to be left out. So why not write new things yourself?"

"Do you know a book *Ulysses*? By James Joyce?"

"Of course, I have it – in Romanian."

"I was told by – by a Romanian friend that *Ulysses* was translated without any changes. And that is a very daring book."

"Yes. And it is a classic. There is never much need to alter anything in a classic – and people will discover if you do. But when it is a novel of our own era –"

"Can you lend me a copy of the Romanian version of Philip Carston's book?" Tim asked. Somehow or other, though certainly not asking Carolina, or Tamasi Ilosz – or Liviu Bobolescu – he would have to persuade someone to go through Carolina's translation and Philip's original, chapter by chapter, page by page, fast, to get at the truth.

"Unfortunately, no. I do not own it."

Suddenly Tim was not so sure he wanted to trust Alexandru's information. It was not that Tim felt he was being deliberately misinformed; the problem was Alexandru's pleasure in rumour and gossip. That Carolina had worked for the Securitate to write or rewrite Philip's novel was inconceivable. Seeing Imre drum his fingers on the tablecloth Tim changed the subject.

"What do you both do for a living in your countries?" Alexandru translated this for Imre immediately.

"We will have a private music shop. Perhaps two or three. We will make and sell cassettes."

"Can you get enough blank cassettes for that?" Tim thought of the record shops in Bucharest and Târgu Alb where everything had been on LP's, on vinyl. Alexandru explained.

"Yes. We will buy the blank cassettes. And we will make our own cassettes to sell to our customers."

"Customers" sounded odd, western, even English on Alexandru's lips.

"With your own musicians?"

"No," Alexandru said seriously, and murmured something in Hungarian to Imre. Imre took a couple of cassettes, not blanks, out of his pocket: they looked like Hungarian pop.

"We will record these on blank cassettes for our customers."

"And you can sell them here?"

They misinterpreted his question. Tim meant sell them within the law without prosecution for piracy. They meant, build up a trade with them.

"*Yes*! The Hungarians in this town want the new Budapest groups. They will buy them."

Tim saw that to pursue the question of copyright would be indiscreet. He nodded, asked,

"But you haven't started yet?

"No. I am a teacher now. I open my shop in the autumn."

So you, Tim thought, a speaker of German and English – and Hungarian – a teacher now, a reader of James Joyce and Philip Carston, will be a retailer of pirated, *stolen*, rock music in the first autumn after the revolution.

"Won't you miss your teaching?"

"Yes, I will miss it. But I will make more money with my shop."

Tim thought he might just as easily lose it. Perhaps something of shock in his expression got across to Alexandru, because the young man smiled, sweetly.

"I see what you are thinking, " he said. "But please – we have had our tyranny, let us have a little decadence."

"Are many people changing jobs after the revolution?"

"After the so-called 'revolution'. Yes. Some of them have to. I see in here a woman who worked for the police who has a private food shop already."

"Where does she get the money to start it?"

"I told you, she was a worker for the police. She had a very good house, she had money in foreign countries. Like many secret police people."

"Money in hard currency?"

"In hard currency. I see here also a man who was lucky to escape prison and he is now a judge." Alexandru spoke softly and gazed over in the direction of Ilie Radin sitting and eating.

"*That* man?"

"Yes, he was a big Securitate official in the city. Now he is a judge." Alexandru almost whispered.

"You mean – " But Tim thought it best to withhold his knowledge of Ilie Radin's name. "You mean the man now talking to a waitress?"

"Yes." So rumour had already elevated Radin from the advocate's table to the judge's seat.

And then – "It is sad, we have to go," Alexandru said suddenly. "We have to 'talk business'."

Tim rose from his half-eaten schnitzel, the others rose, they shook hands, agreed to meet again (which they never would), accepted "good luck" for their projects. Only when they had gone did a vivid visual memory return to Tim, revived by the presence of someone in this restaurant: the Romanian version of *A Time*

Apart lying on the table in the cellar restaurant on top of Ilie Radin's exercise book.

When he had paid the waitress – he discovered that Alexandru and Imre had indeed paid for the wine and felt shame for a moment of doubt – he looked round to be sure the two had left, then rose and went across to Radin. After his conversation with the two strangers he was convinced that he needed to talk with all the participants in Philip's story to check evidence, one by one, absolutely separately and alone. Here was his chance to begin.

It was Radin's turn to be surprised, as Tim had been by the man's call to the Hotel Transilvania on that cold afternoon when he had been asleep and dreaming in his room. When Tim greeted him he looked up over his glasses from the newspaper he was reading as if not believing his own eyes.

"I think," he said slowly, "this is Mr Harker-Jones."

"I thought it was you, Mr Radin. I was dining on the other side of the restaurant."

The band was noisy and Radin had not understood.

"You have come for dinner?"

Oh no, he had had it already; and he was not going to be bought a meal like last time's, under any condition.

"Then you will have some brandy? Please – please sit down." He would have some, and sat down. This level of hospitality he could accept, though his head was light from the wine. Radin looked older; but perhaps his newer suit was just adding dignity, charisma?

Tim told him he was in Târgu Alb with Carolina (that was fair) to see once again, in connection with the Life he was writing – Radin nodded approval – the places Philip Carston had visited, and to talk again to people Philip had known here. Radin heard him with close attention; drumming a heel on the floor.

"I remember you said, 'One day I hope I will read the book in English'," Tim reminded him. But the band was playing a loud, slow tune which many people around them were singing in a rough, slurred maudlin chorus, and Radin could not hear properly.

"They are playing an old Hungarian song," he explained. "The Hungarians are singing it. 'We Hungarians in Transylvania, we suffered in the past, we suffer in the present, we shall suffer in the future, all our history is nothing but weeping.' I exaggerate, but it is something a little like that. It is also a little Jewish in origin."

Tim looked up at him sharply, but took this as fact rather than prejudice.

"It is nationalistic," Radin continued. It was not good to sing it in the era of our last president."

"Your English is very good – getting better," Tim called out, genuinely (though flattery served his cause), across two feet of smokey, clamorous space between their heads. "Have you read Philip Carston's book in English yet? You said you wanted to." Trying again.

"I have it in English now, yes. I have obtained it. And in Romanian." Deafening noise. A misunderstanding? Try *yet* again. (*But Radin had said he now possessed the English original of the novel.*)

"Is there any difference? *Is there any difference?*" shouting.

"Where you *know* it will be different, it *is* different," Radin shouted back.

So what on earth did this mean? Tim took it to mean minor adjustments, bits of toning-down, nothing radical. The band's song reached a climax with a melancholy baritone roar from most of the drinkers. It gave Tim a second to consider how to respond; but what was there to say except, "What *kind* of difference?" The words came out loudly in sudden silence when the band finished, then were swallowed up in applause.

"I mean," Radin said, having heard perfectly, "the difference between the parts Mr Carston writes and what Miss Predeanu writes." He smiled broadly.

"What Miss Predeanu writes?"

"Yes, Professor Bobolescu says she wrote *all* of the book. I say she wrote some things in the book."

"Well – what things?" How relieved Tim was to be having this part of the conversation in silence! But he must get his answer before the band struck up again.

Radin laughed.

"It is perhaps not fair for me to say."

Was the wine and brandy impairing his understanding, or was Radin deliberately talking in riddles? He asked Radin what he was implying.

"*Mr Harker-Jones*! You study human beings, you write about their lives, and you don't understand about *love*?" He was laughing, his smartly blue-grey-suited shoulders were shaking.

"You mean – ?"

"I am embarrassed, and it is not easy to embarrass a Romanian. We are too open. People are embarrassed when they are always having secrets, or – inhibitions, is that the word? – and other people discover them."

"You mean the love affair between Katrin and Richard in the novel?" He sounded to himself as if he was being bold in asking something obvious.

"I mean the deep, true *passion* of Katrin with Richard in the novel."

Tim knew he *had* really heard what Radin was telling him, and implying. The man's self-taught English was clear and exact. As a lawyer he would probably cherish his words, the implications of his words.

"Will you please show me the passages you mean in the Romanian novel? And lend me your copy for the next twenty-four hours?"

He looked at his watch. It was now nine-twenty.

– 3 –

Tim's note for Carolina next morning read:

8 a.m.

Dear Carolina,

I did not sleep well, and when that happens I need to take some exercise to clear my head. I am out for a walk, and if I am not here by ten as we arranged, please go home and I will telephone there as soon as I return. Please accept my sincere apologies for this.

Ever,

Tim (Harker-Jones)

When he was out into the rain he began to hurry. He had undoubtedly slept badly; but his head was remarkably clear about what he had to do. He only wished that his memory was equally clear about how to get to Liviu Bobolescu's house. He was careful always, with a biographer's concern for storing details, to take down addresses; but remembering how they had reached the Professor's house in the snow last time was harder.

People, women in head-scarves and men with hats pulled down tightly over their foreheads, were on their way to work. Tim stopped a man who did not seem in any undue hurry, and uttered the name of the street. "*Nu stiu*," was the reply, with a shrug of sympathy. A woman repeated the name thoughtfully, turned in one direction and frowned, turned in the other, finally let loose a flood of directions and gestures. It began to rain harder, a downpour. Below his tight anorak, its pockets bulging – he trusted their contents would not get wet – Tim's trousers were soaked, already plastered to his shins by the rain.

He thanked the woman, and set off on one of two routes offered by her waving, pointing and circling hands. Fortunately she, and he, were right: he came quickly upon a street sign with the name on it. Less luckily, this was the wrong end, far from the Bobolescus' number, which he realised he could have reached much faster by walking the other way. The villas and their gardens were large. It was a long distance.

And what if, after all this, Bobolescu was not there? Or still in bed (not all Romanians rose early)? Or declined to see him? (Surely he would not do that?) And for Tim to have to present himself like this, without warning and now drenched...

When he eventually recognised the Bobolescus' gate he was stricken by a feeling that the visit was ridiculous, seriously ill-advised – and nearly turned away again. But having come so far, got so wet...

He could not hear whether the bell he pressed rang inside the house. He pressed it a second time immediately, still heard nothing, waited. Then a lock was unchained and the door opened.

Everyone else Tim had met here since the revolution had changed in some particular, but Liviu Bobolescu was the same, even down to the tie he wore when they last met. He was no less shabby and untidy, no less bright-eyed, crafty-looking, apparently indifferent to what people demanded of him but attentive all the same to everything they said or did. It seemed characteristic that – unlike Radin – he should greet Tim without surprise, warmly, and that he should say, immediately,

"Mr Harker-Jones, I am so happy to see you here." Then he added, "But Miss Predeanu is not with you? And this is very early."

He called back into the house to reassure his wife, then stood aside to bow Tim in. The house was gratifyingly warm after the chilling rain.

"You are very wet! You will change? And you will have breakfast because it is obvious you have had none. And I think you are the height of my son, Virgil, though a little more – more 'expansive'?"

Georgeta Bobolescu appeared, smiled almost as if expecting him, shook his hand, was given instructions by her husband.

"Virgil is not here, he is at university in Bucharest," Liviu said. "But he did not take all his clothes with him. Let me take your coat, to begin."

Tim stripped off the sopping anorak, which Liviu draped over a radiator in the hall; the contents of the pockets rang against the metal panels. He removed them, wrapped in their plastic bags, and held them tightly. Georgeta reappeared with a jacket and trousers.

"Not a suit, I am afraid," Liviu apologised. "But respectable clothes. Virgil does not take them to Bucharest University. There you must have 'jeans', it is the regulations! Here."

He pushed Tim, still clutching his wrapped belongings, into the study to change, anxiously asking if his shirt and underclothes were also wet (which thankfully they were not), and closed the door. Here were the crammed shelves Tim remembered, the large desk, the deep armchairs. He removed his wet trousers and stood in his underpants looking round abstractedly for a moment. There was a sharp tap at the door – he took a bath-towel gratefully from Mrs Bobolescu's hand.

Drying his feet and calves he noticed the Romanian edition of *A Time Apart* among numerous books on a coffee table. He saw too that Liviu, or someone, had inserted slips of paper (as he had done with many of the books on the shelves) at certain places...

Virgil's trousers were a little short and tight, but fitted well enough for the present purpose. In order to pull up the zip, Tim positioned himself with his back to the door and leaned over the little table. A telephone in the corner of the study rang loudly, slowly, twice, then stopped; the call had no doubt been answered elsewhere in the house on an extension. Cautiously Tim took the book into his hands and opened it at the marked places.

He could see at once, without much difficulty, that these

were the passages he now knew about – an extraordinary confirmation of Ilie Radin's inferences, or knowledge. *Or investigations?* What puzzled him was that some writing on the slips of paper was not Liviu Bobolescu's (he took out an annotated book from the shelves to check and be sure.) This was a younger hand; but not enough of it for Tim to be able to tell if it was a man's or a woman's.

He folded his own clothes and left the study. Outside the door Georgeta laughed at, and admired him in, her son's tight garments, patted his stomach, carried his wet things away to dry out on another radiator, sent him into the dining-room where only two places were laid. "My wife will not join us, you will prefer to talk alone." Liviu smiled humorously, they were to be conspirators.

Georgeta brought coffee, warm rolls, butter, marmalade, omelettes; they both began eating, eagerly. Looking at Bobolescu, Tim believed he had discovered a truth about the old: the first impressions that age conveyed were no guide at all to someone's continuing strength of character, or ingenuity, or even physical energy, certainly not to their life expectancy. Today Bobolescu seemed set to go on for years yet.

He was talking now about Carolina, before Tim had even mentioned her, declaring what he hoped and believed Carolina would be writing in the future. He seemed ignorant of her ostracism by her colleagues.

"Soon I am going to have to be direct, interrupt this flow and ask questions," Tim decided. Eventually he found the resolution.

"Professor Bobolescu!" he said with steady formality. "We are discussing Miss Predeanu, and there are things I have to ask you. I am told that Miss Predeanu wrote *certain* passages – certain passages *only* – in Philip Carston's final novel. Are you able to tell me exactly which passages she wrote?"

"Mr Harker-Jones, she wrote everything!"

"Professor Bobolescu, I happened to see a copy of the book

just now in your study. If I may possibly fetch it –"

But Bobolescu was ignoring him.

"There is not one word in the novel that Miss Predeanu did not write. Of course she wrote all of it with Mr Carston's guidance, and some help with little points she could not remember when she returned from England. But every syllable of the writing is her own. She translated it for Mr Carston into English and he came to Romania to collect it and polish the English a little. Certain passages –"

"*When she returned from England?*"

"Yes. Miss Predeanu was in England for several weeks in 1985. She met all of those characters, and did all of those things Katrin did, on her visit."

"And she was in love – while she was in England, she – ?"

Tim faltered. He knew he could never ask this question outright of an old man who had probably been in love, in some way, with Carolina himself. Undoubtedly there was a look of sadness passing across Liviu's face, and he paused in his rapid eating. Rain beat even harder than before at the window. Liviu looked at the rain, raised his eyebrows, recovered his poise and smiled.

"Mr Harker-Jones. Fiction is fiction is fiction, as Gertrude Stein would say. Even Proust, who is the most autobiographical of all novelists, invents. Even Proust transfers some emotions he felt to other people altogether. Proust even changes the sex of characters. So a young woman of genius who is in love can certainly imagine the emotion she feels, and which she observes in another, transferred to two characters she has *created*. This is elementary. Miss Predeanu has done that."

There was no getting permission to fetch the Romanian translation of *A Time Apart* from the study. Tim therefore reached for his parcels and unwrapped both books, his own English copy and Radin's Romanian one. Inside both were slips of paper he had placed last night; possibly, though not necessarily, at the same places as those in the Professor's copy.

At this point the doorbell rang.

Whoever was ringing kept a finger on the button a long time, so that a repeating electric peal of which Tim had heard nothing from outside went on and on, and on. Bobolescu looked relieved at this interruption and ignored the books Tim held out to him.

Georgeta was answering the door and Tim heard loud, agitated voices, Georgeta answering and calming them. Liviu rose, went to the dining-room door and motioned Tim to follow.

"Yes, we are all here now," he said with satisfaction. All Tim could see at the end of the short hallway were two large, open umbrellas, one black, one red, momentarily lowered in front of their owners so that they could be closed and shaken; but he certainly heard Carolina's raised voice behind the red one.

The black umbrella folded first, and behind it was Tamasi Ilosz. He, at least, nodded with a smile at Tim, and said, a little aimlessly, "Welcome back to our town." When the red umbrella closed, Carolina's glance at Tim was furious, and came without a greeting.

"Where were you at 8.30?"

"I was out – I – I left a note at the desk."

A note which she would now have realised, if she had seen it, was a lie.

"I telephoned your room at 8.30 to say the only time Tamasi could see you was nine, he would come and take you out for breakfast. There was no answer from your room. I telephoned Professor Bobolescu to ask when he could see you – and he says you are *here*."

She handed the umbrella to Georgeta, who took it with Tamasi's into the kitchen, threw off her raincoat, looked at Tim with sad, fierce suspicion. Liviu began to talk to Tamasi in Hungarian, drew him aside, led him into the dining-room. Carolina and Tim were left alone in the hall.

"Why did you come here alone?" she asked him; quietly, but with even more anger. "You wanted to check on me? Is that it?"

"No," Tim said. But she had guessed the truth.

"You came here to ask questions about the book, I know that," Carolina said. "You are checking on me everywhere. Last night you arranged to see Ilie Radin in a restaurant. Ioana saw you there, talking to him, very quietly." *Quietly*, with that band playing?

"I was there, and I was talking with Mr Radin, but we met by accident when I went to have a meal." Tim felt ashamed all the same.

"Then you went to Mr Radin's house. I know because I telephoned Mr Radin early this morning in case he wanted to meet you – he said he had seen you already. *What are you doing to me?* I bring you to my town to see places you want to describe, I telephone people to arrange meetings – and you are meeting them secretly, to talk about *me*."

The fury was turning to weeping, Tim could see that. He took her arm. Carolina let him hold it, unaware of his grip, crying, trembling. Then she wrenched it away.

"Please – I have things I am nervous to ask you directly," he said; almost the worst thing to say.

"So – you go behind my back, you ask personal questions in private meetings."

"Not personal questions." It was not true; but Carolina was too distressed to hear him. For the first time in his acquaintance with her, her English began to sound strained and incoherent, from grief and anger.

"You do not wait until I am ready – until I find – I find a ready feeling in my – my *heart* for telling you what you wish to know. I am bringing you here in Târgu Alb because you – I am trying to find the strength in my heart to say you the secret things, but I am hesitating, I not know a *time* to tell you, or if I tell at all. And then, we must talk – do I also translate *your* book? I will go to a bathroom."

She wept, silently, speechless now, turned away, ran in the wrong direction, doubled back and disappeared through a far door and locked a bolt noisily. When Georgeta went through from the kitchen with more cups and saucers and coffee on a tray, she assumed Tim was waiting to use the bathroom and looked past him. Carolina was so long he decided to knock; but as he reached it, the bathroom door opened and she came out, calm again, though with an angrily determined look.

They entered the dining-room and Liviu invited them to sit down. Georgeta poured coffee, the Hungarian conversation switched to English for his sake, trivialities were exchanged. Three people whom Tim believed he had needed to meet individually were gathered here all at the same time because of his own bungling. The entire trip was ruined.

"It is not kind of you," Carolina suddenly said, openly. Tamasi made a small gesture to Tim with his two hands, which rested on the table on each side of his coffee cup: it said, I see Carolina's point of view but I sympathise with you and will do my best to help. "It is not kind, because you behave like a spy," Carolina went on. "Perhaps you *are* a spy."

"I am not a spy," Tim said quietly.

"No, you are not even a diplomat," she continued.

"You see, Mr Harker-Jones," Tamasi interposed, "it is not so easy for us in Romania – even now – to be sure about people coming to ask us questions and keep notes of our answers. We had so many years of people asking questions and keeping files. For us, the best way now is to talk everything in the open, and not in secret."

Tim liked him. With immaculate, super-subtle Hungarian panache and tact, Tamasi had restored calm and eliminated most of the embarrassment. Carolina's expression softened a little, Liviu nodded sagely. Tim had the impression that this tactic had been worked out by Tamasi and Liviu together.

"My book is almost finished except for some work on Philip Carston's Romanian connections," he said, not looking at Carolina. "I need just to ask about your meetings with him, your impression of him, what he said and did and what he saw while visiting Târgu Alb."

He would ask these public questions now, at least get Philip's movements and reactions right as these people remembered them; then seek a chance later today to follow up what he suddenly realised – yes!– was Carolina's agonized undertaking, out in the hall, if it still held good, to tell him something more. Times, places, people, subjects of conversations. Trying carefully, with Tamasi and Liviu, not to appear to be checking on what Carolina had told him about Philip's contacts with them. Asking how Liviu found Philip as a guest. What did Philip ask him? What common ground did Tamasi and Philip discover in ordinary talk? Did Philip answer their questions about Romania? About England? And how did they sum up Philip Carston, what did they think of him?

"He was characteristically English," Tamasi said easily, with a smile. "Courteous, kind, rather reticent. Very ignorant of Eastern Europe."

Tim smiled broadly and nodded.

"Also," Tamasi continued, "like you, he accepted criticisms of the English with great tolerance, because in his mind he believed England was superior in *everything*. So criticism from a foreigner would make no difference, nothing at all."

Tim smiled with less pleasure.

"Did Philip make any surprising observations about Romania for an Englishman? Or ask any unusual, untypical questions?" he asked.

It was an innocent question. But it produced unexpected, even alarming, results.

There was a pause, in which everyone seemed to be waiting for someone else to provide this information. An uncomfortable pause. Eventually, Tamasi answered.

"Sometimes he asked about British people in Romania."

"British people *living* in Romania?"

"Yes. Or about temporary diplomats working here. Or intellectuals visiting."

"But – why ask about *them*? What sort of questions?"

"Any sort of questions," Liviu joined in. "He asked if we knew these people, how often we had met them."

Carolina remained silent.

"There was a theory," Tamasi said. "We can tell you now – now that so much is different in our country. We thought Mr Carston was partly sent here to discover if British people living here, or coming here, had too much sympathy for our old political system."

"For the system – of President Ceausescu...?"

"What else?"

"I have a friend in Bucharest, a professor," Liviu said. Carolina listened with an ironically disapproving expression; as if to convey, "Not believe old man's opinions." "He was asked always by Mr Carston questions about the opinions of British diplomats and trade delegates. And, you know –" here Liviu leaned forward with a crafty smile – "sometimes, after Mr Carston went home a particular diplomat was asked to go home, too. It was such a coincidence. And then –"

Liviu began to chuckle and shake so much at the next anecdote that it took him a long time to begin it.

"I have another friend in – what do I call it for you? We call it the 'Ministry of the Interior'. A very unpleasant name, it sounds like the 'innards', yes? The dark labyrinths of the body politic. The intestines. You call it 'Home Office'. Very nice, very cosy, little house with a fire of logs, little cat asleep in front of it. But it is the same as 'Ministry of the Interior'. I explained this theory about Mr Carston to my friend in the Intestines, and he said, we will have a little experiment. There is a British attaché in the embassy in Bucharest, we do not like him, he meets all the people the President dislikes, the lunatic priests, the novelists, the rest. We will ask someone to tell Mr Carston that this man, in secret, is a devoted admirer and friend of President Ceausescu, he has stayed in one of his country houses, he has killed wild bears and wild boars with Nicolae Ceausescu!" Carolina was looking away, not listening. She had taken a slip of paper out of her pocket, was doodling on it, pointedly writing things, apparently to show disapproval of the trend the conversation had taken. Outside the rain had all at once stopped, and given way to weak sunshine. "And so, a Romanian in Bucharest, a strong Communist man, told Mr Carston he had a friendship with this attaché and that he knew this attaché made visits to our President, drank tea with him, listened to records of western music, watched western films in a private cinema."

"Western music?" Tim shook his head in disbelief. "Did Ceausescu like Western music?"

"No, *no!*" Liviu laughed. "The Englishman was a fan of western 'rock-singing', he was sent to promote western 'culture'. And of western American films. So – Mr Carston is informed this young attaché watches American films and listens to rock-singing with the great Conducator, the greatest Romanian in history, in one of his country mansions. It is a joke – an experiment. *Before* Mr Carston is home in England this attaché is *also* home – fired, finished, they gave him a little job writing reports for your Ministry of Fish."

What had happened to the weather? The Bobolescus' dining-room was now filled with dazzling spring sunshine.

Carolina, who had scribbled her name several times on the slip of paper, now threw down her pen. And Tim realised she had been sitting through an anecdote she had heard many times before, deeply bored and irritated, resentful, miserable, not for a moment believing it. When he happened to glance at the writing she had produced, he saw that it was the writing on the slips inserted in the copy of *A Time Apart* in the study. Unquestionably those were for the Professor's information, whether he would believe them or not.

– 4 –

Outside, when they had said good-bye to Tamasi, "The sun is shining," Carolina said, "so we can take the walk I was planning."

The sun was bright and the skies were clear. She strode quickly, as if this weather might not last, and he followed, soon out of breath. In a plastic bag swinging from his left hand were the clothes he had discarded at the Bobolescus', and *A Time Apart* in English and Romanian. Virgil Bobolescu's home clothes felt even tighter in the heat.

They boarded a bus, alighting after three or four stops at a small bridge over a narrow, fast-flowing river marking the edge of some public gardens; everything was radiant and glistening in the sunlight. Carolina looked at her watch.

"Ten minutes before our next bus," she said.

The benches in these triangular gardens were still too wet after the rain for them to sit down. They were seats from which one lick of greeny-yellow paint had faded, and alongside them were dented aluminium litter-bins, low hexagonal concrete flower tubs filled with concrete clippings, no flowers although it was spring. They strolled by the river, along uneven concrete paths which led nowhere, past a heavily elaborate fountain.

"I wanted to show you the park where I was with Philip – there is no time for the Peasant Museum." So that was the same park...

They boarded the next bus at a terminus, a wide patch of stony ground next to a market where tall boards listed fruits and vegetables and left spaces for the regulated prices to be chalked in. Carolina made for a narrow, cool waiting-room where she bought tickets for both of them – for a longer journey? – through a tiny semi-circular aperture at a counter in a corner.

Their fellow-passengers were elderly shoppers returning from an early trip to the market. They got down, singly or in pairs, at stops along this uphill route: High School, Bottle Factory, Statue of the Engineer, Airman's Memorial.

The bus seemed to be climbing the valley of the Târgu Alb river into the forest. Spaces between the houses alongside the road widened, became sloping fields dotted with sheep, of all colours: not only white, black or grey but also brown, fawn, and a kind of sepia that was almost orange. And now they were back into a small village which looked as if it might be the last inhabited place before the mountains. There was a small row of shops with their purpose emblazoned above the windows, in solid letters, in both Romanian and Hungarian: RESTAURANT/VENDEGLO, CONFECTII/KESZRUHA, INGHETATA/FAGYLALT. And a trim wooden shed by the turning circle where the bus finally stopped, with a window for selling tickets, and cool drinks in the summer. They alighted; and first she led him downhill again.

"There is a chance to show you something here before I take you on our walk," she said. "While it is possible."

A hundred yards downhill they turned right, up a narrow, neatly-laid road which Tim had not noticed from the bus. It twisted away almost immediately into the pine trees, out of the sight of the main road, then rose steeply. In a few minutes they came to heavy iron gates, and he saw a wooden porter's cabin set just inside them.

"I telephoned last night," Carolina said. "He will know we are coming."

"Where are we? Is this – somewhere you visited with Philip?"

Carolina laughed ironically, no other response.

A gloomy, probably bored middle-aged man, guardian of the gates, came out with keys and unlocked them. He let them in, shut and re-locked the gates, took them up the road, which now assumed the air of an avenue leading somewhere. He talked to Carolina with the relieved animation of someone who might not have spoken to fellow-beings for days.

Carolina said, "President Ceausescu had at least two houses

like this in every province, one in a town and one in the country."

"You mean Ceausescu *lived* here?"

"It was his Târgu Alb country house that was ready for him, if he wanted to come. He came here just once – for one afternoon. He landed in his helicopter, he had coffee, he asked about bears in the forest. Then he left."

The gatekeeper asked Carolina something, pausing to point through the trees; she answered affirmatively.

"He says, 'Do we want to see some bears?'" Tim must have looked uncertain. "In a cage," she added.

It stood in a small clearing just off the road. The two young bears extended playful paws through the bars. One of them made a mooing noise, not unlike a bullock's but more nasal and less heartfelt. He licked greedily at the gatekeeper's proffered fingers.

"He will lick yours, he says," Carolina said to Tim. "Try him." Tim declined the idea.

Leaving the bears they went on up the sloping road. The house came into view: a large, handsome version of a prosperous country dwelling.

"There is a helipad," Carolina indicated. It was a surprisingly small circle of concrete set in the grass beside the road.

The flat yellowish stones crammed together made the walls of the house look oddly uneven, but Tim assumed it was a traditional style; safe enough if Ceausescu allowed it. The front steps of the house appeared to be marble. Only appeared to be? He remembered the House of the Republic.

The porter produced a key and opened the front door. A narrow, dark entrance lobby opened into a spacious hall, with a wide staircase rising to an upper storey past a tapestry of a bear-hunting scene. In the main reception room on this ground floor was a desk; on it a calendar showing "22nd December 1989", the day the president was overthrown.

"You knew this house was here but you never came?" Tim asked.

"*Of course not!*"

Was her showing it to him now some sort of an apology? For knowing of the existence of such places and not dissociating herself from them?

They passed on into a large meeting – or dining-room with heavy chairs (which may never have been sat in) round a long table. All the interior decoration was done in the expensive, anonymously just-tasteful, style which flatters the rich and thoughtless anywhere in the world.

"He wants to show us the kitchen," Carolina said.

The oven for baking bread was spotless, undoubtedly unused; designed to bake special bread for the president alone, under strict supervision. Tim could see nothing to suggest where it was made, but –

"All of these other things are West German!" he exclaimed. "This cupboard – the cookers – the fridge-freezer – the sink unit –" Every fitting and implement in the kitchen shone. Did they still continue to polish them, even now?

They passed back through the dining-room, out through the hall, and up the stairs to the first floor. The two separate bedrooms, for president and consort, were unslept-in; on the beds the coverlets were turned back in readiness. Beyond each was a bathroom and beyond each bathroom a private lounge, presumably for resting or recovering after a bath or shower. Opening out of each lounge was a dressing-room with fitted cupboards containing numerous suits and dresses.

Occupying corners of the upper storey and facing views across the treetops through wide windows were two private offices, with small desks and neat telephones. Behind the presidential desk were bookshelves of the routine ideological texts, also the endless volumes he had had written for him, and published under his name. In his consort's room were a row of her own ghost-written scientific treatises.

"Is it possible to look" Their guide nodded, and Tim prised a book out of the top row. He saw tables of research data in – in polymer chemistry, possibly?

"Did she *know* all about this?"

"Many people say she knew nothing."

"She didn't try to educate herself in it? So as to answer questions about it?"

"I think – I think she had people to answer questions for her."

Tim bent over to look along the lower shelves: brightly-coloured volumes of fiction.

"But look at this! Virginia Woolf is here." He drew out the book with amazement. "What does this mean – *Noapte si Zi?*"

"*Night and Day.*"

"It's very early Virginia Woolf. Not nearly so well-known as the later... What on earth is it doing here? Did she read novels?"

"It is possible she wanted people to *think* she liked them."

"But she would choose what to have?"

"People would choose them for her."

"But – doesn't it show some sort of intellectual pretension? As if she, or someone, thought it was good to be seen to like a classic modern novelist? And very good to have an out-of-the-way novel? I can't think the British prime minister –"

"Someone just asked the publishing house for some of the latest books."

There was a back staircase, thickly-carpeted, leading down to the ground floor – and passing a small lounge-cinema. Its six seats, arranged in a semi-circle were deep, soft leather armchairs; two had soft pouffes set on the carpet in front of them.

"What films did he like?"

Carolina translated Tim's question for the gatekeeper, who explained something at some length.

"He was only here the one time, so he never saw a film in this room. But there were instructions to find western films to show if he was going to come here."

"What kind of western films?"

Carolina looked impatient; as if Tim had an extraordinary lack of understanding, was just very slow.

"*American* westerns. The 'wild west'."

"So that was true – ?"

At the end of a short warm corridor was a private sauna and a chain of rooms comprehensively dedicated to the presidential health: a chamber with a stationary bicycle and various other devices for light exercise, a bathroom for special mineral baths, a medical room with electrocardiograph equipment.

The gatekeeper was short and stout. He stood on the bathroom scales in one corner of the room, looked down at the number of kilogrammes it registered, passed a remark to Carolina, and for the first time smiled.

"He is saying it flatters him," she said.

– 5 –

Back on the road they walked up rapidly past the bus terminus and were heading uphill in the direction of the forest-covered mountains.

"Why did you take me to that house?" Tim asked.

"Were you not interested?"

"Yes. But you believed in Ceausescu, and now –"

"I never believed in him. I believed in the idea, but that is different."

He could see them conducting the kind of dialogue she – in her account to him of those visits – had conducted with Philip Carston. And he could see himself getting nowhere.

After some moments of silence: "This walk and this place is *so* much to me in my life," Carolina said, suddenly and quietly. "So much has happened to me here."

He found the tact and the caution to let her speak and just to listen.

"This was our Saturday and Sunday walk when I was a child. With my parents," she continued. She stopped to translate a notice for him. "Treat the woods as precious." They walked on. "I could do this walk blindfolded." Beside them, beside the road, ran a narrow-gauge railway on which timber came down from the forest. A Hungarian farm-cart, pulled by two horses decorated with bright ribbons and ringing bells edged them to the side of the road, a grey-haired man with a pinched, tanned face bent at the reins in impenetrable meditation.

It was steeper now, and the trees closed in on either side, though there was still space for an irregularly paved path to run parallel with the road on a higher level.

"You are happy to walk?"

Tim must have looked to her incongruous and uncomfortable: the obvious foreigner, in the tight jacket and trousers, switching the carrier bag containing the wet clothes and books from left hand to right hand and back again. He was more puzzled as to why they were taking this walk than "happy" about it, but, "Yes, certainly," he said. "Certainly."

They were still climbing steeply (Carolina fresh and energetic) when the road, the railway and the paved path all stopped. The only route onwards was a winding track of stone chips, hard to tread with any comfort. They chose the grass verges where they could; though these were damp and they had to walk with care where the road sank away to the right, down a thickly-wooded escarpment into a deep, obscured valley below.

"We come to the view soon," Carolina said. (All this was for a view?) "Up here the path levels out, and this valley opens up, and you see what a wonderful view we have." It was taking longer than a quarter of an hour.

Suddenly – "We are here!" she exclaimed decisively. "'The mountains have all opened out themselves.'"

He was surprised to hear a strange catch in Carolina's voice as she quoted; but then realised, as he caught her up and looked into her eyes as she turned that she was once again weeping.

"Turn round," she commanded.

She turned him round, so that he could see what she wanted

him to see; and not see her in tears. From this spot they could look down over the tops of the trees, in a wide gap in the hills, right out over the green plain on which Târgu Alb stood, a large, ramifying display of civic buildings, houses and tower-blocks, spires and factory chimneys, trees and parks and boulevards, handsome in the sunlight.

"Well, yes," Tim said in bewilderment. "I am impressed. What a fine view."

He felt her hands gripping his arms from behind tighten suddenly. The weeping racked her, left her speechless in a way the angry weeping in Liviu's hall had not. He knew better than to turn round while it went on. It was at last clear to him that this was Carolina's planned climax to the whole trip, the reason for encouraging his visit to Târgu Alb, escorting him, organising people and places for him to see. She had intended from the beginning to bring him to the exact spot of ground on which she had stood with Philip Carston and made her deal with him about the writing of *A Time Apart*. This was where, if she could even now find it in her heart to do that, she would finally disclose that small cluster of facts and truths which she had always so resolutely and skilfully withheld. She wanted the significance of this place for her recorded in Tim Harker-Jones's book.

He felt awed, expectant, apprehensive. He waited for her to speak. He would let her say as much or as little as she wished, knowing by now that nothing he said could influence her. Eventually she released his arms. He took it as a signal, and turned round slowly.

"You know, don't you," she said. "We stood here, and he decided he would write it. And we decided I would help him. We made promises here, and we kept them. He kept them – and *I* kept them."

"The promise to translate the book, and – ?"

"To translate the book. And make my own contribution to the book."

"Yes?"

"To write something for him, a little, myself. It was my request. And he agreed – here, though not on exactly what I would write, at that time. He was very intrigued by the idea; as long as it worked."

"And you wrote passages he included?"

"First in Romanian, then I put them into English and then Philip improved the English. But they were much more mine than his – only a few phrases in them were his."

"And these passages went into *both* books? The English and your translation?"

"Oh *yes*! Of course."

"Please may I ask? Were they *short* passages?"

"What is 'short'?"

"Not a *large* proportion of the book?"

"No. Liviu Bobolescu spreads it around that I wrote everything. No – there were several short passages, of a few pages. And one longer passage."

He waited.

"The longer passage is – it concerns the consummation of the love affair she has with Richard."

"You wrote *that* chapter? That was *yours*?" Tim could not help exclaiming with surprise.

"That was mine. It came into our agreement – later. It was my response to Philip's hints..."

He wanted to say, "Richard is Philip, and you had to consummate an affair with Philip when Philip hinted at that, to write those love-making scenes, didn't you? You implied as much in your story?" But he couldn't say that. Instead he ventured his other daring question.

"Did you go to England?"

"Yes. But it was not as many people imagine it was. Not like that at all. I will tell you later. You will know."

She now turned her back on the view and faced across to a place on the other side of the stony track where a faint footpath led up into the trees, into a darker region of the forest. She kept her gaze fixed on it while Tim waited for her to speak.

First she pointed up into the trees.

"We decided everything finally up there," she said.

He stared at her now, wholly bewildered, embarrassed. Carolina was not moving, not preparing to lead them any farther.

"In the forest?"

"In the forest."

If something all-important, something secret and intimate – Tim would not put Alic Paldrey's name to it in his own mind – had happened in that shaded place under the trees above them, on the other side of the track in these hills where they stood on the rock-strewn grass, was Carolina going to divulge it now? His third and last question... He could not ask it directly.

"That main chapter you wrote, it – it is an extremely passionate and sensual chapter."

"Yes. That is how it is intended," she said tensely.

"Mr Radin knows you wrote some passages – *those* passages?"

"I told Mr Radin. I told him which passages. I wanted him to be my witness in case Liviu Bobolescu made larger claims."

"Mr Radin told *me*."

"I told him I was intending to tell you myself. So he *could* tell you."

They were straying from the subject.

"It surprises me to realise you wrote that part of the book," Tim said.

"Why?"

"Because –"

"Because exactly *what*?"

For the thousandth time in his working life as a biographer Tim Harker-Jones realised that he lacked the elements of combined toughness and charm which could draw the ultimate confidences out of people.

"Because – because Katrin is very real – and if the two of them –"

"Mr Harker-Jones!" Carolina was interrupting him fiercely, with a deeply mocking, ironic – and dangerous – smile. "You have been trying to ask me one particular personal question since we first met, almost. Haven't you? In your prying way, with all your Western euphemisms. You want to know if I 'went to bed' with Philip Carston. If I 'slept' with him. Is not that true? Here, or somewhere else?"

He nearly found the dishonesty to deny it, but held back, and just stood there, shamed and open mouthed.

"I will tell you something," Carolina said. "I want you to listen, and remember it well. I want to tell you this, if you can forget what you assume is truly interesting in the lives of people. I want to tell you that if Philip and I 'slept' together –" she widened her lips on the word with lacerating irony – "it was, literally, *our* fucking business. Not yours."

– 6 –

"You have some dry clothes upstairs? You can dry these out overnight?" She was smiling, at ease, as if something was off her mind.

They were waiting in the empty foyer of his hotel until someone showed up to give Tim his key. The garments inside his carrier bag were still damp. Carolina was being businesslike, concerned about his train ticket back to Bucharest – they had bought one at the railway bureau on their way back from the forest – and anxious lest he had caught cold (he had sneezed several times in the bus).

"If you can change these now I will return them to Professor Bobolescu – no problem," she said, indicating the tight trousers and jacket. "And I can return Mr Radin's book."

She occupied herself with the receptionist, who had finally come to deliver him the key, while he walked upstairs to change.

As he stripped off Virgil Bobolescu's clothes it occurred to him that he was stripping off all connection with these people – the Bobolescus, Radin, Tamasi Ilosz, even Carolina – perhaps for ever. It just remained for him to complete his work from what he had found out, or from what he could conjecture. Carolina might once have been the obvious translator of his own completed book, but now her own precarious position – except that she *had* said... Coming back in the bus she had told him she wished to see the manuscript before it saw the light of print in England, and possibly she – but then she had fallen silent.

When he brought the clothes and book downstairs she was sitting in a shadowy corner in a deep armchair behind opened pages of a copy of *Romania Libera* from the previous day, with *Adevarul* on her lap. Her concentration was so fervent she seemed almost surprised to see him when he stood in front of her. The newspapers only reached Târgu Alb midday next day, she explained, but they had more information than television or radio news so she wanted to scan them.

It was five o'clock. He wondered what she would propose now, or whether he should propose something himself.

But when she had folded and tidied the sheets of the newspapers, she picked up a long envelope which Tim suddenly saw on the arm of her chair, and stood up.

"Mr Harker-Jones!"

When she put out her right hand Tim automatically proffered the bag of clothes. But Carolina took that with her left hand, which was holding the envelope. Her right hand was held out for Tim to shake. And since his own right hand was now free, and Carolina was smiling so insistently, he took it.

"It has been very good to have you in Romania again," she said; with warmth, and yet with a formality he could not believe. She was not simply saying good-bye for the day, expecting to see him again that night, or to-morrow to escort him to the station. "I have arranged with the reception for a taxi to come for you for the train to-morrow – two-fifteen. It will cost only thirty lei. Tell the people if it is late. *Remember to send me a copy of your book.*"

"That's good of you," Tim said weakly, still shocked by the suddenness and firmness of this leave-taking.

"I wish you a safe journey to Bucharest, and to London – and I hope we meet again. And –"

She took the envelope from her left hand with her right hand. Tim saw that it was unaddressed, and thick enough to contain several folded pages.

"And I wrote this for you to read if I did not have a chance to take you to that place today – or if I did not have the strength to tell you things from my heart in conversation. In fact I told you everything I wish to tell you – everything you need. Except for what happened in England. You now have it all in writing. I cannot stop you quoting it. Can I?" Then she laughed; and there was a hint of relief and triumph in it? That she had denied him something to the last?

"You don't have time for – ?" He mumbled something about dinner, a drink, coffee – or breakfast, or coffee, in the morning?

"I am sorry, no," Carolina said with finality. She was dismissing him emphatically, although her manner, with all that she wanted to tell him disclosed, was strangely relaxed. She was continuing to laugh, a spasmodic, almost giggling laugh, nervous perhaps and yet not from stress.

"I wanted to ask you only one more question," Tim said tentatively, wondering whether he could venture this final risk and deciding that he could.

"Even now one more question?" Carolina exclaimed, smiling, her eyes exceptionally bright.

"Yes. I suppose you, yourself – you don't suppose Philip was ever – some kind of skilful spy? As Professor Bobolescu –"

She turned her back on him, went back towards the armchair, stood facing it with her shoulders shaking. For a second, but a second only, he thought she was suddenly locked again in trembling grief, he feared he had trodden clumsily on her dream of Philip.

The next moment he realised she was giggling and laughing, unable to stop and reply to him properly. She sat down in the armchair, helpless with laughter.

"Philip... Philip – a 'skilful spy'? You – you English!" She had to pause to get her breath. "Everyone must be a spy for you. What will you do if you cannot believe in – in 'bugs'? – and cameras in the walls?"

"You thought definitely he never – never was – ?"

"It is all in my letter!" She laughed joyously and stood up. "Mr Harker-Jones, it has been a pleasure to help you." She shook his hand again, and dropped it, still shaking. "I am sorry. This happens to me. It hasn't happened for a long time – Good-bye!"

It was as if she knew she would only be able to stop laughing if she left him at once. So she turned away from him, pushed hard at the glass door and disappeared into the street; head handsomely high, and the warm afternoon sunshine of this day in mid-May 1990 bright on her hair.

– 7 –

I write this (Carolina had said in the letter) in case I do not have the strength to overcome all these mixed emotions – of pleasure, of sorrow, of fear and reserve – and speak these words to you in the place where I plan to say them.

I am very well aware, because I have my instincts and my common sense, that you will wish to find out, as a biographer from England, the most secret personal details of my life with Philip Carston. If I was seeking publicity and money for myself, I could make – or invent – some revelations. It would not matter if I was improving on the truth or telling absolute lies – no one could check the truth of what I was saying.

'Personal confessions' might achieve me some fame and sell more copies of your biography. I know you are not a cynical man or a cynical writer, and you do not write biographies to sell scandal. But you realise you *would* sell more if you had a 'stronger' story to tell. You do not fully realise the strength of the pressures on you to find out a little scandal. Your society calls it things like 'feeding healthy curiosity'. It is 'natural to want to know'.

There is a book, a novel, *A Time Apart*, which is a good or bad book as readers in the future will decide. There was a man, Philip Carston, who decided to place me as a character in a book about a foreign girl in England, which I would assist him with by meeting him when and where we could. I would translate it into my own language. That was 'all' we originally agreed to. I was in love with him in ways deeper than I can explain – and Katrin never manages to explain them about Richard in the book. Those ways transcended physical contacts and abolished distance. Differences of background and contrasts of age and temperament and politics did not matter. If a certain physical act happened between us – in one half-hour, or for three hours, or several or many times, in Bucharest, in Târgu Alb, London – when for seconds we were not people with minds and hearts but just bodies joining, or striving to join – is that more important than any of the rest? More important than larger truths about a relationship? Is whatever physical thing that might have happened in a private house or a hotel or out-of-doors so vital? It is important, if your Western culture is to 'sell' to have the sex in the books and the films, but it is more important for me that your biography puts the larger truth before the private details.

I have hinted that he was very passionate towards me, sexual passion, when he came to this question of giving Katrin in his novel a love affair with Richard.

I 'forgave' Philip this passion and this tactic – I thought it was a bad reason to make love, but a forgivable method of courtship, a distinguished writer asking me to make physical love so that he could make the love between the character representing me and the one representing himself more 'authentic'! When we returned to Valeria's that day during the third visit to Romania, after the sinister encounter with Mr Radin at the Writers' Union, we were very close to each other, and I turned the whole matter into a joke, which he did not mind, because he could see it came from love and not from mockery or contempt. I said that I myself could write *for* him the "passages of passion" as he called them. "Ah," he said. "But I shall accept that offer. It will be fascinating. If you make them very passionate, as passionate as my publishers would prefer, you realise you will be committing a worse kind of act than sleeping with me – an act of *mauvaise foi* as the Frogs would say? You would be catering for Western readers in precisely the way you deplore."

And so he did accept that offer. And I did write them, in my own English which Philip polished for me. I said I would write those passages as truthfully as I could. "It will be dishonest to pretend those are my work," he said. "Eventually I will tell the world they are mine," I said. I would write them with the freedom of an uncorrupted woman writer to deal with the truths of the heart and not feed debased appetites. "My heroine will be reciting collective farm statistics in bed," Philip laughed. I laughed too, because he realised I knew he was talking nonsense.

My visit to England – which was between his third and fourth visits to my country – and whether Katrin in the novel met people *I* met myself, and reacted as *I* reacted in real life: It happened, but I ruined it with my own foolishness.

Can you imagine how a young woman of my age and background might feel about visiting a Western country for the first time in the 1980s? *England*, in the 1980s? Philip could. He had drafted all of that before I went to England. What he wrote about my landing in England was *amended* after I had told him about my experiences at London Airport – but only small amendments because Katrin finally had to go through passport control without too much trouble.

He was altogether right about her disorientation, her feeling that the aeroplane must be delivering her home and not to

England. But he had overlooked one possibility, and when I told him about one thing he resisted the idea of including it in the novel – and I was very relieved. Any flight from Bucharest to London – there are not so many – can throw together people who know each other. I certainly knew Stefan Tonaru.

I missed him at the check-in desk for London at Otopeni. But there he was in the queue in the departure hall downstairs. I was going to pretend I had not seen him, but when I passed him in his seat as I walked up the gangway of the Tupolev, I had to acknowledge him. He was amazed, over-charming, full of questions. The idea that I might see him in London – he was attending a conference, by invitation – never left me; nor did the idea that he might be reporting me.

With Mr Tonaru I walked confidently up to one of two officials at passport control; he went to a parallel desk. My official was neither so young and tidy nor as agreeable as the one in the novel. I was unlucky.

"Your reason for coming?" he said curtly.

"My reason for – ?" Immediately my confidence had gone, he spoke so fast.

"Yes. Your reason for coming."

"I came for – I have an invitation to visit a friend, Mr Carston," I said. "And I have permission from my authorities."

"Is it tourism?"

"It is a private visit."

"That counts as tourism." He was looking so hard at my passport with the British visa in it, holding it so firmly, I did not think I would get it back. "Where are you staying?"

I told him.

"Up north. I see. Someone's meeting you?" And then, with heavy flirtatiousness, "You're young to be coming out of Romania to England at the moment? They usually send the old reliable ones." Out of the corner of my eye I saw Stefan Tonaru moving safely away towards the Customs: old and reliable? "How long are you staying with your friend?"

"Two weeks."

"Man or woman?"

"Man."

"Stand in here please, madam." He kept my passport when I walked through his barrier and stood on the place he indicated.

There were not many others in his "non-E.E.C." queue, and he dealt with them quickly. It was as if he needed to find one person to question rigorously so as to prove his vigilance. When he had finished he got down from his seat and consulted a uniformed man standing near the entrance to Customs. They were speaking almost out of earshot, so I could catch only occasional phrases: "Romanian... boyfriend in the north of England... speaks bloody good English... *Too* good if you ask me."

"You maintain you are Romanian?" said this second individual, tall, moustached, more delicate in voice but very hard-eyed, and talking very fast.

"I *am* Romanian."

"Have you ever been employed or domiciled abroad, in England or the Commonwealth, for example?"

"I have never worked or lived abroad – anywhere."

"And yet your English is remarkably good?"

I said nothing, out of contempt. Why should these men be discussing my life and my linguistic proficiency with me? The silence was another mistake. The first man gave a shrug and shook his head. The second said, "Would you kindly come this way?" I wondered in terror what Philip would do when he failed to find me among the passengers from Bucharest. He might think I had missed the flight. What could I do if he went away again? I had his address and phone number, but only a little English money, not enough for a hotel, or to take me all the way to the north...

I was led to a small room where the second official repeated all of the first man's questions. From there we went out and collected my suitcase (circling alone on the carousel), which I had to open.

It was most thoroughly searched by two women from the

immigration department – neat uniforms, cold eyes, blonde hair combed back and tied in buns. They opened, and smelt, a jar of Gerovital, questioned me about some tablets (harmless and ineffective Romanian aspirins) and even opened up the sheets of newspaper lining the case. They asked about two books I had – poetry, and a novel, in Romanian. They did not look under the screwed-up tissue paper in the plain little cardboard carton in which I had brought the small jar of Gerovital.

"Very well, madam," the man said eventually, without explanation or apology, "you may go through."

I walked out into the terminal concourse with the curious feeling you experience, at that moment, of being released, and yet I felt released into a world which would impose its limits without mercy if you did not obey its rules. At the arrivals exit I went through most of Katrin's reactions to the sights and colours of things when she lands in the West: what greets you is really so different from what you leave – for me, it was the main hall of Otopeni airport, with no commercial advertising, just the calm posters of tourist resorts in my country; and above your head the birds which fly around and chirp and nest under the high ceiling, their cries echoing in the airy space.

Of course Philip had waited, standing very gloomily among a crowd of people with eager, watchful faces, brandishing cards to have strangers identify them. I realised how tense and apprehensive I had been under scrutiny in the immigration office, because I now began to talk, talk and talk, telling him everything and in detail, from Stefan Tonaru onwards. I hardly allowed him to say anything himself, even greet me properly. I suppose I was tired, but the shock of the arbitrary suspicion had upset me, very badly. We wheeled my suitcase away towards the Underground, down Katrin's corridor to Katrin's ticket-office, flanked by the advertisements for insurance.

"I've arranged rooms in a hotel in London for to-night – and for longer, if you like. You can see a bit of London before going to the north."

"That is good," I said; but I wondered why he had sprung this surprise. Philip often said he did not "recommend" London. It had been understood that we would go straight to the north of England, which Philip often said was "infinitely superior to the metropolis."

"There's something else which is a nuisance rather," he said. "I hope you won't mind. I'd like to introduce you to an old friend to-night – we'll have dinner. He's got an extended business trip to Romania happening soon, and would like some practical hints on how to survive there."

"I can *try* to help..."

"I'm really sorry – on our first night. But it was the only time he's able to be in London, and he's been begging me to tell him what I know – which isn't much – and I thought it would be an excellent chance for him to have it from the fountainhead, so to speak."

I began to fear something. But I told myself the airport experience had shaken my nerve, there was nothing to be alarmed about in an old friend of Philip's, due to visit my country. And yet...

Philip reported some progress with the novel, and yet was self-deprecating about it. He said he was eager to see what I had written because it would be so much better. He chatted about it almost as if he wished to change the subject from the evening's dinner. What he said, shouting above the noise of the Underground train taking us rapidly into London competed for my attention with my overwhelming sense of the new world around me.

The hotel, though not large, was very central. I smiled with pleasure, absorbing everything in the calm little foyer: the bell on the desk, the tourist posters and hotel notices (one promising to develop camera film in no more than three hours!), the foreign names in the visitors' book which I was required to sign. Then it occurred to me that this was the sort of hotel in which Stefan Tonaru might stay. That alarmed me deeply, though when I expressed my alarm to Philip in a whisper he was astonished.

"It would be *too* much of a coincidence for Mr Tonaru to be here! That's the kind of coincidence that has the mercy to withhold itself."

As we found our way to our rooms I was quite unable to rid myself of the dread that I might be followed and watched. I would have laughed at, and reassured, any visitor to Romania who expressed that fear, so why did Philip not reassure me in England?

After a couple of hours of "rest" which I requested (Philip said he was tired also), in which I could only lie on my bed, not sleep, in this comfortable little room – though it soon began to seem small and claustrophobic – I dressed carefully for dinner in some new clothes I had brought with me, a wide, elaborate skirt and blouse with just a hint of folk motifs in the pattern (but not enough, I thought, to mark me out as an obvious "foreigner"), stepped out into the corridor, knocked on Philip's door, and went down in the lift with him. We left the hotel to dine somewhere else; and this walk out into a different light (it was early evening) was like a second start in London for me.

Everything I now describe you will please read in the context of the fear and paranoia I had brought from my own country, a worse version of the apprehensions which made Philip want to turn round and go back when he landed in Bucharest.

We were dining in a very quiet, patently expensive restaurant, where Mr Jeff Rogers was waiting when we arrived. He was clothed in that formal English fashion Philip preferred, but in other ways – a smooth, polished confidence, for example – he bore no resemblance to Philip. Mr Rogers said something perfunctory about "school together", but didn't greet Philip with an old schoolfriend's warmth. Neither did he seem much like someone seizing a chance to pick up some advice about handling a visit to Romania. Instead he *seemed* to be telling me things about my own country – such as identifying the "charming peasant design" of my blouse, to my deep embarrassment – a place which he notwithstanding said he had never visited before. Philip took no part in this conversation.

I found the waiters asking my permission to carry away plates of food which I had simply forgotten. I felt too tired, too alert, too threatened, and too distracted to eat. I just had to hope I appeared calm and communicative – non-committally communicative, naturally – about Romania through Mr Rogers' questions about food supplies, the people's opinions of the President, the health of the two Ceausescus, the atmosphere among the workers in the factories and on the farms, the mood of the intellectuals in the cities. He was friendly and charming, and complimentary about my English; but I felt the line of his questioning was becoming personal. "What do you yourself feel about the President?... Well, naturally you have to be reticent... You suffer much from shortages yourself?... I quite understand if you can't divulge your own feelings... Would you ever leave if you had the chance?"

That was where all my apprehensions overcame me and I had to put Mr Rogers right.

"Excuse me, but I am very happy with my country," I said. "No country is perfect, and mine may be less good than some – for the present. But I can live a civilised life in it, with books and music and friends – and it is my own country – and I love it and am loyal to it."

Mr Rogers was all fluent grace and adaptability.

"That does you great credit," he said quickly, (condescendingly, when I thought about it), "And it does me no credit at all that I am one of those crazy, inquisitive Englishmen who inflict direct questions on any foreign visitor within *minutes* of meeting. I am truly sorry. I shall not sleep to-night if you won't – please – accept my sincere apologies!"

He shook his head, grinned, cursed himself, poured more wine, generally played the complimentary fool. I could not have felt more alone than I did at that restaurant table in a strange city. All my sense of security in England rested on Philip and at that moment – though fortunately not for long – I was convinced Philip had introduced me to Jeff Rogers so that I could be sounded out about defecting. *How could I so mistrust Philip?* And be so wrong about his friend? For the rest of the meal Mr Rogers led the talk onto other topics, discussed wine and the weather, asked me why I had come to England just a little too early for the cricket season?

– 8 –

"I am sorry," Philip said when we parted from Mr Rogers in the street. He took my arm, but I made an excuse to disengage myself.

"Philip – I am sorry also."

"Why should *you* be sorry?"

"I am sorry you bring me here for a holiday and you introduce me to a man who wants to make me leave my country."

Philip stopped, and stood open-mouthed in the dark street. Unconsciously I had carried over to England from Romania all the paranoia about colleagues and friends, about family and lovers even, that dominated – I admit it – our daily living. After having travelled with Stefan Tonaru and feared he might be watching me in London, after the incidents at the airport, after all the powerful strangeness of a quite different country, I had then (at that moment I could have sworn it was a fact) been asked about leaving Romania.

Philip laughed, and denied everything until he saw that I was serious and deeply distressed. Then he said he would let me "sleep on it", and we would talk about it in the morning. I was profoundly tired and confused, and I agreed to that. We parted at the door of my room with a plan: I would hang the 'Do not disturb' card on my door, and lie in.

I was so bewildered, felt so ill and uncertain, that I could not sleep at all that night. I imagined that this very comfortable hotel in the heart of London, with its foreign visitors, was probably an official hotel, with listening devices in the walls, cameras even. I knew I was on the brink of throwing away everything I had hoped for from this fortnight, everything I had imagined about it, planned for it. But as I lay awake the risk seemed too great. What if I had been *seen* by someone dining with Mr Rogers, and my shadow knew Mr Rogers was an agent of the British secret services? I was expected to report to the Romanian Embassy in London. What if I did not report that dinner – but they found out? All ridiculous fears and confusions, I decided when it was too late.

I had brought with me the undeveloped camera film I had taken care of for Philip during the Bobolescus' dinner that night, and which he had apparently forgotten, since he never again mentioned it. I had not tried to have the film developed in Târgu Alb or Bucharest; it would have taken too long. I took it out of the little box which carried the jar of Gerovital skin cream, where I had wrapped it in tissue paper. I was not lying in and sleeping that first morning in London. I was wide awake, taking a bath, making myself coffee with the kettle provided in the room – and leaving the film to be developed "in three hours" at the hotel Reception.

To be honest, I suppose I did sleep a little that morning, with the hotel servants not disturbing me; the frail and jumpy sleep you experience when strong coffee is keeping some of your nerves and muscles very much awake. I also watched television a little, letting coloured images and cosy voices from programmes for schools or housewives flow into my confused and fragmentary dreaming. I resolved not to answer the telephone in the room if it rang, in case it was Stefan Tonaru tracking me down.

When I secretly collected and paid for the photographs at Reception – nearly all my English money – I stored them at once in my handbag in case anyone – Stefan Tonaru, or Mr Rogers, or anyone at all – should pass by and see me with them. I went up in the lift, put out again the 'Do not disturb' sign, locked the door, even pulled the curtains in case anyone should see me from windows across the yard, and opened the bright little packet.

The first photographs were the last taken: myself against the background of the view from the track in the forest above Târgu Alb, where "the mountains have all opened out themselves"; and people round the table at the Bobolescus' dinner, snaps I had taken myself with Philip's camera. Everyone, including Philip, looked much more relaxed and sociable than I remembered. How handsome Tamasi looked, I admit that. Liviu Bobolescu, needless to say, had self-consciously posed for the photograph in an instant – erect and dignified, and even spruce, the distinguished elderly scholar.

There were four of these dinner table photos. The fifth photo in the set seemed to have been taken through a narrow gap or hole in a fence. It was a view of the site for the building of the great edifice which President Nicolae Ceausescu planned for the climax of his endless Avenue in Bucharest. It was not forbidden to take pictures of this house while it was under construction; but police had often warned people, foreigners especially, against taking snaps of it, largely because they were sensitive about people taking snaps of *anything*. But here was an only fairly clear photograph of the foundations and the grey beginnings, on an artificial hill, of that immense structure: workers, bulldozers, cranes, trucks loaded with soil and blocks of stone, concrete-mixers. And the next photograph was a scene of demolition, the ruins of a solid nineteenth-century bourgeois house from which yellow dust was rising and being carried away by the wind on a sunny afternoon, like sand clouds in a storm.

There was nothing secret or illegal in what these two photographs depicted. Nor was there in the pictures of lounges and corridors in his hotel, or of a long, smooth train entering a clean, shining Metro station, or of the seven-storey Central Committee headquarters with its classical columns, or even of the telecommunications centre in Calea Victoriei with its roof-message clear against a blue sky: TRAIASCA SCUMPA

NOASTRA PATRIE REPUBLICA SOCIALISTA ROMANIA. What puzzled me was how and when Philip had found time and opportunity to take them, and why he had not shown any interest in photography in my presence until we stood that day in the mountains...

As I continued sifting through these prints I became dreadfully alarmed; though also I was laughing, with amusement as well as nerves.

There were snaps of soldiers parading in Bucharest, and of the brown Militia headquarters. There was a badly focused view of a chemical works, peasant houses, a small line of ancient green military tanks stopped in a siding, this one particularly blurred and hasty. I laughed because all of them were rather bad pictures, taken with obvious speed (some images included the strap of the camera!) by somebody not used to composing pictures. Philip had once said to me, "In my scheme of things 'amateur' is a word of high status." I giggled – out of sheer affection for him – to think of these as the futile efforts of an amateur secret agent; if indeed they were that...

No, they couldn't be. Philip was just not... Except that he *had* introduced me to Mr Jeff Rogers...

Suddenly the full horror overwhelmed me. I had unknowingly brought to England what could be seen by vindictive, suspicious people in my country as spy photographs. I sat there in that London hotel, with curtains drawn and the door locked, shivering whenever somebody passed in the corridor, not seeing the images on the TV screen.

I knew what I had to do. I had to destroy the incriminating photographs while passing on the innocent ones to Philip – in case anyone *did* somehow know I had brought a film into England. Then I had to leave England as soon as I could, on any pretext, before I accumulated more days I would have to report on. If I did not, and the chance of ever seeing him again in Romania might vanish. I had to sacrifice what I most deeply wished for, this visit to England, for the sake of our future relationship, for the sake of my love. And also for the sake of Philip's novel, which I told myself was even more important. That was how I analysed it that morning in London. All this I could tell Philip later – and did, and laughed about it; although I never lost a certain suspicion (which made him all the more attractive and intriguing to me) that Philip could have been, all the time, a typically incompetent English secret agent! To leave his illicit photographs in my care and forget all about them...

Feeling ridiculously superstitious about it, I invented a story about a telephone call back to Târgu Alb which brought me unexpected bad news of family illness and other problems. Philip believed me, as I did not revert to the topic of my suspicions about Mr Rogers, and was clearly distressed for my sake, felt – as he put it – "let down yet again by fate." He then performed wonders of organisation for me, pleading with the London agent who had sold him the ticket (I had picked it up in Bucharest, and it was an open ticket) to let me return (this was Thursday) on the Sunday flight. There was no time to go to his north of England. I never went there at all, or met any of the models for the people Katrin met. It was not necessary to go there to write about her love affair. That could have happened in Bucharest, or Târgu Alb. Or London.

We made the most of my remaining time in London: I saw (and I gathered Philip was also seeing for the first time) several of the traditional sights – I recognised them all from pictures in childhood encyclopaedias! We travelled on the top decks of buses, we became experienced in the rigours of the Underground.

Of course I never saw Mr Tonaru again. And when it was too late, and everything was arranged for me to return on the Sunday, I began to be certain that all my fears were equally unfounded. In sixty hours I lost nearly all my apprehension. Mr Rogers made no further appearance. Philip only referred to him once, and apologised for his questioning and manner: "It's just his way," he said. I said nothing. I began to feel so very deeply ashamed of suspecting Philip. And we seemed to be closer in the anonymity of London than we had ever been in Romania. But I did not show him the photographs until we were at Heathrow for my return flight, with time to spare.

I had taken them out of their wrapper and put them in a hotel envelope. Most of them, that is, because I had disposed of any which just might conceivably be of use to a foreign government (soldiers, tanks) by tearing them up and dropping the pieces, wrapped in another, screwed-up, envelope in a litter bin in Oxford Street.

"I have a little surprise for you," I said to Philip when we had at last found two seats on the terminal concourse. He raised his eyebrows and smiled, very sadly; he had just said his spirits had been sinking all morning.

"You don't remember taking these – do you?"

"But how – ?" He looked at them astonished, shook his head, shuffled them, dropped a couple.

"You don't remember letting me take care of a film out of your camera?"

"No, I don't. Yes I do – vaguely. But where?"

"At Professor Bobolescu's? During dinner?"

"Yes! Well – I forgot completely." I watched his reactions with close attention as he looked at each print a second time, a third; especially the views. Then he said,

"But I thought I took more than this. How many are there?"

"I haven't counted."

"Do you have the negatives?"

"I have something to confess," I said. "I lost them." In fact I had destroyed them, burnt them in the washbasin in my hotel bathroom, under the extractor fan, washing away the ashes.

"I am *certain* I took more than this. It was thirty-six." It may be that he gave me a rather sharp, and anxious look; but I could have been imagining it.

"Where were they developed?"

"Here, in the hotel."

"Ah." He seemed relieved. "They wouldn't have lost any.

Perhaps they didn't come out. It doesn't matter – I can't remember what they were."

We could see my flight announced on the Departures board. Suddenly I felt so stupidly and abjectly ashamed and penitent I couldn't speak. This feeling deepened when I was back in Romania and could reflect on my folly. I had denied myself all but a fraction of the pleasure I could have had by overcoming my fear and paranoia. I had shown ingratitude to Philip, who had gone to great personal expense to book a hotel and show me London.

I could now easily understand why Philip had felt so insecure in Bucharest, having crossed the divide in the other direction. He had years behind him of a similar instruction in dread and suspicion, subtly and constantly cultivated.

Only much later, after Philip's two further visits to my country, probably after Philip had died, did Liviu Bobolescu begin to retell (to invent? He had so many fantasies) stories about Philip's reporting on British people he met in Romania. Every kind of story, about everyone, passed around and was believed in those years. Some people, in the East and the West, believe them still; it will be a long time before we learn not to listen to these stories.

Mr Harker-Jones, I have now told you everything you need to know. I hope you can see why I kept that shaming, and not very important, matter of my only trip to England to the very last. It has given me pleasure to meet you (English courtesies! Tim thought. She has no high opinion of those, either) and I shall look forward to reading the biography.

TEN

– 1 –

From Simon Stonehurst
Theatre Director

CONFIDENTIAL

Dear Mr Harker-Jones,

(I note that you mark your own letter "confidential" so I will do the same.)

I can well understand that your biography of Philip Carston has proved, as you term it, "quite a considerable undertaking" and that "various problems" which you do not specify may have arisen. I am bound to say nevertheless that I find your attitude of non-cooperation so far in this matter very bewildering and disappointing, to say the least.

May I remind you that I promised the utmost confidentiality about any information which it might be regarded as premature to divulge in advance of the book's publication? I also promised complete discretion in my treatment of the relationship between Philip Carston and Carolina, having regard to the fact that the latter is still alive.

As I have mentioned before, it is not practical for me to visit Romania. Therefore I – and Nick Tillitt – are dependent on you for a little help with details about the places and times these two people met, the names of some of Carolina's friends (and persecutors) in pre-revolution Romania, etc, etc. Nick Tillitt's script is excellent on the Romanian background, but the personal detail about Carolina herself he cannot supply, because he never met her while he was there, nor did he ever meet Carston.

I am therefore totally reliant on you for information which will help me, with Tillitt and the actors, to flesh out these people. Carston and Carolina are basically, to me, wonderful symbols respectively of Western democracy and of the flame of the spirit which went on burning in Romania in spite of Ceausescu's abominable, godless tyranny. The overriding purpose of my production will be to bring this out. But it will be a *better* production if I can get my mind round these people as day-to-day human beings and know more about the experiences they shared in Romania.

May I put it to you another way? I sincerely believe it would in no way *pre-empt* your book (in case you fear that) if the information you give me went into my production. Basically it would *help* it. I have plans for the play after its première up here, and don't intend to confine it to the provinces! I have very promising contacts in fringe theatres in London. If it succeeded on the fringe, such a topical theme as this would enhance the hope of a West End transfer. None of this could do the reception of your biography – when it finally happens – any harm.

I ask you, please, if you would reconsider your refusal to meet and discuss these matters? I have had a very deep respect for your work for some years, and would be honoured to receive your assistance and advice, which would of course be acknowledged with gratitude in the theatre programme for the production(s).

Yours sincerely,

Simon Stonehurst

– 2 –

Simon posted it that morning on the way round to the theatre for the rehearsal. They were at an early stage, and there was still time if Harker-Jones responded quickly.

It was a characteristically cold English April morning and Simon pushed his hands deeply into the pockets of his donkey jacket, as he liked to do when he went around the leafy streets of this respectable northern town, Philip Carston's home, on one of what he called his "thinking walks." Perhaps the posture itself encouraged him to adopt his slow, brooding stride, head down under the grimy little black hat, chin protecting his exposed neck above the T-shirt against the cold. In his very new, tattered, stone-washed jeans and soft-soled trainers he would not have stood out in a crowd in a larger city; but here on the bridge at nine-forty on a weekday morning he looked, if not actually mad, at least incongruous, especially because Simon had the habit of growling things to himself as he walked.

While he was walking and thinking he would sometimes also stop abruptly, frown, and reflect; or alternatively, lengthen one stride of his long thin legs as if stepping over an invisible puddle, the latter gesture usually signifying the solution of a problem. All the time his elbows were pressed tightly into his sides as if they served to contain an energy – or an anger? – which could not be permitted to burst out *yet*. This was the way he paced his study at home; but it looked odd in the respectable shopping mall in the centre of town.

When he turned down the narrow pedestrian walk of Upper River Street, past the Oxfam shop and the crafts emporium and the newsagents', he lifted his head and prepared himself for the first conversations of the day. Inside the stage entrance of the theatre he noticed that Ken, the doorkeeper, cleaner, and general factotum still failed to accord him the respect he had found on his occasional engagement in the big cities, in London particularly.

"Greetings, Ken!" he said rigorously, but received only a preoccupied nod. In London, Simon thought, Ken would have replied, "Good morning, Mr Stonehurst. Miss Duncaster wanted a word before rehearsals" – or given some message of that sort; as any London doorman would. Not so in small provincial theatres. If only he could get this production to London; not with the same cast though... "Greetings, Derrick!" he called out to the fifty-year old hidden behind The *Guardian*. Derrick Ramsley shook the paper in a cursory Monday-morning response. "Greetings, Malcolm!" he shouted to the stage manager, flat on a bench in a favourite posture of meditation.

"Greetings, Sophe! Greetings, Em! Greetings, Paolo!" One-by-one salutations, as he always gave when arriving for rehearsals, going round the room, expecting everyone to have arrived before he did. These last three, sixth-formers aspiring to drama school, were attending three half-mornings a week to learn about production before their interviews, and had easily adopted the friendly abbreviations and nicknames Simon had bestowed on them. "Black, lots of sugar, Paolo," he called out to Paul at the coffee machine, fishing for coins to drop into the honesty box for both himself and the boy (Simon was not an ungenerous man in small particulars.) Sophie and Emma never drank coffee.

The problem, as usual, was: Jane Duncaster, cast as Carolina, was not here yet. She had always been, irritatingly, a little late, every morning so far. Simon liked to talk, "to discourse," to impart, to teach, over this coffee. Rehearsals always started late, it was a tradition he, for one, was determined to graft onto this provincial theatre; the twenty minutes between arriving and starting was one in which "to set the working mood." But he liked to have the *entire* cast around him to do that, and without the female half of this two-hander...

Nevertheless he began to expatiate over his black coffee, stirred with a tiny thin plastic spoon which he then, as always, licked and dropped into his hat.

"So what did *you* think of it, Sophe?" An item of TV drama

everyone (except Derrick) had watched the night before.

"I liked it," Sophie said. Simon (not unkindly though) began to explain to Sophie why she should not have liked it, how lacking in verve and originality the direction had been, how tired the camera work looked. Then Jane Duncaster came in, ten minutes later than Simon, smiling, unapologetic, dropping her bag neatly on a chair, turning her back on Simon – deliberately, he thought – as she worked the coffee dispenser. Simon deliberately concluded a paragraph of his discourse before exclaiming, with contrived surprise, "Ah – greetings, Jane!"

"Good morning, Simon," she replied; composed, and ready for anything. She had his measure. She had it better than Derrick Ramsley, who probably needed the part of Philip Carston more than Jane needed the part of Carolina Predeanu.

"*However!*" Simon suddenly exclaimed, well before Jane had finished her coffee; his signal that serious business was about to begin. He looked pointedly at Jane's coffee cup as she carried it into the theatre; Ken had *told* her cups were to be left outside.

"Rear stalls," Simon said to the three sixth-formers. He told himself he was going to oblige Jane and Derrick to be "visible and audible" this morning. The two actors took up their places, scripts in hand, on chairs stage right and stage left.

"Right, then," Simon called out from half-way up a side-aisle. "Spots on both, Malcolm," he called to the stage manager, at the lights. Malcolm came out of another relaxed, meditative posture, house lights went down, spots duly appeared, Jane looked prepared and defiant under her illumination.

"Right, then. Right. Boom-boom! Fourth scene. From the top. Remember how we finished Friday – Philip is just, *just* beginning to sense that he has to supply, like, not *only* Carolina's need for love, but a deep *spiritual* craving. Jane – Carolina – you think you have his love to believe in, but you have nothing else to believe in, you are a controlled person in a controlled society which tells you what books and music you must admire – you live your life in terror, and in a spiritual vacuum."

"Yes?" Not *dumb* insolence, but in her tone a monosyllabic insolence; which Simon overrode by ignoring it.

"Day-to-day living is a kind of starved servitude for you. Philip is a hand lifting you out of that abyss of physical hunger and spiritual despair."

"Yes?"

"Derrick – Philip – you have to be aware of what you represent for Carolina on that spiritual plane." Derrick, unsure but more submissive, nodded thoughtfully. "Basically you are *meaning* for her. You are *hope*."

"You –"

"Simon!" Jane was leaning forward in her chair with provocative earnestness, addressing the director in clear, doubting tones, loud enough to let the young students in the rear stalls know she was questioning his authority.

"Jane!" Indulgently, he would consider whatever it was she wanted to say. Jane riffled through the pages of the script.

"Simon – this is not how it is in *A Time Apart*."

She had been here when he explained all about that, but he would do it all over again.

"Jane, these are the real people who *inspired* the characters in the book, not the fictitious characters. Philip and Carolina are *not* Katrin and Richard. These are the author and the real woman."

"O.K., O.K." Jane went back to her script. "Now, I'll buy the possibility of the love thing happening in life as well as in the book. And I'll buy the shortages, and power cuts, and the fear, and paranoia, and all of that. What I *don't* buy is Carolina being such a bloody wimp."

"Who said she's a wimp?"

"*You* say she's a wimp. You say –" But Jane was not hearing his reply, her thoughts were running on, she was expounding her doubts unstoppably now. Christ, we haven't even got started today yet, Simon was thinking. We haven't covered one fucking speech and she's trying to undermine me.

"You say," Jane declared, "that Carolina lives in a state of ongoing spiritual desolation, or whatever. With nothing to believe in until Philip the White Knight turns up. I say she *must* have had things to believe in if she was so intelligent. She can't have been without friends and lovers if she was so attractive."

Unfortunately Simon could see that; but given the terms of the script could not admit it. So he tried another tack. He tried pretending that this was where his interpretation of the script had been heading all the time.

"*Yes*. Yes, of *course*," he replied, thinking hard about what he could say next. "Underneath – deep, *deep down* – basically – Carolina has reserves of strength, and power –"

"– which don't help her at all with this spiritual despair?"

"– reserves of power which you must show *reaching out* to Philip's understanding and compassion."

"So he falls in love with her out of compassion? He's *sorry* for her? Is that it? He doesn't know she's got this colossal power deep down? You want me to be pitiable and powerful simultaneously?"

Simon looked round the darkened auditorium for an answer to this challenge, took in the faces of the three students, pale accusing blobs in the rear stalls, and knew he would have to have a one-to-one row with Jane Duncaster before this production could make any further progress. Then he saw something else, a figure entering the theatre from the vestibule and leaning on the brass rail that ran along the back of the stalls. This was the end! This was Nick Tillitt, author of the script, "dropping in from London", as he had threatened, "to see how the rehearsals were going".

Simon guessed Nick would start pressing his own meanings and intentions on the production in the tedious, obtrusive way authors usually did, confusing the actors, hampering the director. And Nick's knowledge of Romania would give him the right to start dictating matters of detail, changing things – Simon knew by instinct he would not be content with just hovering in the background to help if required.

At least here was an excuse to halt the proceedings and shelve the inevitable conflict with Jane until later.

He called Malcolm out of his semi-trance to raise the house lights, and suddenly the little theatre was plain and ordinary, lacking all atmosphere, rows and rows of well-worn seats, the magic abolished.

"Greetings, Nick!" Simon barked. The young, grinning, awkwardly effusive figure in the long light raincoat sauntered towards him. "This is a great surprise. Wonderful to see you." Was it, hell! He beckoned to Sophie, Emma and Paul to come down and meet the newcomer. "Everything stops for the playwright," he said, generously. Jane Duncaster came down off the stage with a curious, enigmatic little smile. Derrick Ramsley, too heartily, shook Nick's hand and said, "This is a lovely script – lovely, it really is." Tillitt smiled boyishly at everyone.

Simon Stonehurst went into overdrive on introductions and explanations. When these were over, Nick Tillitt felt obliged to mark the occasion – his first meeting with the first cast of his first play – with a little, formal address of thanks; his diplomatic training suggested that this was something his hearers would both expect and appreciate. After that, embarrassingly for Simon (who was directing this play, wasn't he? He didn't want to encourage a habit of consulting Nick on things) – Sophie asked Nick a question.

A conversation began about the meaning of the play, with Tillitt thoroughly delighted to expound in his eager, high-pitched tones, Simon standing aside, casting glances up towards the stage, looking at his watch. Yes, it was mainly about East and West, he told the students pleasantly. And these two characters, who it seemed may have fallen in love across the divide in real life, were representative of the two halves of Europe before the fall of Communism. Sophie looked unsatisfied. What about dramatic *conflict*, she wanted to know? Tillitt hesitated, not clear what Sophie wanted to know. He said it had seemed to him very dramatic that Philip Carston had reached out into Carolina's darkness and touched a chord of freedom in her. With the flame of one candle you can light a thousand candles of liberty – you saw how people banished the darkness of Eastern Europe with such candles after the fall of the Berlin Wall? Emma and Paul nodded, but Sophie pressed Nick on dramatic conflict, and political occurrences, and such a list of other issues... Simon Stonehurst had his hands in his jeans pockets and was cudgelling his sides with his elbows and looking most impatient. Nick Tillitt was saying that it was a *most* dramatic thing that a celebrated English writer had fallen in love in his last years with a beautiful young woman suffering under the evil empire of Communism, and thought that love had kept the flame of freedom alive in her soul. Of course his play, he explained, was unashamedly a romantic "faction" – did Sophie know that word? – a fiction based on facts. No, he hadn't been able to meet Carolina, who was still alive, nor had Simon, but...

And so on.

As the three young people listened and questioned, and Nick Tillitt explained, and Jane Duncaster sent looks in Derrick Ramsley's direction which he felt it was tactful not to return, and Simon Stonehurst fumed in silence as he saw the foundations of his production shaken, the level truth in all its subtlety and oddity, in all its diversity and with all its qualifications, all its hidden corners important or trivial, that level truth about individuals that really did require to be found and described and spread abroad if you were to understand races and nations and governments, receded even further into the distance, into rhetoric and propaganda and delusion, wafted away by self-interest and self-deception and by a sheer inability to comprehend; though in this group of the ignorant in one northern English provincial city Jane and Sophie were doing their best to salvage the truth from history and take a look at it.

Meanwhile one person was not party to any of this. Up above, at his lighting console, Malcolm waited and waited, looking out and down through his little window at the group standing and rabbiting on at the point where the centre aisle started sloping down from the middle of the stalls. Well, when they wanted him, they could call him. And perhaps he would hear. Shuffling sideways off his seat he cleared a space on the floor of his little cabin just big enough to sit down and assume the first position of yoga.

By the same author

NOVEL
The Way You Tell Them

POETRY
The Railings
The Lion's Mouths
Sandgrains on a Tray
Warrior's Career
A Song of Good Life
A Night in the Gazebo
The Old Flea-Pit
Collected Poems 1952-88
The Observation Car
In the Cruel Arcade

FOR CHILDREN
To Clear the River (as John Berrington)
Brownjohn's Beasts

WITH SANDY BROWNJOHN
Meet and Write 1, 2 and 3

AS EDITOR
First I Say this
New Poems 1970-71 (with Seamus Heaney and Jon Stallworthy)
New Poetry 3 (with Maureen Duffy)

CRITICISM
Philip Larkin

TRANSLATION
Torquato Tasso (from Goethe)
Horace (from Corneille)